Journey to Tracer's Point

Sundowners
A Division of
Treble Heart Books
1284 Overlook Dr.
Sierra Vista, AZ 85635-5512

Published and Printed in the U.S.A.

ISBN: 978-1-932695-74-8

Thank you
for choosing
A Sundowner's
Western Selection

Live the adventure!

Gwyn Ramsey

Journey to Tracer's Point

by

Gwyn Ramsey

SUNDOWNERS

a division of

Treble Heart Books

Dedication

To my husband, Kenneth Ramsey, for his faith in my dreams and patience to see me through them.

Also, to my dear friend, Virginia Czaja, for her steadfast guidance and in-depth editing, who is always there for me.

Acknowledgement

I'd like to thank my dedicated critique group, Mary Schoenecker, Marge Brooks, and Madelaine Ginsberg, who so diligently edited each chapter with a critical eye.

My special thanks to Cindy Sandell and the Women Writing the West organization for their generosity in sharing their knowledge on the history on the west.

I would also like to extend my gratitude to the Tampa Area Romance Authors for their incredible workshops on writing techniques.

Without all of the above people and organizations, this novel would still be a dream instead of a reality.

Prologue

Tracer's Point Valley, California, late fall 1848

Lying on his stomach in the chilling mud behind a fallen log, the miner shivered as his breath kissed the cold winter air. Two hours of rain had soaked him to the bone. His innards growled as he waited, waited for the men in the tent to fall asleep. Hands shaking and teeth chattering, all he could think about was the food he saw lying on the small round table through the open tent flaps. A piece of bread or a dry biscuit, it didn't matter. He hadn't eaten in four days. Money was scarce and his gold claim had shown no yellow in months. No money, no food, no place to sleep, and the constant cold rain were wearing him down. Miners were dying from dysentery and starvation. He wanted to go back home to Kentucky, but he knew that would never happen. *Oh, sweet wife, why did I ever leave you for this pipe dream of gold?*

Peeking over the top of the log, he noticed the oil lamp was out. Only a few more minutes, he could wait that long. He needed to be sure the two men were asleep. Finally, he rose onto his stiff knees, a blast of cold wind penetrating his worn, muddy clothes. Trembling, he pulled his shredded shirt around his shoulders. His swollen hands showed signs of chilblains. He looked at them in disgust. Maybe while he was inside, he'd steal a shirt or a jacket. A pair of socks would be nice.

Slowly he got to his feet and staggered toward the tent door. He heard loud snoring inside. Grasping the canvas, he stopped to listen one more time before entering. The short one lay on his side, the skinny one on his back.

One slushy step at a time, he made his way toward the small center table. Half a slice of bread, a few sips of coffee, and scraps of meat lay like diamonds, beckoning him. Reaching out, he grasped the cup. Placing it to his parched lips, he downed the beverage. As it hit rock bottom, he scooped the biscuit into his hands and backed out of the tent.

"You gonna take that food or pay for it," boomed a voice behind him.

Panicking, he shouldered his way into a bear of a man who blocked his way of escape. The tent occupants, now awake, jumped to their feet.

"Kill the bastard," yelled the short man.

"What's he think he's doing, stealing from us?" shouted the skinny fellow.

Big John stood in the doorway, clutching the thief around the chest, squeezing him tight as he picked him up off the ground.

The man wiggled and squirmed, squealing like a pig. "Put me down. Don't hurt me. I'm hungry. Oh, God," he begged, "please, don't hurt me. I only wanted a little bit to eat."

The skinny man pulled his knife, while the short man grabbed one of the thief's hands. The biscuit dropped into the mud. The two men laid the poor devil's hand across the table while the big man held him in a vise grip.

"A mucker like you doesn't deserve a full hand of fingers."

Hysterical, the thief's eyes widened in horror as he wailed a piercing cry, "No, no!"

Tormented screams echoed through the valley of Tracer's Point.

John Anderson tugged his collar up to shield his neck from the chilling rain dripping off the brim of his hat. Leaden clouds hovered over the valley. Even though his slicker kept most of the rain off his buckskin, his hands were already numb and he still had two miles to Hangtown.

"This weather is not fit for man nor beast. Late fall here is one nasty soggy mess."

Approaching a bend in the trail, he heard moaning up ahead. John slipped his rifle from its sheath and made ready in case of an ambush. The trees thickened on one side as the trail began to dip into a ravine. He urged his horse forward, holding his rifle with his right hand, the butt tucked under his arm.

As he rounded a small outcropping, he spied a man nestled in the brush on the side of the trail, curled up, his knees to his chest. His shirt was tattered and splattered with blood. John dismounted and edged closer. He nudged the gaunt miner with the toe of his boot. The man moaned again, one hand bled profusely.

John laid down his rifle, reached into his jacket pocket

for a handkerchief, and wrapped the man's bloody hand. He lifted the injured man, threw him across his shoulder, then made his way back to his horse, where he placed the miner over the saddle. After retrieving his rifle, John headed toward town.

Stopping in front of Sadie's Hotel and Bath House, he dismounted and entered the large, dimly lit lobby. "Sadie, where in the hell are you?"

She came out of the back room, carrying a stack of towels. "What's all the yelling about, you big baboon? Can't you tell this is an upright hotel? Keep your voice down." She laid the towels on the chair next to the staircase. "Now what's your problem?"

"Got a man out here bleeding to death. Need your help."

"Somebody got himself into trouble again?" she sniffed. "Seems to be more of that going on these days since the gold played out. Why don't ya take him to Doc Henderson?"

"He left town about two weeks ago. He's not back yet."

"Well, don't stand there you long-legged galoot. Bring him in, and don't drip blood all over my good floors."

"The floors are only wood, Sadie," said John, giving her a what-for look.

"Get your butt out the door and quit sassin' me. We'll put him in this first room down here. Now hurry before he dies on your horse. Then we'd have to explain it to that stupid sheriff we have here."

After carefully bandaging the miner's hand, Sadie covered him with a quilt. She picked up the water pan and all the dirty rags, including his shirt. "That's the best I can do for him right now until Doc gets back into town. Sure is an ugly thing to do to any man, cuttin' off three fingers."

"What do you suppose he did to get himself mutilated like that?"

"Seems this morning, Michaels told me Winger caught a

miner stealing food from his tent. Guess this is the feebleminded idiot."

"Jeez, anyone but Winger. Well, I have to go." John tossed some coins on the side table. "Maybe that will help him. Feed him and get him a clean shirt. Poor fool."

John left the hotel, mounted his horse, and headed out of town. He had a plan to spring on his brother back in Virginia. Yes, a mighty good plan, but a bit devious. Whistling a snappy tune, he headed southeast to the trail across the southern part of the mountains.

Chapter One

Rockbridge County, Virginia, Spring 1849

"Hello, Caroline. You're as pretty as ever. Have you missed me?"

Caroline Anderson spun around, recognizing the voice she dreaded to hear, and aggravated for being taken off guard. The prodigal brother-in-law, John Anderson, stood in the cabin doorway, still charming with a dash of disrespect.

"Hello, John. You're looking well."

"Thank you, kindly. Can't complain."

He leaned against the doorframe, arms crossed, as though he owned the whole world. His dark eyes raked over her, from head to toe, causing her stomach to knot and her palms to sweat. *Why can't he stay away?* His casual bearing triggered old painful memories, making them more vivid.

"How's life been here in Virginia?" A crescent moon grin spread across his handsome face. A shock of unruly hair hung over his brow, deepening his dark penetrating eyes.

"It's been *fine*, John," she said, trying to remain calm.

He raised one eyebrow.

She could tell his demeanor hadn't changed a bit. His long dark hair cascaded in untamed waves over the shoulders of his buckskin shirt. The stains and the cracks in his boots showed evidence of many hard miles and bristling adventures.

Caroline forced a smile. "Come on in. Alexander and the children should be here soon."

She wasn't afraid of him, only leery and uneasy. Pretending his presence didn't bother her, she stirred the beans in the kettle and put the floured fish into the fry pan.

He lifted his pack off the porch, threw it across his shoulder, and stepped across the threshold. "I'll just make myself at home," he said.

She had trouble concentrating on her work at hand. His masculinity unnerved her with his intoxicating woodsy smell.

"You've done the cabin up good, Caroline. Real comfy like," he said, as he moved in closer.

Her heart beat a little faster. "Thank you," she replied calmly as possible.

With him standing directly behind her, she refused to turn and face him. Suddenly, he placed a light kiss on her shoulder. Startled, her body went rigid. Gently, he nuzzled the back of her neck, his unshaven cheek scratching her skin.

"Stop it, John. Behave yourself."

He snickered.

She couldn't move. Her legs wouldn't cooperate with her mind. She was trapped, between his body and the fireplace. Knees trembling, she stood her ground.

His lips touched her earlobe. "Mmmm, something smells good."

She froze, incapable of moving, not knowing what to do. His cat and mouse trifling were a game to him, but

Caroline silently vowed never again to allow his charm to sway her. Trying to keep her voice steady, she turned and glared at him. "Would you like a plate of food?"

"Don't mind if I do," his voice husky. Cocking his head to the side, John lifted an eyebrow and moved back, giving her room. "A ladle of beans will do nicely along with a piece of your fine corn pone."

She desperately tried to regain control of her emotions. "Sit down. I'll set you out a plate."

Stretching his long legs over the wooden bench next to the table, John closed his eyes to ease the ache in his groin. The smell of her sweet fragrance only excited him more. *How many years have passed since the three of them left Pennsylvania and journeyed to Virginia together? Seems like only yesterday.*

He heard the ladle tap the tin plate as she dipped out the food. Famished, the delectable aroma aroused his hunger, causing his stomach to growl. This was his first meal under a roof in weeks. He knew the food would beat his own disgusting trail cooking. "Just put the juice on a bit of the pone."

She carried the plate over to him.

"Sure looks tasty." He watched her hands tremble as she set the plate in front of him. He shot her a mischievous grin and took a spoonful of beans. The morsels melted in his mouth, tasting like a bit of heaven. He loved brown beans and corn pone. Picking up a hunk of bread, he sopped the juices from his plate, all the while studying her graceful movements about the room.

"These vittles are mighty delicious," he said.

She sat down at the butter churn, her back to him. "I'm glad you like them."

Enjoying himself immensely, he smiled. He'd

probably be wearing the food instead of eating it, if Caroline had her way. "Could I bother you for some of that good smelling coffee?"

She rose from her chair, took a cup off the shelf, and poured the coffee.

The gentle sway of her hips captivated him. Her skirt moved like prairie grass in a light wind. He loved the way she pulled her long auburn hair back and tied it behind her neck with a piece of ribbon, accentuating the fine features of her face. Her lips, full and tempting, could smother a man and take away his breath. Her pale blue eyes reminded him of a clear mountain lake, and her small nose had an appealing gentle slope. He wanted to feel the soft skin of her breasts against his bare chest.

She carried the cup to the table. The thought of holding her to his body sent a shiver through him. He wanted to reach out and touch her. The same old longings invaded his thoughts. Her haunting image had plagued him these last twelve years, and seeing her today brought back memories of another time shared before she married Alexander. *If I had paid enough attention back in Pennsylvania, she could have been mine. But back then, I didn't have a lick of sense.*

The blush on her cheeks made him realize his gaze unnerved her. He didn't care, as he breathed in her clean scent mixed with lavender. He recalled a bear was the last feminine thing close enough to hug this trip, and she hadn't even been pretty.

James Anderson flew out to the field, yelling at the top of his lungs. "Pa! Guess what? I saw him! I saw him! Uncle John's here. He looks like a big, wild, hairy bear. Come on, Pa. You gotta see him." He turned and raced to the cabin as though the devil was after him. He didn't want to miss one minute of his uncle's presence nor his stories. Passing the hen house, James spied his sister, Sarah, out feeding the chickens.

"Hey, Sarah. Uncle John's here," he shouted, dashing past her.

"Wait for me," she yelled, dropping the chicken feed pan and racing after him.

Reaching the cabin, the boy burst through the doorway at break-neck speed, crashing the wooden door into the log wall. The door rebounded, hitting James' shoulder and knocking him sideways into the room.

"I'm James," said the nine-year-old lad, stepping up to the table, rubbing his shoulder, not a bit afraid of the dirty, unshaven, buckskin-clad man. The child's dusty brown hair flopped onto his forehead nearly covering his big brown eyes. The mischievous look matched his nature.

John reached out and grasped the boy's small hand. "Hello, James."

Quiet as a mouse, Sarah slipped through the partially opened door and stood behind her brother. John caught a glimpse of her in the shadows. He could feel her staring holes through his worn shirt.

He twisted around, catching her off guard. "Hello, little lady. And who might you be?"

Embarrassed at being caught staring, Sarah lowered her soft blue eyes. Her auburn hair hung to her shoulders, loose strands falling across her face. Trying to think of an answer, she stuttered and blushed red.

"Oh, that's only my silly sister, Sarah," answered James. "Are you really Pa's brother? Did you come all the way from California? Did you know Daniel Boone?"

"Yes, I am and I crossed those big mountains from California *just* to come see you. Now, about Daniel Boone,

I'll tell you later about ole Daniel and me." He paused a moment, rubbed his chin, and grinned from ear to ear. "Would you like to see my 'Injun' scalp?"

Wide-eyed and excited, James gasped, "Yecsss."

Sarah gasped in horror.

Appalled, Caroline swiveled around from the fireplace. "John!" Her eyes flashed a warning signal to him.

He only laughed and waved his hand. "Only kidding, Caroline." Then he winked at James and mouthed, "Later."

Alexander Anderson flung open the cabin door. He couldn't believe his eyes. After years of separation, here sat his older brother.

Rising, John took three gigantic steps, greeted Alexander with a huge bear hug, almost lifting him off the floor.

"Alex, how in the hell are you?" John's voice was a husky murmur.

Choked with emotion, Alexander struggled to speak. "John."

Standing back a step, John grasped his brother by the shoulders to view the man who was now his equal. Silence lingered in the big room, broken only by the ticking of the grandfather clock. Strong emotion gripped both men,

"It's good to see you again," John said.

"Likewise. How've you been?"

"Fine. Health's good."

Alexander noticed a few changes since the last time they were together. A few lines tugged at the corner of his brother's eyes, giving an older and more rustic façade to his nutmeg coloring. "Your hair's a bit longer and a little wilder. At least it's still yours and not on some Indian's shield."

John grinned wide. "Yes, and I still have all of my teeth." Laughter filled the room.

Alexander wondered if his brother's roguish manner and devil-may-care attitude helped him survive the rough life he'd carved out for himself. *He looks so much like our mother.*

"I'd say you've gotten older since I last saw you," said John. "You're taller and a bit more muscular." *My brother has a gentle nature about him, probably comes from easy living here in Virginia. I wonder if he's up to going to the gold fields.*

"Who gets you out of trouble now when your back's against the wall, little brother, or do you get your ass stomped once in a while?" John asked.

"Your speech is still rough as ever." Alexander placed his hands on his hips. "How many times did the two of us go to the woodshed for what Pa called a 'serious talk'?"

John smirked and shook his head. "More than I care to remember."

"We need to eat before everything gets too cold," Caroline said, retreating toward the fireplace. "Sarah, help me set the food out."

Her husband moved the bench out from under the table. "Come and grab yourself a place, John. Let's eat."

James squeezed onto the seat next to his father and uncle as his sister placed the food onto the table.

"Sure looks like we're having a feast tonight," said John, rubbing his hands together. "I've already sampled the beans and corn pone."

The noise around the table buzzed with excitement. Eyeing Alexander from across the table, John listened to the laughter and conversation. He knew it wouldn't be hard to convince his brother to leave the farm. He could see it on his face. The hungry look in his eyes. As Alex talked about the farm and some of the problems he was having, John glanced toward Caroline

She sat there so beautiful and desirable, avoiding his

attention, concentrating on her food. His heart was troubled. Ever since he first laid eyes on her in Pennsylvania, she'd fouled up his life totally. Now her escape from his foolproof plan would be impossible. He'd bide his time until after supper.

Chapter Two

"Remember all the trips I use to make to the Pennsylvania Mountains searching for that once-in-a-lifetime adventure? I never found it there, but I kept on looking."

James, Sarah and Caroline paid attention to the two brothers smiling across the table at one another.

"Aye," replied Alexander. "I remember you're being gone forever. Ma use to say, one day you'd get lost and never return."

"I did." John paused for a moment. "But I also remember promising I'd share my one big adventure with you when I found it. Didn't I?" He bent his arms and rested them on the table in front of him, giving his brother a mischievous smile.

"Did he, Pa?" asked James. He waited for his father's answer, huddling as close as he could to his uncle, touching the buckskin shirt.

Alexander leaned forward on the table, clasping his hands in front of him, interlacing his fingers. "Yes, he did," he replied.

John ruffled James' hair and winked. "I never break a promise, especially to my brother."

Alexander smiled. "All right, then tell me about this promise you never break."

"Right over those mountains the country is beautiful, the land's wide open. Land like nothing you've ever seen back home as a youngster. Good and fertile for the taking. Valleys so green it almost hurts your eyes to look at them." John eyed his brother's expression. "Some of the land lies flat with prairie grasses so tall you can get lost in them. Farther west, there's mountains higher than these here in Virginia, with snow on top of them."

James sat, mouth open, completely mesmerized by his uncle's tale.

Sarah gave her mother a questionable look. "Snow! Our mountains have snow on them in the winter."

John turned around to face Sarah. "Yes, little lady, but on the highest parts of these mountains, snow falls almost everyday, even in July. The Indians call them the Shining Mountains. They're beautiful."

He stopped, letting them digest the information. He needed to be convincing as hell in order to entice his brother with a plan Alexander couldn't resist. Having his brother as a partner in California helping with the box would ease the workload. Caroline being there would make it delectable. His conscience told him he could never have her, yet he needed her near.

Caroline listened to John's words. *How suave he is with his big talk. He's persuasive as ever. Fertile land, lush and green. I wonder what he's leading up to?*

She glanced at her husband. Cold chills danced down her spine. *He's hooked like the fish he brings home for supper.*

As John wove his magical adventure story, she wondered

if another woman had ever entered her brother-in-law's life. Why did that question bother her?

Interrupting his glowing story, she asked, "What do you do out in California?"

"Oh, a little bit of everything, Caroline." A sardonic grin spread across his face.

Alexander leaned his elbow on the table, cupping his chin in his hand. "Is the hunting good?"

"There's so much buffalo and wildlife out there, it'll keep meat on your table for the rest of your life. Some of the buffalo herds stretch for miles," John answered.

James leaned a little closer to his uncle. "What about the Indians?"

"I'll get to them later. Now let me tell you about my trip to St. Louis." John cleared his throat. He didn't want to push ahead too fast and spoil everything. He'd start out by telling them about his travels over the Appalachian Mountains to Louisville, Kentucky.

No one spoke as he told his tale of the journey west.

He continued with his boat trip down the Ohio River, describing the gamblers and river pirates he met along the way, telling about the pitfalls and traps, and how to avoid them.

He stopped talking for a moment, gazed up at the ceiling, trying to recall something special. Then he stood up and spread his arms in a wide semicircle.

"St. Louis, Missoura. What a place," he said, surveying the little group around the cabin table. "The city streets, paved with cobblestones, with elegant coaches traveling over them, and people dressed as if they were in Boston. Sidewalks line both sides of the street, keeping people out of puddles and the ladies' dresses clean. Some of the buildings stand three stories high, made of fancy carved stones." He halted once again, to get a second breath. *Yes, they're still with me.*

"There's hundreds of people coming and going at all hours of the night, gussied up in their Sunday best. Even the river's busy. Fifty or more steamboats arrive each day with a swarm of people and supplies."

Awestruck and unable to move, James sat enthralled with his mouth opened wide and his jaw slack.

"There's more. The west has busted wide open. People arrive by the wagonload, traveling to the territories and California. There's adventure out there, Alex. A whole new beginning for you and your family." Hooked by the magic word, *adventure,* John continued. Lowering his voice, he leaned forward to divulge his secret. "Now, the most important news..." He stopped and looked around. A hush settled over the room. No one moved. "Out in California, they've discovered gold."

Everyone gasped.

"Gold?" Alexander cleared his throat and sat up straight. "Where do you find this gold?"

John licked his lips. "Last year, I was out near Sutter's Mill on the American River by Sacramento when some man by the name of Marshall discovered a huge nugget. I immediately went and claimed me a piece of land at Tracer's Point and started panning for the yellow stuff myself. It's the nuggets that bring the most money, but hell, gold dust and flakes are as good."

He dragged out a small, dirty pouch from beneath his buckskin shirt and poured yellow lumps and soft glittery powder into the palm of his calloused hand. Everyone leaned closer to get a better view, as he passed his hand in front of each one.

"This is worth twice the money you use back here. You can't depend on that paper stuff. Gold is dependable and so easy to get. You pick it right out of the stream." John chose all the right words. Alexander scooted forward for a better look. Mission accomplished. John knew the second part would be a bit trickier. He glanced toward Caroline. She would require more work, an enjoyable, one-on-one, intimate discussion.

James stuck a small finger into John's palm to stir the glistening powder. "Could I do it? Get gold out of a stream?"

His question interrupted John's fantasy. "It's not hard. You have to have the know-how and the tools. And it so happens I've got both. The land I own has a stream smack dab in the middle of it. What do you think of that?" His eyes moved from face to face, soaking up the admiration.

The glint in Alexander's eyes cut straight to Caroline's heart. She could tell John's description of St. Louis excited her husband. However, the tantalizing gold her brother-in-law held in the palm of his rough oversized hand hypnotized her husband, like a carrot dangling in front of a donkey.

She didn't trust John and his hair-brained scheme about easy gold. *Something is wrong with his story, something is missing. And here he is, irresponsible as ever, proposing we pull up our roots and leave everything we worked so hard for, to travel thousands of miles across unknown trails by wagon. He's lost his mind. And, if he thinks we're going, he's crazy.*

Caroline studied the mesmerized faces of her husband and children. John had done his homework well. She listened as he enthusiastically wove his web, ensnaring her family with tales of gold. Holding her breath, she wondered if obtaining gold could be so easy. He made going to California sound exciting. Yet, she knew this irresponsible man never followed through on anything.

Rising to her feet, Caroline walked to the small table in the corner to light another lamp. "James. Sarah. It's time for bed."

"Ah, do we have to go now? I wanted to hear more stories about Uncle John's gold," begged James.

"Can't we stay up a little longer? Please?" pleaded Sarah.

"No, it's bedtime. Say your goodnights." Caroline stood at the foot of the loft ladder, waiting.

They kissed their father and hugged their uncle. "Good night Pa. Good night, Uncle John."

Reluctantly, the children crept up the ladder, tarrying as long as they could at the top, before she heard them scurry across the loft floor. She knew they would lie quietly, listening to the discussion below.

With James and Sarah in bed, Caroline sat in her rocker by the fireplace to do her mending, leaving the men alone to talk freely. Her head bent over her work, she eavesdropped on their conversation. She'd have her say with Alexander after her brother-in-law went to bed.

Leaning closer to his brother, John wasted no time getting down to a more detailed discussion.

"Alex, there's so much I want to tell you. I have a partner in California keeping an eye on the claim. Right now, not much work's going on with the mountain rains and snow. Even with that, I'm taking a chance on losing everything coming here. I can't stay long, so listen." John paused, taking a long breath to emphasize the seriousness of his meaning.

"There's plenty of gold out there for both of us. We'd have to work for it. Hell, it's worth it. Think about it, gold lying in our stream, Alex. *Our stream.* All we'd have to do is dig it out."

John waited a few minutes for it to sink in as he scanned his brother's face. He'd tell him later about the major strike they might make.

"Shoot, it takes more than my partner and me to handle the Long Tom box. It's a ten-to-fifteen-foot trough. Two men do the shoveling while the third throws out the rocks. You're the third man." He eyed Alexander, studying his face. "The best part is the gold you pick up and put in your bag. All yours."

"There's a lot to consider, John, what with my family and all." Alexander shut his eyes and for a moment before continuing. "You mean, we're gonna shovel this gold right out of a stream?"

"Yep." John repeated, "right out of a stream." No doubt about it, his brother was hooked.

Alexander stared at his hands, lacing his fingers together, all the while muttering, "Gold." He lifted up his head. "Just sitting there in our stream. Easy pickings."

"That's right." John didn't need to say much. The westward adventure for gold hit his brother hard, consuming his very fiber.

Alexander's head spun, his heart pounded. Right over those mountains, the dream of all dreams waited for him: adventure, freedom, and opportunity…gold.

Turning abruptly to his brother, he asked, "Why didn't you write and ask me to come out?"

"'Cause I didn't want to take the chance you wouldn't come," John replied. "Besides, I have some important unfinished business to tend to back in St. Louis. So I'll be moving on soon."

Shooting his brother a wide grin, John sat up straight on the bench. "How about I meet you there?"

"In St. Louis?" asked Alexander.

"Yes."

Excitement caused his hands to tingle. "I always wanted to see what was over those mountains. I guess now's as good a time as any."

John leaned forward. In a hushed tone, he said, "Now, here's what we need to do."

Engrossed in their discussion, the two men forgot Caroline existed.

John pulled a wad of crumbled paper from his buckskin shirt and laid it on the table. He gently smoothed out the wrinkles on the crude map in front of him.

"Made this for you before I left California. Now, after you cross the gap, you'll travel across Kentucky." He pointed to various spots on the paper, including rivers and towns.

"There's steamboats in Louisville. It'll cost, but it's the fastest way to St. Louis." He went on explaining about the trail through Missouri, the Oregon Trail, and others that led to his place in California.

"When you get to Independence, we'll make sure you get a good trail master. The trip west is rough. The worst thing that can happen is not to have enough water. I'll be there for you, I promise." He went on describing the river crossings, camping sites, and inns.

Alexander's eyes glowed, absorbing all the information.

Caroline fiercely rocked in her chair, trying to keep her composure. Free...that was the key word. Last time the two of them got together, it only took one week before they packed up their wagon and headed south to Virginia. Now children were involved.

She lifted her eyes and observed the brothers with their heads together, in deep discourse. *It's happening all over again, only this time there's more to lose. This is our home, built with our own hands. We've invested twelve good years of our lives clearing this land. Would he actually consider going to California for gold? I can't believe he would throw it all away.*

Glancing cautiously at the two men at the table, she

waited for Alexander to tell his brother no, he wasn't interested in this zany venture. However, she could tell by the look on her husband's face he devoured every word John said to him.

Alexander darted a glance her way, then quickly resumed his conversation with John.

Change hovered in the air, chilling her to the bone. She didn't want any part of it, not now. She pulled her shawl closer about her shoulders. The idea of jostling across thousands of miles through all kinds of weather over dusty trails and living under the stars had never crossed her mind. The insurmountable dangers of traveling west horrified her. She looked around at several family heirlooms, memories of her past. If this journey materialized, much of what they owned would be left behind. No, the fanciful dream of moving west did not excite her.

She wished she had the gumption to stand up to Alexander and shout, "Forget it. I won't go." What could she do? Stay here without any support. No family nearby. She and the children would starve. She knew she would go with her husband.

Alexander leaped up from the bench, knocking it over, and grasped John's hand, pumping it up and down. "Partners," he shouted.

Caroline jerked her head up as her husband shouted, her shawl slipped off her shoulders. She clutched the rocker arms so tight, her knuckles whitened and cramped. *I can't believe I heard him say that. Partners. Oh, Lord help me.*

John ducked his head a little, but she saw his mischievous grin. She wanted to wipe that smirk off his face.

Alexander turned to her and pounded the table with his fist. "Caroline, we're going to California."

Chapter Three

"Alex, lift that side a little higher. I've got the tongue on a block of wood. There, we're ready now," said John. "James, roll that wheel over here."

Taking the wheel from the boy, he moved it to the back end of the wagon. Suddenly, John shouted, "James, get out from under there. If your father drops that end, you'll get hurt."

The boy scuttled out from under the wagon.

Alexander stood with his back to the wagon box, hands gripping the bottom. Perspiration trickled down his face.

"Hold it. A little more," shouted John, sliding the wheel hub onto the axle shaft. "All right, that's good. You can let it down easy." He grabbed a rag to wipe his hands.

Alexander swiped his face with his shirtsleeve.

James squirmed underneath the wagon for a better look. "It's looking good, Pa."

Caroline stood in the cabin doorway and leaned her forehead against the doorjamb. So much work to get a wagon ready for this journey. She needed to get excited about this trip. However, the miles to California distressed her.

Sarah stepped up on the porch. "Ma, can I—"

"No, I need you to take a container of starter over to Mrs. Lacy." Caroline went inside and returned with a small package. "Now don't play around. I expect you back in two hours."

"Yes, Ma." Sarah skedaddled off down the road, happy to leave.

Caroline headed toward the barn to join the men. The wagon's rectangular shape intrigued her. The bed measured four feet wide and twelve feet long. Eight bent hickory bows would eventually support the rain-proofed canvas covering Sarah and she sewed on each day.

"How's it coming along?" she asked.

"John's about to drop in the linchpin. Now all we have to do is grease the hubs and the wheels are in great shape." Alexander stood tall and proud of the work they had accomplished.

"We still have to caulk and pitch the wagon to make her watertight." John winked at his brother. "Then she'll sail across those deep rivers, dry as a man's whistle without a drink. Yep, it's starting to look real travel worthy."

Alexander stepped back to admire his work. "What do you think?"

"It's, ah..." Caroline paused for a moment. "It looks like a home on wheels," she replied as she stretched the truth a little.

"Sarah and I are almost finished sewing the covering. We doubled some of the material, hoping to make it more weatherproof. It should be ready by the end of the week."

"That's good." Alexander nodded toward James and John, "We're gonna take the small wagon into town in a bit. Need to purchase some pitch and tar to mix with the tallow for the grease bucket. We'll be stopping at Wilson's Store. Need anything?"

"Yes, another spool of heavier thread, a yard of oiled canvas, and two needles. Mr. Wilson'll know the size." With one last glance at the men's handiwork she headed back to the cabin.

Caroline walked about the chicken coop, carefully collecting eggs, making sure to leave one next to the small nesting rock in each box. With her mind on items to pack for the trip, she didn't hear the door creak.

"You sure are beautiful with straw stuck in your hair."

Caroline jumped, dropping several of the precious eggs onto the floor.

"I thought you went into town with Alexander and James."

"No. I decided to stay." John took two steps toward her. "Damn, you're beautiful."

"Leave me alone, John. Go away."

"Oh, I plan on leaving, but first we need to talk…you and me with no family around."

Stepping closer with every word, his body now almost touched her. Stopping short by a few inches, he flicked the straw from her hair, and then lifted her chin with his hand.

Jerking away from his touch, she dropped the egg basket, breaking a few while two eggs rolled across the shed floor.

"Darn it, John, look what you made me do." Caroline wasn't sure what he had in mind, but she knew it spelled trouble for both of them. Glancing up, she found his face so close, she saw her reflection in his eyes.

"Caroline, why didn't you wait for me back in Pennsylvania?"

"Wait for you? You were never around," she said matter-of-factly.

"I loved you, woman."

"How was I to know that? Did you ever tell me you loved me?"

"No. You knew I did. I would've married you."

"When? Did you ever mention that you wanted me as your wife? Did you?"

"No…no, I didn't. I thought you understood how I felt after we—"

"John, a woman needs to be told those things. Besides, you have to ask a woman to marry you. You just can't take her for granted."

"Damn it, I cared. You should have known that. I wanted you. Then you go off and marry my brother." He slammed his fist into a nesting board and splintered it into pieces.

"It's too late John. I'm married to Alexander and have his children," she said. "It's too late."

"Do you think I don't know that?" He paused for a moment, rubbing his clenched right fist. "It doesn't change the fact that I still love you. You have no idea how much I think about you." His deep brown eyes narrowed in a threatening expression. "I had you once, remember? You were mine."

"No, John. I was never yours because you never asked me. You took my self-respect, my dignity, and all you gave me was heartache and worry." She shot him a defiant stare and started to leave. "I'm sorry John, you'll—"

He grabbed her roughly by the shoulders, yanked her toward him. Grasping her in his arms, he wrapped them securely around her body, crushed his lips onto hers, taking her breath away. Stunned, she melted into his embrace, overcome by his passion as he greedily devoured her lips, his tongue slipping into her mouth.

Time stood still as years of longing aroused the passion, cascading over them. She couldn't breathe, blood raced through her veins. His muscles twitched with anticipation against her body.

She couldn't let this happen. Not now. Shoving him away, she ducked from his reach as he grabbed for her.

"Stop it! Enough." She gasped for air. "Leave me alone, John. This is no way to treat me. I'm your brother's wife." Shaking, she stood her ground, trying to get her thoughts together. "We talked about this before you went west."

"We didn't talk," he retorted. "You said, go away and I did. If I had any sense then, I would've taken you with me."

"John, I won't have any of this. You're my *brother-in-law*." Caroline paused for a moment, raising her arm in defense. "Stay away. Listen to me. I love Alexander." With her anger building, she took a wide stance. Placing one hand on her hip and shaking the other in his face, she shouted, "Leave…me…alone! You mean nothing to me anymore. Nothing!" Regaining control, she coldly stared him down. "You need to leave. Tomorrow isn't soon enough."

Quickly, she escaped the chicken coop before she changed her mind. She could still feel the warmth of his arms around her, crushing her against his chest. Her heart still raced. Her hands shook. The taste of his smoldering kiss made her knees weak. Surprised by her overwhelming desire for him, she staggered to the cabin to find refuge, leaving the overturned egg basket on the chicken shed floor.

Ya stupid fool. John pulled his foot back to kick the egg basket. Staring at it, he bent over and rescued a few unbroken eggs off the floor, placed them in the basket, and set it on the shelf. *You've made a mess of things again and this time you've lost her for good.* He left the shed, slamming the coop door. Across the way, the cabin door closed behind Caroline. No final gesture, no wave, no second look. She had discarded him like an old shoe. His anger exploded.

He stomped off into the woods, following the path along the crooked creek. Infuriated and riled, he thrashed his way through the brush, shoving aside branches with his arms and body, barely aware of the thorns. He needed to think. All the old memories flooded back, causing him unbearable anguish and pain. If he could only bury these feelings, he could think straight. The woman made him crazy. He dreamed of wrapping his arms around her body, holding her close, feeling her warmth. He wanted to smell the freshness of her hair, feel the softness of her skin next to his. He had desire walled up inside like a bag full of rattlers.

Picking up a fist-sized rock, he threw it as hard as he could and heard it bounce off a tree. Hell, she didn't even want him. He hated it when his plans backfired on him. He'd figured that when he got her to California, things might be different. No, nothing would change for him except more misery. He had muddled the whole affair pushing too hard. She would never be his. To make matters worse, he'd invited Alexander and his family out west to work the gold fields. Trapped by his own doings, he'd set himself up for a big fall.

"Here's to my brother and his beautiful wife." He flung a stick across the creek, yelling, "She should have been mine."

Before first early light, John stood on the porch, talking to Alexander, his pack resting against his leg. "Well, I have to be moving on. Time's slipping away and I need to get back."

"Won't be long we'll be in California with ya. We should

be leaving here in another two or three weeks. You'll meet us in St. Louis? Right?"

"Yes. At the City Hotel on Third and Vine. Can't wait long, so you gotta hurry." John paused for a moment. "If something should happen and I'm not there, I'll leave you directions to the next meeting place."

"I don't want a note on how to get from place to place. I wanta travel with you. I'd feel safer, with the family and all."

"Whoa. Trust me," John replied, a bit testy. "Have I ever let you down?" He stepped off the porch. "Say my good-byes to your family and your sweet wife. You're a lucky man, Alex. Remember that."

Alexander watched his brother disappear down the road, engulfed by the early morning darkness. The mangy black mare he rode needed some meat on her bones. They traveled together from California, he guessed they'd make it back home.

Won't be long now. Once we get the wagon packed and sell the land, we're California bound. Nope, won't be long at al. The excitement welled up inside him, sending shivers down his spine. *I wonder if I can push a little harder. Heck, we can probably be ready in two weeks, if I can only sell the place.*

"Did John leave?" Caroline quietly stepped through the doorway with a blanket wrapped about her shoulders. A light patch of fog twisted through the valley in the chilly morning air.

"Yes. Said he needed to be going. He sure seemed in an awful hurry to get out of here. Yesterday, he talked as if he wanted to stay a few more days. This morning he packs up and takes off. I don't understand him."

I understand him. It's over. That's the end of it. Relieved,

Caroline strolled back into the quiet cabin to warm herself by the glowing fire. Feeling at ease and safe for the time being, she nestled into her rocker. Heat from the fireplace enveloped her body.

Alexander followed her. "I can't believe we're so close to leaving. Won't be long and we'll be heading down that same road." He walked to the fireplace to pour himself some coffee. "You know, Sarah sure favors my brother."

Caroline's muscles tensed, cold gripped her heart. With a slight quiver in her voice, she said the first thing that popped into her head. "I wouldn't say that. She looks more like your mother to me."

Chapter Four

Perspiration trickled down Alexander's forehead, dripping off the end of his nose. Removing his hat with his free hand, he wiped the sweat away with the sleeve of his shirt. *Phew, March is a little too warm this year.* Raising his hand to shield his eyes from the sun, the brilliant light brought back images of the golden lumps and dust his brother had held in his hand. Gold. As his thoughts drifted to California, he envisioned the lumps lying on the bottom of their stream. Waiting.

"Pa, how soon will we start out to see Uncle John?" James kicked the wheel rim, dislodging dirt from his boot.

Startled back to reality, Alexander answered, "Ah, hopefully in a couple of weeks or so." Walking around to the back of the wagon, he hung the grease bucket on the rear axle.

"There, that does it. Everything looks good." He scrutinized his workmanship on the sturdy wagon made of seasoned, maple wood. The hickory bows bent high over the inside. Squatting, he checked the undercarriage. John had helped him with that part. "All we need to do now is load her up and head for the 'land of milk and honey'. Don't want to get caught by the mountain snows."

"Will we sell our two cows?" James stared at his father waiting for an answer.

Alexander shook his head. "Son, I think you're more worried about the work involved on the trail than the poor old cows. Yes, we're selling everything we can, including the livestock. We're only taking what's necessary to California."

James began to fiddle with something under the seat, stretching across the bench, his bottom sticking up and his head down, wedged next to the footboard and jockey box.

Coming around to the front of the wagon, Alexander caught sight of his son as he squirmed under the seat. "I swan, you're a little too inquisitive for your own good. Serve you right if you get stuck under there."

"Aw, Pa."

Walking up behind them, Caroline brought three cups of cool water from the spring. "Why don't you two rest a spell?"

"Mmmm. Sounds good." Alexander removed his hat, chugged down the cup of water, then wiped his mouth with the back of his hand. "Ah, that tasted good." Handing the cup back to Caroline, he asked, "What do you think?" Pleased as a peacock, he spread one arm in front of him, displaying their future home on wheels.

Patting him on the back, she felt the dampness through his shirt. "It looks good. When will the wagon be ready?"

"It's ready now. All we need to do is stretch the canvas top on and load'er up." Alexander paused for a moment. "I'm going into town in a bit and talk with Nelson again. He's interested in buying the place. Should get a nice price for it, what with all the outbuildings."

"What about the livestock?"

"Need to talk with Peter Johnson tomorrow. He definitely wants to buy all we have."

"That's good." She stood quietly, gazing at the wagon.

Alexander looped his arm around her waist. "Not bad," he said. "Not bad at all, if I do say so myself."

"When you get through admiring your work, I have a list of food you need to buy for this trip."

"I'm sure you do." He held her close as they walked toward the cabin.

"Let me see. We'll need sixty pounds of coffee, two hundred pounds of beans, forty pounds of salt…"

Time slipped away, faster than Caroline anticipated. The wagon was ready. She looked about the cabin. So much to do and so little time left. For the past week, she and two neighbor ladies had sewn shirts and trousers, pantaloons, several pullover dresses, and petticoats. They sewed three changes of new clothes for each family member from the forty yards of cloth she wove.

"Ma, can I use these scraps for my quilt?" Sarah held up several remnant pieces of cloth. "Please?" she pleaded.

Caroline smiled. "Yes, you may have them. How are your Nine Patch squares coming along? Be sure you alternate the four dark colors with the five light ones."

"I am. I had to rip out two pieces, but I finished three. See." Sarah showed her handiwork.

"They look nice. Think of all the time you'll have to sew the pieces together while on the trail. Now put your sewing away, we need to get our chores done before your Pa gets back. You can start with the pan on the table."

Sarah threw the dishwater out the door. Setting the pan

on the table, she asked, "Ma, do we have to go so far away? I don't wanna leave Rebecca. Besides, I hate sitting and eating off some old, dirty ground. I like the feel of a bench on my bottom, something comfortable and clean."

"We will do what we have to do," said Caroline. She didn't want to make this trip either. "When a man makes up his mind, there's no changing it."

Sarah fisted her hands on her hips. "Phooey."

"Think of the new and wonderful places and things we'll see." Caroline tried to make it sound exciting to keep her daughter's spirits up.

Sarah lowered her eyes and screwed up her nose. "What's the use? No one ever listens to me." She yanked her bonnet off the peg, jerked it over her head, tied the ends in a knot under her chin, and stomped through the door in a huff.

"Don't forget the basket. You need to collect the eggs." No sooner had Caroline muttered the words, than memories of the chicken house with John came flooding back, sending shivers up her spine. *Blast you, John. Just wait. I'm gonna make your life miserable.*

Days passed and crucial preparations brought Caroline face to face with heartaches. She picked up a blue and white teacup and stroked it gently with her fingers.

"Ma, didn't that belong to your grandmother?" asked Sarah.

"Yes, it's the tea service she hid during the Revolutionary War. My mother gave the set to Pa and me as a wedding present." Caroline thought about the beautiful cup and her wedding day, remembering how surprised she was when her mother handed the set to her. Now she must leave it behind. There wasn't enough space for frivolous belongings.

"Preacher Henderson and his wife want to buy it," she said. "I'm sure they will take good care of it."

"What about the clock?"

"Esther Marshall wants it."

Sarah stared at the grandfather clock, ticking away the minutes of her life in a familiar place. "That's sad."

Many years ago, Caroline's father had made the clock and now, it too, would be left behind. She'd miss its mellow tones that gave her comfort during the many dark nights she'd sat holding poor baby Jane before she died.

The decisions were heartrending. She settled comfortably into her rocking chair, mentally and physically exhausted. Packing had turned into a trying experience. Parting with many of her beloved keepsakes emotionally drained Caroline.

Gazing out the window, she caught a quick glimpse of the canvas flap in the wind, a bright addition to the dark rough wood. Alexander stood next to the jockey box beneath the seat, carefully selecting the necessary tools for the journey. Whatever additional tools her husband needed out in California, he'd make later.

"Sarah, get the candles from under my bed." Turning back to her work, Caroline picked up an empty box.

Carefully, she rolled each candle in toweling and packed them side-by-side, stuffing patching material into the open spaces. Next, she wrapped the family Bible in a soft cloth and placed it on top of the packed items, putting rolled linen between and around the Bible to keep it safe. Recorded in its pages were the family births and deaths.

"Now, let me see. I guess we need to pack the soap next."

Sarah leaned against the rocker. "How much are we taking with us, Ma?"

"All ten pounds. Staying clean will be a challenge. We'll need to do lots of washing on the journey."

Sarah snickered as she helped her mother pack the homemade soap. "James won't like that. Bathing isn't one of his favorite things."

"We won't tell him." Caroline reached up and handed Sarah several spools of thread and two packages of needles. "Here, put these in the pockets we sewed on the inside of the canvas cover. What a clever idea you had. It will keep all of our sewing items handy."

Sarah dashed out to the wagon.

"Let me see," Caroline said, making a mental note of items to remind Alexander. "We need to pick up the food supplies from town. I wonder if Alexander got the vinegar and the salt bag."

Her daughter returned, stepping through the doorway. "Pa put 'em over in the corner next to the tea and the pickles."

"What about the saleratus? We'll need that to make the biscuits rise."

"James put it over there, too." Sarah placed her elbows on the table, while cupping her chin. "This packing is a lot of work."

"Yes, and there's still lots to do."

Caroline pointed toward the fireplace. "Hand me that bag on the chair over there."

Using both hands, Sarah struggled with the heavy bag. "What's in here?"

"This is gonna be our medicine bag."

Sarah plopped down next to her mother, stretching her neck to see inside.

Caroline looked at each item. "Let's see, there's laudanum and camphor, hartshorn for snakebites, quinine for malaria, peppermint essence, and of course, citric acid for scurvy. We need to pack the castor oil."

Sarah wriggled up her nose and stuck out her tongue. “Yuck. Can’t we leave that behind?”

Caroline smiled. “Maybe we won’t need to use it.”

Sarah got up and ran out the door on her way to tell James about the Castor Oil.

“I still need to pack several bottles of Alexander’s ‘medicinal’ libation. I only hope there’ll be some left when we arrive in California. Maybe I should hide a bottle or two.” Exhausted, she sat back in the rocker and shut her eyes, resting her head against the bare wood. *So much to do and so little time to get ready.*

A week later, Alexander went over some of the items lying on the porch. He hoped he wasn’t forgetting anything important. The food he had ordered from Wilson sat in a corner of the cabin, all ready to go. The tightly-packed clothing trunks waited in another corner. The hand-sewn canvas tent, their sleeping quarters for the next six months, rested on the porch and would be loaded last. Inside the cabin, more boxes littered the floor. He needed to pack the butter churn, a washtub, and several other large items. He stood with his hands on his hips. Would it all fit?

Gazing across the land, he watched the sun slide behind the mountains. The peaceful sunset nestled lightly in the dips of the hills. The colors ranged from rose and pink to blue, caressing the stately treetops and sending shadows into the valley. Today the crisp March breeze penetrated his woolen jacket, chilling him as the day receded.

Inside the cabin, Caroline sat quietly in front of the fireplace, working on her hand sewing. The lighted lantern cast shadows across the walls. Leaning against the doorframe, he said, "God made some beautiful land. We've settled Virginia and proved our mettle. Now we have another challenge. California."

"Yes. We do have a challenge ahead of us." She took a couple more stitches.

"Tomorrow I have a few more debts to collect. We're gonna need every cent we can get. I'm sure there'll be expenses that will crop up along the way. Probably have to buy supplies before we make Independence." He paused for a moment. "Independence. What a far-sounding destination. The 'jumping off' place they call it."

She continued her needlework, too tired to contribute to the conversation tonight.

Sarah and James ran into the house. They plopped down on the bench at the table.

"Pa, when are we leaving?" asked James.

"Everything should be completed by tomorrow afternoon. In two days, we'll be packed up and on our way."

Caroline sat up and raised her head. *Two days! Lord have mercy. We're leaving in two days*

Chapter Five

"Okay, Pa. Stop," yelled James, kicking the tailgate down. Alexander and Peter Marshall, a neighbor, chocked the wheels and placed the wagon tongue on a wood block. James jumped onto the porch. The rear end of the wagon now faced the cabin doorway.

"The canvas top looks fine, Carolinc," said Esther Marshall.

Caroline stood on the porch, admiring her handiwork. "Sarah and I worked many days on it."

"Do you think the wagon will hold everythin' you wanna take?"

"Alexander seems to believe he has things under control. We've sold all of the furniture and many of the household items we can't take with us, keeping only the things we need."

Esther stuck her hands into her apron pockets. "So you're leavin' in the mornin'."

"Yes. Right after breakfast."

For over five years, Caroline and Esther had quilted

together, shared troubles, and helped each other when their children got sick. Now, she was leaving, traveling over three thousand miles away.

Esther touched Caroline's shoulder. "You look tired and a little peaked today. This must be very hard for you."

"Yes, there's so much more to do." Caroline sighed. She clasped her hands together in front of her apron. "Still have to cook extra food for our nooning meal tomorrow."

Esther glanced sideways at her. "I guess we need to get busy. Looks like the men have plenty to do." Boxes, sacks, and barrels crowded the Anderson porch.

Caroline turned and headed for the doorway. "I want to thank you for coming over and helping us out."

Esther followed her. "Peter and I wouldn't have it any other way. You know the old sayin', 'Four hands are better than two'. At least somethin' like that."

The women disappeared inside the cabin.

"Peter, let's pack those six double-canvas flour sacks forward in the wagon, on the left side," said Alexander. "Then we'll put the sugar bags against the opposite wall to even the load."

"Those India-rubber bags you got through Wilson should keep your sugar dry." Peter ran his hands over one bag. "Must be somethin' new."

"Pa, here's the two bags of dried fruit." James put them down on the porch, propping them against the post.

"How many more fruit bags do we have?" asked Alexander.

"About four." James kicked a stick off the porch. "Sarah's bringing out the sacks of *little britches*. Green beans will taste great on the trail. All we have to do is soak 'em a little. Yum."

"Peter, put the wash tub up forward. We can pack the dried food sacks in it." Alexander stood for a moment contemplating the available space. "The loom goes in next. It's in the cabin."

"Has it been knocked down?"

"Yes, did that last night."

"I'll go get it." Peter jumped off the wagon onto the porch. "Come on, James, you can help me."

"I'll lash the water barrels on. We'll fill 'em in the morning." Talking to himself, Alexander ran over the list. "Now let me see. We still need to remove the bacon and lard from the smoke house. We can use bran to pack it. Hmmm, and there's…"

"Sarah, take this churn out to your Pa."

She stopped frying doughnuts, dipping out the last two, and picked up the churn.

Esther covered four loaves of bread on the breadboard. "We'll let these rise. If you'll stop by in the morning on your way out, I have some crackers made up for ya."

"Oh, Esther, how nice. I didn't have time to make them. Thank you."

"Well, I know you'll need 'em." Esther carried the baking utensils over to the wash pan.

"Tonight, I'll stew some dried fruit. It will be a nice dessert for tomorrow evening at our first layover." Caroline stood looking down at the packing box by her feet. "Six to seven months on a trail. I hope we have enough supplies to get us through."

"I hope it will be an easy trip for you," Esther said. "Now what do you want me to do next?"

* * *

Caroline woke before dawn. Stars still filled the sky. She lit two lanterns and aroused the children. Already dressed, Alexander moved about the cabin raring to get on the road.

"Sarah, James, collect the bedding and stack it near the door." The children descended the ladder half awake, carrying their pillows and blankets.

"I'll take 'em out." Alexander grabbed an armful and walked through the doorway. "I'll be back to get ours."

"James, take a lantern outside for your Pa so that he can see what he's doing. Sarah, strip my bed while I get this food prepared."

Alexander stepped through the doorway. "Are there any more boxes to take out?"

"No."

"Good. James, Sarah, start filling the water barrels while I feed the horses." Staring at the empty barn, Caroline heard Alexander say, "Sure looks bare since Johnson took the livestock."

"I know. I had to borrow eggs from Esther yesterday."

Alexander walked over and stood by the table. Caroline looked up. "I have a surprise for you. I've packed the wagon tight and found a small amount of room. How would you like to take your rocker along?"

Caroline dropped the bowl of fruit on the table. "Yes." She threw her arms around his neck, startling him. Squeezing her husband as hard as she could, she began to sob.

"Oh, Alexander." She hung on to him as all the anxiety flowed from her body. Tears streamed down her cheeks, soaking his shirt.

Not exactly sure what to do, he put his arms around her and held her tight. He knew she loved that rocker and it would have broken her heart to give it away.

"Ma, what's wrong. Don't you feel well? What happened?" Sarah stood in the middle of the doorway, shocked to see her ma crying and her pa hugging her, all the while twirling in the middle of the room.

"Ma wanted to dance. She's a little strange this morning."

Alexander kissed Sarah's forehead, chucked her under the chin, and then made a fast escape to the barn before she asked any more questions. He knew women were emotional, but he'd never seen Caroline like this before, happy and sad all at the same time. *Maybe this trip is too much for her and the children. That crying makes me feel uneasy, all over a silly rocker. This woman stuff is getting to me. Next, it'll be Sarah.*

As first light ribboned the sky, the family ate breakfast, cooked extra food, packed it away for later, and washed the dishes, placing them into the side box on the wagon. They worked quickly to finish packing a few small items into the wagon.

"Put it over there, James. No, not there. Between the little box and that large trunk. Oh, find a place and stuff it in." Tired and irritable, Sarah stamped her foot. "You're impossible."

Caroline brought out two small boxes. She knew the children were still sleepy. "Why don't we stop awhile and let Pa look over what's left to pack."

"Suits me fine," said James. He flopped down on the folded tent, bottom first with his feet in the air.

Testing the canvas like a cat softening its bed, he picked out his traveling spot with a bird's eye view. Suddenly, he rolled off the tent, arms and legs flinging every which way, and almost fell off the back of the wagon.

As he clung to the gate rope, feet dangling over the edge, Sarah broke in fits of laughter.

"That's not funny, Sarah," said James, embarrassed by his ungraceful maneuvers.

"Are you hurt, James?" asked his mother.

"No, I'm all right," he answered, rubbing his elbow.

He sat on the back of the wagon with his knees propped up. Sarah took a seat on the porch, placing her feet on the porch step and wrapping her arms around her knees. Caroline sat down next to her. They waited.

Alexander walked out of the cabin, carrying another small trunk, packed with clothes. He hoisted it off his shoulder onto the tailgate. "I have one smaller trunk to bring out. We should be about ready to leave."

James knelt on the tailgate to help his father shove the trunk up into the wagon.

Caroline stood up and walked toward them. "Place one over here. The smaller trunk goes over there and the medicine bag on top. James, Sarah, go get the two boxes off the table. We'll put the cooking pots and utensils in the grub box." Caroline opened the box on the side of the wagon. She moved the coffee pot and Dutch oven to make room for the other items the children brought to her. "Let me see. Oh, Sarah, don't forget the rolling pin and the coffee mill off the lower shelf by the table. And the smoothing iron."

"All right, Ma." Sarah ran inside the cabin.

Checking on her spinning wheel, she made sure it was secure and in place.

Alexander stood with his hands on his hips. "Are we all packed? Everybody ready? Let's go. Daylight's slipping away."

The moment had finally arrived.

Bursting with excitement, James shouted, "Let's go!"

Sarah climbed into the wagon, a small wooden box

with all her valuable keepsakes in her hands. She strategically stuffed it between some of the bedding to secure its safety. "There, that should hold it from bouncing around this old wagon."

Caroline knew Sarah had mixed feelings about leaving and didn't know how to express her misgivings about the trip. Her daughter was a martyr to the end as she sat down and gently spread her dress about her, placing her folded hands in her lap

Tension filled Caroline's body as she looked at the wagon, her home on wheels for the next six or seven months.

Alexander hitched up the horses and rechecked the wagon for the third time, in case he'd missed something crucial.

As a farewell gesture, Caroline reentered the cabin to say her personal good-byes. She loved her home and her heart ached. Memories flooded back as her eyes swept the naked interior. The emptiness crushed her. A sad hush settled within the cabin. It wasn't the same without their belongings in place and the family's presence inside. Now the Nelson's would be moving in soon.

"I wish them love and happiness," she whispered. "It's a sturdy cabin and will serve them well."

She and Alexander had taken much pride in raising it, with the help of their neighbors. Now, it was time to leave and start anew.

She stepped through the doorway and closed the door.

"Ready?" Alexander asked, sitting with the reins in both hands.

Never looking back, she climbed up onto the seat next to her husband. "Yes."

"Then let's go." He stirred up the horses. "Gee up." The wagon rolled south, down the dusty road.

Caroline turned to view a small lonely cross on the hillside. *Good-bye, Janie.*

Chapter Six

St. Louis, Missouri

John Anderson stood at the railing of the crowded ferry, viewing the angry, muddy water lap at the floorboards. His thoughts were totally occupied by a dog-eared letter tucked away in his buckskin pocket. It was written by D'Alene Dubois, the most beautiful woman he'd ever known, a woman who shared part of his life once. Their affection proved to be more of a sexual desire, a convenience for survival. He smiled. What a convenience.

Standing at the railing, looking down at the whirling water, he puzzled as to how the letter tracked him to California. Must be fate. He'd had left no destination or forwarding address when he had departed St. Louis in a hurry ten years ago. After all this time, she needed his help and he couldn't refuse. It was time to pay the piper.

The panoramic scene of St. Louis drew nearer, memories

flooded back to a turbulent time John tried to forget. Leaning against the rail, he rubbed his brow. It had all started with a love affair in Pennsylvania that went bad because he'd never told Caroline how much he loved her. That was the reasoning she had given him, before she demanded he leave and never come back.

A log twirled in the water, thumping the ferry hard, jolting the passengers. John gripped the railing. The last time he had arrived in St. Louis, the water ran high and fast, like now. The good old muddy Mississippi whirled and lapped at everything in its path. Old Muddy was a mean, meandering river that reclaimed the land when the banks overflowed. With all its flaws, it was still the best catfishing place ever. Fish nested in rock and mud ledges along the banks of the river. He remembered the stories an old man had told him about fishing naked in the water, shoulder high.

"Yes, siree," old Joe had said. "I stuck my right hand in that there catfish's mouth, gigged him with the hook in my left hand, and pull him out of the hole upside down. But, ya have to watch out for those three pointy spines. If they git ya, it sure is painful. Won't kill ya, but you'll surely hurt a while."

John chuckled. That must have been a sight, seeing that old man naked as the day he was born, weighing a little over 300 pounds, wrestling a 50 to 75-pound catfish to the bank.

Looking into the dark water reminded him of the angry and resentful mood that had settled over him when Caroline rejected him. Leaving Virginia in a huff, he arrived in St. Louis, hostile and belligerent. He had found solace in a bottle of raw whiskey and the arms of a beautiful mulatto woman, D'Alene Dubois. She was a slender, soft-spoken Creole from New Orleans who didn't ask for anything or inquire about his past. The affair was doomed from the beginning, and he didn't care. He needed a warm body. They had spent two wildly passionate years together in her elaborate boudoir until one spring day the money ran out and the whiskey wore off.

Sitting in a bar, broke and completely sober, John had met a few of William Ashley's Rocky Mountain Fur trappers. They were heading up to the Green River rendezvous in the western territories. Their adventurous stories about trapping and hunting in the wide-open spaces had excited him and stirred his soul. He'd rushed to his room, packed up his gear, and joined the buckskin hunters for a canoe trip up the Missouri River. His short note had told D'Alene he'd be back. What he hadn't realized was the fur trapping days were over. When he arrived up in the mountains, there was nothing much to trap except bear, coyote and such. The beaver had played out. No one in Europe was interested in that type of skin anymore. So he'd wandered the Sierra Madre range and ended up in California. He could've returned to St. Louis, but didn't. He'd become distracted with all his adventures and time slipped away.

As the ferry neared the landing, he reached for his horse's reins, walked to the front rail, and stood next to the ferryman.

"The city sure has grown since I was here last. There's buildings everywhere, as far as the eye can see."

"Yep. They keep extendin' the city limits further out every year. If they keep goin', it'll reach St. Charles one of these days."

John leaned on the ferry railing. "Don't remember the levee being so crowded. The cotton and hemp's stacked higher than the workers."

"Everyday, there's more and more people a-buzzin' round here like bees at a honey pot. Can't get the work done these days with all this activity." The ferryman walked away, mumbling to himself.

Steamboats were docked everywhere, with hardly any

room available at the landing. He wouldn't stay here long, too crowded for his way of life. He needed room to breathe.

With a thud, the ferry stopped and the gangplank clunked onto the levee. Disembarking, John mounted his horse and headed for a nearby tavern. He needed a strong drink to quench his thirst, and partly to build up his courage so he could face D'Alene. He had used her and wasn't proud of it. After she saved his life, he'd walked away without saying good-bye. Now he needed to own up to his cowardice and bite the bullet. Yes, he needed a tall drink fast.

John rode along the bank, made a couple of turns, searching for some of his old haunts. Ahead in the Irish part of town named Battle Row stood a tall two-story, brick building housing J. O'Donnell's Saloon. He tied his horse to the hitching post next to a few buggies.

He walked through the door into a smoky room buzzing with activity. A room full of regulars crowded the bar while a piano player plunked out a raunchy tune, adding to the din. Upstairs at the gambling tables, the patrons' shouting drifted down the staircase. Looking around and selecting a table in the corner, he planned to lose himself in here for a couple hours.

After John ordered a mug of ale, a brightly dressed matronly lady sashayed over to him.

"Hi, handsome. My name's Maggie. Ya want company?"

John looked up from his drink. The lady's makeup started with overdrawn red lips, bright splotches of rouge on her cheeks, and a heavily powdered face, giving her a white pasty look. Three side curls cascaded down from her high piled disheveled red hair. The lace trim from the neckline of her purple off the shoulder dress needed repairing.

"No, not tonight."

"It'll only cost you a drink."

He wanted to be alone, drink until his mind went numb, he didn't want conversation. "No. Go find another table."

John lowered his eyes, looked into the dark Irish ale. Returning to old haunts made him uneasy. Slowly he sipped the brew, some of it trickled down his chin. Wiping it away with the sleeve of his buckskin shirt, he set the half empty mug on the table and closed his eyes. Another full mug arrived, then another. Time slipped away. He didn't know how much he drank nor did he care. He put down his coins and lifted the mug. Music blended with the chatter as his temperament mellowed.

His mind conjured up D'Alene's beautiful body. Aroused by the memory of her smooth caramel-colored skin, he wanted to stretch out his hand and feel her satiny texture beneath his fingers, smell her rose scented hair. His passion for her came swimming back, filling him with heated fervor. Maybe he did love D'Alene at one time. On the other hand, the affair had been short-lived, not strong enough to keep him in St. Louis. He had changed, moved on to wilder, more exciting times. Nothing is forever.

Rolling the ale mug between his hands, disturbing memories of a fatal poker game in a backroom whirled through his mind. He couldn't remember the name of the tavern. It really didn't matter. His winning streak had been good that night, Lady Luck stuck with him. Earlier in the evening, he'd won enough money to get into Beckett's high stakes poker game. They were playing 32-card poker, lowest card a seven.

There were five players at the table and the biggest loser was Dr. Beckett. The good doctor's face flushed from too much drink, his condition worsened with each losing hand. The pot grew with each deal. John picked up the cards, one at a time, placing them in order, side by side. He held three queens, a seven and a nine. He kept two queens and discarded the rest. "Give me two." Slowly he picked up the first one. It was an eight, then another eight. He was holding a full house.

"I'll raise you two hundred," said Beckett, puffing on his cigar. He stared at John across the table as he placed his money into the pot.

"I'm out," said one player.

"Me, too," said another.

"So am I. Too rich for my blood." The third player threw in his cards.

John stared at Beckett, gave him a devious smile, and pushed his money forward, into the pot. "Call."

Beckett leaned forward, sneering as he laid down his cards. "I've got a flush."

John pretentiously placed his cards onto the table. "Full house." He stood and racked in the $1,200 pot.

Beckett's face flushed red as he roared, "You filthy cheat. I hate card sharks. They're not wanted in St. Louis." He stood up and leaned across the table. "You better get your ass out of town. Someone just might cut your throat before the week's out." He turned, knocked over his chair, and staggered out of the room.

John left the tavern with a wad of money in his pockets and walked down the dark street toward D'Alene's place. Turning into an alley, he stopped to stuff most of the bills into his boots, making them extremely tight. It made walking difficult, but the money was safe. The rest of the bills he wadded into his pockets. Rounding a corner four blocks away, someone grabbed him from behind and stabbed him in the shoulder. His assailant kicked and beat him, then robbed his pockets.

He couldn't remember how long he lay in the alley. Pulling himself up off the ground, he stood leaning against the wall. In excruciating pain, he staggered the rest of the way home, hanging onto whatever he could. The last thing John remembered was falling in front of D'Alene's door.

Weeks later, she told him how she found him, crumpled up in a heap. He almost died from loss of blood. She nursed him back to health, keeping his wound clean until it healed. Even though his pockets were empty, his boots contained most of his winnings. They lived high until they spent every last cent....

He tried to forget that living nightmare, but couldn't. It still rolled around in his head. Now his past came to haunt him through her letter, pleading for his help.

If you ever loved me, if you ever cared, you will come. I need you....

Here I sit, all because of a woman and a debt to repay. Downing the last of his drink and quite inebriated, John stumbled across the room, out into the fading sunlight. As the shadows grew longer, he needed to locate the City Hotel. Tomorrow he'd tackle finding D'Alene. Right now he needed sleep.

Morning came early, too early. His mouth tasted like dry, gritty desert sand with tumbleweed rolling around inside. He pulled the covers over his head to ward off the sunlight sneaking through the slit in the shade covering the window. His bad breath gave him cause to pull back the covers and sit on the edge of the bed, head in his hands. How many brews did he drink? Seven...nine? Who knew?

He stumbled over to the dry sink and poured water from the pitcher into the basin. A roach floated on its back across the partially filled basin.

"You couldn't take it either, huh?" He flipped the bug onto the cabinet top, scooped up the cold water with his hands, and splashed it on his face. "Whoa, that could wake the dead." He was wide-awake now. In fact the cold water gave him a headache. He ran his wet hands through his hair, trying to control the wild wispy ends. Before he put any more energy into cleaning up, he desperately needed coffee. Placing both hands on the dry sink, he leaned forward and gazed into the crackled mirror. Lines ran every which way, distorting his image.

"Good morning, handsome. Have a good time last night? You look bright eyed and cheerful this morning." He grinned, the image grinned back. "We both look bad this morning. Why don't we get some strong coffee that we can cut with a knife?" He leaned closer to the mirror and winked. "All right?"

He felt horrible and smelled worse. He needed a bath, but that wasn't a priority. "If I'm gonna be civil, I need my coffee first." He opened the door and spied a young lad, about eight, walking down the hallway.

"Hey, boy."

"Yes, sir?"

Tossing a half-dime to him, he asked, "You think you can round me up a large mug of coffee and bring it back here? You can keep the change, if there is any."

"Then you better give me another one. Coffee's ten cents here."

John tossed him another coin. *Expensive place to visit. Glad I'm not staying.* While he waited, he combed his long hair and tied it back with a thin strip of rawhide.

"That looks at least halfway decent." He glanced into the pitcher to see if anything else was floating upside down. Taking a mouthful of water, he swished it around and spit into the bowl. Pulling a towel off the rack, he wiped his face and hands.

Sitting down on edge of the bed, he bounced once then flopped onto his back, flung his arms over his head and rested them on the blanket. "Squeaks a bit and a little short. Not half bad." Shutting his eyes, he drifted into a softer world.

A sharp knock at the door interrupted his slumber. Jumping to his feet, he yanked the door opened.

Startled, the boy held out a steaming mug. "Here's your coffee, sir."

"Thanks, son." John tossed him a half-cent.

Catching the money in midair, the boy replied, "You're welcome," and hustled down the hallway.

Closing the door, John blew into the cup. The first careful sips were hot, bitter and hit rock bottom in his gut. Growling came from above his belt. Either he was hungry or his stomach was complaining about last night. "I hate it when I drink that Irish brew. That thick black stout gets to me every time."

He sat on the bed sipping the contents of the cup and formulated a plan. He needed to find D'Alene, locate a bath and change his clothes. Lifting his arm, he took one sniff.

"Phew. First a bath. D'Alene deserves better. Wouldn't think of approaching a prairie dog looking and smelling like this." He drained the cup, set it down on the dry sink, grabbed his saddlebags and headed down the hall.

John stood in the midst of garbage and slop, facing a tumbledown shack on Commercial Alley. Pulling the envelope from his pocket, he reread the address, just to be sure. Thin wooden slats covered the only window, letting some light filter through. The door hung at a crooked angle. These deplorable conditions weren't fit for humans, let alone his horse. John gave the door a push. It swung inward, scraping the floor and filth with it. Stifling stench filled the dark room.

How could D'Alene have fallen so low? He tried to remember the grand days they spent together in her elegant boudoir with its high ceilings, crown moldings, and yellow painted walls. That room had dwarfed a huge four-poster canopy bed. Red velvet curtains with golden tasseled tiebacks hung from two ten-foot windows. A brocade settee and chair sat in front of the windows, while a delicate white French provincial desk occupied one corner. Thick lush carpeting covered the floor and a large stone fireplace with a marble mantel had stood opposite the door.

Standing in the doorway, John surveyed the interior of the shack. What turn of events had brought D'Alene to this hovel? A single wooden chair leaned against the wall, part of the back leg missing. A thin mattress lay on the floor. A person's backbone would feel the floorboards. A cracked empty oil lamp sat on a small dusty table in the corner. These were meager wares for a once gracious lady. A small pile of dark brown stained rags lay next to the door. John kicked them to be sure no varmints hid underneath. He picked one up to examine it. Old blood. It fluttered to the floor.

"What are you doing here?" The question was sharp and loud.

John spun around to face a small boy, about ten or eleven, standing in the doorway with a stick in his raised hand. They stared at each other for a long moment. Thick, tousled dark hair hung to his shoulders, a few stray strands shading his green eyes. His once-white shirtsleeves rolled up to his elbows were tattletale gray and covered with splotches. Faded red suspenders kept dark dirty pants from sliding off his slim hips. With unlaced shoes and no stockings, he looked like a street urchin. However, the challenging look on the boy's face made it clear that John was the intruder.

"I came to see Miss Dubois. Do you know where she might be?"

"Uh-huh." The statement was short. The boy glared at John.

"Where is she?"

"Who's askin'?"

The boy taxed John's patience. Irritated, he tried once more. "I am. My name's John Anderson, a friend. Who are you?"

The boy narrowed his eyes, hatred written on his face. "My name is Micah." He paused for a moment with a defiant stare. "Micah Anderson." With a venomous bite, he added, "I suppose you're my Pa."

Shocked, John took a deep breath and stared at the boy.

"My son?" He stood in disbelief, then realized why D'Alene desperately needed him to return to St. Louis. "Where's your Ma?"

The boy stood quiet for a moment. "She died last week."

John felt like a buffalo trampled across his heart. "Dead?" he repeated. Silence surrounded him. He broke into a sweat. His mind reeled, racing from one thought to another, continually coming back to *dead*. "Have you been living here by yourself?"

"Yep. I can take care of myself." The proud look on Micah's face cut to his heart.

"What have you been doing to earn money since your Ma's passing?"

"I clean the spittoons at the tavern around the corner. Sometimes I clean out the slop jars." He raised his head and straightened his shoulders. "I don't need you. I make enough to feed myself."

My kid cleaning spittoons and slop jars? That's not right. John looked around the room. He needed to think. Why hadn't D'Alene written and told him he had a son? Hell, he wasn't ready for this type of responsibility. His way of life was footloose and fancy free, not babysitting a kid.

John eyed him wearily. "How old are you?"

"Why?"

"Answer the question."

Micah twisted his mouth and shut his eyes.

"Well." John's impatience began to show.

"I'm ten." The boy crossed his arms and glared at John who moved his fingers one at a time. "What are you doing, counting the years? I don't like being your son anymore than you like having one."

The boy was sassy. He could leave him here to fend for himself, but what would become of him? He recounted the years and it kept coming out the same. His son! Those bright green eyes stared back at him, D'Alene's eyes. What was he going to do? Guilt set in as memories flooded his mind. The boy needed help, someone to care for him. John removed his hat and raked his fingers through his hair. The only honest thing he could do was take the lad with him, a decision he might regret further down the trail. What he didn't need right now was a kid to take care of.

Sliding his hat on, John stepped toward the doorway. "I have a proposition for you. I'm leaving for California tomorrow. Have a gold claim out there. You can come along with me and I'll make sure you won't ever have to clean another spittoon." He eyed Micah for a reaction. The boy sneered at him.

"You can get an education if you want and even buy yourself some good clothes." John raised his eyebrows and stared straight at the boy. "How's that sound? You work along side of me and I'll make sure you have a decent life."

Micah stuck both hands into his pant's pockets and stared down at the floor, twisting his mouth back and forth, thinking over John's offer.

After a few inaudible moments, he lifted his head. "All right, I'll go. Don't expect me to call you Pa."

"You don't have to. My name is John. Is there anything here you want to take with you?"

"Nah. Ma's gone. The rent ran out yesterday. Nothin's left."

"Then let's go, boy." John stopped for a moment, wishing he could take back the word. "I mean son."

Micah gave him a sideways glance. "I heard ya the first time," he said as he headed out the door.

John shook his head and followed the lad, not looking back at the shambles behind him.

Mounting his horse, John reached down. "Give me your hand. You can ride with me."

"What if I don't want to?"

"Don't be contrary. We have a long, difficult journey in front of us. Come on, take my hand." He pulled Micah up behind him and headed for the hotel. The journey back to California was not going to be easy.

A father? How in hell am I gonna be a father? As bullheaded as the boy is, it's gonna be a real chore trying to figure out this youngster.

Back at the City Hotel, John walked up to the desk. "I'd like to leave a message for my brother. He'll be passing through here soon."

"Yes, sir, we can do that. We'll keep it for him. Here's a piece of paper and a pen." The clerk hesitated for a moment. "Mr. Anderson. We don't, ah, allow niggers in the hotel, sir."

John turned and acknowledged Micah. "First of all, he's a Mulatto. Second, he's with me. Third, he's my partner."

"I guess he can stand in the doorway."

"That's very *kind* of you." John glowered and lowered

his head. The message was harder to write than he thought. The words didn't want to come. How do you explain a son to your brother in a short note, when you hadn't even known you had one? He hoped Alexander would understand why he couldn't stay and wait for him in St. Louis. He wrote straight to the point.

Alexander,
Ran into a small problem.

He turned and looked at Micah leaning against the doorframe. Small problem indeed.

Meet you in Indi…

"How do you spell Independence?" he asked the clerk.
"I-n-d-e-p-e-n-d-e-n-c-e."
"Thank you."
"You're quite welcome, Mister, ah—"
"Anderson." John finished the note, folded the paper, wrote Alexander's name on it. He handed it to the clerk, who placed the message into a pigeonhole on the wall behind the desk.
Micah leaned nonchalantly against the hotel doorframe, enjoying the status of a privileged Negro. During the whole transaction, the clerk kept a diligent eye on the boy.
He'd crossed the line by entering the hotel. Only John's presence allowed him to stay inside.
John paid for his room and pocketed the receipt. Satisfied with leaving the message, he picked up his saddlebags and headed out the hotel door with Micah trailing behind.
"Thank you, Mr. Anderson. Do come back again."
John didn't acknowledge the statement.

He climbed into the saddle, offering his hand to his son. "Come on. We need to get moving."

"What're we gonna do?" Micah stood thinking for a moment. He didn't cotton to bouncing on the back end of a horse.

"Micah!"

The boy grabbed his father's hand, swung his leg over the saddle, shifted his weight and grabbed onto John's shirt.

"First of all, we need to get you a horse."

"Where're we gonna get a horse from?" Micah pointed to his left as John turned north on Fifth Street. "The road west is that way."

"I know that. I have a friend in Baden who owns a stable. He should be able to help us. Now stop fidgeting and sit still. We have a ways to go."

"Well, this is uncomfortable. Besides, do we get to eat today?"

"Later."

"I didn't know I'd have to starve."

"Look. It's still early. We'll stop for a noon meal soon. Now sit still or you'll walk to California." *Patience, John. He's young. Maybe I could tie him up and throw him over the rump of my horse. It'd be a lot easier that way and cheaper. Nah, that wouldn't work.*

People stared as John and Micah continued their journey down the street, heading north. They were strange-looking traveling companions.

Once they reached Baden, John stopped at a clothing store and bought Micah new dark brown trousers, red suspenders, a butternut muslin shirt, new undergarments, and a pair of black ankle-jack boots. Taking the boy around behind the building, Micah changed into his new clothes.

"Told ya they wouldn't let me in the store." Micah snapped his suspenders as he looked at his new pants.

Aggravated with the narrow-minded clerk, John slapped his hat against his pant's leg to dislodge some dirt. "Quick, finish dressing before we have a crowd back here."

The boy pulled on his new boots and stepped lively in the dirt, taking giant steps and lifting his knees high.

"You're prancing around like some pony. Showing off, are you?"

Micah beamed from beneath his new hat. "These new duds fit fine." He held his head high.

"Let's go. Need to buy a horse and then we'll eat. Maybe we'll stay in town tonight."

Micah bundled up his old clothes and strutted behind John, swinging each arm in step with his feet.

Down the road at the stables, John purchased a six-year-old strawberry roan, about fifteen hands tall. The mare was well broke, with her legs and hooves in good condition.

"What are you going to name her?" asked John.

"I don't know. Does she have to have a name?"

John lifted one eyebrow and stared at the boy.

"Lizzie. That's what I'll call her."

Micah wasn't overjoyed about owning a horse. Being from the city, he had never ridden a horse before and the large animal intimidated him. He grasped the end of the reins and led the horse around the corral, making sure he didn't get too close.

The next morning, Micah tried his best to keep his seat in the saddle as they headed up the hill out of Baden. He fell off twice before they reached the crest, only hurting his pride. Once the animal took off across a plowed field, the boy's legs flapped in the air while he gripped the horn tightly with both hands. Another time Micah grasped a handful of mane, leaned across the neck of the horse, and hung on for dear life while the reins trailed on the ground.

Furious, John caught up with him. "Lesson number one, you *never* let the reins out of your hands. Do you hear me, *never*? You have to be in control of this animal at all times. Take command."

"I hate horses and I ain't goin' to California," Micah yelled back.

"That doesn't matter," John retorted. "This horse is going to California. From the way things look, you'll be walking." John lowered his voice and enunciated each word, "You're going! You hear me?"

Infuriated with himself for letting a young boy provoke him into losing his temper, he grabbed the reins and led the mare along the dirt road. Holding onto the horn, Micah wobbled in the saddle. John's patience hit a new low, but he was determined to win the battle of wills with his son. Neither one spoke. Stubbornness ruled between them.

The day wore on as they made their way toward St. Charles. John gave detailed instructions on horsemanship and guiding maneuvers.

"Don't give her a weak knee. Keep the toe of your boot in the stirrups, not your whole foot." The boy's legs were so short, the stirrups looked like knee holders.

John acknowledged they were both experiencing something new. He needed to learn patience and Micah might learn to take orders. Maybe. The boy was extremely bull-headed. John smirked. With more than a physical resemblance, it was like fighting with himself.

After several riderless jumps and a few wild rides, Micah finally took control of the reins. His son did ride a little better, yet there was plenty of room for improvement. It was his inexperience that concerned John. The long trip ahead was treacherous. With only a short amount of time remaining, Micah needed to learn to ride on the trail west.

They reached St. Charles by dusk, exhausted and hungry. Too tired to complain, Micah grumbled to himself. Hoarse and needing a good stiff drink, John knew sleeping accommodations were more important. A grueling day awaited them tomorrow. Their destination—Independence, Missouri.

Chapter Seven

Virginia Road

"This road is a bone shaker with all of the ruts," complained Caroline, feeling each jolt jar her body from neck to ankle.

"It could be worse. After that downpour yesterday, we could have mud up to our axles."

"True. How far have we come?" she asked.

"I'd say a little over three hundred miles, give or take a few."

Caroline sighed. *My bottom would guess a lot more than that.*

"Look," shouted Alexander, rising out of his seat, waving his hat in the air. "There lies the cross roads to Kentucky. The Cumberland Gap and Promised Land should be only a few days away!"

"What's Kentucky like, Pa?" asked James. "Have you ever been over the mountains before? How long will it take us to get into Kentucky?"

"Slow down, James. I can only answer one question at a time."

Caroline chuckled. "He's eager and the ride is already boring."

"Well, he's got a *long* way to go. These are foothills, son. When we get into the mountains, the grades'll get steeper. Now settle down. We'll be nooning soon." Alexander halted the wagon. "It's time everybody walks. Need to save the horses."

Caroline carefully stepped onto the wheel and down to the ground, followed closely by Sarah. James jumped off the back end, yelping and carrying on like a puppy unboxed.

"Look, Pa," Sarah pointed behind them, "there're more wagons behind us."

"They're heading west like we are. Everybody's stretching their legs looking for land these days."

"James, stay close so you don't get snake bit or fall in a hole," Caroline shouted. She knew he paid no heed to her remark.

"Gee up," shouted Alexander to the horses.

Caroline grabbed her daughter's hand. "Let's walk on the other side so we don't get so much dirt thrown up on us from the wheels."

"When do you think we'll get to California?" Sarah shuffled her feet as she walked, kicking at little stones in her way.

"I'd say in about six or seven months."

Sarah wrinkled up her nose and gave her mother a disgusted look. "That's a long time. I'll be old by then."

Caroline suppressed a smile. "With your birthday coming up, I'd say probably one year."

Sarah grinned. "My birthday. I almost forgot." She took off running down the road to catch up with her brother.

Later that afternoon, Caroline walked along the rocky road and listened to her son's and husband's babbling discussion about the mountains ahead and gold they'd find in California. As she followed the wagon, dreams of smoother ground, a table and chairs for mealtime, and warm water to bathe in floated through her mind. *Oh, it's going to be at least six months before I see any of those familiar comforts of home.*

The steep, rutty switch-backed road of the Allegheny foothills stretched upward for miles, sometimes hugging a sheer tree-lined drop-off to a creek below. Topping the crest, Caroline took in the awesome view. The thoroughfare dipped into a rolling valley with green pasturelands, layers of wild flowers, and cool spring breezes.

Her skirt swished above the ground at her ankles like a feather duster twisting above a dirt floor, around and around, back and forth, creating small dust swirls about her feet. Looking up at the horizon, dusty blue-green mantles covered the crusty slopes surrounding her. In the distance, she saw the road rising again into the foothills of the rolling mountain peaks. Tired of walking, Caroline's feet hurt, and her body cried for rest.

Carrying a fistful of wildflowers, Sarah ran up to her and looped her free arm through her mother's.

Caroline graciously accepted the bouquet, "These are lovely."

"I guess so. Do we have to go to California?"

She looked down at her daughter. "Yes. We talked about this yesterday."

"I know. This isn't much fun and I'm tired. I really miss Rebecca." She heaved a heavy sigh. "I wish we were back home in Virginia. I want to sleep in my own bed, not in that old tent."

Caroline pulled her daughter close and kissed the top of her head. “I miss our home, too.” She tweaked her daughter’s pert nose. “And for your information, we are sleeping at an inn tonight.”

“With real beds?”

Caroline laughed, “I hope so.”

Sarah fell silent for a moment before she asked, “Wasn’t Pa happy back in Virginia? Do you want to go to California? Can’t you talk Pa into going back home?”

“Sarah, there’s no turning back. Besides, you might like the west.”

Jerking away from her mother’s embrace, she stamped her foot in the dust. “I’ll never like it. I won’t.” She ran off in a huff.

She understood her daughter’s feelings. She also wanted to turn back. Too many unknowns ahead frightened her. Gritting her teeth, she whispered, “John Anderson, you better be true to your promises.”

Alexander halted the horses. “You want to ride a little bit while we’re in the valley?”

Sarah and Caroline climbed on.

As the wagon rolled forward, James ran to catch up, throwing rocks at nonexistent enemies hiding behind trees, almost tripping over his own feet as he turned around. He jumped onto the opened tailgate, let his legs dangle and sway, as the wagon jostled along the uneven road. He managed to crawl to the middle of the wagon. “Pa, can I get this gold that Uncle John has? Can I, Pa?” he asked. “If I find those little round things he had in his pouch, can I keep one? Just one?”

“Yes,” replied Alexander, “you can keep one, maybe two.”

“Could I buy me a horse? You know, like the one Andrew has back home for racing? A fast one, Pa, so when I ride, the Indians can’t catch me.”

"We'll see." Alexander changed the subject. "You know Daniel Boone and his men blazed this trail right through the gap and into Kentucky. He's a Shenandoah man, like us."

Caroline sat lost in her own thoughts. *Mountains, that's all the men ever talk about. I wonder if Alexander will be satisfied once we cross over them? What would men do if God had made this country completely flat, with no mountains to challenge them? They might decide to stay put in one place and tend the land.*

"I doubt it," she said.

"You doubt what?" Alexander asked.

Embarrassed at being caught out, she blushed. "Oh, nothing important."

Crawling to the back, James stretched his legs over the backend, shooting his imaginary gun at birds and other creatures that accidentally crossed the trail behind them.

"James! Be careful. Don't fall off," Caroline admonished.

"I won't. I'm huntin' bears and wolves. Pow! Pow! I'm gonna shoot them and bring 'em home for supper." His hunt went on. He jumped off, ran out into the road and climbed back on one more time before he settled himself more securely against the side panels next to his sister.

"You pest." Sarah shoved her foot at him.

He screwed up his mouth to spit at her.

His mother turned in time to catch him. "James. No."

Bored with pretend enemies, he shouted, "Can I ride up front now?" He made his way to the front on his hands and knees. "I want to drive the horses again, Pa. Can I, can I?" he chanted, trying to get his father's attention.

Alexander motioned him forward, anything to quiet his mischievous son. "Come on up here."

Caroline moved over to make room for her rambunctious child. "Be careful. Don't step on your sister."

"Ouch," cried Sarah, with indignation.

"Aw, I didn't touch you." James stuck his tongue out at her. Stepping over her legs, he kicked her on purpose, as he hopped upon the seat.

"You dratted nuisance," shouted Sarah.

"That's enough, little lady," reprimanded her father.

Bending her head, Sarah pouted and whispered, "I want to go back home."

Alexander carefully placed the reins between James' fingers and patiently guided his son as he sat up straight and tall with the air of authority. "Now, take it slow and don't pull, son. Be patient. That's right, hold the reins the way I taught you."

He continued, looking pleased. "So far, the trip has been uneventful."

"Yes. Wouldn't it be nice if it goes this smoothly, all the way to California," replied Caroline.

"We've only had a couple of little rainsqualls. Spring usually brings those heavy rains. So far we've been spared the flooding and constant muddy conditions."

"Except for the downpour yesterday." Caroline loved early spring. Warmer days and cooler nights made for easy sleep.

"Look at the mud puddles over there. Musta rained here earlier this morning."

"Where?" James' head swiveled to the side.

Alexander grabbed his son by his ears, turning his head forward. "Drive and keep your eyes on the road. We want to make the inn in one piece."

As the sun kissed the mountaintops, sending shadows through the valley, the Anderson family pulled in front of Martin's

Inn. A man with bright red, wavy hair and a face full of freckles stood on the porch, leaning against a post, smoking a pipe. Alexander jumped down from the wagon and heard a booming voice.

"Howdy. Ma' name's Michael O'Brien." The man grasped Alexander's and pumped it twice. With a wide grin plastered across his face, he continued, "I hail from Lincoln County, North Carolina. Now, where ar' you from and where might ya be goin'?"

"Same to you, my friend. I'm Alexander Anderson and this here's my family: wife Caroline, daughter Sarah and son James. We're from Rockbridge County, Virginia and headed for California. Where are you headed?"

"I'm takin' me wife, Annie and our four darlin' children out to the Willamette Valley in Oregon where me two brothers live. Come on over and I'll introduce you to me family."

The Anderson children exited the wagon quickly, with Caroline following close behind. The entourage accompanied Michael O'Brien to his wagon, while the men continued their conversation.

"How was the trip up from Lincoln County? Any trouble?" asked Alexander.

"Nah, only a little dusty, ya see. Sure enough need the rain down there."

"I know what you mean." Alexander brushed some dust from his trouser leg. "We had a bit of rain on the way. Hit one dousing. Enough to wet us down and make the road muddy, in spots. But all in all, the trip's been good."

As they drew near the O'Brien wagon, a woman wrung out a piece of her wash as she eyed the approaching visitors.

Laying the wet shirt over the wagon tongue, she dried her hands on her apron. "Now, who do we have here, love?" the woman asked.

"This lovely creature is me wife, sweet Annie, who has the patience of Job to put up with her husband, three Irish ruffians, and one dainty princess."

A fairly tall, square-shouldered woman with curly brown hair, Annie smiled broadly.

O'Brien turned and grabbed a tall boy by the shoulder, a spitting image of the man, down to the color of his hair and freckled face. "Over here standin' so tall behind me, is our John. He's sixteen and a mighty fine apprentice. One day he'll be a fine carpenter like his father, if God's willin'." Michael laughed at his last remark.

"You're braggin' again, husband. The wee people be listenin' to your blarney," said his wife.

"Ah, Annie, I only speak the truth." He stopped for a moment, roared loud and slapped his knee. "You can see, our poor wagon bulges at the sides with all of our tools and belongin's. It's filled to capacity. All we have ta do is get everythin' and ourselves to Oregon."

Alexander glanced at the O'Brien wagon. Tools extended out the tailgate, more were strapped and tied to the sides, giving the impression of a carpentry shop on wheels.

"Now, here he comes carryin' his rifle, an empty hand, and nothin' for our supper. This strappin' young man dressed like a bear is our Patrick, age fourteen goin' on forty. Sometimes he thinks he's a frontiersman, a bit adventurous he is, with a keen eye for huntin'. He never misses a shot and keeps our table supplied with game. He enjoys the outdoor life a wee bit more than need be." Michael lowered his head, looked at his second son from under his eyebrows, grinning from ear to ear.

"Oh, *Da*," Patrick said, disconcerted by his father's statement. "I'm usually around to help out."

"Uh-huh. Usually. Hmm. Well, I am sure he loves the

idea of goin' to Oregon more than anyone else in the family, besides meself."

Michael stepped to one side, making a deep bow. "And now, I'd like to introduce Her Ladyship, Elizabeth."

"Father!" Indignant at her father's introduction, Elizabeth O'Brien's body language told everyone she totally approved of the honor her father bestowed upon her.

"Elizabeth is twelve. She'd like everyone to believe she's enterin' adulthood. Look at her now, she's still me wee little girl." He waggled his eyebrows at her and continued, "And, she is goin' to stay that way and not be playin' patty fingers with any young beaus for a while. Not until I say she can."

"Ah, Michael, you're near to impossible. These kind folks don't even know us. Why, they'll be thinkin' you're a big bag of wind," Annie chided her husband. "Besides, her Ladyship is still too young to be seekin' beaus."

"Mother!" exclaimed Elizabeth, her eyes opened in horror. "How embarrassing."

"Now, now dear. Don't take it to heart. Your father's Irish wit is takin' over again. You know how he likes to quip."

"Honestly." Elizabeth stamped her foot and glared at her parents.

"Now here comes himself, our youngest son, Joshua," Michael continued. "Joshua is ten and his energy knows no bounds. Neither does his mischievous nature, which of course usually gets himself into all kinds of trouble."

"Not lately, *Da*."

"Ah, yes, how true, not lately. Then again you've been confined to a wagon these several days with no other companionship except for your sister and brothers. Ah, have a look now. I spy a young man close by about your age." Michael lifted one eyebrow, and with a smirk on his face, he looked at James. "With two heads together, I am sure there's a bit of mischief afoot."

Joshua grinned at James.

Turning back toward his wife, Michael announced, "Now, family, these lovely people standin' here so patiently are the Andersons. They're headed to California. This tall distinguished lookin' man is Alexander. He'll be sayin' the names of his own family to ya."

Not quite as eloquent and jovial as Michael, Alexander introduced his family, one at a time to the O'Briens. He told the reason for their trip west and what they planned to do there. When he reached the point of his story about why they were heading west, everyone listened, spellbound.

The children, tiring of the adult discussions, dashed off. Joshua and James made tracks for the nearest trees, continual noise radiating from the gregarious and noisy twosome.

Elizabeth and Sarah walked and chatted in endless conversation.

Patrick and John joined a small group of older lads who hid out at the back of the stables, a secret gathering of young smokers, trying to spread their wings. One boy kept to the side as lookout, in case a parent happened to drift nearby.

The men departed and headed for the Andersons' wagon. Michael helped Alexander unhitch the team, tether and bed down the horses for the night. Leisurely, Michael lit his pipe and drew on the stem. Catching up on political events and happenings, their conversation turned to the trail that lay ahead of them.

Caroline and Annie sat in two rockers on the wooden porch, waiting for the men to return.

"I hope Alexander hurries. We still need to eat supper and purchase a room for the night."

"They should be strollin' in any minute now, unless me husband gets the gift of gab. Then they might not return until the rooster crows."

"Oh, my. That's a long time. Why did your husband decide to go to Oregon?" asked Caroline.

Annie sat back in her chair. "In spite of what they say about the lovely mail, letters from friends and relatives can be challengin'."

Caroline shook her head, "I understand exactly what you're saying. I guess it didn't take him long to decide to head west."

Annie continued, "No, we lived poorly, constantly grubbin' in the dirt. Most people don't have any respect for the Irish. So, when my dear sweet husband received his brother's letter about the wonderful land in Oregon, you know *the land of milk and honey*. It didn't take himself but a minute for the idea of travelin' west to set into his head. I knew when I married him he was a wanderer. From pillar to post, we've been. First to Pennsylvania, then to Virginia and North Carolina. Seems we hardly put down our roots and up they come to plant them again somewhere else."

"I understand. Men. They're never satisfied," said Caroline. "It's so nice to know you're journeying west, too. I was a little worried about, you know, going to the bushes for privacy."

Annie stood up and grasped both sides of her skirt, pulling it wide as a feather fan. "I'll hold out me skirt like this and make a screen to keep pryin' eyes away."

Alexander stepped up onto the porch.

Michael stood next to him and leaned against a post, rubbing his chin. "Wife, would you be dancin' so late in the evenin' with your skirt held out so? Or have ya gone daft so far from home?"

Both women giggled.

"I don't believe I'd ask if I were you, Michael. Looks like trouble to me," said Alexander. Then he turned to his wife. "Come on, let's all go eat. I'll call the children."

The Andersons and O'Briens decided to travel together. The journey slowed to ten or twelve miles a day up the rugged mountain foothills. Women and children walked the uneven rocky terrain, hugging their coats closed. There was a slight nip in the air as the brisk wind whistled through the trees.

Spring, dressed in its finest glory, greeted them. Patches of yellow daffodils and lilies of the valley blanketed the hillsides, mingling with unopened blooms of flame azalea. Low-growing Indian Pipes, a scale-like leafy plant with nodding, waxy yellowish-white flowers, sprinkled the rocky slopes. Trailing arbutus grew profusely under trees and around boulders, its creeping stems bearing clusters of newly-opened, blushing pink blooms. The white flowers of the mountain ash peeked out at the world against the background of the brown hardwood trees.

Suddenly the wagons turned the bend. James yelled, "I see it! I see it!" He jumped up and down in the front of the wagon, hanging over the side. Alexander grasped his pants' straps to keep James from tumbling headlong to the ground.

"Easy, James," Alexander said. "You want to get there in one piece, son."

"There it is, Pa. Do you see it? There! There!"

James pointed to the limestone formation in the distance. The majestic white outcropping towered above the valley. Only one day's journey stood in their way to reach the Cumberland Gap. The Andersons and O'Briens stopped their wagons side by side for a brief moment. The gentle mountain slopes stretched as far the eye could see, blending with the foothills, lying behind them. A small gurgling creek wound its way between the hills and into the valley.

"Isn't that a grand sight to feast your eyes upon," remarked Michael O'Brien.

As the afternoon shadows grew longer, Alexander selected a campsite near a clear-running creek. After the animals were fettered and the meals cooked, the travelers settled down to eat. Alexander sat cross-legged next to Michael.

"Well, as I see it," said Michael, "we still have a small distance to go. With a wee bit of Irish luck, we should cross the gap by late afternoon."

"I'd say around noon, depending on how hard we push," replied Alexander.

Michael took another spoonful of food.

"It's been a grueling day," said Alexander. "Tomorrow, descending these mountains will be trying. We need to be up and on the road by early light."

Michael O'Brien rubbed his belly. "I do believe my eyes were a wee bit bigger than me stomach." Then, speaking louder for all to hear, he said, "Ah, my, such delicious tastin' food. Would ya believe it was prepared by such dainty fingers?"

"Oh, get on with ya now, Mr. O'Brien. You been nippin' the medicine bottle again?" Annie shot her husband a cocky smile, before she turned toward the fire.

"Mr. O'Brien," pleaded Sarah, "please play your squeezebox for us tonight."

"Yes, love," said Annie, holding her skirt out as she did a

little Irish jig. "We need a bit of your lively Irish tunes to keep us warm tonight."

"I'd love to do the honors for you ladies. But first, I need me pipe. Come along, laddie, let's escape before the lovelies put us to work."

The sun slipped behind the trees, casting long dark shadows onto the campground. Alexander leaned against the wagon wheel, stretching out his long legs, relaxing his body, bruised and battered from sitting on the hard wagon seat all day. Mesmerized by the flames dancing toward the sky, he thought about the events of the day. The wagons were all in good shape, there had been no problems, and no accidents.

He watched his children playing with the O'Briens, running around the wagons, jumping off the wagon tongues, and wrestling in the dirt.

Caroline joined Annie sitting near the fire. Many a good recipe or home remedy would be shared tonight, and most likely there would be a discussion about their men. Every once in a while he heard a giggle or soft laughter coming from the ladies' area. It did his heart good to see Caroline having time to relax and visit with Annie.

Michael ambled off a-ways, smoking his pipe.

"Now then, Alexander," shouted Michael, "will ya be joinin' me or oglin' the womenfolk all night?"

Chapter Eight

"Steady, steady," bellowed Alexander. "Pull more to the left, John. Pull hard, it's going over. Caroline, hang on."

"I can't hold it much longer," shouted John O'Brien, digging his heels into the dirt. "It's sliding over the edge. Jump! Jump!"

The panic in the boy's voice brought chills to Alexander. "Lay low, Michael, and dig in." Alexander's command echoed through the valley. "We need some help up here. Hurry," he called out to the women below.

"Lean back a bit, John, and pull, son. Pull hard." Michael dodged small boulders and rubble in his way, fighting to keep his footing. The projecting mountain walls scraped his back and arms with their sharp chiseled edges, slicing at his clothing. He murmured to himself, "Aye, we can do this. Lord, Almighty, we can do this."

Alexander shouted a sharp remark, "Save your breath, Michael, and pull."

"Aye, laddie, I am," he replied, "I am."

"The ropes are slipping," John hollered at the top of his lungs, straining to keep his grip on the ropes.

"Hold on. Don't let go. Hold it." Alexander's voice trailed off as he slid along the steep rutted road, trying to keep his footing on the rocky rubble.

"The wheel pole's gonna break. Hurry, need help up here." With his rope attached to the wagon's side, John hugged the mountain wall as close as possible, endeavoring to keep it from careening over the sheer cliff edge and sliding down to the rocks below.

John's firm grip on the rope inched slowly from his bleeding hands, wetting the rope. With terror in his voice, he yelled, "The rope's slipping. I need help."

A pole, strapped and wedged through the wagon's back wheels, held them stationary to keep them from a rapid downhill course or plunging over the side. They were reduced to using ropes on the wagon's final descent. The cargo's deadweight made this undertaking extremely hazardous.

"The wagon is almost to the bottom," John yelled.

Pulling on the wagon's back ropes, Alexander and Michael O'Brien put their body strength into trying to slow the wagon's accelerating downhill journey. They leaned backwards and dug their heels into the dirt road. Wrenched forward and jerked about by the heavily loaded wagon, the men slid along the ground on their bottoms, rocks and dirt going up their trousers legs, tearing at their skin and sticking to the hairs on their calves.

John screamed, "The wagon's tilting. Watch out it's going over!"

Alexander bellowed, "Pull hard, Caroline! Keep the horses under control." He feared that she might be tossed onto the road and trampled.

Caroline lay flat-out backwards over the bench seat, trying to keep her balance.

John cried out, "Hold on, Mrs. Anderson. We'll make it to the bottom."

Annie and Patrick rushed to his side, all out of breath. They hugged the jagged cliff walls, dodging horses and wagon.

"Grab the rope," John ordered, "quick!"

Annie seized the loose end of the rope, dug her heels into the rutted road, the hem of her dress shoved up around her knees.

Patrick reached and grasped at the rope between his father and mother with one hand, running along, trying to stay up with them. Finally, he wrapped his free hand around the rope, stumbling from side to side endeavoring to keep his balance. One after the other, the travelers were dragged down the rutted mountain road like rag dolls, bouncing and flailing from side to side. Even though the wagon creaked, groaned, and wobbled, it stuck to the road, rolling down the last portion of the well-worn furrows with all of the human ballast trailing behind.

Alexander sprawled in the soft green grass with his eyes shut, taking note of every ache and pain in his body. Too exhausted to move, he panted heavily. "It's taken three grueling hours...to get the wagons down."

"Aye, it has at that. Faith and saints preserve us, we've come through safe and sound." Michael raised one arm, then another. "If I'm not mistaken, I do believe we are, at the present time, lyin' in Kentucky." Slowly, he eased both arms out to his sides, stretching the tight muscles cramping in his biceps and shoulders.

Alexander chuckled. "I believe you are correct, Mr. O'Brien." He tried to move one leg and grimaced. "You know, the first wagon wasn't all that difficult to get to the bottom."

"I for one am glad we got the young'uns down first." Annie sat across from the two men, massaging her reddened, stiff hands. "At least they were out of harm's way. Patrick. John. How are my big strappin' lads doin'?"

"We're fine, Ma," they said in unison.

John lay on his back, knees bent, breathing hard. Patrick sat rubbing his palms together.

"Now ya know," said Michael, "I thought me wagon was goin' to cause the most trouble. Sure enough now, it's packed as tight as a corset. Why you can even hear it moan."

"Michael, have a care your language," admonished Annie.

He chuckled. "Now, now, me Annie. Beware. I believe it was a bit of an ankle I saw ya showin' up there, me girl. Not bad for a woman who's so proper.

"By the way, laddie," he continued. "Were ya gettin' a bit rough with me up yonder? It never hurts to call on the good Lord above for help, ya know."

"Sorry, Michael. My only concern was for Caroline." Alexander placed the back of his hand over his eyes. "All I could think of was how close she came to going over the edge. Losing her, well..." He lay there for a moment.

"I think the trouble all started when the wagon gained too much momentum. We lost leverage near the end." Alexander made a meager attempt to sit up. Every bone in his body hurt. "My wagon surely posed a challenge. Next time we cross a mountain or a rough spot, we unload everything. Don't care how long it takes us. It'll make the crossings and downgrade trips easier."

"Aye, the truth be known, it was hard work, all right. Everythin' workin' against us all the way." Michael winked. "Although, ya might say we had a wee bit of help from The Man above."

"You're probably right." Alexander smiled. "Okay, we're through the gap and I for one am glad it's over." He looked over his shoulder at the rock-strewn and rut-worn steep road. "Now, we need to check to see what has to be fixed and get goin'. We might not make a station tonight."

He sat up, pulled his boots off, and shook out the debris. Then he removed the grass and rocks from under his trouser legs. He looked at his hands. Not too bad, a few minor burns. He'd tend to them later. Lifting his eyes, he looked over at Caroline. She lay on her back, a bit past Annie, with her eyes shut and hands placed over her stomach. His heart almost stopped. Quickly he pulled on his boots.

"Be back." With great effort, he got to his feet. Making his way over to his wife, he knelt down and tenderly brushed the dislodged strands of hair from her face.

Her eyes fluttered open and she smiled. "I'm fine. Just tired."

"Lie there for a while. We have time." He stared at her soft facial features. *Have I been fair to ask my family to travel over 1,200 miles to a place not one of us has ever seen?*

The expression on his face caught Caroline's immediate attention. "Don't think about it. There's no turning back now." She placed her hand gently over his. "The only way to go is forward."

Her reassurance relieved him of some of his guilt. It would take a lot to make him turn back now. The challenge deep in his heart pushed him forward. Sitting down beside her, he took her swollen hands into his. "I'll have Sarah fetch you some water to soak them. We need to get the swelling down." He raised her right hand to his lips, placing a gentle kiss on the palm. "You did a fine job controlling the team."

Caroline lay there astounded. He had never kissed her hand before. She stared up at him, knowing the gesture came from his heart. Embarrassed, color rose into his face.

Alexander stood up, "I'll, ah, be right back. Need to look after the children." He headed for the wagons.

Michael struggled to his feet, working out each kink in his sore, overworked muscles. He glanced sideways at his wife brushing dirt and debris from her dress, checking for any tears.

"Would you look at that, now?" she said, shaking her head in disbelief. "In spite of that excitin' downhill trip, we didn't lose a thing and no one was badly hurt."

Michael was aware of her every move. "Yes, except for our dignity," he added, absentmindedly. With her hair mussed, patches of dirt on her face, and her dress disheveled, she reminded him of their courting days back in Ireland when he chased her through the fields of heather. *Ah, she ran me a merry race, she did, and always trying to be so prudish.* His heart beat fast as he watched her. *How beautiful she is with those ample hips and lovely brown eyes.*

Annie caught her husband scrutinizing her. "Now, Mr. O'Brien, what would you be thinkin', starin' at me these good few minutes? I do believe you've had your fill, especially if you've got some big notion in that Irish head of yours. Maybe you should move on. Or, should I be savin' me breath." Her eyes twinkled as she stood there, hands on her hips.

My, she is one good-looking woman. "Well, now, I think I'll be takin' meself over to the wagon to check out the team and see what needs mendin' before I get meself into trouble." He patted her rump as he passed by.

Approaching the O'Brien's wagons, the excited children surrounded Alexander, whooping, hollering, and raising such a ruckus, they almost spooked the horses. Their high-pitched voices reached a crescendo, reverberating through the valley.

"Wow, Pa." James waved his hands up and down, jumping around excitedly. "The wagon slid down the slope this way and that way. It almost went over the side with Ma."

"Calm down, James." Alexander placed his hand on his son's shoulder.

"Is Ma all right?" asked Sarah. She stared at him, big blue eyes filled with fear.

"Yes, she's fine," her father answered. "But, she's very tired and needs our help. Sarah, fetch a pan of cool water. We need to soak Ma's hands to get the swelling down."

Sarah dashed away without being asked twice.

Alexander ruffled his son's hair. "Let's go, I need your help."

"Next time can I drive the horses down? Can I, Pa?" James pleaded. "Can I? I know I can do it. I'm strong enough."

"Ah, you're too little," replied Joshua, coming up behind him, clipping him on the back of his head. "You're still a baby."

"No, I'm not," said James, punching the older boy. "Take that back. I'm not a baby. I'm only a year younger than you."

"Stop it, Joshua," admonished Michael O'Brien, approaching the quarrelling boys. "There's enough time for horseplay later. Let's tend to the animals. Off with ya now."

Strolling toward his wagon, Alexander inspected the front wheels as Michael walked up behind him.

"Me wagon's in tip-top shape except for a few tools that worked loose on the way down. Nothin's badly damaged. How did ya fair, my friend?"

"The left front wheel needs to be changed. Three of the spokes are cracked."

Michael slapped his hands together. "Well, then, me good man, let's get to fixin' it."

"When we're finished, we'll be nooning on the way," said Alexander.

Michael asked, "Maybe a little nip to wash down the food wouldn't hurt any, 'ay?" He nudged Alexander in the ribs with his elbow then shut his eyes, savoring the thought of the smooth golden elixir. "Mmm, I can almost taste it."

Later, repairs made, Alexander shouted, "Let's go. James, get into the wagon. Ready Michael? Let's move 'em out."

Anderson, the self-appointed wagon master, headed north toward the Ohio River and Louisville. As the wagon lumbered on, he sat hunched over with every muscle and joint of his dirty body aching. Hundreds of miles to travel and already his body talked to him.

Leaning over to his wife, Alexander asked, "Why don't you break out some food? I know the children are hungry and my stomach is kissing my backbone."

Caroline distributed jerky, morning biscuits and sweet cool water to the children in back. Sticking a piece of jerky into his mouth, Alexander switched the reins to his left hand, gnawed off a piece, and stuck the rest behind his ear.

He stared at the horizon and the land around him, lost in thought, eating bits of biscuits Caroline stuck in his mouth.

She held out a cup of water to him. "You're awfully far away. Good or bad thoughts?"

"Oh, thinking about the Gap. It proved to be more of a challenge than I anticipated."

"It certainly was. Here, drink," she said. Taking the cup back, he continued, "We did good. Everyone came down safely, even the animals."

"True." He paused for a moment. "You know, that whole experience pulled everyone together, and all of us were strangers not so long ago."

"Does that surprise you? Have you ever heard of farmers not giving a helping hand when needed?" She gave him a sideways glance, a little surprised at his statement. "How many times did we pitch in to help others?"

After passing Yellow Creek Station, the Cumberland River lay ahead. Michael O'Brien pulled up next to the Andersons and jumped down to join Alexander on the riverbank. "Now, I'd say that crossin' this here river will be smooth sailin'."

"Yes, the water is at the halfway point," said Alexander. "My brother warned me, if the water rises over the crossing rock, fording the river's too dangerous."

Michael took off his hat and ran his fingers through his red hair. "We'll take a bit of time doin' our crossin'. No need to hurry."

"Strange, isn't it the way the river flows east to west?"

"Aye. Makes me think the wee people are playin' tricks on me eyes."

Alexander placed his hands on his hips and took one more careful look along the riverbank. "Looks fine to me. It could be a bit tricky over on the other side."

"Saints preserve us, if I wasn't gonna say the same thing meself." Michael headed back to his wagon.

Smiling at Michael's Irish wit, he climbed up onto the seat next to Caroline.

"Even though the river's running a little fast, it's not high enough to give us any trouble." He stirred up the horse and slowly entered the water. "Once we get across, we should be thinking about finding a campsite."

Days passed. The ladies walked the serpentine roads through rolling hills, thick wooded valleys, and steep coves, keeping a vigilant eye on their young offspring. The heavily loaded wagons bucked and rattled, worse than a green horse.

Walking with Annie one morning, Caroline twisted and turned to get the kicks out of her back. "Ah, how heavenly to get away from that spine-jostling wagon. Oh, look at all the tiny purple and blue flowers, like a blanket covering the ground."

"I'd be thinkin' more like the wee elves spreadin' their magic." Annie gestured with both hands in front of her. "Their little faces peekin' out between the grasses as far as the eye can see."

"Listen," said Caroline. "Did you hear that? The noise from the woodpecker's tapping travels all around the forest. It sounds like a hundred birds pecking at the same time out there."

"Now, would you look at that?" Annie pointed ahead. "There's a clearin' and, I do believe I see the sun a shinin'."

"I spy a few small buildings," Caroline said, glancing about. Several of the cabins seemed to be abandoned. "I guess this 'Manifest Destiny' they've been preaching about has people on the move. Seems strange to see a home so deserted like that."

"I am sick of the talk of it." Annie scowled, a gloomy mood settling about her. The forsaken lonely structures served as reminders of what they each had left behind.

Caroline changed the subject. "I'm happy not to be pregnant. Can't imagine dealing with bearing a child on the trail."

"Aye, that would be a challenge. It's been a while since we've had a baby about the O'Brien family." Annie smiled, shaking her head. "As far as I'm concerned, me strong husband can take his small member and place it in his toolbox. A wee bit of rust on it, now, wouldn't hurt it a bit."

"Annie, how you talk." Caroline feigned shock.

They burst into hilarious giggles.

Ahead, black-bottomed clouds bumped into each other and soon the sky opened up. Rain drenched the scurrying walkers as they hurried for cover. Dresses plastered to their bodies, mud up to their ankles, bonnets drooping over their faces, the women and children crawled over the tailgates to escape the downpour.

Later that afternoon, Alexander halted the wagon. "I believe everyone can walk again. The sun's out, so off with you."

Sarah jumped down to join Elizabeth who stood waiting by the road's edge. The two girls dashed off, chattering and collecting flowers along the road, placing them into their bonnets.

The boys ran alongside the wagons. Puddles from the rain created an irresistible opportunity to make mud pies to throw at each other.

"Why are they so rowdy?" asked Elizabeth, with a sophisticated air. "Can't they grow up?"

Sarah shook her head. "I don't know." She pressed her lips together in disgust. "They're stupid."

Out of the corner of her eye, Sarah caught sight of Patrick O'Brien riding in her direction. His woodsy attire and bearing attracted her attention. Her heart skipped a beat. She stood tall, patted her hair and straightened her dress in a lady-like manner. As she walked gracefully along the road, she suddenly realized that Elizabeth watched her with disdain. Blushing, her face turned crimson.

Splat! Out of nowhere, a hurling missile made a direct hit, squarely on her chest, splattering her dress and face with mud. She let out a horrible high-pitched scream, dropped her bonnet and flowers. She grabbed her skirt above her knees, making tracks after the culprit who dared to muddy her dress.

Poor Joshua O'Brien could not move fast enough to find a safe haven from this maddened creature with big wild eyes, who chased him as though demons propelled her. "She's gonna kill me. Help me, somebody, please help me. I don't want to die." Legs pumping as fast as he could move them, Joshua made a beeline for the wagons.

Screeching at the top of her lungs like a wild creature, Sarah streaked after her assailant, blood in her eyes. She wanted to annihilate the little monster, rip out his heart.

Alexander heard the screams and pulled sharply on the reins to halt the horses. "Oh, my God, one of the children's been run over." He jumped from the wagon and dashed to the back.

"Oh, hurry, Alexander," shouted Caroline, trying to descend from the bench seat.

Joshua flew as fast as his small feet could carry him around the O'Brien wagon, careened into Alexander.

"Oh, save me. Please save me. She's gonna kill me," he cried, climbing up Alexander's frame, snuggling close and holding on for dear life.

Sarah appeared around the end of the O'Brien wagon. Her red face spotted in mud and her dress covered with brown splotches, she presented a bizarre sight. Strands of her once neatly braided auburn hair fanned out from around her head in an eerie halo effect. Breathing heavily, she marched up to her father. Clenching her teeth, she hissed. "Give him to me. I want to rip out his liver."

Joshua hung onto Alexander's neck for dear life. "I only threw a mud pie. I didn't mean to hit her. I was aiming at James."

Where was his friend? He needed him. All he could remember was James falling over backwards in fits of laughter, holding his stomach.

Sarah made her way to her father and yanked on Joshua's leg, pulling as hard as she could to dislodge him.

Caroline rounded the wagon in time to grab her daughter and shake her gently. "Sarah! Sarah! Stop and listen to me."

"I want to—" was all Sarah could manage to say. Uncontrollable tears cascaded down her cheeks. Her overwhelming embarrassment humiliated her.

Caroline wrapped her arms around her daughter and hugged her to her bosom. "Shhh, you'll be fine."

Sarah wailed and sobbed as her mother walked her toward their wagon.

Joshua released his grip around Alexander's neck and escaped with great haste, running to his father's protective arms. Reaching his safe haven, he noticed his father's grave face. Joshua knew he was in deep trouble.

Michael O'Brien grabbed his shoulder and pulled him along to their wagon. "All I did was have some fun and now everybody's angry with me," Joshua wailed.

James climbed up into the bench seat next to his father and the wagons rolled again. Looking over his shoulder into the interior, he leaned close to his father.

"You know, Pa, girls are really strange," he said, in a whisper.

"James, someday you won't think so. A bit of advice, don't ever try to figure them out. You'll drive yourself crazy doing that, son." Alexander looked down at the young boy's questioning gaze. "One day, you'll understand what I mean."

James plopped his hat onto his head. "I don't know, Pa. I guess so."

Caroline sat precariously in the back among their personal belongings, gently holding Sarah. For the next hour everyone heard the heartrending sobs from the Andersons' wagon.

As the travelers set up camp near a cool mountain creek, eight miles shy of their next station, the sun slipped behind the mountains. Tents pitched and meals prepared, they spent the rest of the evening socializing. Music and singing echoed through the valley.

Sarah sat with her back propped against the front wagon wheel, head lowered, hands grasped together around her bent knees. The picture of a small waif, dejected and forgotten.

Joshua hid behind the rear wagon wheel, undecided whether he should venture over and apologize to her. With her bonnet in one hand and her wilted flowers in the other, he cautiously approached her. He didn't want to deal with another wild attack. Standing a few feet in front of her, he cleared his throat and tried to talk. Nothing came out but a squeak.

She lifted her head. "What do you want?"

"Sarah, I'm, I'm really sorry about your dress. I was aiming at James and, and—"

"What?" She glared at him.

"I'm really sorry." Quickly he extended his hands. "Here's your bonnet and your flowers." In his shaking hands, he held crushed purple and blue flowers, their heads all bent and many of the petals missing.

Sarah's anger changed to admiration for the courage of this young boy who stood before her. Afraid and shaking, Joshua didn't budge an inch. When she stood up and approached him, he cringed, and then squinted his eyes, waiting for her to lambaste him. The grimace on his face made her smile. Gently taking the bonnet from his small fist, she placed it on her head. Next she took the flowers, and holding them in both hands, she leaned over and placed a gentle kiss on his forehead.

Joshua jerked his body back in total surprise. "What did you do that for?"

"Because you're very sweet and I forgive you." Sarah turned and sashayed toward the campfire.

A whimsical smile of bewilderment on Joshua's face

betrayed his confusion. He stood there dumbfounded. "Sweet? She forgives me? She has to be daft," he muttered, shaking his head.

With the campfires banked, the travelers dispersed to their protective tents, settling in for the night.

Alexander peeked in on the children, then closed the tent flap. He stared at the stars blanketing the sky with the quarter moon resting on its backside. "We might get a little rain tonight."

Standing at his side, Caroline placed her arm around his waist, nestling close. "Kentucky's absolutely beautiful. Maybe we should stay here." She knew what the answer was going to be.

He placed an arm across her shoulder. "It's beautiful all right and plenty of game, but John's waiting for us. I'm sure California's as good as Kentucky. You'll see. I promise."

They heard the children whispering and rustling about inside the tent, making themselves comfortable. "It won't take 'em long before they're asleep."

Caroline moved away from the tent opening.

Alexander moved his shoulders around to work out the kinks. "I think I'll turn in, too. It's been a long day. You coming?"

"I'll be in soon. Have a few chores to finish. Remember, stay on your side." Caroline smiled. "Last night you wound the blankets around your tired rump."

With a sheepish grin, Alexander replied, "Now woman, you know I save you half the covers."

"Is my half the part under your bottom or the half twisted around your legs and arms?"

Alexander laughed. He lifted the tent flap, and bowed deeply, waving his arm inward, raising his eyebrows at her. "Come in and find out."

She grinned and flipped her hand at him. "Later. All I ask is that you leave me room."

He entered the tent, the flap falling behind him.

Caroline stared up at the sky. Wisps of hair fluttered across her eyes and ears as cool night breeze caressed her face. She clasped her shawl around her shoulders to keep in the warmth. Wild flowers scented the air, mixed with fresh spring grasses. Far into the woods, an owl hooted a soft night tune.

Walking to the fire scar, she retrieved her skillet and stored it in the side box. Carefully she checked the area one more time before entering the tent. James lay awake. "You better get some sleep, son," she whispered.

"Okay, Ma. Nite."

"Good night."

Caroline rolled in next to Alexander, inching the covers from underneath him. She heard James sleepy muttering as he toss around for a minute. Finally he settled down.

A soft spattering of rain tapped against the tent roof. Her eyes fluttered closed several times and finally sleep conquered her, as ribbons of water trickled under the canvas tent.

Chapter Nine

Caroline awoke with a start, cold and wet. A chill coursed through her body. Rain saturated everything: clothing, blankets, and bedding. Quivering, she rose, put her damp coat on, and hurried outside. Smoky gray fog enveloped the wagons, tents, and valley, while a black funeral shroud covered the sun. She grabbed a few dried pieces of kindling stored in the back of the wagon, and hurriedly started a fire. She didn't need anyone to get sick with a chill.

Alexander came to the fire carrying an armful of wood. "The animals are fed and the wagon's ready. We won't be able to dry anything out until we're down the road a piece."

"Glad we put some of the wood into the wagon last night. Everything is soaked." The fire finally caught and she laid two logs onto the kindling.

"Got an armload from the O'Briens. They have everything in that wagon of theirs. Never saw such a hoarder."

"It's nice to have a fire this morning. Could you get the children up? I'll start breakfast. Have them change their clothes in the wagon."

"Okay. We'll take down the tent later." Alexander turned to leave. "Good morning, Annie."

"Mornin', Alexander." Annie moved closer to the fire. "Are the Andersons' as wet as we are?"

"Not a dry stitch on any of us." Caroline shook her head.

"Aye, us either. Be careful and don't be gettin' sick. I need to be tendin' me crew. Be back later." Annie grinned. "I sound like me *Da*. He was a fisherman, you know." With that said, she shouted directions to her children who stood around their wagon.

Caroline quickly prepared the meal, fed her family, cleaned up the utensils and area. After a bland, soggy breakfast, Alexander and the children folded up the wet tent and stored it in the wagon. Mud stuck to their shoes and clothing.

Alexander grabbed James by the collar before he hopped up onto the tailgate. "Don't sit on the tent. We'll unload and dry it out this afternoon."

As the children climbed into the wagon, Caroline wiped them down the best she could. "Take off your muddy boots and sit up front. Try to stay out of the rain."

"The rain's misting through the canvas." Sarah cuddled next to the wagon side.

"Take a shirt or something and cover up with it, and be sure to wrap your feet up," said Caroline. "Button up your coats or you'll get sick."

Alexander stood next to the wagon. "Let's get 'em together."

He climbed up next to his wife. "Okay, let's head 'em out." He stirred up the team and slowly moved forward.

"The fog makes it hard to see the road's edge." He wiped the moisture from his face with the back of his hand. "It hangs in the air. You can cut it with a knife."

"Everything's wet back here," cried his daughter.

Alexander lost his patience. "Be still, Sarah. We're all wet. Now settle down and try to get some sleep if you can. Otherwise, you're walking."

"The muddy road's going to make traveling slow," he said. "What a miserable morning."

For the first time, he wished for open flat land instead of the damp creek bottom. He felt guilty for pushing his family so hard in these conditions. "I promise, if we don't get out of this fog before noon, we'll stop and start a fire."

"I'll be giving this family some spring tonic tonight. We don't want anyone getting' the ague." Caroline knew the odious spring tonic wasn't her family's favorite medicine.

James heard tonic and ducked his head under his pillow. "Oh, no."

Alexander made a face and changed the subject quickly. "Haven't heard much from the O'Brien's wagon this morning. They all can't be sleeping. "

"I doubt that, very much." Caroline looked into the interior. "The children are grouchy, cramped, and uncomfortable."

Alexander mulled over the mileage. "With a little bit of luck, we can make Hazel Patch by nightfall." He smiled down at Caroline. "Hazel Patch. Strange name, isn't it?"

"Yes." Caroline gently laid her hand on his leg. She felt too tired to continue the conversation. Her only wish at this moment was to see the sun. A nice cozy fire wouldn't be bad either or a place to stretch her legs.

The wagon jolted and swayed along the rocky, potholed road. Glancing over her shoulder, she saw James burrow into a small niche, wrapped in a coat like a cocoon. She could only see the tip of his hat as he snored in his sleep.

Sarah was like a cat trying to find a soft spot among all

of their personal possessions. She poked and fluffed, and poked some more. Finally, she settling on an area at the back by the gate and curled up with a blanket.

Shivering, Caroline tucked her skirt under her legs, pulled a small lap blanket over her knees, and tugged her coat tighter around her body. She tried to keep her mind busy, thinking about what lay ahead, what California might look like. Yet, small fleeting pictures of their warm, comfortable cabin back in Virginia invaded her thoughts instead.

It stopped drizzling about mid-morning. The sun shyly peeked out from behind the clouds, bringing some warmth to the crisp breeze. Scooting closer to Alexander, she laid her head on his shoulder. He nuzzled her hair with his cheek. Damp, but happy, she smiled, feeling content. Shutting her eyes, she drifted into a softer world.

Bam!

Everyone in the Anderson wagon went flying in different directions. Alexander held onto the reins, trying to control the horses and stay anchored to the seat, while he made a desperate wild grasp for Caroline to keep her from pitching out onto the road. She fell forward, landing in the footboard area, halfway out of the wagon, looking down at the ground behind the horses.

Personal belongings and loose items in the back flew through the air amidst cries and howls. The debris covering James stifled his shouts. High blood-curling screams caught Caroline's attention. Crawling up from the footboard, she grasped the seat back in time to see Sarah tumble out the open tailgate onto the muddy road.

Alexander pulled the horses to a stop, jumped to the road, and dashed to the rear of the wagon. Sarah sat upright in the middle of the road, covered from head to foot with brown gooey mud, wailing at the top of her lungs, kicking her feet as though movement might solve her problem.

"Why me? Why is it always me? I hate this trip. I hate this wagon. I hate mud. I want to go home. I want to go back to Virginia, now."

"Out of the way! Out of the way!" Michael yelled as he yanked the reins, taking a hard right and running off the road's edge into a gully, barely missing Sarah. The O'Brien wagon teetered precariously.

His family made a quick escape. Annie was the first one to put her feet on the ground, making her way to Sarah with a small blanket. She began talking softly, trying to calm her. "Oh my, are you all right my dear? Are you hurt? Here lassie, let me help you up." She gently gathered Sarah to her bosom, wrapped the blanket around her small dirty body.

"There, there, my love. You'll be fine, I'm sure. Come with me now, me girl. We'll get that old ugly mud off your pretty face. Now, don't you be cryin'. You'll be fine in no time at all."

Alexander helped Caroline down. Her face was pale, her right cheek red from being slammed against the footboard. "Are you all right? Here, hold onto my arm. You took a nasty tumble." He gently pushed the loose hair away from her face.

As her knees buckled, she grasped the side of the wagon for support.

He quickly grabbed her and pulled her into his arms. "Be careful now. We don't want you in the mud, too."

"I'm fine, Alexander. A little shaky. Nothing broken that I can see or feel. Only my legs won't hold me and my right shoulder hurts."

"You have a small knot on your forehead and a few scratches on your check. Are you sure you're all right?" he asked.

"Yes, I'll be along in a minute. Go see to the children."

Alexander hurried to the back where everyone gathered.

Clutching the side of the wagon, Caroline tried to acclimate her unsteady legs.

James escaped from underneath the debris and stood on the open tailgate viewing the mayhem.

"Are you all right, son?" asked Alexander.

"Yes, Pa, I'm fine." He dabbed the cut on his forehead with his hat and tried to brush the drops of blood on his shirt.

"You stay put and don't go anywhere. Do you hear me, son? I need to check on your sister."

"Yes, Pa." He plopped down on the back of the wagon, placed his head in his hands.

Patrick and Joshua raced up to investigate the accident.

"Wow," said Joshua. "That sure was something."

"You okay?" asked Patrick, helping James down from the wagon. "Looks like you've been fighting. Your jacket sleeve's torn."

"Yeah, I'm fine," said James, still a little dazed. "My head really hurts."

"Sarah looked like a flying bird." Joshua laughed and spread his arms in a mocking gesture.

"No, she didn't," retorted Patrick. He gave Joshua a warning look that shut his younger brother up immediately.

Taking several steps, James wobbled a little. "Can't get my feet to work right." He leaned against Patrick to steady himself, almost falling into a water puddle. The brothers quickly grabbed him.

"Easy, James," said Patrick.

Joshua tugged on his friend's arm. The boys could hear Sarah sobbing her heart out. "Let's go back and see what's going on."

Michael O'Brien checked the horses for injuries, looking in disbelief. The right side of his wagon was stuck axle deep in mud, tilting to one side. For the moment, he stood there, his hands on his hips, and shook his head.

Alexander walked up next to Michael, both men contemplating the job ahead of them.

"Well, me lad, looks like we'll be doin' a bit of muscle work. With the heavy load I'm carryin', we'll have to unload in order to get me wagon back on the road."

"Yes," replied Alexander, "and there goes most of the day."

"Aye. What a mess and all because of a bloomin' pothole. Wouldn't it be nice ta have smooth roads, no matter what the weather conditions."

"That's a long time coming. Maybe one day the good roads will stretch all the way to California." Both men laughed at the bizarre idea.

"Aye, that's a dream, it is. But for now, we have a wee bit of work cut out for us. I'll round up me two oldest lads."

"The women and children can help unload the light pieces." Alexander kicked at a rock along side of the road.

"Let's go tell 'em," he said. "You know, seems like a man's work is never done. It's challenges like this that will break your back."

"Oh, it's only a wee bit of a setback." Michael cocked his head and grinned. "Ah, laddie, we'll have it done in no time. First, we need to see how our flyin' angel's doin'."

Making their way to the wagon, the two men looked at each other and laughed.

"Flying angel?" said Alexander. "Now, that I'm not so sure about. Maybe the angel should ride in your wagon for a while."

Michael feigned shock. "And here I thought you were me friend."

John O'Brien stood by the horses, waiting to greet the two men walking toward him. "*Da*, how much damage is there?" he asked.

"From what I can assess, Alexander has a broken wheel and we need to unload our wagon in order to get it out of the mud and back on the road."

Patrick O'Brien joined the men and listened to the discussion about what had to be done, as they went to join the women.

Michael grasped his son's shoulder. "John, you're a strong strappin' lad. Go fetch our extra wheel for Mr. Anderson."

"I'll help ya," volunteered Patrick, following his brother.

"Thanks," said Alexander. "Once we reach Hazel Patch, I'll have the wheelwright fix mine, if they have one."

Caroline sat on a stool next to the O'Brien's water barrel. Alexander stepped up next to her. "How are you doing?"

"Still a bit shaky. I'll be fine."

Alexander tried not to smile. "How's our flying angel doing?"

Caroline put her finger to her lips. "Don't you let her hear you call her that." They both smiled.

Behind the wagon, Alexander spied Annie rinsing his daughter's hair. With most of the mud washed from her arms, legs, and face, Sarah looked like a girl again. She'd change clothes when she got back to the wagon.

Over to the side, Elizabeth attended to James' cuts on his forehead and arm. Joshua entertained everyone, talking animatedly about James' battle scars and wild experience. All the while, James sat with a silly grin on his face, paying attention to Elizabeth's every move.

Cutting the right size trees for poles took time. Alexander gave directions on how to use them to keep the wagon from falling onto its side. At first the work progressed slowly.

Finally, the women and children dug in to do their job, removing the lighter items from the O'Brien's wagon, leaving the heavier ones for the men. An hour later when it was totally emptied, the men double-teamed the horses to pull the wagon out of the mud while the women and children used their weight to push it back onto the road. Michael O'Brien carefully supervised the reloading of his prized possessions, his tools.

With the wagon back on the road, Alexander surveyed his damaged wheel.

Taking a deep breath, he wiped his face on his shirtsleeve and turned to his son. "James, go ask Mr. O'Brien to bring his boys along. It'll take all of us to switch wheels. Also, ask him to haul up some of those logs we used."

He stood holding the extra wheel, disappointment on his face. *Another wheel. Can't afford any more breakdowns until we get these fixed.*

"Well, now, do I see a long face of discouragement hangin' there in midair or is that face left over from the mornin' gloom?" Michael's sense of humor was aggravating sometimes, even though Alexander knew he meant well.

"Here it's noon and daylight's slipping away. There'll be no need to hurry. We probably can't make Hazel Patch by evening, we've lost too much time."

"Ah, think, me friend, how much fun we've had handlin' this catastrophic situation. Why, I thoroughly enjoyed meself this mornin', cuttin' trees down, sloshin' in the mud, puttin' blisters on me hands and other places ya can't see. Why I could almost dance a jig if me meager physique allowed it."

Alexander chuckled. This stubborn Irishman had a gift of the gab and could turn a phrase so well. "Let's put some of that gusto to work."

After changing the wheel, everyone ate in silence. Only the children seemed to enjoy the free time to romp. Alexander sat quietly, contemplating the turn of events and questioning what arduous challenges lay ahead.

Annie and Caroline huddled together trying to keep warm. The chilly air seeped through every fiber of their clothing, buffeted by the cold damp wind. A small fire would be welcomed right now, if there was time.

"How do you feel, Caroline? You look awfully peaked."

"Oh, I'll be fine. Still feel a little shaky."

"Quite a tumble you took back there." Making light of the situation, Annie asked. "Now, how interestin' did the horse's rump look from the footboard?"

Wrinkling her nose, Caroline said, "It was broad, dark and a little smelly. Not exactly the best view from the wagon, to my way of thinking."

"Would ya ladies be talkin' about the loveliest end of the horse? I said to meself, not a better view could be had. I do believe we'll be followin' that part of the horse to Oregon."

Giggling at her husband's pompous stance, Annie said, "Ah, Michael, you're talkin' rubbish. Be off with ya now."

With a decision made, Alexander stood up, his voice filling the air. "Everyone, listen up. If we pull ourselves together and push hard, maybe, just *maybe* we'll make Hazel Patch by nightfall. Let's get it together and roll out."

"Aye, that's what I wanted to hear," shouted Michael. "Good old determination. Saints preserve us, we're pushin' hard."

"Michael, me love," said Annie. "You're the devil in sheep's clothin', you are. I can't live with him and I can't live without him."

Smiles and laughter replaced all their frowns. Alexander's spirits rose as he climbed up next to his wife. With the children settled in back, he patted Caroline's knee and stirred up the horses.

Chapter Ten

The pain in Caroline's chest and shoulders plagued her most of the day. Tired and lethargic, she pushed it aside the best she could. As the wagon jolted and bumped over every hole in the road, it renewed the pain. She tried to walk. Lack of energy played against her and she climbed back into the wagon. She hurt all over. She barely listened to Alexander's ramblings.

"I do believe we're gonna make Hazel Patch before nightfall. We'll sleep at the inn and tomorrow I'll have both of our wheels fixed. Hopefully, the wheelwright can get to them in the morning."

Trying to think of something other than the pain in her chest, she asked, "Then after Hazel Patch, what are our next destinations?"

"Let me see. Crab Orchard and Stanford, then about five or six days to Louisville." He paused for a moment. "Louisville. What a sight that will be with all those beautiful steamboats on the river."

"Can't wait, Pa." James loved listening to his father's stories about what lay ahead of them. He never missed a word, unless it involved work. Then he turned a deaf ear.

"I think it's time you and your sister walk." Stopping the wagon, the children jumped onto the dusty road. He clicked his tongue and flicked the reins, the horses responded, moving forward at a slow gait.

"You know," he continued, "I hear the inns in Louisville are quite comfortable. Some of them are downright beautiful and expensive."

"That's nice." All the bumping about in the wagon increased her pain. She prayed for a smoother road. Gripping the seat board and shifting her weight, Caroline made an effort to breathe slow and easy, hoping Alexander didn't notice.

"I'm sure you saw a few more wagons joined us this morning," Alexander said. "We'll probably see more later on today."

"How could I miss all the noise? More wagons mean more children."

"I know our two are happy. There must be a dozen or so young'uns out there on the road. Makes me nervous when they get too close to the wagon." Suddenly he reined in the horses and yelled, "Hey, you three boys get away from the animals. Do you want to get run over?"

Jostled from side to side, Caroline grabbed her midriff and sat straight up on the seat. "Oh, Alexander."

"I know, I shouldn't yell like that." Alexander looked back over his shoulder. The children scurried out of the way of another wagon. "That's right, boys, stay on the side of the road."

"Alexander!"

He faced Caroline, "You know we are— What's wrong?"

"I'm...in...pain." She sat up straight to relieve the pressure. Grabbing her ribs, she moaned, "Ohhh!"

He slowed the horses. "Do you want to stop?"

"No. We'll be there soon."

"Are you sure? I can get Annie to help you. Better yet, lie in the back. You'll be more comfortable."

"I don't want to move. Keep going." She tried to smile and failed miserably.

The road took a steep downhill descent, winding through a thick wooded area with a shear drop-off on one side. Below, a fast, tumbling creek wove its way parallel to the road. The wagon jostled over the rutted road, wobbling from side to side.

Alexander yelled to two men walking his way, "Hey, how far to Hazel Patch?"

"Not far, friend," a man shouted back. "Down the road yonder, around the bend, then straight ahead. Can't miss it."

"Thanks." He turned to Caroline. "See, we're almost there. Hang on."

"I'll make it," she whispered.

They followed the road down and around, winding through the trees.

"Look ahead," he said. Then he shouted to the O'Briens behind him, waving an arm, motioning ahead of him, "Look, Hazel Patch."

A few small cabins nestled among the trees along the hillside. Below, in a wide-open area, stood the station inn. The children started shouting, running forward trying to out run each other, hoping to reach the station first.

Alexander shouted, "James! Sarah! Be careful and stay away from the horses. We're almost there."

"Okay, Pa," they both answered, running to catch the other children.

The pain became more intense. Caroline moaned and leaned to her right, grasping the back of seat with her left hand, her knuckles turning white from the grip.

Alexander whipped the horses up and pushed them, leaving their children standing by the roadside in bewilderment.

"Out of the way," he yelled. Thc children scurried to safety to avoid being run over.

"Where ya goin', Pa?" shouted James.

"Stay with the O'Briens."

"He left us," muttered Sarah.

Seeing Alexander whip up his horses, Michael O'Brien pulled his wagon to a halt. "Come on, get in. We'll catch them."

"Somethin's up." Annie bit her lip and looked at Michael.

Caroline tried to catch her breath. The pain crept up her back and across her chest, making it hard to breathe. As the wagon flew down the hilly road, pitching from side to side, she collided with Alexander. Straightening her legs against the footboard for balance, she clutched Alexander's arm with her left hand and clenched her teeth.

"Slow down. I can't take all this jostling." She dipped her head, tightening her grip on her husband's arm, digging in her nails.

Alexander pulled up in front of the inn. He heard the O'Brien wagon roll up behind him. The banging and clanking tools, pots, and pans on their wagon's side made an atrocious noise.

He needed to find a doctor. Jumping off the wagon, he turned to assist his wife.

"Alexander." She scooted across to his side of the seat and slumped forward. He caught her and pulled her down into his arms.

James and Sarah jumped from the O'Brien's wagon, ran toward their father, and stopped short.

"James, go get Mrs. O'Brien and tell her I need her. Run son, run. Sarah, go inside and get some help. Hurry, girl." Sarah disappeared.

"Ahhh!" Caroline screamed, then grimaced and gritted her teeth.

Michael O'Brien rushed up to Alexander's side with Annie close behind. "Let's get her inside. Easy, lad, we have precious cargo here."

Annie shook her head. "My goodness, she must have really hurt herself when she hit that footboard a-ways back. Get her inside. Ah, me poor lassie. Easy, easy, don't drop her."

"Now, Annie, we're doin' the best we can. Quit talkin' woman and go open the door." Then Michael turned back around and shouted, "You boys do what ya can for the horses."

Sarah stepped inside the inn, the door banging shut behind her. "Help us. Help us, please! My mother's hurt and needs help. Pleeeease, somebody help us!"

The owner of the inn dropped the pan he had in his hands and headed to the entrance. Annie threw open the door. As the men stepped through the doorway, carrying Caroline, the innkeeper's wife cleared off the table and moved the benches to make room for her. Many of the patrons milled around.

"Do you have a doctor close by?" shouted Alexander, gently laying his wife on the table.

"No, he went to Boonsboro yesterday, won't be back for two more days." The innkeeper stepped away from the table and shook his head, his eyes gazing over the woman breathing so laboriously.

The innkeeper's wife drew close to Caroline, gently running her fingers through the loose hair, pushing it away from her face. "Here, honey, what's the matter?"

"My ribs," she whispered. "I think I broke something."

"Out with ya all. Everybody out except the women." The innkeeper's wife shooed the men outside and shut the door. "Don't need the help of any man in here." The innkeeper's wife pointed to Sarah, "Sit here and hold your ma's hand."

Later, Annie came outside to join the family group. "Caroline's doin' fine. A little sore. She cracked some ribs so we wrapped her up good. Tomorrow she can travel. Sleepin' in the wagon for a few days wouldn't hurt her."

"That's good news," said Alexander. "I had no idea she was hurt that bad."

She started to leave, then hesitated. "Oh, by the by, you'll be needin' to carry Caroline to your room." With nothing else to say, she walked away, shouting directions to her children.

The inn door opened and Innkeeper's wife waved her hand at the men standing around the Anderson wagon, beckoning to them. "Come along with ya now, ya big strappin' men. We need your help in here. Be quick about it."

Sarah came outside.

"What's wrong with Ma?" asked James, kicking at the wheel of the wagon. He made a face and screwed up his mouth.

"She cracked a couple of ribs when we had the accident a while back."

"Is she going be okay?" he asked, stretching his neck to catch a glimpse of his mother before the men shut the door.

"She'll be fine. Let's go get some of our things together for the night. Afterwards, we can go play with Joshua." Feeling proud of herself for helping her mother, Sarah ushered James toward their wagon.

The cool morning breeze rustled the leaves and chilled the travelers as they huddled around the wagons. Caroline pulled her jacket tighter and furrowed her brow. She stared ahead, deep-seated resentment for her brother-in-law increasing by the minute. She'd love to inflict a little pain his way right now. Her ribs ached and her legs were weak. She needed to sit down.

Alexander stood behind her, massaging the back of her neck with one hand, letting her soft hair fall between his calloused large fingers. "Are ya okay?" he asked.

"Yes. A little tired and sore," she said, placing her hands on the small of her back.

"You need to rest a spell. Here comes Annie." He touched the brim of his hat. "Good morning. Maybe you can talk my wife into sitting on the porch with you while I go talk with Michael. We'll be leaving soon."

"Well, now, there's nothin' I'd like better than a nice sit down. What a fabulous idea. Come on, we'll chat a while." Annie placed her arm through Caroline's.

"Be back in a bit," said Alexander, heading toward the wagons.

Walking side by side toward the porch, Annie asked, "How are you farin' today?"

Settling comfortably in a high-backed rocker, Caroline answered, "I'm fine, as long as I don't try to bend over or pick up anything heavy." She placed her hand against her ribs. "Feels like I'm wrapped in swaddling clothes."

"That'll give you good support in that bouncin' wagon." Annie looked up and spied the men heading their way. "Well, now. I'm sure me husband will be havin' somethin' to say the way he's wavin' his hands around. It's his Irish, you know. He expresses himself with so much energy. Aye, you should see him after he's had a nip or two."

Michael O'Brien approached the ladies, placed one leg on the porch and leaned forward. "My, aren't they pretty a-sittin' here like flowers in a field waitin' to be plucked and tended to."

"You haven't been in the medicine chest, now have you,

Mr. O'Brien?" Annie laughed and gave her husband a mischievous grin. "Look at you, all smiles and full of it."

"Not a nip, my love. Not a nip." Taking off his hat, Michael bowed deeply. Raising his head, he winked at Alexander. "Could it be these fair maidens are waitin' on us?"

"Oh, Michael, take your blarney somewhere else." Annie got up from the chair and shooed him with her hands like she would a flock of chickens. "Git away with ya now."

Alexander suppressed a chuckle and cleared his throat for a more serious note. "We need to be pushing on within the hour. Enough time's been spent here making repairs and taking on supplies."

"Here, here," agreed Michael.

Annie sat back and said, "Let's be calling the children in to eat. *Then* we can be on our way."

The wagons traveled from Hazel Patch, heading for Louisville. Caroline reclined on a pallet Alexander made for her in the wagon. Every bump and shake caused her agony, making the day seem ten times longer. Nighttime did not come fast enough.

Eventually she grew stronger, able to tolerate the jostling ride on the seat. She leaned against her husband's shoulder, gripping his arm. "What a beautiful day."

"Yes," he nodded in agreement. "I personally like those fat clouds. It's the black bottom ones telling me we're gonna get some rain soon. Sure would cool things down for us."

Caroline pulled at her bodice. "It is a bit sticky for this time of the year. I'm almost sorry we aren't in the mountains anymore. At least it was cooler there."

"I agree. Maybe the rain will cool things off."

As the day wore on, Caroline decided to walk. She touched Alexander's sleeve, "Stop and let me get down. Exercise might do me good. Besides, I miss Annie's Irish humor."

"Okay. If you get tired or begin to hurt, holler loud. With all the children scampering around, the noise is earsplitting today." A din rose from the children as they chased a rabbit into the field.

Pulling his team up, Caroline climbed down and hurried over to join Annie.

"Isn't it somethin'? The fields are dressed in their finest glory."

"Yes," said Caroline, stopping to take in a deep breath. "It's absolutely beyond anything I ever imagined."

"Aye. Now look at ya, rosy-cheeked and smilin'." Annie's spirits were high today.

"Alexander told me this morning, we'll be in Bardstown tonight. Then our next stop is Louisville. Can you believe it? Sometimes it seems we've been on the road for years." Caroline gazed off into the field, keeping an eye on the children. "I hear Louisville has wicked establishments where women are only half clothed. In fact you can see their limbs."

"Ya don't say now. That's a bit darin' if you ask me. Of course, I'd be right curious to sneak a peek into one of those places." Annie raised her eyebrows up and down.

"For shame," exclaimed Caroline. "What would Michael think?"

"Ah, my dear, if it were up to me husband, I would be seein' him sittin' right in the middle of it enjoyin' himself."

Caroline laughed. "Land sakes, Annie! I swear that even makes me blush." Then added mischievously, "Do you think their undergarments are like ours?"

"I don't know, but I'd give two bits to see."

Chapter Eleven

Lovely brick and frame houses lined the dirt streets of Bardstown. The Anderson wagon joined a parade of vehicles moving along the road into town. People milled around, bartering with hawkers on the sidewalks with carts full of wares.

Alexander halted in front of an inn on the main thoroughfare and went inside to make arrangements.

Civilized comfort at last. Caroline waited for her husband and Michael as they sauntered toward her.

"We have a delightful room down the hall from yours," said Michael. "What a pleasure it will be to sleep on those lovely white sheets tonight. My Annie will be in all her glory."

Caroline stepped down to join Alexander, while the children escaped through the wagon back. "Let's at least go in and see our accommodations."

Inside the room, she scanned two full beds fitted snug against the far wall with four goose-down pillows and two woolen blankets. Across the room stood an oak washstand with a blue-flowered pitcher and bowl, white towels and washcloths hung on the side rack. One small window faced the street. Hawkers, pedestrians, and animals paraded by.

"How lovely," was her only comment.

"Shall we see what else is available," Alexander asked.

Caroline nodded and followed her husband and the children into the hallway.

A large bulletin board hung on the main entry wall. Rules and regulations were posted for all lodgers to read. Rule Number Three stated:

Meals are served in the dining room.
Breakfast is served at 7:00 A.M.
Noon meal at 12:00 sharp and dinner
at 4:00 P.M.
Don't be late if you wish to get a place at
the table.

Next to the rules, Caroline noticed an advertisement posted for a May Dance. "My goodness. A frolic would be delightful to attend. We need some spirited diversion."

Sarah eyes widened with anticipation. "Oh, Ma, could we go, please? I could celebrate my birthday there. Can we go, please?"

"Is there gonna be food?" James' one-track mind worked overtime when it came to eating.

"Pa, can we go?" begged Sarah.

"Seeing it's your birthday and all, I believe we can. Besides, kicking up our heels would do us good." Alexander winked at Caroline. "Especially since you are turning twelve tomorrow."

Sarah twirled around and around, then ran toward the inn door. "I'll be right back." Heading outside, she shouted, "Elizabeth. Guess what?"

The two girls walked away, heads close together.

"James, please shut the door." asked Caroline.

He slammed it closed.

"Easy, son," said Alexander, ruffling his son's hair. "Our daughter, the town crier, is announcing our participation tomorrow night."

"Alexander, shame on you," chided Caroline. "She's excited."

"I'll never understand girls. I'm excited, but you don't see me running around town screaming at everybody. What's she so happy about anyway? It's only a dance." James flopped on the bed. "Besides, the food's the best part."

Patting his son's shoulder, Alexander tried to hide his smile. "You keep thinking that way, son, and you'll be fine."

Sarah fidgeted with her dress, played with her hair, and fiddled with her stockings.

Her exuberance exasperated Caroline. "Sarah, please be still. How will I ever get your hair braided?"

"Oh, Ma, can't I wear my hair straight tonight. I feel so much older. Besides, braids are for little girls. I'm almost grown up." Smiling into the mirror, she lifted her chin, pushed back her shoulders and folded her hands at her waist.

Caroline stared at her daughter. Somewhere along the trail, Sarah had grown up. The image tugged at her heart.

"Let's pull your hair back with one of my ribbons." She rummaged in her valise. Pushing Sarah's hair behind her ears, Caroline tied the ribbon on top of her head.

"There, you look lovely."

Alexander walked into the room with a box under his arm, followed by James, who held his hands behind his back. "You do look pretty." Handing her the box, he wished her "Happy birthday, young lady."

"Oh, Pa, for me? What is it?"

"Open it."

James' patience exploded. "What's takin' you so long? Here, let me help you." He took one step toward her.

Sarah moved the box away from him. "No, I can do it myself. It's my present." She sat down on the bed and placed the box next to her. Carefully lifting the lid, she smoothed back the paper inside. A new crisp pinafore lay folded neatly.

"It's beautiful. Oh, thank you, thank you." She wrapped her arms around her father's waist, giving him a big hug. Then she gently picked the pinafore out of the box. She slid the shoulder straps and bodice piece over her head and turned to her mother. "Please tie it for me."

Standing in front of the mirror, Sarah smoothed the pinafore downward from her waist, straightening the creases. Turning around, she asked, "How do I look?"

"Enchanting," Caroline answered.

"Quite grownup," was her father's reply.

"Hmm, I guess," said James. "I have a present for you, too." He brought her boots from behind his back and shoved them at her. "I cleaned them up for you. They were a mess." Then quickly he added, "Besides, Pa made me do it."

Sarah held them in her hands. "Thanks, James, how nice."

"Yep, I know. Just remember that," he quipped, embarrassed by her attention. Not sure what to say, he told her, "Happy Birthday." Then he quickly disappeared from the room.

Alexander looked at his maturing daughter for a moment

and grinned. "I think I'll join our diplomatic son. Don't be too long. People are starting to gather down the street and they'll be serving food soon."

As her father shut the door behind him, Sarah faced the mirror one more time. "Ma, do I really look pretty?"

"You look beautiful."

Feeling quite grownup, she smiled at her reflection in the mirror. Staring beyond the image, her heart held an innermost secret, a dream she relived over and over. Tonight Sarah hoped with all her might it would come true. Fluffing her dress and straightening her pinafore one more time, she walked outside and down the street with her mother to join the festivities.

Tables and chairs surrounded a large open area between two buildings. A fair-sized dance floor lay in the center, made of flat boards placed side-by-side on the ground. A raised platform to one side held four men playing their instruments, along with Michael O'Brien with his squeezebox. The spirited music, mixed with people laughing and socializing, created a foot-stomping time.

Over to one side, Sarah's dream-knight stood dressed in his finest, dashing and handsome as ever. New strange feelings confused her. Light-headed and floating on air, she pinched herself to be sure she wasn't dreaming. Suddenly, he glanced her way and smiled. Her legs turned to rubber. Heart beating fast and butterflies filling her stomach, every nerve in her body tingled alive.

Across the dance floor, Patrick O'Brien caught a glimpse of a beautiful young girl in a crisp white pinafore. His gaze followed Sarah. She looked different tonight, more grownup with her auburn hair flowing around her shoulders. A yearning hit the pit of his stomach, making him feel queasy. Standing in a daze, he stared at her, music and conversation softly drifting away. Gathering up his courage, he crossed the space between them.

"H-hi," he stammered. "You look real pretty tonight."

"Thank you." She hung her head in shyness.

"Ah...would you like to dance with me?"

"Yes,"thank you.

Patrick held out his arm, escorting her to the dance area.

A week ago, he remembered her ranting like a child, sitting in the middle of the road kicking her feet, covered in mud. Tonight an angel walked next to him, her arm through his. When she smiled, her youthful beauty took his breath away. His knees wanted to buckle as he grasped her hand to dance the Scamperdown.

The wide turnpike from Bardstown to Louisville accommodated comfortable travel. Alexander enjoyed the smooth macadamized road made of crushed stones, water-bound for tightness, and compacted by a heavy roller, locked it all together The first-class road delighted the women and gave them an excuse not to ride in the jarring wagon. The only catch was an occasional tollhouse.

Sitting next to his father, James squirmed and fidgeted. He was bored and anxious. With the end in sight, his son's patience evaporated into thin air.

His humming, tapping, and constant motion undid Alexander's tolerance. "James! Let me tell you about Kentucky."

"Already heard all your tales about that."

"Did you know buffalo roamed free here a long time ago?"

"Buffalo?"

"Yes. And men like Simon Kenton and Daniel Trabue crossed these mountains on foot."

"Don't forget Daniel Boone." James cocked his head to look at his father. "Does Uncle John really know him?"

"Could be. You'd have to ask your uncle that question." Alexander suppressed a smile. His brother's wild stories would get him into trouble one of these days. "Anyway," he continued, "Kentucky wasn't a state back then, only wild animals and Injuns. I remembered stories my Pa told me about the British trying to keep us out of this land."

"Was there a war?"

"Yes."

James sat silent for a moment pondering the information. "Pa, did Daniel Boone ever go to Louisville?"

"Yes. He also lived in Missouri. Maybe we'll see his cabin."

"Really." Taking off his hat, he stared ahead.

The wagon rolled by several handsome farms with large two-story stone houses. Fences sectioned off land into neat squares. Horses roamed the rolling fields of blue-green grasses. *If it weren't for John, I might consider settling in Kentucky. It's a man's land.*

James jolted his father back to reality. "Pa, how long will it take to get to Louisville?"

"A few more hours."

"What's Louisville like? Is it big?"

"It's a large city with lots of streets, fancy buggies, and people everywhere. Down at the levee you'll see steamboats docked, loading and unloading goods." He glanced at his son, who sat staring at him with mouth agape and his eyes wide. "It's a beautiful sight, I'm sure. While Uncle John stayed with us, he told me about the boats. Remember, he rode one from St. Louis when he came to visit."

"Wow," whispered James. "Pa, what does a steamboat look like?"

"Let's see. It's the size of ten large cabins sitting side by side with ten more stacked on top of 'em. There're two big paddle wheels, one on each side, churning water like the old mill back home, only three times bigger. It has two tall stacks like chimneys high as trees, puffing smoke into the air. Each white boat's painted with red, blue, and yellow designs. Some have frilly decorations and flags all over 'em."

James sat quietly for a moment. Suddenly the boy shouted, "I wanta get out now, Pa. Stop!" As the wagons slowed to a stop, James jumped to the ground. "Hey, Joshua, Wait till you hear this."

After passing through the Knobs, the women spent the morning walking, enjoying the warm breeze and gossipy companionship. James rolled and gamboled in the fields with Joshua while Sarah rode with her father.

By afternoon the weather turned warm and humid. Perspiration trickled down Caroline's neck, soaking her hair and bonnet, making her clothes stick to her. She unbuttoned the top two buttons of her blouse and one on each cuff. Even though the bonnet shaded her eyes, the glaring sun reflected off the road making her feel sluggish and exhausted.

"Glory be, I do believe my body's beggin' for a little water. My whistle's dry and puckered," said Annie.

The women waved their husbands down. When James and Caroline climbed on board, Sarah hopped over the seat to settle in back and sew on her quilt pieces.

Toward mid-afternoon, Patrick O'Brien cantered up along side the Anderson wagon. Alexander stared ahead, grumbling, "Doesn't that boy have a family he can ride with?"

Sarah lowered her head and smiled coyly.

Caroline stifled a grin, amused by the smitten boy's anguish.

"What's Patrick looking so silly for?" asked James. "He's been acting mighty strange. Maybe he ate something bad and isn't feeling good."

"Oh. He's been bitten by the bug," answered Alexander, keeping tabs on the rider.

"What bug? Is he sick?"

"Not exactly," replied Caroline, giving Alexander a cautious glance.

"Maybe he's queer in the head, like being stomped by a horse or something." Patrick's behavior baffled James.

"It's something like that, son," retorted Alexander.

James made his way to the back of the wagon and hopped off to join Joshua. He needed to talk with his friend.

He jerked his head in Patrick's direction. "Your brother's acting awfully odd today."

"I know. Been like that since last night."

"My ma says he was bitten by a bug."

"What bug?" Joshua looked concerned.

"Don't know. We need to keep an eye on him. Come on. Let's catch up with the others."

"I'll beat ya," yelled Joshua, shoving James aside and dashing ahead.

"No, you won't." James took off after him as fast as his legs could carry him, thoughts of Patrick wiped from his mind.

Late in the afternoon, farm wagons, carryalls, and buckboards congested the road. Once a fashionable double-brougham pulled by two beautiful Cleveland Bays passed them.

"Alexander, did you ever see such a beautiful wine-colored carriage?"

"Nope." He looked over his shoulder. Agitated, Alexander exclaimed, "Dad-blame it. Here he comes again."

"Alexander! The children."

Patrick rode up close to the wagon front. "Won't be long now, Mr. Anderson. my pa says Louisville is just over the ridge. Hello, Mrs. Anderson. Mighty fair weather we're having today." He tipped his hat to Sarah and smiled. With politeness aside, he quickly took off in a gallop to catch up with the other riders heading for the ridge.

"At least his manners aren't lacking." Caroline shook her head and lowered her voice. "That poor young boy is really smitten with Sarah. She can't decide whether to act her age or be a young lady with a beau."

"He's been following us like a lovesick puppy all day. Maybe I need to talk to that young man. As far as I'm concerned, he can keep on riding."

"Alexander. Now don't go making too much over it. This infatuation has a long way to go before you need to worry."

"Good grief, Caroline, she's only twelve."

Caroline nudged Alexander in the ribs, whispering so Sarah couldn't hear her. "I know, she's your baby."

They stood at the crest and viewed the city of Louisville, sprawled in panoramic splendor, industrial stacks puffing huge billows of dark smoke along the horizon.

James stood in the road, with the other children blocking the wagons, pointing toward the northwest. "Yahoo! There it is, straight ahead. Look." He was beside himself. "Won't be long now," he shouted, waving his hand at his father.

Sarah leaned over the seat between her parents. "Oh, Pa, isn't it beautiful."

"We made it." Caroline gave a sigh of relief. "What a smoky city."

"Lots of industry. We'll be in before nightfall." Standing up on the seat, Alexander shouted, "Let's get going. We need to get in before the sun's down."

Slowly the wagons descended the rolling hills.

Following the road into Louisville, the wagons turned onto Main Street, the hub of the city. With wide-eyed interest, James' head turned from side to side. There was so much to see. Never in his wildest dreams could he have imagined so much commotion.

Cobblestone pavement and wide sidewalks stretched as far as the eye could see. There were barbershops, hardware stores, clothing and millinery emporiums, tinware and cooper shops, inns, and taverns. People attended to late afternoon business, while carriages and wagons congested the thoroughfare. Street vendors and peddlers hawked their wares from handcarts shouting "Scissors and knives to grind", "Fish! Buy your fresh fish here," or "Stttrawbbbberrrries, fresh strawberries. Get 'em while they're fresh." The continual noise filled the streets with people selling wood, newspapers, and even matches.

Standing on the corner of First and Main Streets was a tall, thin chimney sweep, all sooty with his stick and brooms. Children gathered around, shouting at him while adults tried to avoid his dirty condition. A lamplighter walked across the street carrying his ladder and lighting stick to ignite the next gaslight. In the background, church bells pealed.

Suddenly, a Concord Stagecoach passed the Anderson wagon, clamoring down Main Street at crack speed, stopping abruptly in front of the Old River Tavern.

Pointing up past the coach, Caroline asked, "Isn't that the inn you were looking for?"

On the north corner of Second and Main Streets, stood the Galt House, John's recommendation for a comfortable night's lodging. It looked to be a modest inn. Any accommodations were a welcome sight. Alexander's tired, sore body cried for relief from the hard bench that beat his buttocks all day. Once the family settled in, he'd find a livery for the horses.

Under the lamp light on the sidewalk, Alexander watched the street activities. A cabriolet, driven by a hackman, rumbled along the cobblestone street headed for the exquisite Louisville Hotel. Illuminated gaslights and smoke from surrounding foundries blotted out most of the stars in the sky. Crossing the street, Michael O'Brien dodged a couple of carriages.

"Well, saints preserve us. A man could get himself run over in this fair city." Michael took off his hat and brushed his red hair back with his fingers. "Took a few cups at O'Reilly's Tavern over yonder. Gettin' the feel of the land, ya might say. We've somethin' of a crisis, me lad. The news I have ain't good."

"Oh, did the *fair city* run out of ale, Michael?"

"Now be holdin' your tongue there, my good man. What I have to tell ya is mighty important. You'll be thankin' your lucky stars I took a few at the tavern tonight."

"Well?" Alexander waited. Michael was not to be rushed, especially after drinking.

"Hmmm. Like I said before, the news isn't good. In fact it's downright mean. Seems this lovely city is besieged with a sickness ya can't see." He stopped for a moment to catch a glimpse of a lady sashay invitingly down the sidewalk across the street. "Would ya look at that now? I'd say that cost a pretty penny for a night's entertainment."

"Michael, get on with your news," said an exasperated Alexander. "Sometimes getting information from you is like pulling teeth one at a one."

"Is that right? Oh, yes, where was I now?"

"The sickness, Michael. What is the sickness and how bad?" Alexander placed his hands on his hips.

"Oh, it's really bad, really bad. Cholera. I say we should be leavin' the first thing in the mornin'. Seems many of the people are vacatin' the city in fear of the disease."

"Cholera?"

"Aye, and it's bad, from what I hear."

Dead silence. Finally, Alexander asked, "Do you have enough supplies to get you through to St. Louis?"

"My supplies are in good shape."

"Good. Then tomorrow we locate a steamboat and leave. I'm going to get some sleep. See you in the morning." Alexander strolled toward the inn.

"I'll be followin' ya as soon as I smoke me pipe." Michael eyed the lady in red standing under a gas lamp across the street. She lifted her head and stared straight at him.

"Not tonight, me sweet thing. I fancy ya, but definitely not with me wife so nearby," he mumbled, pulling his pipe from his shirt pocket.

Chapter Twelve

Independence, Missouri

"How come all them wagons are drawn up behind each other? What're they waitin' for?" Micah tried to make himself heard above the shouting and yelling. He scanned the area in astonishment. Wagons, people and animals milled about everywhere. Never in his whole born days had he seen such a sight. All this upheaval made him nervous.

Wagons lined Lexington Street in front of the Independence Courthouse Square, one right after the other on both sides of the road. More rolled up and down the dirt street, congesting the thoroughfare. Stock roamed the streets, braying and bellowing while drivers cussed at them.

"Welcome to Independence," John shouted, leaning over his horse toward Micah, to be heard over the deafening noise. "They're all waiting for their names to appear on a wagon train list so they can travel on to California."

Not impressed one bit by all the activity, Micah asked, "Is this what we came for? These people are crazy and have lost their stuffin's." He glanced about slowly, scrutinizing faces around him. There weren't any blacks or dark-skinned people anywhere. He pulled his hat down over his eyebrows, trying to be inconspicuous.

John caught his gesture and understood. "Don't give it another thought. Just stay close so you don't get separated in all this hubbub."

He turned right, onto Main Street, dodging cattle, wagons, and pedestrians, heading for the road behind the courthouse square. Handcarts, farm wagons, oxcarts, wheelbarrows, and many other unusual makeshift vehicles packed with cherished possessions, stretched completely around the block.

"We need to find a livery stable."

Micah pointed, "There's one."

After stabling their horses, they walked down Maple Street to Colonel Noland's Tavern and Inn.

John pushed open the door to a noisy room full of cigar-smoking, tobacco-chewing, and whiskey-drinking men. The bar was lined three deep. The racket inside blended with the ruckus outside. Crossing the room, he walked through the entrance of the inn, signed for a room, and headed up the stairs, saddlebags slung over his shoulder. Micah followed, glancing at the stares behind him.

Tired and dusty, they entered a small, but adequate room. "We've made Independence as I promised," said John wearily, dropping his bags on the floor.

"Oh, pshaw!" Micah looked around the small room, one bed, a dry sink, and one chair. Exhausted, hungry, and apprehensive about going West with this rough white man, he showed signs of indignation. "It's cramped in here. Couldn't we get a bigger room?"

John ignored the boy's comment. "Are ya hungry? If ya are, let's clean up and go eat." They managed to share the washbowl.

Micah tried to tame his wild hair to no avail.

John grabbed a piece of thin rawhide. "Here, let me help you." He tied the mass of soft locks behind the nape of the boy's neck. "Now you look presentable. Ready?"

Micah nodded, a little nervous about going to a restaurant, but as long as he was with John, maybe it would be okay.

After eating, they returned to their room. The boy flopped across the bed spread-eagle, raising little puffs of dust. The springs squeaked as he wiggled about. It beat sleeping on the floor.

John counted his money and slipped it into his jacket pocket. "I'm going out. I'll be back in a little bit. Listen to me. Stay here and don't leave the room. Do you hear me?"

Micah glared at him, and caustically repeated, "Do you hear me?"

"Don't get snippy with me, son," he said gruffly. Raising one eyebrow, John stared at the boy, then left the room.

Micah walked over to the window and slid his backside down the wall. Outside, the street activity proved to be quite interesting this time of day. He saw two fights take place, one on the sidewalk, the other in front of the courthouse. Across the street a man and woman were arguing. In front of the bar, a drunk fell face forward and lost his bottle as it broke into a million pieces.

"Looks like tempers are awful short here. They're all liquored up tonight. I wonder where Pa went." He hugged his knees and rested the back of his head against the wall. This was better than St. Louis, he guessed. At least rats didn't run through the room. No one had asked him to leave the table when he ate tonight. All in all, it wasn't half bad.

Leaning forward and resting his forehead on his knees, mental images of his beautiful mother floated through his mind. She had been awful sick for a long time and suffered so much. He did the best he could for her, but he didn't earn enough money for opium or medicine to make her better. *I wish she were here with me now.* His heart hurt, he yearned for the comfort of her warm arms, the gentleness of her melodious voice. She made the hurt go away. A lump swelled in his throat. Tears welled up in his eyes. Strong men don't cry, but he was only a kid. Tonight the desolate loneliness made him feel vulnerable.

Hearing children's voices outside, he whipped his head up, staring down below. Near the corner, several boys played baseball with a stick and rocks. It was a new game in St. Louis that Micah was familiar with. He jumped up and raced out of the room. Reaching the street, he strolled toward the boys, staying close to the building a while. The group finally moved to a side street to avoid being run over. He joined in without anyone objecting. At first, he missed hitting the rock. It didn't take long for him to catch on, though. The hard part was dodging the rock when it was thrown at the runner. It sure hurt when contact was made with his backside.

"Hey," shouted a boy named Peter. "Let's do something different. How about a game of mumblety-peg?"

"Good idea," said another.

Micah searched his pockets for his knife, withdrew it, and opened the blade. "Don't mind if I do."

For a while the game went smoothly. They threw their knives in various positions, sticking the ground. When a boy missed, he pulled a peg from the dirt with his teeth, face full of grit.

With Micah's turn, he was winning. His expertise and agility made a boy named Gus, mad. As he held the knife to toss it in the air, Gus nudged him with his shoulder, causing Micah to miss. He jumped up and yelled, "You did that on purpose."

Gus smiled. "Whatever do you mean, black boy?"

"You heard what I said, stupid."

"Listen, nigger, go shine something. Or better yet, kiss my—"

Red-faced, Micah tackled Gus knee high, knocking him over backwards. Fists flew as they rolled in the dirt punching and cussing up a storm. The other boys formed a circle around the fight, shouting instructions.

"Hit him harder."

"Kick him."

"Bite him. Hit the nigger again."

"Give him a real black eye." This remark brought laughter from the small group.

John left Miss Nellie's establishment and walked across the street feeling relaxed. Every man needed a bath at Nell's place. Now he needed to set his plan into action. He heard shouts coming from the side street. Turning the corner, he saw Micah take a punch at the taller lad who out weighed him by a good ten pounds. John grabbed the boys by their collars and shook them hard. The boys' wild punches found John's midriff as he separated them. Micah stuck his foot out and tripped the older lad, sending him into the dirt.

A man with a red face and a bulbous nose rushed into the side street, huffing and puffing. "What's going on here?" he gasped, out of breath. He helped the older boy up, dusted him off, and straightened his shirt. "Gus, are you hurt?"

Gus pointed a finger at Micah. "He started it. He was cheating."

"That boy's a menace. He should be taught some manners. What's that nigger doin', playing with these white boys anyway?"

"He's no nigger. This boy is a mulatto and he's my son."

"Well, take his black ass away from here. Come on, Gus, let's go."

Micah started charging at the man's back. John quickly grabbed him by the shirt. "Easy there, fellow. There's plenty of time for that. Pick up your knife." He grabbed Micah's hat and plopped it on his head, shoving him in the direction of the inn.

"Don't push. I can walk. Besides, he started it."

"I don't care who started it. I told ya to stay in the room. Didn't I? If you had done what you were told, none of this would have happened."

Micah turned around and belligerently said, "I know. I'm always wrong. But, I could have finished him. I hit him with a good sockdologer right in the stomach."

"Yes, and you were probably lucky. Right now we have other things to do besides fighting." John grabbed him by the shoulder and led him through the inn door, shoving him up the stairs.

The man behind the desk looked up. "You got quite a mean little nigger there, fellow."

John stopped and glared at the desk clerk. "He's a mulatto."

The man turned around to avoid John's stony stare.

Upstairs in their room, John asked dryly, "So how did the fight start?"

"You heard 'em. Just like the man downstairs," Micah blurted out. "He called me a nigger and wanted me to kiss his—"

"Yes, I know where."

"I ain't kissin' no one's butt."

"Good for you. I wouldn't either." John gave Micah a big friendly grin. "Besides, it looked a bit dusty."

John sat down on the bed, eyeing him carefully. "Did you cheat?"

"Does it matter?" Micah twisted his mouth, glaring at John, waiting for a reprimand. Then he added brusquely, "No, I wasn't cheatin'. I played fair and square. I was winnin'."

John lay back and clasped his fingers together under his head. "I'll accept that answer."

Micah sat next to his father on the bed, grabbed a pillow, punched it a couple of times and crunched it into his lap. "Did you love my mother?"

The unexpected question took John totally off guard. He'd known one day he'd have to stand up and answer his son's questions. He had hoped for a little more time to get an explanation together. What were his feelings for D'Alene? Did they use each other for comfort and convenience? He wasn't sure. They never lacked passion, no question about that. He smiled. Living, breathing proof to attest to their amorous behavior sat next to him. The question was, how much did he really love her, or was she a replacement for Caroline?

Caroline. Another problem to face one day.

His son's glaring eyes told him, his past had caught up with him. His reckoning day had arrived.

"Well?" Micah punched the pillow again.

"Micah, I loved your mother. I can't honestly tell you how deeply." John sat up, scooted up to the headboard and leaned his head against the wall. He bent one leg and rested his forearm on it. "I remember her as a kind and beautiful woman. She made me laugh at the world and at myself. Most of the time, we didn't have enough money to buy the fancy things she deserved. Other times we spent money like pouring water out of a boot. The memories of your mother are good ones."

He paused for a moment to reflect on his life with her. Shutting his eyes, he saw her lovely lithe figure, her flawless caramel skin. "She was part of my life and my past. I won't ever forget her. In fact she saved my life. Maybe someday I'll tell you about it. In the meantime, remember, I loved her in my own way and she loved me the same."

He looked at his son for some understanding for his past discretions. "I could sure use a drink right now."

"What do ya need, courage?" Micah asked sarcastically.

"No, just a drink. All right. Somewhere along the way I lost all perspective on life. I struck out and did what I wanted to do, when I wanted to, wherever the adventure took me. I can tell you, it's no way to live. It's mighty lonely. You can get yourself killed living life on a whim. I've been extremely lucky."

Micah lifted his chin, defiantly, and said, "I was wonderin' why you left us."

"First of all, there wasn't an *us*. Only your mom and me. I didn't know she was pregnant. She never told me."

"You didn't give her time. How was she supposed to tell you? You just up and vanished."

John pondered Micah's statement for a moment. He did leave them high and dry.

"Look. I'm not proud of my past. I've done a lot of stupid things and leaving your mother was probably the most ignorant thing I've ever done."

Micah glared at him. "Yep, it was."

"Okay, so we both agree."

"If someone told you she was gonna to have me, would you've stayed around?" Micah scrutinized John's face for a truthful answer.

He faced the boy. "From my heart, Micah, yes! I'd have stayed and raised you the best I could."

Quiet prevailed as the two sat pondering the truth. Raw sores that had chaffed for years were cleansed. Healing had begun both father and son.

John broke the silence. "Son, and I do mean son, no matter what happens from now on, I promise, I will stick by your side." He extended his hand and waited for some type of acknowledgement from the lad.

Micah twisted his mouth, mulling over all he said. He wondered, could this man truly be trusted to honor his pledge? There was no way to know except to trust him.

He smiled and extended his small hand. "All right, I'll try to be the best son you'll ever have." Then he wrinkled his nose with a sideways glance. "I sure don't look at all like you. You're much lighter than I am and your hair's straight."

Laughing, John grabbed his son and pulled him down on the bed next to him. "Can't do anything about my hair. Maybe we can borrow some boot black from the old man on the corner. How's that sound?"

If the bar hadn't been so busy, all the patrons downstairs at Colonel Noland's could have heard the laughter and the foot stomping from their room. They wrestled for a while until John became winded.

"Okay, enough's enough. Look, I need to go out tonight. Have a little work to do. This time, *stay put*. No messing around outside. It's dark and dangerous out there, and you don't need to be getting into any more trouble."

"Why do I have to stay here and you get to go out? It's hot and borin' in here."

"Micah, there are men out tonight who would love to cause you trouble. I can't protect you if you're out there by yourself. You're safer in our room. Please be patient with me right now. Stay put. We can use some extra money and I intend to win playing poker. Now promise me you'll do as I ask."

The boy sat cross-legged on the bed, his hands resting in his lap, head bent, pursing his lips together. He wasn't a bit happy about being left alone again with no one to talk to, nothing to do. He'd spent most of his life on his own, and now he had a father, he liked the company. Micah looked up and realized he approved of this man. His pa. He smiled. *Yep, that's what I'm gonna call him, like the other boys. I know my maman would approve.*

"Did you hear me?" repeated John.

Defeated, Micah answered, "I heard you. All right. I'll stay here. Don't be long. And, don't get yourself shot. It's too far for me to go back to St. Louis by myself."

"Okay, I promise to be careful. Now lie down and go to sleep." John faced the mirror, combed his hair, and tied it back.

"Yep, you look pretty." His son could not resist laughing at his father's primping.

"Pretty?" John flopped on the bed next to Micah and rolled him.

"Stop, stop. You're gonna mess up your…"

"My what?"

"Your shirt."

John stood up, straightened his clothing and headed for the door. "I'll be back soon, I promise."

Tonight, the lucky feeling crept through John's bones. Why, he might even get luckier if he won enough for a good night's entertainment. She'd have to be pretty. He stopped in mid thought and looked up at the window. Micah waved to him. On second thought, he'd made a promise and he wouldn't break it. Business only tonight.

Even at this hour of the night, people crowded the streets

of Independence. Crossing the road, he dodged several wagons before turning down Third Street to O'Shay's Tavern, a quieter section off the main thoroughfare.

He entered the tavern and looked around. His palms itched, his pulse raced, and his mouth felt dry. He savored the action of a card game. Lady luck sat in his pocket. Life couldn't get any better. He'd acquired a son, a partner to guide over life's pathways, and his brother and family were somewhere behind him, traveling to California. Yes, life had turned around for him.

"So, what do ya have?" bellowed Big Mike.

Only John and the enormous dirty creature sitting across from him were still in the game. He knew he'd won, by paying attention to Mike's eyes and facial expressions.

"I have a full house," he drawled. Big Mike threw his cards on the table. John reached across the table to rack in his winnings.

His opponent grabbed his wrist with one hand and raised his pistol with the other. "You cheatin' son of a…."

"Here, here now. I never cheat." Trying to remain calm, John turned his free hand palm up. "I played the cards the way they fell. In fact, you dealt, if I remember correctly."

"I know you cheated. You can't be that lucky, especially with my money. This here pot is mine." Mike pulled the hammer back and pointed the gun at John's head. "Right?"

"Since you put it that way, I guess the pot is yours."

Mike smiled a toothless grin, lowered the hammer and replaced his gun into his holster. Then he racked in the money with both arms. "I knew you'd see it my way."

Thwack! John slammed his fist hard into Mike's face, knocking him onto the floor. Before he could get up, John flew over the table at him, belting him again. Coins spilled across the floor. He brought his bloody fist back to hit Mike again. Behind him, he heard a bottle smash. He quickly jumped to his feet and dodged, avoiding being jabbed in the back. Turning, he slugged the second assailant with his injured knuckles. The fight became a free-for-all. Patrons walloped each other, breaking chairs and tables, spilling broken glasses and pitchers across the floor.

John crawled around the floor dodging bodies and trampling feet, collecting paper money and coins, stuffing them into his pockets. He wasn't leaving without his money. Standing up next to the piano, he punched a few more men who stood in his way and shoved a couple back into the fight as he eased his way to the door.

He viewed the shambles behind him as he stepped through the doorway, glad to escape with only a ripped jacket and bleeding knuckles. The money would buy some extra necessities. He'd won it fair and square this time with no cheating. Hell if he'd let Big Mike take it away.

"Wake up, Micah. Come on. Wake up. We have to leave."

Micah rubbed his eyes. "What? We have to leave now? It's still dark."

"I know. I'll explain it to you later. Get dressed and be quiet."

John washed his knuckles in the water bowl and wrapped them in strips of cloth torn from an old shirt. Grabbing up his saddlebags, he and the boy hastened down the stairs and out the door. They sprinted for the stables. He had to get out of town before Big Mike and his crowd found him. He had a son to think about now.

They reached the stables, saddled their horses, and left fee money in the box tied to the post.

As they rode out of town, Micah broke the silence. "Are we gonna eat?"

"We'll get food and water at the Shawnee Mission."

"How far is that?"

"About fifteen miles."

Micah gave a disgusted sigh.

"When we reach Fitzhugh's campground, we'll rest a spell. We need to pass New Santa Fe before noon."

"Why?"

"If the law is hunting for us, they can't reach us beyond there."

With nothing else to say, they rode in silence.

Chapter Thirteen

Louisville, Kentucky

Captain Montgomery raised his voice. "Ya can't take your wagons aboard my boat, I tell ya. The Pike Number Nine is short handed due to the cholera epidemic here in Louisville. Besides, there's no room."

The heated conversation on Preston's Landing drew a crowd. Michael and Alexander were determined to board the steamboat. The captain politely tried to tell the two men why his wooden-hulled side-wheeler could not accommodate them. The discussion was going nowhere as tempers sizzled.

Michael's neck and face went from pink to red as he scowled at the captain. "Now, laddie. Are ya telling me we've traveled all this way and we can't get to St. Louis except by land?"

"Correct. Every boat you see along the landing is booked." With a sly smile, the Captain added, "If you want to travel to St. Louis on my boat, you'll have to sell your wagons, some of your wares and your horses. Then get your personal belongings and supplies aboard. Go back across the bridge and purchase your tickets quickly, we've nearly reached capacity and we leave in one hour."

"I don't mean to be bullyraggin' ya, but how long does this overland trip take and what are the road conditions?" Michael took a step closer to the captain, clutching his hands nervously.

"Take the Albany Road south to Portland. There the ferry crosses the river below the falls. The road's a bit steep on the other side goin' out of town, but it's in good condition. Then head east toward Vincennes and on to St. Louis. Ya can't miss it."

Michael rephrased his question slowly and deliberately, gritting his teeth, the muscles jerking in his neck. "I asked how long it would take."

The captain's eyes narrowed. The angry man in front of him was a mite younger, more agile, and twenty pounds lighter. Besides, many of the roustabouts standing around waited for a good brawl.

"Settle down, Michael. Exactly how long will it take us to reach St. Louis by wagon, Captain Montgomery?" Alexander patiently waited for an answer.

The captain looked up, as Michael moved closer. "With the road and weather permitting, about fifteen days."

Michael shouted and stomped about, waving a hand in the air, trying to comprehend the time involved. "Fifteen days! Fifteen days!"

"Easy, Michael." Alexander stepped in closer to the captain.

"I'm not kissin' the back of his trousers," Michael shouted. He moved to one side and swung, squarely landing his fist on the captain's jaw, knocking him to his knees. Alexander jumped in between, trying to separate them.

Someone in back of the crowd shouted, "Fight! Fight!" A full-fledged riot broke out. Many of the onlookers stepped into the melee, swinging to protect themselves. The situation grew dangerous.

A short stocky bystander cut loose with a powerful swing, missing Alexander by inches as he tried to extricate Michael from his seat on Captain Montgomery's chest.

"He's comin' around at ya," hollered Michael.

As Alexander reached for the captain, someone wheeled him about and landed a punch into the pit of his stomach, knocking the air out of him, causing his knees to buckle.

"Here's a face full of knuckles," yelled Michael, swinging at a ruffian in front of him. The man dodged and landed a lucky punch connecting with Michael's nose. Another rowdy grabbed Michael from behind, holding him, while a big ugly roustabout landed a solid punch to his mid-section. Michael slid from the man's grasp and hit the ground, blood spurting from his nose and mouth. He lay curled like a pretzel, holding his ribs and stomach.

Bodies sprawled across the levee, the wild brawling continued, reaching a crescendo of grunts and cursing.

The fight made the horses skittish. Annie and Caroline jumped from their wagons to steady them. Clopping their hooves on the slick levee stones, the animals shifted their weight, jerking the wagons.

The children stuck their heads from under the canvas and shouted to their fathers, encouraging them. Excitement escalated with every punch.

"Hit 'em again, Pa," James yelled, fists flailing.

Joshua hung over the edge of the side. "Clobber 'em. Hit 'em hard."

Pandemonium prevailed as the fight spread across the levee and up the wharf to Canal Street.

As John and Patrick jumped down to help their mother calm the horses and back the wagon away from the fight, a man grabbed John and pulled back his fist. Whap! Annie smacked the man in the back of the head with a piece of driftwood she'd retrieved from the levee. He collapsed at her feet.

"Good going, *Mam*." Patrick patted his mother's shoulder.

"Get our wagon away from this mess," Annie demanded. "John, go help Mrs. Anderson back up her horses. She's right in the middle of all the fightin' over yonder. Hurry."

Caroline held the reins tightly, praying Alexander would not be seriously hurt. A man fell at her feet, knocking her against the horses. Desperately, she clung to the reins as the lead horses reared up, pulling the back two horses sideways. Shaking from side to side, the wagon began to edge closer to the Ohio River on the slippery levee.

Sarah's screams reached a piercing crescendo that could be heard above the noise. White as a ghost, James stood stock still behind the bench seat, holding on for dear life.

John O'Brien leaped over a man lying on the ground, dodged several groups of fighters, before reaching the Anderson wagon. "Let me help you, Mrs. Anderson." To the children, he yelled, "Stay in the wagon and sit down."

He grabbed the reins from Caroline and pulled vigorously to keep the wagons from turning over and the horses from plunging into the river, all the while keeping his feet anchored solidly on the cobblestone landing. "Easy, there. Whoa, me beauties, whoa. That's it, easy there, easy." The horses settled down, snorting and pawing the ground.

Suddenly shrill whistles blew as two levee policemen briskly elbowed their way through the crowd, breaking up the fight.

The crowd dispersed quickly.

Michael knelt on the levee, head bowed, hands on his thighs. The knuckles on his right hand were cracked and bleeding. His left knuckles red and swollen. Cuts slashed his cheeks; a deep gash gaped crossed his forehead and the bridge of his nose, with one eye a mere slit. A partial strip of shirt clung to his midriff.

"Would you look at ya now? You're bleedin' and tore apart. You and your temper will be the death of us all. Ya act like there's not a brain in your head," Annie lashed out at him, all the while wiping his face with her apron and cuddling his head against her bosom.

Alexander helped a roustabout walk Captain Montgomery back toward the steamboat. A stoker relieved him, half-carrying the Captain up the gangplank. Alexander returned, surveying the area. *What a way to begin the day.*

"Here, now. What's goin' on? I don't suppose you could be tellin' me who started this ruckus?" Two burley Irish officers eyed the men suspiciously.

"It's a slight misunderstandin' that's been settled with fisticuffs." Michael stood up, leaning against Annie for support.

"There doesn't seem to be anyone filin' a report." The officer waved his hand to move them along. "Get yourselves together and be off with ya now, all of ya. Don't want to see your smilin' faces around here anymore today."

Alexander shook his head.

The officer looked around. "I hope ya'll be keepin' your noses clean and no more fightin'. I mean it now."

"We're leaving." Alexander went to the wagon where Caroline stood waiting for him. "How are the children? Did you get hurt?"

"We're fine. John O'Brien helped me with the horses when the fighting surrounded the wagon. He certainly isn't like his father, thank heavens." She took her kerchief from her pocket and wiped the blood from her husband's lips.

"We need to go before the officers change their mind and arrest us," Alexander said. "I have no idea how long it'll take us to get to Portland and cross the Ohio." He helped her into the wagon, climbed up behind her, and looked around. "You ready?"

Michael settled onto the seat of his wagon. "Ready here."

"Move 'em out," Alexander shouted.

Alexander's black mood tolerated no tomfoolery. "Sarah, stop sniffling. Both of you children sit back and be quiet until we get through the city."

"What a fight!" James sputtered, *"Pow! Pow!* You gave them what for, Pa."

Alexander swirled around and glared at his son. "James!"

His father's stern expression scared James enough to shut his mouth and sit back. Being in trouble seemed to be part of his life lately.

Sarah sat grinning at her brother like she just ate the last piece of apple pie.

James shoved his boot at her.

Avoiding his kick, she tilted her head and kept smiling.

"James, I don't want to stop this wagon, but I will if I have to. Behave," Alexander said as he turned in his seat.

Caroline took Alexander's hand, gently wiped away the blood from around the cuts and between the fingers. "How in the world did the fight begin?"

"A misunderstanding and a hot Irish temper."

The Albany Ferry rocked at its moorings, crowded with wagons, passengers, and animals. Over thirty vehicles waited at the landing for a turn to load and cross the Ohio River. Michael and Alexander made their way to the boat dock, signed their names to the bottom of the list.

Sitting in the wagon, waiting, Alexander scanned the dock. So many in front of him and the trip across the river took forever. Every bone in his body hurt. *I would give anything for a warm comfortable bath and a soft bed. If I could only shut my eyes for a half an hour and rest undisturbed, I would feel like I'd died and gone to heaven.*

"Sarah, hand me the medicine bag." Caroline selected salve and bandages from the case. "Let me have your right hand. It needs tending to. It should be soaked to get the swelling down." She began dressing his wounds, first one hand then the other.

"We don't need all this delay in crossing the river." Miserable and tired, Alexander sat mesmerized as the water rushed past the levee.

Even James sat quietly in the back, too afraid to say a word. He whispered to Sarah, "Pa's in a black mood."

"Well, all your whispering won't help," she hissed. "Be quiet."

Water lapped at the cobblestones, pushing debris and driftwood onto the landing. The noise grew louder as animals and wagons rattled by, interspersed with hawkers calling out their wares.

Alexander's head buzzed. The sun boiled overhead. Humidity hung in the air. Sweat trickled down his neck and back. His hair was pasted to his forehead. For three hours he waited and swatted the flies buzzing around his head.

Michael stood leaning against the side of his wagon. He noticed John and Patrick standing next to the tailgate, probably discussing the fight.

Surrounded by boxes, packages, tin pans and tools,

Elizabeth and Joshua hid in the cramped vehicle, too afraid to make any noise that might set their father off again.

Annie sat looking down at her lap, hands twitching nervously. "Today is the first time I've felt uneasy about this journey west, almost like a premonition, a dark cloud hangin' over us. It's makin' me skin crawl."

"We'll be fine, girl." Michael mumbled a few more inaudible words. He grabbed the side of the wagon and leaned his forehead against the board. *Waitin', always waitin'.*

"Are ya all right?" she asked.

Irritably, he snapped, "Yes." He took a deep breath and exhaled. "I'm sorry, me beauty. My poor body hurts, me temper is short, and I'm tired of waitin'."

Annie fell silent. Her gay mood of yesterday had disappeared.

He broke the silence. "Fifteen more days of land travel before we reach St. Louis." He kicked at the wheel, dislodging some dirt from his boot. "Now additional supplies need to be purchased, cuttin' into our reserve money. These unexpected expenses crop up at the worse time."

He lifted his head. "I can't believe I lost my temper back there."

"Humph!" grunted his wife.

He glared at her.

Suddenly a bell rang four times. "Yo, hear this," bellowed the ferryman. "Bacon, Smyth, Anderson, and O'Brien now loading."

Alexander jumped up and grabbed the reins. "Let's go."

They crossed the swift river, slowly making their way to the other side. Once on solid ground, they made purchases at the general store before rolling forward on an uphill trek. The climb out of New Albany, Indiana proved slow. The sky grew dark with huge fat clouds. A light drizzle began to fall.

"Ah, look at it now. The sky decided to add to our miseries by drownin' us in water. Soon, the roads will be a quagmire. Indiana's no better than Kentucky."

Annie knew her husband's black mood matched the color of the clouds. A bit distraught, she placed her hands on her hips, leaned forward and stared him down. "Stop your blubberin'. We're all in one piece. As I see it, we've made our way out of Kentucky without your losin' any part of your body."

"If I had wings, I'd fly to St. Louis," he shouted. "Fifteen days. That's a lot of miles to add to this journey. Could put us into the mountain snows."

"The whole township will hear ya, your kingship, if ya keep yellin'. I'm sick of the talk of it." Annie bit her tongue, trying to control her temper. Making him cross would not help the situation. "Ah, me love. We'll talk to Alexander tonight."

Annie intended to speak out tonight. All of this fussing and spouting off got her husband nowhere. Her family huddled in the wagon like refugees, bedraggled and disheartened. Alexander and Michael acted as though they had fought a war.

The soft drizzle turned to a light rain, slowing their progress. The hills dropped into a small plateau, only to lead back up into more rolling hills. After two hours, the rain stopped and the sun came out.

When they reached the night accommodations at Floyd's Knobs, they cornered Alexander.

"Can we make it to St. Louis in good time?" asked Annie.

"I truly don't know. If we rise early, start out right away, and eat on the trail, maybe."

Michael rubbed his chin. "Me question is, can we beat that lovely blanket of snow before it covers the mountains?"

"I can't answer that one either. We'll have to try. If we rise at two o'clock and roll out by four, we might be able to cut off a day or two. That means no resting on our laurels at night. We'll camp at dusk. The mornings will be dark and a little dangerous. Do you want to try it?"

"Aye, the O'Briens will be ready, me lad. No two ways about it," volunteered Michael.

Both families scrambled to their rooms. Morning would definitely be early.

The next two days of dismal rainy travel dispelled the joy of going west. One evening at a camp gathering, Alexander stood before the depressed group and spoke like a traveling Baptist Minister.

"What's happened to us? Where are our dreams? Are we going to give in to a little let down?"

Downhearted, Michael asked, "Where will fifteen days put us, Alexander? Can we make Independence in time?"

"Where do you want to be in fifteen days, Michael? My family and I want be in St. Louis. If we keep our hopes and dreams stuck in our back pockets, we might as well make Indiana our home." Alexander pounded his fist into his hand. "If you're with me, then we'll push a little harder. These macadamized roads aren't as bad as we thought. We might be able to make St. Louis in twelve days. Do you want to try?" He paused for a moment, waiting for some inkling of enthusiasm.

Michael bent his head and scraped the toe of his boot in the dirt.

"Do you think you can do it? Are you with me? If you're not, stay here," Alexander shouted, pounding his fist in his hand. "I'm going on without you."

Annie poked Michael in the ribs. He lifted his head and looked at her. She gave him a wide smile and winked. In her sweet Irish lilt, she said, "Ya know we can do it, love. Nothin' ever puts the Irish down. So a bullheaded man once told me a long time ago."

The O'Brien children began to shout in unison, "We can do it. Can't we, *Da*?"

He smiled and shook his head. "Aye, we can do it. An Irishman never gives up." He jumped to his feet and shouted, "All right. By all the saints that's precious to me father's memory, we can do it." He grabbed his squeezebox and began to play a high-stepping melody. The fast and lively music diffused the anguish of the day. Enthusiasm ran high.

Caroline linked her arm through Alexander's. "Can we do it, Alexander?"

"I don't know, but we sure as hell are going to try. The way I figure it, the days will be long and the nights short, making conditions hard on humans and animals alike. Our best friend will be good weather. Pray we don't see much rain on the way." He patted her hand, tapped his hat and slowly walked away, skirting the open area, and headed to the back of their wagon.

She understood he needed a little 'medicinal' help right now and he knew right where to find it.

Amazed at his stamina and courage, Caroline admired her husband, the way he pulled the group together. His wisdom and inner strength totally baffled her. When did he develop this leadership quality? She smiled. *Now if he can only stand up to his brother when we reach California?*

A shrill voice broke her train of thought. "Oh, Ma, isn't this fun? Mr. O'Brien is so silly. Look at the way he's dancing." Sarah stood behind her, giggling and pointing across to the dancers.

"Yep, he looks like he's got bees in his pants." James laughed and slapped his knee.

"His legs do look a bit rubbery," said Caroline. "I believe he's doing an Irish jig."

"Does Pa dance like that?" asked James.

Caroline ginned. "No, he doesn't. He has two left feet. Now go have fun."

"What did she mean by that?" she heard James asked, as he and Sarah ran to join the jubilant falderal with their friends.

Caroline laughed at Annie and her eldest son flat-foot stomping around the area in time to the music while the younger children jumped in the air and twirled in circles. They didn't have a care in the world.

Michael O'Brien played the pied piper. The dancers followed him as he weaved about the area. The gay, rowdy tunes were invigorating.

Alexander returned, a simpering smile on his face. She glanced sideways at him.

"Sometimes a small amount of courage from the medicine chest helps to clear one's mind," he said. He kissed her neck and sat down on a stump to enjoy the merriment. She grinned. *Yes, I'm sure it does.*

Morning brought Alexander renewed energy with the thought of St. Louis ahead of him. Towns, with churches, taverns, and a multitude of inns to ease one's aching body after a strenuous day's travel, grew closer together.

When they reached the bluff, the city of Vincennes lay below. Much to their delight, the travelers had cut a day and a half off their travel time. Alexander had pushed them hard to achieve the goal. Tired and exhausted, a good substantial meal and a comfortable night's rest were the only items on his agenda, after taking care of his animals and wagon.

The wagons rolled on each day, ever closer to Salem, Illinois. They crossed the wide Wabash River, Skillet Fork and the Little Wabash River.

Alexander sat in awe of the graceful vegetation swaying in the wind. "Look at the grasses, as far as the eye can see. They have to be five or six feet tall." He sat still for a moment, enjoying the tranquility. "One rippling wave after another."

"The wind brushes across the tops like a gentle kiss," said Caroline. She placed her arm through his and rested her head on his shoulder. A comforting silence embraced her.

"The roads are a lot straighter now, making travel easier."

"Do you think we are going to make it?" she asked.

"Yes," he said, emphatically.

Caroline decided to walk with the children. Alexander stopped long enough for them to exit the wagon, before urging the horses on.

Across the horizon, billowy clouds, like clotted cream, blended into one another. Underneath, unconnected layers of dark blue to gray stretched across the sky. The rolling mass gave vent to openings where fingerlings of rays touched the ground. Far ahead, a dull gray curtain of rain fell from the sky, shielding the sun.

Pointing, Alexander said, "Looks like we're in for it." Clouds bunched together, forming irregular shapes, blotting out the sun, giving them welcome relief from the heat and humidity. The temperature dropped.

Suddenly, the wind picked up, tumbling brush and leaves across the flat land, blowing dirt swirls across the road and fields. Gusts of wind whipped the women's skirts about their legs, tousling their hair, blowing their bonnets over their shoulders. Lanterns swung and thumped loudly against the wagon's sides as a prairie storm approached.

Caroline shaded her eyes with her hand trying to block the dust and flying debris.

In the far distance, jagged streaks of lightning illuminated the sky, followed by resonating thunder.

"Get the children together," shouted Alexander. Pulling the wagon to a halt, he signaled for the others to do the same. Caroline called to the children and ran to the wagon.

Sarah hid inside. Burying her head under a blanket, she covered her ears with her hands. Caroline knew violent storms scared her and made her sick to her stomach.

James stood next to his father, enjoying the lightening display in the distance. The noise and jagged fingers of light excited him.

As the sky grew ugly, Michael walked up behind Alexander. "I don't like the color of the sky."

Alexander nodded in agreement. "The storm's moving in fast. We better batten down everything that's loose and find cover quickly. This could be bad."

"I'd be hoping it's not one of those wild tornados I hear tell they have out here," said Michael.

Caroline gasped, "I hope not. We don't have much protection."

Alexander put his arm around her shoulder. "Now don't worry. The sky looks bad, but it's probably only a small prairie storm. Go check on Sarah, take James with you. I'll be there shortly."

Green intermingled with black and orange, filled the sky as the storm rolled in to greet the travelers. Bright flashes of lightning preceded the ear-splitting thunderclaps, directly overhead. The clouds burst open dropping hailstones the size of a man's thumb, sending everyone scurrying for shelter.

Hail pounded the canvas, bounced against the seat, pelting the occupants inside the wagon. The wind flapped the canvas openings. Caroline grabbed the heavy material beating against the hickory bows like rugs on a clothesline. The wagon rocked, hanging items clanged together or fell from their perches. The horses struck with ice pellets, whinnied and pawed the ground, jerking the wagon. A deluge of rain fell from the sky, filling the side ditches and potholes in the road. Water seeped through the covering, soaking Caroline and Sarah.

Alexander lay on his stomach under the wagon with James. Rivulets of water and mud soaked them through. Hailstones rolled underneath. James grabbed a few ice balls and stuck them into his pockets.

Abruptly as it all began, the storm abated. The black clouds rolled on, giving space to the sun, beaming bright and warm. Steam rose from the ground, melting the hail. Scurrying from their hiding places, the soaked travelers surveyed the damage to their wagons and checked on their horses. After changing into dry clothes, Caroline raised the canvas covering, wrung out the clothing, and hung them over the sideboard to dry.

"People, let's get ourselves together," shouted Alexander. "We need to push on. No time to waste."

The dampness from the storm lingered while the sun overhead beat down on them. Oppressive humidity smothered them. They pressed on, pushing hard, bearing whatever came their way. Alexander was relentless, yet no one complained or slowed down. They were headed for St. Louis, Missouri.

Day after day, determination drove them as the wheels rolled closer and closer to the beautiful city John had told stories about. Only a few more miles lay between them and St. Louis.

"Pa, how much farther?"

"Won't be much longer, James." Alexander's heart beat like the rhythm of a tune Michael O'Brien had played the night before. He sat tapping his foot against the footboard.

Caroline glanced at her husband's fancy footwork. "Have you taken up dancing for the horses?"

"Do you recall the name of the music Michael played last night?"

She laughed. "No. It sure was a foot-stomping piece."

"The tune is very catchy. Maybe he'll play it again for us."

"Oh, I am sure he will if you ask. Michael never passes up an opportunity to play his squeezebox."

Finally, the wagons topped a bluff and rolled down a hilly road, surrounded by black bottomland. Across the open plateau, farms dotted the countryside with oak, maple and spruce trees surrounding cabins and stone houses.

"Pa, look," shouted James, pointing ahead. "We're almost there."

Gazing into the smoky distance, Alexander heaved a weary sigh. "Yes, son, we made it."

Chapter Fourteen

St. Louis, Missouri

"Look how fast the water's moving." Caroline stood, stunned, on the banks of the mighty Mississippi River and observed the awesome sight. Muddy, chocolate-colored water churned and tumbled past the shoreline with a vengeance. Adding to the debris, the children began chucking rocks and sticks into the water to see who could throw the farthest.

"Whew." Michael O'Brien shook his head. "Ya know this here is one wild river we'll be tacklin', and not to my likin'. From the looks of it, nothin' can tame it."

"We've been here three days and the river's getting worse." Alexander watched the water lap at the bank, ingesting the riverbank into its main flow, swallowing it up forever, and greedily continuing on. Small shrubs and mighty oaks unlucky enough to be growing on a piece of land the river wanted, moved toward New Orleans and the Gulf of Mexico.

"Surely must have been some rain they had up river last night causing it to swell like this," he said. "Look at all the flotsam and driftwood floating in and out among those whirly things."

"Those are whirlpools, my friend," said a man standing behind them. "They're mighty dangerous in this here river. They'll suck you straight down, never giving you a chance to swim ashore. Nobody can save you."

"Hmm. Nasty little buggers, to my way of thinking," remarked another traveler. "Been waiting neigh onto twelve days for a crossing. Who knows when we'll get over. There's at least a hundred families camped here, all headed west. Now the river's in no condition to navigate."

Alexander and Michael stood in silence on the Illinois side of the river. *A hundred wagons...*

"Looks like it's gonna be a while before we get across," Alexander stated.

Michael gave a heavy sigh. "Aye. I hear tell it'll take more than a month to get half the wagons across. If the weather gets better and holds for awhile."

The fellow in front of them rubbed his head. "The ferryman says they'll have to work them three ferries from sunup to sundown, and more people are a-comin' everyday. Could be weeks before any of us get across." With his shoulders slumped, the man stuffed his hands into his pockets and walked away.

Michael whispered, "Not if I can help it, me lad." Looking around to be sure only Alexander heard him, he spoke low. "Ya know, yesterday I met a blessed ferrymen. He's from the neighboring Waterford County back in Ireland. Since I'm from Cork, it's like we're brothers." Michael smiled broadly. "Good old Irish luck, I'd say."

Alexander gave him a puzzled look. "How will that help us?"

"Well, now, let me tell ya, laddie. An Irishman never let's another Irishman down. Why he'd travel a hundred miles to help his countryman out."

"Don't stretch it too far, Michael." Alexander chuckled. "Your blarney's getting knee deep."

"He might not go that far. Come tomorrow, I'll take meself over to the dockin' area again to have a wee bit of a chat and offer a drink or two to Timothy O'Flannagan. See if we can't get us a little help to reach the top of that bloomin' list, if ya know what I mean."

Alexander quirked one eyebrow and smiled. "I understand exactly what you mean. Just be careful. If any of the others waiting to cross hear you, I'll have to come and save your bragging hide. That is, if you remember our last scuffle."

"Saints preserve us, don't remind me of Louisville. My Annie's been my conscience since we left Kentucky. I've eaten crow every night."

"All right. I'll give you some breathing room, but beware is all I'm telling you." Alexander turned away from the water. "Looks like the rest of our family's gone on back to camp. What do you say we join 'em? We need to get a fire going before light's gone. Do you think we can talk you into some music tonight?"

Michael's eyes twinkled. "Oh, now I'd say there's a sweet possibility."

The miserable campsite lay open to a flat treeless area. During the following days, the sweltering sun and humidity plagued the travelers, with hordes of mosquitoes and flies. The marshy ground of thick mud coated their shoes. The waiting was the worse part of each day for Michael O'Brien. Waiting for clean drinking water. Waiting for dry firewood. Waiting for a call to board the ferry.

The next day, Michael stopped by Alexander's tent.

"Me patience is about gone," said Michael, bored and agitated.

"Were you able to talk with your countryman about our crossing the river?"

"Aye. He told me to come around later this afternoon. It slows down around six o'clock when the sun's close to settin'."

"Maybe he'll have some good news for us. In the meantime, let's go do some repairs on your wagon. Then I need to tackle mending some of my gear."

Michael glanced at the fire scar. "Looks like the women'll be washin' today." He spied his sons leaving the area. "John. Patrick. Need your help boys. Where's Joshua?"

John pointed behind him. "He and James are up the road looking for more firewood for *Mam*. She sent them out a while ago."

Michael waved the boys over. "You husky lads follow us. We're in need of your expertise." Then he added, "Unless you want to be helpin' your *Mam* with the clothes."

The two boys stopped in their tracks. Appalled at the idea of helping with the wash, they quickly followed their father.

Caroline and Annie watched the men head toward the wagons. Taking the two buckets Patrick and John hauled from the river, the women poured the dark water into the hot pot. Annie shaved pieces of soap from the bar then chucked a few wood chips into the fire to keep it going. The flames licked the pot sides, flaring up.

"Be careful, you'll catch your dress on fire!" shouted Caroline.

While Annie stirred the water, Caroline placed several pieces of clothing into a tub of cold water. She rinsed and battled each piece across a log. After wiping her forehead with the back of her sleeve, she pushed loose wet strands of hair behind her ears. "What a wretched day to wash. Between the heat from the fire and this oppressive humidity, we'll be wringing wet before we're done."

Stirring the pot of hot water, Annie lowered her voice and looked at Caroline from under her eyebrows. "Well, if we don't do it today, we might not get a chance tomorrow."

Caroline picked up the short paddle. "Do you know something I don't? Come on, tell me, Annie. The way I feel right now, I need some good news."

"We might be movin' on tomorrow. Me husband's workin' with a ferryman, tryin' to get us on board sooner than what's expected." Annie slowly stirred the boiling water. "The water's ready."

"If only he can. I don't know about your family, but Sarah and James are constantly bickering at each other. I'll be glad to be back on the road to anywhere as long as we get away from this slop hole." Caroline dropped several items into the pot, one piece at a time.

"Aye, I understand. My Joshua and Elizabeth aren't exactly what Father O'Neil would call angels from heaven. Not by any means."

"I sure do miss my wash area back home. Why did we ever leave?" asked Caroline, standing up straight for a moment to ease the pain in her ribs.

"Men. It's always men," Annie snickered, working the items down into the water. "Ya have to love 'em."

"Here, let me stir for awhile." Caroline hiked up her skirt, tucked it into her waistband, and took the paddle handle.

"Are ya sure?" said Annie. "Be careful now. You're still under the weather, lassie."

"I'm fine. Doing clothes in this muddy river water is like not washing them at all. They'll never come clean again. Look at 'em."

"Your clothes? Look at me hands: nails broken, callused palms, rough red skin." Annie turned her red hands over and stared at her grimy nails. "They look like they belong to Old Matt Henderson back home. He was constantly grubbin' in the dirt. Down right filthy, he was."

"Dirt. It's all around us, day in and day out. I'm so tired of being outside all the time. I guess I'm grumbly, exhausted, and I still hurt." Caroline uttered the last sentence soft and slow, placing a hand across her rib cage.

"We have a right to growl and be short-tempered. This trip will get the better of us if we don't get angry about the conditions. Caroline, we look like scouring maids, with our filthy soiled dresses."

"It isn't my appearance bothering me. It's all the extra work. I'm totally exhausted when I bed down."

"I couldn't agree more, lassie," said Annie. "Less work would make me extremely happy. Unfortunately, I can't see that in the near future for either of us."

"I have an idea." Caroline offered. "Maybe we could exchange a nice padded rocking chair for the wagon seat. Then we'd be riding in style like queens. Are you ready for me to dunk some of these shirts?"

"You're a bit of a dreamer, ya are," giggled Annie, rinsing out a few more items. "Aye, put them in that pan over there. Glad we're doin' the wash together. Havin' two rinse pans make it easier and faster.

"Now," said Annie, wiping her hands on her apron, "here's somethin' I fancy: a cook to get the meals, serve the food, and clean up the mess."

"What a wonderful idea. Imagine having someone do the cooking."

"Aye," said Annie, shaking her head. "It's all that cookin' over an open prairie fire we'll have to do once we reach Independence that bothers me. If ya know what I mean. Here's the last of the clothes."

"Oh, don't remind me," said Caroline. "I don't even want to think about what lies beyond Independence. I'll be so glad to get to California."

"Do ya want me to stir for awhile?"

"No, I don't think I'd be able to shake out the rinsed pieces. Go ahead and finish. Lay them over the bushes or wherever you can find a place. I'll have these ready in a minute."

"Me poor mother'd be horrified to see the color of this wash water," said Annie.

"There, that's the last of them. At least they're clean, for awhile." Caroline wiped her forehead with the bottom of her apron. "Here, let me help lay these out."

"Once we reach our destination, we'll look back and say 'look what we did'."

"Not me. When I get to California, instead of wringing pants, I'm gonna wring someone's neck."

Annie wrenched one fist in a circle. "You mean like a chicken?"

Both women laughed until tears streamed down their faces. "Let's bail out this dirty water and dump the rinse pans," said Annie. "Then we're done."

"Wonderful idea. It'll be nice to sit for a minute and put our feet up." Caroline placed her hand on the small of her back.

From up the road, a young lady covered in mud ran crying and wailing, flinging her arms about.

"Oh, my. I believe that's Elizabeth," said Caroline.

"Would ya look at her, now?" Annie rushed to meet her

daughter. "Elizabeth, darlin'. What in the world happened to ya? Are ya hurt?"

"He— Oh, Ma!" she cried. Heartbroken and filthy, Elizabeth grabbed her mother around her waist and buried her face into her white apron, smearing mire all over her.

Standing in the road, Sarah rushed to her mother.

"What happened to Elizabeth, Sarah?"

"We were out gathering more wood for the fire, when these three big nasty boys came up and started picking on us. Elizabeth talked back to them. They shoved her a couple of times and then pushed her real hard into a mud puddle. They started to kick her, but I hit them with a big stick and chased them down the road."

Patrick came up behind his mother holding a saw and hammer he had retrieved for his father. "Who did that to my sister, Sarah? Tell me who they are."

"I don't know their names."

"Now, Patrick. Don't get angry. We'll let your *Da* handle this." Annie didn't want anymore fighting from the boys.

Without a word, Patrick stomped off toward the men.

Annie gave a heavy sigh. "This is what I mean. Fights all the time. I personally can't wait to leave."

Caroline hugged Sarah. "Annie, go ahead and take care of Elizabeth. Sarah can help me here."

"I'll be back as soon as I get me daughter out of these dirty clothes. Looks like I have more wash to do."

Elizabeth's crying slowed to soft sobs as she and her mother walked away to their tent.

"Sarah, help me gather our stuff together."

"All right, Ma."

Annie returned, carrying her apron and her daughter's dirty dress. "Elizabeth is dressin'. I'm sure she'll be out soon. I believe the only thing crushed was her Irish dignity. I checked and didn't see any cuts or bleedin'."

"Here let me rinse those first," said Caroline.

Joshua and James returned with four sticks of wood each. "This is all we can find."

"I can tell the two of you hunted *real* hard," said Caroline, eyeing both boys.

"Honest, we looked everywhere. There's nothing big or thick, just this little stuff." James hung his head.

"Go see if you two can help the men over by the wagons." Caroline kicked the stick as she dropped Elizabeth's dress and apron into the wash water. "Four measly pieces of wood. Not enough to build a fire. Sure is getting scarce around here. Too many people."

"Aye," Annie said. "It's not only the wood we're short of. Our drinkin' water's low, too. Don't know about you, but we're almost to the bottom of the barrel. We'll have to be stretchin' what sweet water we have until the crossin' takes place. Hopefully that'll be soon."

"With all these wagons pouring in, people have taken to drinking the tepid river water," said Caroline. "Once the sediment settles to the bottom of a filled bucket, they drink the beige stuff."

Annie made a face. "No! Glory be that's not good. People'll be gettin' sick drinkin' that ugly brown stuff."

"I wouldn't doubt it."

"Oh, my, that's nasty." Annie shuddered, dropping Elizabeth's dress into the clean rinse water. "Makes me ill to be thinkin' about it."

Caroline stood up and stretched. "Sarah, come help me. We need to dump this dirty water."

Patrick joined the men at the wagon, giving a high sign to John. Working their way around to the other side, Patrick told his brother what had happened to Elizabeth.

"Don't know their names, but I'm sure we can find the boys."

John stood quiet for a moment. "I'll make an excuse to *Da*. Go to the back side of the Anderson's wagon and stay there until I join ya."

Patrick made his way to the wagon. A few minutes later John joined him.

"What did you tell him?"

John smiled. "I told him someone caught a big fish up the river a-ways, and you and I wanted to try our luck."

"You think fast. Let's go." Walking away from the wagon, Patrick said, "Ya know, we'll be in trouble for fighting."

"Won't be the first time." The boys smiled as they searched for Joshua and James.

Soon the O'Brien boys spied James being manhandled by three older rowdies. They held James by his collar. One boy cuffed his ears, while another hit him across the shins with a switch. James howled while Joshua tried to help by pelting the bully with his small fist, hitting him on his arms and back. All the while the older boys laughed at Joshua's efforts.

"Why don't ya pound on me instead of the little fly you're holding on to?" yelled Patrick, hopping from foot to foot in his best pugilist dance, shoving his fist out one at a time. "Come on. Come on. What, are ya afraid of me?"

John hid a thick rod behind his back. He eyed his brother's antics and waited patiently. "What's the matter?" He pointed at Patrick. "My younger brother's a mite smaller than you. Why not take him on? Looks to me like he needs some trimming down."

One tormentor dropped James and shoved him aside. Joshua ran to him and they huddled together, neither wanting to leave. The O'Brien boys were in action.

"Let's get the feisty devil that's all mouth." The three boys made a move toward Patrick.

"You wouldn't be the boys that pushed a wee girl in the muck, now would ya?"

"So what?" they answered in unison.

"Come on, you hair on a donkey's ass," taunted Patrick. "Come get me. Or are you still sucking your Ma's tit?"

Two of the bullies lunged at Patrick. He dodged one and landed a fist squarely in the other boy's face, breaking his nose. The tormentor screamed and fell to the ground, holding his face. Blood spurted everywhere.

John swung his weapon catching the biggest ruffian behind the knees, knocking him to the ground. He swung one more time, for good measure and connected with his arm, hearing a deadly crunch. With only one assailant facing him, Patrick glared at him.

"I want you to remember me. If, and I say *if* you three ever bother my little sister or brother again, or his friends, you'll have to answer to me." Patrick took a breath. "And I can get real mean and ugly. This is only a taste of my temper."

John stood next to his brother, slowly tapping the rod against the palm of his left hand. Together they presented a menacing image.

Patrick turned his back on the three. The last bully stood staring at both of them for a moment. Suddenly he lunged at John. "We'll get you for this, you son of a…."

Thwack! Patrick turned in the nick of time and sucker punched the ruffian. He hit him square in the midriff and again in the face. Down he went, rolling in pain, moaning like a sick dog.

Caustically, Patrick said, "I guess you didn't understand me a minute ago." He stood over the three injured boys. "Don't *ever* come around this area again."

Then, pointing at James and Joshua, he said, "You two get back to the wagons where you belong, and keep your mouths shut."

The two small boys shoved each other, making tracks down the road. John and Patrick stood silently eyeing the three on the ground.

Motioning to his brother, John said, "Let's go. Don't believe we'll have any more trouble from these nincompoops."

Chapter Fifteen

"Alex, we're movin' out. Get the tents down and gear up," Michael yelled as he rushed between the wagons. "Saints preserve us, we're on our way."

Alexander stopped sawing on a table leg, rushed to pick up his tools and boards, and threw everything into the wagon. "Let's go!" he shouted. "James, hurry. Help me with the horses. Sarah. Caroline. Strike camp. Move. Move." His family scurried about, gathering all of their belongings, rushing to be on their way to the 'promised land.'

"We don't want anyone to be takin' our place. Hustle!" Michael helped John throw the tent and personal items into their wagon. "Get in, we're leavin'."

Excited, Alexander drove his wagon down to the sandy levee, O'Brien directly behind him. They sat in line and waited.

Then came the call. "All right. You two," the man pointed, "on the 'Rhinoceros.' Bring your wagons on up."

Fully loaded, the ferry pulled away from the Illinois bank.

The boat rocked, fighting the current, endeavoring to stay in line with the landing on the other side. Four ferrymen poled and another used the sweeper oar. Reaching the middle of the rolling river, Alexander leaned against the railing and looked back over his shoulder. The shoreline gradually diminished.

Angry water surged over the floorboards, spraying those standing by the supports before rolling back into the river. Even with his feet soaked, Alexander didn't feel uncomfortable. His mind dwelled on the journey ahead. Soon he and his brother would be traveling together, sharing an adventure.

Michael approached his two older boys from behind and startled them. "Well, now," he said, "I hear tell you've been fightin' again. Your lovely *mam* is upset. Seems the story goes ya whipped three lads back at camp. True?" He stared at the boys and raised his voice. "Now, I've told ya once and I'll be tellin' ya no more. No fightin'! Do ya understand me? Or I'll give ya a thrashin' ya won't soon forget."

"Yes, *Da*," the two answered, heads bent, looking down at their boots.

Turning to leave, Michael cleared his throat. Looking out over the water, he whispered, "By the by, lads, well done. Couldn't have done better meself."

Giving each other sideways glances, smirks spread across the boys' faces. Their father approved of their actions. The berating was for their mother's peace of mind.

Caroline leaned against the railing in horror and disbelief. The once glorious waterfront she had heard so much about from John, lay in ruins, blackened by the fire.

"Oh, how terrible," she whispered. Her heart sank. Feeling chilled to the bone, she snuggled closer to Alexander.

He put his arm around her, pulling her close. "I heard the

stories about the fire back at camp. This is worse than I expected."

"What a horrible thing to happen," said a woman standing next to Caroline.

Barely audible, Annie asked, "I wonder how many people died?"

"I don't suppose you can tell us how it happened?" Michael O'Brien asked Jonas, the ferryman.

"I remember it well," he answered. "In May, tons of hemp and cargo were stacked high on the cobblestone levee for the night. Around ten that evening, the steamboat, *White Cloud*, caught fire. The strong northeasterly winds pushed her into another boat, the *Edward Bates,* docked south of her."

"Couldn't they release the burning boats and stop the fire?" someone asked.

"Oh, they tried. But, one boat was pushed into another, spreading the fire until two boats were shoved onto the levee." Jonas shook his head. "That's when the real trouble began."

Silence surrounded him as he continued with his story. "I was across the river, standing by the shoreline. It wasn't until the shanties caught fire, that it spread through the city." Jonas swept his hand in front of him. "It lit up the sky as far as the eye could see. Yep, it looked as if the earth was on fire, everything blazing red. You could hear the voices yelling and the bells ringing all the way to the other side of the river.

"The fire jumped from street to street. To make matters worse, the water supply gave out and the fire departments began drawing water out of the river. The burning steamboats kept getting in the way," said Jonas, totally engrossed in his story.

"I'm surprised the whole city didn't burn down." Caroline shook her head, feeling compassion for the people who had suffered during the horrible disaster.

"How long did it take to get it under control?" Alexander asked.

"It was finally put out the following morning. By that time, twenty-three boats and almost fifteen blocks of the city were destroyed." Jonas looked at the waterfront. Pointing, he said, "As you can see, the waterfront's gone, but they saved our Court House and the marketplace, except for its roof."

The ferry reached the levee at Vine Street, and Jonas threw several lines to the dockhands to tie down.

Moving part of the front railing, the ferryman said, "The real tragedy was Captain Targee, a volunteer firefighter. He was eating his meal when the bells began ringing. He rose from the table, telling his wife he'd be back." Jonas threw another rope on the landing. "He was planting a keg of gunpowder when it went off. Blew himself up, he did, trying to put out the fire. Sad. Real sad."

Alexander and Michael rounded up their families and boarded their wagons.

"Piece of advice," Jonas shouted to Alexander as he waited to disembark from the boat. "If I were you all, I'd travel as quickly as I could to the other side of St. Louis. The city's plagued with cholera. There are close to fifty deaths a day now. It's gonna get worse with the summer heat coming on."

He waved farewell, then turned, making one last remark. "You won't see the dockhands staying around too long. Everyone's afraid of strangers these days, with the cholera and all." Then he walked away, head hung low.

Caroline shuddered. "Cholera! Oh, Alexander, I thought we left that behind in Louisville."

"Now, don't panic, we won't be here long. Once we locate the City Hotel where John's staying, we'll get out of town fast. We can pick up supplies on the other side of the city."

Wagons and patrons bustled about the levee. It was business as usual. Nothing seemed to be out of place or disturbed except for the hulls and rubble of businesses that had thrived earlier.

The two wagons lumbered up Vine Street and crossed Commercial Alley. The street was narrow, crowded and lined with deplorable shanties.

"This is terrible," said Caroline. "There's garbage everywhere, and look at the rats scurrying about."

James wrinkled up his nose. "Phooey, what stinks, Pa? Smells like something died."

"The odor's from a slaughterhouse nearby."

"Ohhh, that's bad." Sarah covered her nose with her bonnet.

"Settle down, we're on our way." Alexander pushed the team forward.

Behind the Andersons, Michael O'Brien shouted, "Yo, Alexander. Catch up with you later. Need to stop and locate an 'old friend'." He put his hand to his mouth and lifted his elbow, smiling mischievously.

Alexander watched O'Brien turn his team south toward Main Street. "Meet you at the City Hotel," he yelled. "Just ask for directions."

Michael waved and rolled away.

"Hope he knows where he's going." Sometimes Alexander worried about Michael. Right now, he couldn't concern himself with the man. His main objective was to locate the hotel and his brother.

Passing the massive Missouri State Bank on Main Street, Alexander headed away from the burnt section of the city. Crossing Clay Morgan Alley, they saw children milling about the street, playing in the filthy garbage.

"How can they live like this?" asked Caroline.

"The poor are more or less forced to live here. Jonas told me immigrants arrive daily. There aren't many jobs for them."

She whispered, "God be with them."

"I'm sure these conditions contribute to the spread of cholera." Alexander solemnly shook his head. "We certainly need to be thankful for what we have."

Suddenly a loaded beer wagon, in front of them, broke down, blocking the street. Several cracked barrels rolled across the cobblestones, spilling the contents everywhere.

Pulling to a halt, Alexander growled, "I can't believe this. Since we can't move, I might as well help." He handed the reins to Caroline and jumped to the street. "Be back as soon as I can."

He and several men cleared the street and fixed the wagon. With the work completed, he returned tired, hot, and smelly. "We've wasted more time." Then he grinned at his wife. "The beer sure smells ripe."

"I'd say you're quite fragrant." Caroline waved her hand in front of her face to ward off the odor. "Did you roll in it?" she asked, laughing.

"It's all over my trousers and boots. Won't be able to change until this evening, so get used to the smell."

James wrinkled his nose. "You're kind of smelly, Pa."

"He doesn't like to drink it, he just likes to wear it." Caroline chuckled. The children joined in teasing their father.

Embarrassed, Alexander said, "The smell is pretty awful. At least we're rolling again. Need to find the hotel and the O'Briens. Don't know which will be the hardest to locate."

Approaching the Second Street crossing, Alexander noticed the buildings had become more elegant and massive as the city surroundings improved. There were no more alleys with garbage, the stench from the factories disappeared, and people seemed more refined. Elegant apparel mingled with coarse backwoodsmen's buckskins. Farm wagons and superb buggies congested the streets. The people seemed totally unaware of the disease threatening their everyday existence. Only the church bell's occasional tolling and frequent funeral procession announced the hovering cloud of sickness hanging over the city.

Nearing the corner of Third Street and Vine, Sarah leaned over the wagon seat and pointed. "Pa, is that what you're looking for?"

On the corner stood the stately City Hotel. Alexander reined the horses to a halt in front of the iron hitching post.

The stone building, with its impressive carved façade, rose several stories. Citizens milled around the sidewalks and crowded the hotel steps.

James shouted, "Look Pa, there's Uncle John!"

Alexander stretched his neck for a quick look at the buckskin-clothed man. He hesitated for a moment. "No, son, it's not your uncle."

He jumped down from the seat and tied the reins to the hitching post. "I'll be right back. It shouldn't take me long." Alexander stepped onto the sidewalk, elbowed his way through the crowd and walked into the hotel.

The short note John had written disappointed Alexander. He contemplated his next move, as he reread the message.

Alexander,
Ran into a small problem

"Hmm, I wonder what kind of a small problem? How important was it that he couldn't wait here for us?" He read on.

Meet you in Independence at Noland's Inn.
John

He shook his head. His brother was unbelievable.

The clerk looked up. "He had a dark boy with him."

Alexander looked at the clerk. "Did he say anything like where he was going?"

"Nope. Said the boy was his partner. Kind of strange, if you ask me."

Frustrated, Alexander exited the hotel. How was he going to explain this to his wife? Making excuses for his brother's actions was not going to make Caroline happy.

"Hello, there," Annie shouted, as the O'Briens pulled up next to the Anderson wagon.

"Howdy, Alexander. Knew we'd catch up with ya all. As I was sayin' to me lovely wife, it might be a little hard in findin' ya. Lo and behold, here ya are." Michael was extremely inebriated and slurred most of his words.

"It warms the cockles of me heart to see yer smilin' faces. It's the luck of the Irish, you know." He climbed down from his wagon, slightly unsteady on his feet and joined Alexander on the sidewalk.

"Ya should have seen the Planters Hotel on Fourth Street. It's as big as a steamboat and fancy as a whorehouse," bellowed Michael.

Horrified, Annie shouted, "Michael O'Brien, take care of your loose tongue, what with the children about and all. Have ya lost your senses, man?"

With a mischievous grin, Michael said, "I do believe my lovely wife has admonished me for poor behavior." With a swish of his hat, he bowed. "I beg your humble forgiveness and apologize for my uncouth manners and language."

Caroline suppressed a smile. "You're totally forgiven, Mr. O'Brien."

Leaning forward, Michael sniffed Alexander's shoulder. "Seems to me you're wearin' me favorite cologne or have ya been visitin' the most revered place, the brewery?" He sniffed again. "Ah, what a heavenly scent."

Alexander tugged on Michael's sleeve. "Be serious. I need to talk with you privately. Turn around here and listen."

Backs toward the wagons and heads bent, the men held a discussion for a few minutes. Cautiously, Alexander glanced in Caroline's direction, and then quickly lowered his eyes and continued his conversation.

She froze. The grim expression on her husband's face disclosed her worse fears. The news was bad. She twisted the reins in her clammy hands.

Alexander shook his head. Michael shrugged his shoulders. She bit her lip, closed her eyes, and grasped the reins tightly in her hands. She knew John had left St. Louis without them.

Darn you, John. Why can't you be dependable? I hate you for your ignorant independence. Back in Pennsylvania, I loved you and needed your help desperately, but you up and left me without a word. Now you're doing it again. I can't believe you'd strand your brother. You promised to be here. I should have known your promises were all empty. You are the most despicable person I have ever known. What are we to do? We've come too far to turn back. Strength, don't leave me now.

A tap on her shoulder interrupted her thoughts. "Ma, where's Uncle John?" asked James.

"Did Pa find him?" asked Sarah.

"Hush, children. Let's wait and see what your father has to say."

"Hey, Joshua." James interest changed, as he tried to escape by swinging his leg over the seat board.

His mother grabbed him by his shirttail, managing to waylay his departure from the wagon. "Wait, Joshua's coming over to join you. See."

The O'Brien boy climbed up on the wheel. "Hello, Mrs. Anderson."

"Hello, Joshua. Why don't you boys put down the tailgate and sit back there until we're ready to leave?"

James scrambled across their belongings, shoving Sarah aside, while Joshua ran around to the back.

"Don't push, James. It's not fittin' to treat me that way," Sarah screeched at her brother, kicking him in the butt. "What's your all-fired hurry, anyway? It's only Joshua, the little gallinipper."

"Sarah Anne!"

Sitting in the back, dangling their legs over the edge, Joshua asked, "Did you smell the stink?"

"Yep. Did you see the burnt buildings? This city is—" James suddenly heard an eerie ghostly sound of tinkling bells.

The boys gaped at a horse-drawn hearse draped in black, rounding the corner. Neither spoke. A hush settled over the crowd, heads turned to watch the final departure of some poor soul who had lost the battle with death.

"Where are they going?" whispered James.

A bearded man standing next to the wagon, explained, "They're headed for the new Bellefontaine Cemetery, son." Cynically, he added. "Seems with so many deaths these days, we fill cemeteries up faster than we can develop 'em."

After the cortege passed, conversations resumed, people bustled about their business unaffected.

The boys stared at each other. "I'm not so sure I like this city," said James.

"Me neither." Joshua slipped off the gate, put his hands into his pockets, and crept back to his mother.

Caroline gazed at the cold white stone of the hotel in front of her as she sat deep in thought. Problems had plagued their trip from the very beginning. A shadow of misfortune dogged their heels along the journey. She agreed with the boys. She didn't like this city, either. The black-draped hearse slowly made its way further down the street and turned the corner. A chill danced up her spine.

"All right, I'm behind you." Alexander startled her as he climbed aboard.

Caroline nearly jumped off the seat. "Good gracious, Alexander. You gave me such a fright." She closed her eyes, placed her right hand over her heart, and gripped the seat with her left.

Taking a deep breath to calm her rapid heartbeat, she asked, "Did you see the funeral procession?"

He nodded. "Yes. It's a sad part of life."

"It makes me feel very uncomfortable." She wrapped her shawl closer about her body. "I feel like the finger of fate is pointing at us."

He reached over and took both of her hands into his. "Don't worry about it. We're fine. We'll make it to California. Besides, you might upset the children."

Suddenly, remembering the purpose of their stopping at the hotel, she removed her hands from his, squared her shoulders, and met him eye to eye. "Well? Where is your *dependable* brother?"

He took a long deep breath, smiled, and tried to formulate a convincing explanation in order to win her over. "Seems we're on our own."

"What?"

Alexander put up both hands in front of him. "Wait. John's note explains that a small problem came up. He needed to go on to Independence. We're to meet him there."

"A small problem indeed! With your brother, it's a constant problem."

Trying to be cheerful, he said, "I know. It'll all work out. Now don't fret. Michael made some inquires at Murphy's Tavern on Battle Row. From what he tells me, the roads from here to Independence are in excellent condition. We shouldn't have any trouble. He indicated most of the inns along the trail are clean and the food is good. He also says there's a printed pamphlet we can purchase, describing the trail to California. So between John's actual written information and this publication, we should have no trouble at all."

Sitting straight and stiff, Caroline stared ahead, gritting her teeth. Her face resembled a marble statue he once saw in a book, sober and expressionless. She was understandably upset with him and his brother.

Trying again to relieve her of any anxiety about getting to Independence without John, he put his arm around her shoulders, pulling her to him. Hugging her close, he pointed ahead. "All we have to do is follow this street straight on out to St. Charles. Once we cross the Missouri River, the road on the other side will lead us straight onto Independence."

He sat silently giving her a chance to mull over the last few sentences, trying to come to terms with their situation.

She cocked her head. With a determined stare, she lifted her chin and said in a cold, steady voice, "If it's that easy, then we need to be moving on. Since your brother is so unreliable, we don't need him. We can do this on our own."

"Of course we can." Looking over his shoulder, Alexander spied the children visiting with the O'Briens. "Sarah! James! Let's go. We're moving on." *When I find my brother, I'm gonna have a heart-to-heart talk with him about responsibility. Probably won't do any good.*

When Caroline spoke the words, 'we can do this on our

own,' she had wanted to sound convincing, yet doubt flooded her mind. Traveling across country alone, without John, worried her. If she pegged him right, he probably wouldn't be waiting for them in Independence either. She wished she could sock him real hard, maybe beat him senseless with a thick knobby stick. What little respect she had for her brother-in-law disappeared.

Sarah and James, fussing with each other, climbed into the back of the wagon, closed the tailgate behind them.

"You stepped on my hat." James poked his cap back into shape.

"Don't have a conniption," Sarah said, peevishly.

"Settle down back there. We're on our way to St. Charles." Alexander waved to Michael O'Brien as the wagon rolled forward.

James made his way to the front and leaned over the back of the seat. "Where's Uncle John, Pa?"

"He's waiting for us at the jumping off place."

"Independence!" hollered James.

Alexander nodded. "That's the beginning of the trail west, son." He tried to make light of the situation. However, Caroline's mood did not include drivel about trails.

She sat, hands folded in her lap, mulling over each event leading up to their journey west. First, there was an innocent letter from John. Then he dangled a tantalizing small bag of gold in front of them with the promise of a better life. The worst part still haunted her, the confrontation with her brother-in-law in the chicken shed. She couldn't shake the feeling of his arms wrapped around her, holding her tight against his chest. His crushing kiss had left a burning sensation she couldn't ignore. Caroline placed her hand over her lips.

What diabolical scheme did John have planned? Did he really want Alexander to help him in California or did his insidious plan actually involve her? Frightened, Caroline decided to confide her fears to Annie once they arrived in St. Charles. The more she thought about the string of events, the more she understood they were being lured into a well-laid plan, an entrapment, and there was no way to stop it. With Alexander's mind set on moving forward, she couldn't tell him about his brother's aggressive behavior without revealing the past.

Glancing at his wife, Alexander noticed the grimace on her face. With her dander up, John was in for a tongue-lashing he'd never forget. Alexander loved and admired his brother, but John needed to change his immature and irresponsible ways. That would take a miracle.

Reaching over, he patted Caroline's hands clutched in her lap. His touch softened her expression. "I know we've made the right decision to go west. When we reach California, I'll build you a three-room cabin. You'll see. And if this gold thing with John doesn't work out, we'll get some land in one of those fertile valleys he told us about and start us a new farm." His wife was a good woman and stood faithfully beside him. A man couldn't ask for better. He loved her deeply.

Suddenly, Patrick O'Brien rode up, tipped his hat to Sarah. "Good day," he said, passing the wagon. Sarah blushed. Lifting one eyebrow, she gave him a teasing smile. He tossed her a daisy then rode ahead.

Startled, Alexander glared at the young man. "Thought this funny business was over with. I need to have a talk with him."

"Suit yourself. I think you're making too much out of these carryings-on," said Caroline.

* * *

Outside the city limits, the Saint Charles Road widened into a well-traveled dirt turnpike, with lush green landscape and sweet fresh air. Three-story palatial houses, surrounded by spacious verandas, overlooked well-manicured grounds.

Ahead, another funeral procession wound its way toward a cemetery on their right. Alexander shook his head. "Look, three graveyards in a row. Two too many as far as I'm concerned."

Whoops and yells behind the Andersons' wagon caught his attention. Michael O'Brien pointed across the road to several buildings on his left.

Michael yelled, "Let's make a stop and get some supplies."

"Oh, Alexander, let's do stop," pleaded Caroline. "It's such a lovely place."

"Please, Pa," begged Sarah.

"All right. We'll noon here." Alexander motioned to the O'Briens to follow him to an open grove next to the grocery store where several other wagons had pulled up.

James piped up. "That's a good idea, Pa. I'm a little hungry."

"Me, too," stated Sarah.

The children exited through the tailgate to join a group of youngsters in the field. Their prattle resounded through the trees.

Michael and Alexander strolled over to talk with three men at the hitching post. Being too old to join the younger children, Patrick and John O'Brien tagged along behind the men.

Michael O'Brien licked his lips, eyed the tavern, and announced. "Gentlemen. I do believe it's time to wet me whistle. Anyone care to join me in a pint or two?" He looked around, waggled his eyebrows, and smiled deviously.

"Sounds good to me," said a fleshy man, rolling a cigarette.

"Might as well stay busy while our women spend our money," was a jovial comment from another gentleman behind them.

They walked toward the Rising Sun Tavern with Patrick and John in tow. The boys weren't allowed to enter the tavern, but could enjoy a sarsaparilla outside, while they eavesdropped on the conversations.

Glancing over his shoulder before slipping through the doorway, Alexander spied Caroline and Annie with their heads together off to one side of the women's group. Annie patted Caroline's arm, then they made their way into Burgess' Grocery Store.

Wiping his hand across his mouth, Alexander pushed the door open. *One drink won't hurt any.*

The next morning, the Andersons and O'Briens pulled out from the Prairie House Inn with only eleven miles standing between them and 'Les Petites Cotes du Missouri,' as a man at the tavern called Saint Charles.

Alexander followed the lead of several wagons ahead of him on the congested road. "We just passed Fee Fee Church. We're getting close."

When they finally reached the Missouri bluffs, below them stretched the sloughs and sandy river bottomland. Beyond lay the town of Brotherton and the Belland Ferry to Saint Charles.

Chapter Sixteen

St. Charles, Missouri

"There're people everywhere," said Alexander.

Horses and oxen plodded along the narrow, congested dirt streets of the city, pulling a variety of vehicles.

"Land sakes alive! How'll we ever get through this maze?" Caroline was bewildered by the pandemonium.

Alexander shook his head and laughed. "Don't rightly know. I'm surprised the thoroughfare can accommodate everyone. More people are getting off the ferry behind us."

He followed closely behind the wagon in front of him. "Seems all the shops are doing a grand business." The noisy din surrounded them. Kicked up from all the activity, dust swirled across the street and sidewalks.

"My goodness. Look at the people standing in the doorways of the shops," said Caroline. "It's like they're giving goods away."

"Look, Pa." Sarah pointed to the wagon next to them. "They've got their name painted on their canvas. Isn't that pretty with all those bright colors?"

James piped in, "There's one with 'Oregon or Bust'. We should paint ours with 'California or Bust'. Can we, Pa?"

"By golly. Never thought of that, son. What a grand idea. Of course we can."

Awed by her son's suggestion, Caroline said, "Why, that would be befitting. Might as well let 'em know where we're headed."

"All right!" chorused the children.

Alexander's interest honed in on three men, dressed in buckskins, standing next to their horses, passing a bottle of liquor without a care in the world. Pack animals, loaded for the trip west, resembled fat pumpkins ready to burst. Coarse language and wild carryings-on left much to be desired.

Children dashed across the road in front of them, dodging wagons on their death-defying trip to get to the other side, yelling at each other in order to be heard. Parents shouted directions at their youngsters to no avail.

"Be careful!" Caroline screamed, pulling at Alexander's sleeve.

Sarah covered her ears and hollered, "My ears hurt."

"It's like a holiday with everybody celebrating," said Caroline, fascinated. "I can hear music from somewhere."

James pointed over his mother's shoulder. "It's coming from there. See that lady. She hardly has any clothes on."

A tall, thin woman leaned against the doorframe of a tavern. Her red dress stopped at her knees, her bosom nearly escaped the black lace material confining it. Blonde hair was coiled high atop of her head, ringlets cascading down one side. Large rouged circles of bright red on her cheeks stood out, paling her complexion.

"James," his mother scolded. "Keep your eyes forward."

Bottom lip stuck out, he pouted. "I was only going to say that I like the music." Quickly he snuck another peek.

Alexander chuckled. "I'm sure Mr. O'Brien will be enjoying the music, too. I'd be surprised if he didn't want to stop for a 'pint or two.'"

"Hush, Alexander. Behave yourself." Caroline suppressed a smile. Looking back through the wagon's interior, she caught a glimpse of the O'Briens behind them. "That's strange. Michael looks disinterested in all this commotion. Seems awfully quiet for the Irishman we know."

Sarah piped up. "Maybe he ain't feeling good. Could be something he ate."

Alexander smirked. "Or something he drank."

"It'd serve him right. Don't believe he's missed one tavern since we left Illinois." Caroline declared. "Michael O'Brien loves his ale."

"Woman, we've only stopped twice," Alexander protested. "He's trying to catch a few before we start the trail west. That'll be a dry run for everybody."

A man dashed across the road, halting in front of the Anderson wagon.

"Whoa!" yelled Alexander, straining hard on the reins. "You'll get yourself killed doing that."

Waving his hands back and forth in front of his face, the man hollered, "Sorry," while jumping onto the wooden sidewalk. "Lost my sense of direction in this here rip-snortin' town."

Alexander shouted, "Can you tell me where I might find a good inn for my family to stay tonight?"

"Western House is to your right on Chauncey Street. This late in the afternoon, they're probably full. I'd try the Westenkuehler Inn at the top of Lick's Hill. Good German food and reasonable."

"Thank you kindly." Coming to a standstill, Alexander jumped from the wagon, dodged a passing vehicle, and made his way to talk with the O'Briens.

"The man over there says the Westenkuehler Inn up on top of the hill is a good place to spend the night. I think we should try for it." Michael appeared a bit peaked to Alexander's way of thinking. Lowering his voice, he asked, "Michael, you feel okay?"

Michael bent forward so no one else could hear him. "I'm a wee bit tired." Then raising his voice, trying to be his jolly self, he replied, "Aye, sounds good to me. Let's go. Be nice to stay a day or two if we have the time."

"All right." Alexander pointed forward, "Follow me. We're heading up Lick's Hill. Keep your eyes peeled." He hastened back to his wagon and climbed aboard.

Crossing South Main Street, they made their way past Blanchette Creek, up Boone's Lick Road. Finally reaching the top of the hill, they spied Westenkuehler Inn ahead, a sign over the veranda.

As the wagons rolled up to the inn's entrance, a huge tolling bell with deep melodious tones tolled, surprising the approaching travelers. Some of the workers gathered outside, playing German music to welcome them. The stout mustached innkeeper, Hermann Westenkuehler, joined the musical group with his violin. Showered with so much attention, the noisy spectacle astonished and embarrassed the arrivals.

James stomped his feet and moved his shoulders, keeping time to the music. "Wow, that sure is loud, thumping music. Look at the large squeezebox." His eyes riveted on the man's nibble fingers dancing across the shiny keys, as the bellows moved in and out.

"I believe they call that an accordion, son," said Alexander. "Sure is strange looking."

In a flash, James jumped to the ground and hopped around to the music.

"Stay nearby and don't run off," shouted Alexander. He leaned over and whispered in Caroline's ear. "We need to put a cowbell on that lad. He disappears so darn fast."

"I think you're right," replied Caroline, laughing at her husband's statement. Exhilarated, she grabbed his arm, hugging it tight. "Oh, Alexander. What a lovely greeting."

"It seems a bit much." All this falderal made him uncomfortable. "Whoever heard of so much fuss over guests and a few wagons?"

"Ma, listen. Isn't it lovely? I like this place." Sarah slipped down from the wagon to search for Elizabeth.

Spying Patrick tying his horse to the rail, her knees shook. *He's so handsome.*

Slowly, he turned, smiled, and winked at her.

Sarah flushed, turning hot and cold at the same time. Her feet felt stuck to the ground. *Did he really wink at me?* She averted her eyes, not knowing what to do. When she raised her head, he had disappeared. Her emotions vied between disappointment and relief.

Elizabeth crept up behind Sarah and grabbed her by the shoulder. "Caught ya."

Startled, Sarah jumped, her heart beating wildly. "Darn, Elizabeth. You scared me silly."

"Sarah, your language," teased Elizabeth. "I saw you eyeing my brother. Are you sweet on him or something?"

"No." Sarah said emphatically, clearly embarrassed at being caught gawking. "Oh, never mind. Let's go listen to the music." Sarah wanted to forget the whole incident. She knew Elizabeth wouldn't.

"Maybe we'll come across Patrick along the way."

"Elizabeth!"

Her friend giggled as they ran toward the inn.

* * *

Wagons arrived by twos and threes behind the O'Brien's, adding to the confusion and noise. Families mingled on the front lawn, exchanging news. Children ran across the veranda and out into the field, playing tag. With evening coming on, Michael and Alexander fed their horses and hobbled them. Annie and Caroline gathered their valises and a few extra clothes to spend the night.

The stout innkeeper stood on the veranda and bellowed, "Velcome to the Vestenkuehler Inn. You come in to the dining room. The evening meal is to be served." He ushered the guests to several tables.

Mr. Westenkuehler cleared his throat to get everyone's attention. Once the room became quiet, he announced. "First, I vould like to explain about the noise you heard as you arrived. Ve velcome our guest vith music and our lovely tolling bell. Ve like a little 'pomp and circumstance.' It's a tradition here at our inn. The meal vill now be served. Help yourself."

Workers carried heaping bowls of boiled potatoes, green beans seasoned with bacon, and buttered squash. Platters piled high with squirrel in brown gravy, succulent roast pork, and stewed dove breasts were placed in the middle of each table. Later delicious bread pudding, white cake, and flummery were passed around. No one left hungry.

After dessert, Michael joined two other men and strolled outside to smoke. Caroline and Annie sat on the veranda, discussing their children and home remedies. Other families headed to their rooms for a good night's rest. Caroline and Annie relaxed in two high-backed rocking chairs. As the sun slowly set over the horizon, several mothers corralled their children and took them off to bed.

Alexander joined the smokers under a large oak tree to

discuss the trip and what to expect ahead of them. Michael sat with his head back, resting against the tree trunk, eyes closed.

Bending over, Alexander grasped his friend's shoulder, "What's ailing you, Michael?"

"Don't rightly know. Me head feels like a large drum and me legs are a trembling like an old bowlegged horse. Could hardly eat me supper tonight. I'm feeling poorly and weak."

"Maybe you should call it a night. You'll probably feel better in the morning."

"Aye, I do believe you're right." Michael stood and wobbled a bit, trying to regain his balance.

The next day, the children played among the tall oak trees, rolling in the short green grass, enjoying themselves with newfound friends. Caroline sat with several women on the porch, exchanging recipes or medicinal remedies, all the while keeping one eye on James and Sarah.

Near the wagons, a few men exchanged information about the trail west, deliberating about accommodations further down the road, and discussing the cost of merchandise.

Alexander made his way to the side of the veranda behind the women, trying to appear inconspicuous. Caroline sat near the railing with her back toward him. He leaned near her and asked, "Have you seen Michael O'Brien this morning?"

Without turning her head, Caroline whispered, "No, I haven't." She paused for a moment, moving her head, keeping her voice low. "Now that you mention it, I haven't seen Annie either."

"Think I'll go upstairs to see what's keeping them. It's not like Michael to miss a meal."

"If you need me for anything, I'll be right here."

He walked around the corner of the veranda, tipped his hat to the ladies, and headed for the inn's entrance. After last night, his concern deepened. *There's probably a logical answer why they weren't at the breakfast table.* James barreled out the door, running into his father.

"Easy, James. No running inside. Is Joshua outside playing?"

"Yep. He's with Elizabeth and Sarah. "

"Where are John and Patrick?"

"Down by the stables. Can I go now?"

"Yes, but slow down."

James bolted across the veranda and jumped to the ground, shouting at the other children.

I think I wasted my breath on that one.

Alexander climbed the stairs to the O'Brien's room.

Distressed about her husband's well-being, Annie dealt with what she knew. She took the children down to breakfast, then shooed them outside to play. The commotion from their antics only upset their father. A knock on their door brought Annie to her feet. Stepping through the doorway, she greeted Alexander.

Hat in his hands, Alexander said, "We didn't see you or Michael at breakfast. We wondered if something was wrong."

"Michael isn't feelin' quite himself this mornin'. I'm extremely worried about the dear man. Please send John up here to me. I think we need to send for a doctor. I'm at my wits end."

"Is there anything we can do to help?"

"No," she answered. "At the moment, we're doin' our

best. I have to go. Thank you for your concern. Don't forget to tell John I need him."

Silently, Annie returned to her husband's side, praying he'd get better. His coloring scared her. She sat next to the bed holding his hand, trying to remember when he began to feel ill. Michael was up most of the night with diarrhea. When he did come to bed, she felt the heat from his feverish body. The night proved long for both of them. This morning he had complained of nausea and severe abdominal cramps. She gave him sodium bicarbonate water to drink, in hopes it would settle his stomach. She had also bathed his face and neck, trying to keep his fever down and make him comfortable.

John barged through the door. "Ma—"

"Shhh."

Speaking softly, John moved closer to his mother. "Mr. Anderson says Pa's not any better. Want me to go for a doctor?"

"Yes, son. His condition is worsenin'. Here are directions to find the doctor."

"How did you get these," asked John turning the paper over in his hand.

"Never mind. Go and don't tell anyone. Now hurry, love."

John raced out the door, taking the steps down two at a time. The door slammed behind him.

From the upstairs window, Annie watched him ride toward the city at a full gallop.

Oh, Lord, be with us today. I'll be beholden to ya, if you'll heal my husband. I'm not askin' for much. Please, he's too young to die. Tears filled her eyes, rolling down her cheeks. Annie muffled her cry with her hand, trying not to wake her husband. She didn't want him to catch her weeping.

"Annie," Michael gasped. "The pain…my legs…they're crampin'." She knew he was too weak to move. Gently she massaged his limp legs, one at a time, and then rubbed his hot arms. He grimaced and whimpered. Frightened by his rapidly deteriorating appearance, Annie panicked. Where was the doctor? Why was this happening?

"Water." His raspy voice faded.

She raised his head and put the cup to his lips. He tried to sip the water. Swallowing proved to be difficult for him. She lowered his head onto the pillow as he shut his eyes. His rapid pulse and returning fever worried her. Suddenly, he began to cough and vomit violently. Weakness prevented him from lifting himself. She slid her arms under his shoulders, turning him toward the bucket.

Michael finally settled back. She rushed out the door and down the steps to the lobby. "Please send someone for a priest," she yelled at the desk clerk. "My beloved husband's dyin'." The clerk stared at her in astonishment, as she bounded up the stairs to her room, holding her dress above her knees.

Michael's life hung on a thin thread. She sat in a chair staring out the window, waiting. Minutes ticked away, one at a time. Who would arrive first, the doctor, the priest, or Death? She jumped each time Michael moaned. Nervously, she twisted the ring on her left hand, her rosary coiled on her lap.

Staring out the window, she spied Caroline walking in the direction of the veranda. She raised the sash and shouted at her, desperation in her voice. "Can you meet me on the landin'? I need your help." Bolting across the room, almost falling over a small table, she ran out of the room. Halfway down the stairs, she met Caroline, rushing up the stairs to meet her.

"I am so glad I found you. Me husband is extremely ill. His condition is gettin' worse. I'm so afraid I'm goin' to lose him. I've sent John for a doctor and asked the desk clerk to get a priest. Can you please keep the children until we find out what is wrong?" Annie trembled. "I've never been so scared in me whole life."

Caroline held Annie in her arms. "Of course, I will. Don't worry about your children, they can stay with us. In fact, Patrick is helping Alexander. Joshua and Elizabeth are playing with our two out in the field."

Caroline took her handkerchief out of her pocket and began to wipe the tears from Annie's face. "Is there anything else I can do for you?"

"Not right now. I have to go. Thank you," she called over her shoulder, rushing back into her room.

Caroline slowly descended the stairs and crossed the lobby to the doorway. As she placed her hand on the door, the doctor's buggy pulled up in front with John in tow. She hurried outside to meet them.

"Cholera?"

"Yes, a man upstairs has Cholera." Whispers echoed through the inn. Guests panicked. The news spread quickly.

When the doctor broke the horrifying news, Annie collapsed into the chair next to Michael's bed. "Cholera. Oh, my. Why?" There was no answer to her question.

A knock at the door brought her to her feet. Opening it, Father Ryan introduced himself. He talked with Annie for a moment before walking to the bed to administer the last rites, praying for Michael and his family.

Annie returned to her chair. Her head hurt, her thoughts jumbled. Nothing made sense.

Staring at the bed, she sobbed, "How can this be? I don't understand. Isn't there anythin' we can do for my husband?" Michael's lips were blue, his breathing labored.

Doctor Johnson closed his medical bag. He rolled down his shirtsleeves, buttoned the cuffs, and put on his jacket. "I'm truly sorry, Mrs. O'Brien. Your husband has very little time left. No matter what you think, you must keep your children out of this room. We don't want anyone else coming in contact with the disease."

"I understand," she whispered. Her whole body and mind were exhausted.

The doctor continued, "Father Ryan and I will stay with you until the end. I will notify the undertaker. I apologize for having to talk to you so bluntly, but the arrangements are very important because of the disease. Your husband will be wrapped in his sheet and buried quickly. All linens and used clothing must be burned out back, including yours. You will have to collect the items yourself."

"Mrs. O'Brien," said Father Ryan, "I am sure the innkeeper will request you to leave as soon as possible. I know a woman back in town who will be more than willing to give you and your family room and board."

"Thank you both," she murmured. Tears welled up in her eyes and slid down her cheeks. By morning, she would be a widow.

Caroline Anderson sat in their room with the younger children, trying to comfort them and answer their questions. Elizabeth and Sarah cuddled together and cried themselves to sleep. James and Joshua talked for a while, then crept under the covers and shut their eyes.

John and Patrick sat in the corner of the room, forearms resting on their thighs, hands clasped and heads bowed. The leadership of their family now rested on their shoulders. They knew cholera meant certain death for their father. Alexander tried to ease their burden. He didn't have answers to all of their questions. Silence prevailed, except for the continual heavy breathing from the younger children and the ticking clock on the mantel.

Alarmed for the safety of her family, Caroline checked for signs of fever. Satisfied all were fine, she took off her shoes and curled up next to them.

The German innkeeper was livid. "How dare they bring cholera into my inn? Look, my guests are leaving because of the sickness. The O'Briens must leave. Out! Out vith them immediately."

It was barely eight o'clock in the morning. Alexander and Caroline made sure the children were fed. Afterwards, they kept everyone busy outside. When the younger ones tired of chores, they went to play.

Worried and extremely nervous, Caroline asked, "Alexander, how did this happen to Michael?"

"The way I see it, he contacted it back in St. Louis when he stopped at a tavern on Battle Row. We were together at the Rising Sun and I feel fine." He smiled to reassure her that his health was good. Yet, he was worried.

"Did you hear the innkeeper this morning? He wants the O'Briens to leave his establishment *now*. There's no way Annie could move her husband right now. Besides, where would they go?"

"I wouldn't worry about Mr. Westenkuehler. The doctor won't let him evict them."

John O'Brien stepped out onto the veranda. His news was devastating. His father had passed away. When the other children saw John, they came running. Trying to repress his emotions, John spoke with Alexander. "What am I going do? How can I take my father's place? He was a great man."

"John, your father taught you some good skills. Use them."

Realizing Alexander was right, he said, "Yes. I have the tools."

"With your mother's help, you will do right by your father, son."

"There is so much in front of us." John shuffled one foot in the dust. "I don't know if we can handle going to Oregon without Pa."

"I believe that's something you and your mother need to discuss."

"You're right." John hung his head. "Thanks, Mr. Anderson." He walked away.

Elizabeth ran to Caroline, grabbed her around the waist, sobbing uncontrollably. Caroline nestled the young girl against her chest, gently stroking her hair.

"I'm scared," Elizabeth cried, hiccupping between sobs. "Pa's left us alone."

Sarah huddled close to her mother, not knowing how to comfort her friend. Tears tickled down her cheeks. She reached out and touched Elizabeth's arm with her fingertips.

Joshua threw himself onto the grass, pounding the ground with his small fists. "I hate God. What'd he have to take my Pa for? *Dang* it anyway!"

James fell silent, mouth open, and eyes wide, shocked at the words tumbling out of his friend's mouth.

Alexander rushed over to Joshua, grabbed the boy by the scruff of his neck. "Enough, young man. Your father'd be ashamed of your language, and in front of the ladies, too."

"He's gone and I want him back," Joshua howled. "He had no right to leave us."

"I understand how you feel. But, your blaspheming won't bring him back. Now settle down. Your mother needs your help."

Joshua jerked away from Alexander in defiance. "Let me go. You're not my father." He bolted across the ground, yelling at the top of his lungs.

Patrick raced after his younger brother. Joshua rebuffed his efforts.

Exasperated with Joshua and angry over his father's death, Patrick stopped in his tracks and turned around. Anger consumed him. He screamed, "What did he have to die for? I don't understand." He grabbed a handful of rocks and threw them hard against a tree, making the bark fly.

"Caroline," said Alexander, "I'll take Patrick with me and go find Joshua. Can you care for the rest of the children?"

"Yes. John will help me," she said, smiling at him while gently patting Elizabeth's head. Sarah held her friend's hand in both of hers, trying to comfort her.

Patrick shuffled his boot around in the dirt. He wanted to cry like Elizabeth or cuss like Joshua. Something inside wouldn't let him. "They want to bury Pa right away."

Caroline knew those were hard words for him to say.

Alexander squeezed Patrick's shoulder. "Let's go find your brother." They headed to the open field.

Elizabeth lifted her head. Caroline wiped the child's eyes, dust and tears making small smudges on her face. "Mother's getting our things together," she sniffled. "We have to leave." She lowered her head and began to bawl again.

"John, I need you to stay on the veranda with your sister. Alexander and Patrick will be back with Joshua. I'm going upstairs to help your mother. I'll be back as soon as possible."

She instructed her children. "Go to our room and wait for me there. I won't be long." When no one moved, she added sharply, *"Now, go."*

Shocked by the harshness in her request, Sarah and James stared at their mother for a moment before dashing off like the devil was after them.

* * *

Only a handful of people gathered around Michael O'Brien's grave to say farewell to the brave Irish man, that damp and hazy morning. Annie and her family huddled together off to one side, gathering comfort and strength from each other. Annie's pale and swollen face showed the stress she shouldered. When the men began shoveling dirt onto the coffin, she turned her family away and headed for their wagon.

Caroline's heart ached for her. To have traveled so far from home only to have tragedy strike them down. A soft scuffle at her side brought her attention to the warm hug around her waist.

"Ma, what will they do now?" Sarah asked. "There's nobody to take care of them. Where will they go?"

Yes. When a husband dies and leaves behind a family, who does take care of them? Who really cares what happens to them? "The Lord will help Annie, and she will take care of her family."

"Does this make John the father now?" she asked.

Caroline paused for a moment. "Yes, I guess it does." The question made her think. Instead of the O'Briens, this could be her family. She shuddered to think of the consequences Alexander's death would bring to them, thankful she didn't have to make the decisions Annie now faced. She climbed aboard their wagon with her family and proceeded toward the inn, with the O'Briens following closely behind.

Halting in front of the veranda, Annie climbed down. "Now stay here. I will be back as soon as I pay our bill."

Crossing the threshold, she waited at the counter for the desk clerk to return.

"Mr. Perkins," Annie called. "I would like to settle up my bill with you."

The man hid behind the half opened door. "Mr. Westenkuheler says for you to just leave. He doesn't want your money. And don't touch my counter."

Insulted and crushed, Annie stared in disbelief. Behind her people shied away, making a wide berth and some very rude remarks.

"What is she doing back here?"

"You'd think she'd have the sense to stay away."

"Hmm. Someone ought to tell her she's not wanted here at the inn."

"And she's Irish."

"No wonder."

Standing on the last step of the staircase, Caroline's temper rose. She walked over to her friend. Looping her arm around Annie's shoulders, she said loudly, "Let's go out on the veranda where the atmosphere is a bit friendlier."

Sitting at the far end of the porch, Caroline asked, "How are you doing?"

Annie raised her chin and stared ahead. "I'm gonna be fine. The children and I've been talkin' about what to do. Whether we should go back to North Carolina, stay here or go on to Oregon."

"That's a big decision."

"Yes, and it wasn't easy. If we stay here, we have enough money to start with. We can sell the wagon and the tools, if necessary. However, if my John wanted to be an apprentice to a carpenter in town, he would need the tools."

"How do the boys feel about living here in St. Charles?" Caroline glanced up to see Annie's expression.

"Well, they all wanted to stay, except Patrick. He wants to go on to Oregon, but I can't let him go by himself. Besides, I don't feel we should travel on right now. Maybe we can make the trip later when we sort things out a little more."

Caroline patted her friend's arm. "If that's how you feel, you've made the right decision."

"Is there ever a right decision in life?"

The women left the veranda and walked to the O'Brien's wagon. Caroline missed the gay whoops and hollers of bygone days. Elizabeth and Joshua hid in the wagon. John sat tall in his father's place, holding the reins. Caroline glanced up at him and smiled. What small hands to take on such a large job. Patrick was nowhere to be seen.

Annie climbed up to the wagon seat.

"Where will you live in St. Charles?"

"Father Ryan located a lovely room for us at a boardin' house on Second Street. The landlady is in need of help in the kitchen and the boys can get jobs at the stables. It will be small, yet adequate, until we can get ourselves together to make bigger decisions."

Caroline stepped back from the wagon. "Well, I'm sure you will all be fine. Good luck and God bless." Slowly, she walked away feeling lost and alone without Annie. *So many miles to go and no one close to share it with, other than my family.*

Alexander rushed out of the inn door, excited and waving a paper. "Caroline. Look at what I purchased. A guidebook to California."

He handed her *The Emigrant's Guide to California* by Joseph E. Ware. She should have felt impressed and happy, but the sadness of the day still filled her heart.

He started explaining how he heard about the book and where he purchased it. She was halfway listening. Suddenly, somewhere in his explanation she heard a statement that froze her heart.

"We leave early tomorrow morning. Now we don't have to worry about directions anymore. They are all here in this wonderful book. It was the last one left. Can you believe it?"

Tomorrow, did she hear him correctly? Yes, tomorrow they would be departing for Independence, Missouri.

Patrick waited patiently next to his horse, reins in his hands. Sarah stood quietly next to him, trying not to cry.

"I won't ever see you again, will I?" she asked.

"It'll be a couple of years before I can make it out to California. I promise, I will come." He paused, flipping the reins in his hands, lost for words to express how he felt. "I'd write, but I don't know where you'll be. Right now I don't have an address either."

Sarah looked down at the ground, choking back her tears, her heart broken.

"I have to go, Sarah. Ma's waiting for me." He waved to his mother, letting her know he was headed out. He dropped the reins, stepped forward, grabbed Sarah around her waist, and kissed her long and deep.

He slowly pulled away, a little embarrassed at his actions. He toed the dirt with his boot. "I won't apologize for the kiss."

At a loss for words, Sarah replied, "I…don't."

He climbed into the saddle. Holding on to the horn, he bent over and extended his hand to Sarah. "Here, this is for you to remember me by. Keep it near your heart. I made it especially for you."

In his hand was a small cross, made of braided wide-blade grasses, bound by a long, thin piece of twine. He reached forward and slipped the cord around her neck, letting it slide down onto her chest. Then he rode away, yelling over his shoulder, "One day I will find you and I want it back. Remember, I will find you no matter where you are."

Sarah touched the cross with her fingertips. "One day," she whispered, hoping in her heart he would keep his promise.

"Thank you," she murmured, tears trickling down her cheeks as she watched him ride behind the wagon. He turned once more and waved. She didn't move until he disappeared from sight over the hill, all the while hugging the small cross to her chest.

When she joined her mother on the veranda, neither spoke. Sarah slipped her arm around her mother's waist. Caroline wrapped a protective arm around her daughter's shoulder. They walked into the inn together, seeking comfort from each other.

With her free hand, Sarah cupped the cross hanging around her neck, gently caressing it with her fingers.

"Forever," she whispered.

Chapter Seventeen

On The Trail to Fort Laramie

John Anderson's teeth felt hairy, his mouth dry as tumbleweed. He'd give a week's take of gold for a shot of good whiskey, a warm bath and a long-legged woman. On second thought, he preferred the whiskey. "Won't be long before we reach the fort."

"I'll be glad to stop a while," grumbled Micah. "My butt's sore."

John smirked. "Know what you mean. We'll be there before sundown."

Curiosity piqued, Micah asked, "What's Fort John look like? A man back in St. Louis once told me about a castle made of stone where kings lived. Is it like that?"

"Not sure about a castle. Never saw one myself. Fort John-on-the-Laramie is pretty big. There's high walls made of adobe bricks and..."

"What's adupee?"

"Not adupee. Adobe." John replied. "Bricks made of straw, manure, mud, and dried grass. It's all mixed together, then slapped into a frame and left to bake in the sun to harden."

Micah wrinkled his nose. "Manure? Bet that's stinks."

John murmured to himself and shook his head. Changing the subject, he said, "I need to take a piss, Micah."

"Me, too."

They stopped long enough to relieve themselves and grab some jerky from their saddlebags before climbing back onto their horses. Light began to fade across the horizon.

A soft, warm fuzzy feeling settled over Micah as his body swayed with movement of his mount. The horse's hooves plopped onto the sandy loam, reminding him of the water under the bridge back in St. Louis where waves lapped at the wharf bricks, slap, whoosh, slap, whoosh, slap.

"Hey," John shouted, jarring him awake. "You're gonna fall off your horse, closing your eyes like that."

"I only shut 'em for a minute," Micah snapped.

John clamped his jaw, lowered his head, and glared at his son. "You got an attitude problem, boy?"

"So it's *boy* again?" Micah stared back at him.

"Micah!" John's temper exploded. "Knock that chip off your shoulder right now. You listening? If we're to get along, you have to cooperate."

Tears welled up Micah's eyes as he choked back a sigh. "Got it."

They rode in silence for a while. Finally Micah said, "In St. Louis it was, '*Boy* do this', or 'Oh, *boy*, get me that'. I was always beneath them because I was a dirty old Creole."

"Get that nonsense out of your head. You're not a dirty old Creole. Your ma was a gentle, loving woman. A rare beauty, indeed. Be proud of who you are. And, don't worry what others think. There are a lot of stupid people in this world."

John cleared his throat. "Now, about that word *boy.* Well, we'll throw that one away. There's no need for it."

Micah lifted his shoulders and straightened his hat. "All right. Why don't ya tell me about this fort we're goin' to visit?"

"Back on questions again?"

Micah shrugged his shoulders. "It'll help this prairie go by faster."

"See what ya mean." John smiled. "What do you want to know?"

Micah thought for a moment. "Who owns it?"

"An old frontiersman, William Sublette, and several of his partners built the fort. Can't recall their names. Anyway, they use to own the stronghold."

"Never heard of him." Micah didn't want to hear anything about some old codger. "Are there any Indians there?"

"Yes. They're usually camped around the outside of the fort."

"Damn!"

John jerked his head, glaring at the boy.

"Oops." Micah stared ahead.

John accepted the off-handed apology, and continued. "Sublette and his men used to go up to Green River for a wild rip-snorting, liquor-drinking rendezvous every year, trading furs for liquor and supplies. Those old timers must have had a lot of adventures trapping back then.

"When I rode through last time, Jim Bridger owned the fort." John rambled on. "Rumor has it he's not doing too good since the rendezvous stopped."

Micah scratched his forehead. "Thought ya said this other man owned the fort, not Bridges?"

"Bridger. No, Sublette sold it to Big Jim quite a while

ago." John flexed his stiff shoulders, trying to work out the kinks.

"This Bridger. He's old, too?"

"The greatest mountain man ever. Could bite the head off a rattler, or so it's said."

"Yuck. That's not much to brag about. Who'd want to put a snake in his mouth?"

John laughed hard and loud. "Have to agree with you there."

Micah's next question stopped John stone cold. "Are you old?"

"Hell no. Not yet, at least," he retorted, pushing the brim of his hat onto his forehead. "Old indeed."

Come to think of it, his body talked to him more now than it use to. Maybe his mind was old. He'd left a long trail of stupidity behind him. For instance, making a pass at Caroline in the chicken coop. Dumb, real dumb. Where did that get him?

He thought of how he'd wasted most of his years chasing after dreams and women. He could have had more by now: money, farm, family. He'd had two chances for a lovely wife. He bungled both opportunities, one in Pennsylvania and another in St. Louis. The summation of his past could be rolled up like tobacco in paper. Lighting it would give off a trail of smoke and ashes. Nothing else. He was a pipe-dreamer.

The greatest thing to come along, in spite of all his stupidity, was a boy who claimed to be his son, and he couldn't even take credit for this remarkable achievement. He hadn't been there for D'Alene or the boy. Now he had a chance to turn his life around. Maybe this time he could get it right. The young lad riding next to him deserved better. But fatherhood?

Glancing at Micah, John marveled at how the lad's

horsemanship improved. He didn't even look like the same rag-a-muffin from St. Louis. At the beginning, John had worried about reaching Independence, let alone Fort John, together. He envisioned Micah leading the horse west.

"You've come a long way in handling your horse, son. I'm proud of you." *My son! Nothing has happened the way I planned it. Strange the way it all worked out. Well, I guess I wouldn't change anything, well, maybe one. Caroline.* Her soft hazel eyes and rich auburn hair haunted him. The thought of stroking her ivory skin caused an ache in his groin.

"Are ya fallin' asleep over there or thinkin' about that red-headed Virginia woman you told me about?" Micah knew his pa was thinking about her by the look on his face. Jealousy raged within him. *I'll bet he never thought about my* maman *like that.*

He hated the world for what he was. White father, Creole mother, nigger kid. He didn't fit anywhere. He was a mistake that couldn't be corrected. People looked past him like he was invisible. He might be brown and smelled bad at times, but he was a human being.

His hatred grew when he thought of the men who had mistreated his beautiful *maman*. Her work angered and embarrassed him. Men visited at all hours of the day and night. She had made good money, but not one of them had respected her. They'd used her until she got the bloody flux. The last two long years Micah had struggled to get food for them to eat and keep a roof over their heads. Even though he got kicked around on the streets, giving up had never entered his thoughts. His *maman* needed him.

No one had come around to help out while she was sick, except old black Molly. She'd brought whatever she could salvage from the rich folk's garbage. It hadn't been much, yet they'd made do. He remembered when he was a little shaver, he'd sit in Molly's lap while she rocked and hummed tunes from the South. He remembered feeling safe and warm when he cuddled up to her breast. She had cared for him and kept him safe while his *maman* worked. Old Molly had died three years ago. Seems like everyone he loved left him. Then suddenly, his white father showed up to take him to California. Life sure is odd.

"Where're you at, Micah. You daydreaming again?" John's eyes twinkled with mischief.

Micah grunted, "Huh, like ya haven't done that the whole trip. Who is this redheaded woman you keep thinkin' about? Is she your wife or somethin'?"

"Are we back on that subject again?" John's mouth twisted. "Why are you so gawlderned interested in my redheaded woman, anyway? Why don't you ask about your ma and me?"

Micah's anger flared. "I don't want to know about that." He rode in silence for a few minutes. "I want to talk about somethin' besides your gold, the weather, or that old man, Bridges." Micah purposely provoked him.

"Bridger!" John shouted. "All right. I'll tell you about my Virginia woman. I want no interruptions. Do you hear me?"

"Don't get huffy. Just tell me your long-winded story."

"Okay." John shifted in his saddle, a little uneasy. "There was a girl I once knew in Pennsylvania." John wove his tale telling Micah about Caroline. "You see, I cared about her a lot, but I didn't pay her much attention, thinking she'd always be there for me. When I got…"

"Ya mean ya treated her like my *maman*?"

John paused for a moment to reflect on Micah's statement. "Guess I did."

"You're not very good with women, are ya?"

"You gonna let me finish?" John growled. He went on with his story about how his brother married Caroline, leaving out a few details that didn't concern his son. On and on he talked, riding into the long shadows.

Finally, Micah could take no more, especially when John skipped over the part of his going to St. Louis.

"I'm gettin' hungry. Can we stop and eat soon?" Micah shifted his weight in the saddle, wishing for something softer to sit on besides this bouncing animal.

"Yes. We're only about an hour's ride out of Laramie," said John. "I'm sure someone is cooking up some vittles. Be ready to chow down."

"Can't be soon enough for me. My belly's rubbin' against my backbone. What's this fort really like?"

"Last time I stopped there, it was busier than a beehive dripping with honey. There's farmers, doctors, all kinds of folks traveling west in search of gold or land. Wagons everywhere. Indians pitch their teepees outside the walls looking to trade with the travelers. It's one bustling place and the prices are high."

"Are we gonna sleep inside the fort or camp outside?" Micah's backside told him a soft bed might be nice. "I don't cotton to sleepin' on the ground. Back in St. Louis, the rats used to scurry across my covers at night, searchin' for food. Nasty little critters."

"Ever eat one?" John asked, curious about his answer.

"No. Peg Leg Willie did. Did I ever tell you about him? He and I were buddies. I'd meet him down on the levee, and then we'd work the city. Willie could talk people out of their pants if he had a mind to. So we'd tell them Willie lost his leg in a war. I'd dance while he sang and clapped his hands. I'd collect the money they'd toss on the street."

"This Willie character. Did he stay with you and your ma?"

"Nope. We'd traveled the streets earnin' money the best we could. Sometimes he'd let me keep it all. Willie'd drum up business and I'd run errands. Some days, we'd just fish." Micah talked on and on about the bars, their patrons, and the work he did.

John surveyed the swollen waters of the Laramie River lapping at the banks.

"Isn't that the fort over there?" asked Micah.

"Yes. There's the parade ground ahead. Looks like we can't cross here, water's running too fast. We'll have to follow the bank and cross on the west side."

Micah followed John as he made his way south, along the river's edge. Finding a good spot, they entered the churning water. Before they were halfway across, the water spilled across their saddles, soaking them to the skin.

Reaching the other side, the horses clambered up the steep bank, scrambling to keep their footing as the ground shifted under their hooves. As they topped the rise, Fort John loomed before them.

Micah stared at the stronghold. High, stately red adobe walls rose twenty feet tall with thick vertical pointed cottonwood poles forming an awe-inspiring fortress. A blockhouse perched on top of two corner walls diagonal from each other, extending two feet out from the wall. The main entrance was a gaping hole cut in the stockade. More cottonwood poles, stacked in piles, lay on the ground.

"Looks like they're finally going to make the opening large enough to drive a wagon through. Sure are a lot of uniforms around."

As the sun dipped behind the formidable walls, a ghostly

shadow outlined its contour. The land encompassing the fortress lay barren except for several hundred teepees crowding the area, smoke trailing through the top openings. People moved about the grounds carrying newly purchased supplies. Frontiersmen and a handful of garrison personnel milled about the palisades. Dogs and children ran unconcerned and carefree over the dirty scrubby ground.

"Ever seen anything like this before?" asked John.

"Nope. Never." Micah pointed to one side of the fort. "Look at all the wagons over there and there."

"More camped on the other side for about a mile or so." John nodded in the direction of the river. "That group of wagons is just sitting and waiting to travel on. Sure is a hell of a lot of farmers going west these days." *Easy, John,* he chuckled, *your brother's one of them.*

"What so funny?"

"Oh, thinking about all these people moving west. If it keeps up, there'll be a neighbor every twenty miles. Nobody'll have any peace of mind."

Peace of mind. The thought conjured up a picture of Big Mike's gang from Independence. One day they might come looking for him. When their paths did cross, he'd be ready. He needed to get Micah to California before he confronted those river ruffians. He patted his saddlebag where he's hidden the money.

Leading their horses, they walked past the sutler's supply post, through the entrance hole, and onto the quadrangle. People crowded the center of the complex. On one side of the area, twelve flat-roofed houses formed part of one wall, each with a window and a door facing the center of the fort. Across the open area and attached to the opposite wall stood a blacksmith shop, a storehouse, and a public house for entertainment. Toward the front, a tall adobe wall hid the horse corral.

They stabled their horses, and then headed for the public house. Gruff voices, tinkling music, and high-pitched laughter emanated from the brightly lit doorway. Entering the swinging half-doors, John elbowed his way to the makeshift bar, followed closely by Micah. He grabbed Micah's collar to keep him from being sandwiched between two burly drunks. He shoved the boy in front of him up close to the wooden counter and pushed him down to the floor where he'd be safe.

"Barkeep, give me a double of your best and a glass of water for my short partner here," he said, pointing below the bar.

The bartender leaned over to see what he was pointing at. "Hey, that's a kid. He's not supposed to be in here."

"He's with me. He won't be any trouble. Besides, he's like a fly on a horse's ass. If he causes any ruckus, we'll sweep him outside."

Everyone laughed, except Micah, who sat all scrunched up at John's feet.

The drinks arrived and John passed a glass down to the lad who had his arms wrapped around his bent knees. John straddled Micah so no one could step on him.

"Hey, Anderson," came a shout from the other side of the crowded smoky room. "Whatcha doin' way out here in no-man's land? You get lost or something?" An over-sized hulk of a man made his way across the room. He towered over John by four inches. His wild hair appeared to have never seen a comb and his whiskers traveled down his chest. A hat dangled from a piece of rawhide off his shoulders, his buckskin reeked. A mean-looking hatchet was tucked in his belt. A knife hilt stuck out of his rawhide-tied knee-high moccasins. Fringe slapped in the air as he pounded John on the back, leaning against the bar.

John coughed, "Is that you, Joe Walker? You look like you've been rode hard and got hung up wet."

Joe smiled. "You old puke-faced son-of-a-dog. Where ya been?"

"Back east visiting my brother and his family. What are you up to these days?"

Joe scratched his beard. "Headin' to the high country to visit some kin. Thought about leavin' tomorrow."

He waved his hand at the barkeeper. "Whiskey."

Noticing a movement down around his knees, he reached down, grabbed a handful of hair, and yanked a yowling Micah from his hiding place. "What'd we have here?" Laughing, he said, "Doesn't look eatable to me."

Swinging his fists at the giant of a man as he dangled in his grasp, Micah yelled, "Put me down, ya hairy ape. You're pullin' my hair out."

"Joe, meet my son, Micah. Son, this is the best frontiersman you'll ever meet. Joseph Walker."

Walker dropped Micah onto the floor. He reached over and dusted off the lad. "Sorry, young man. Didn't mean to rough ya up. Thought I had me a new varmint crawling up ma leg." He turned to John. "This here boy's got grit."

"I thought I might be supper." Micah stood a little closer to his pa just in case this wild creature decided he liked barbeque Creole for a snack.

Joe lifted his glass and gulped his drink down. Wiping his mouth on the back of his sleeve, he asked, "Been here long?"

"Nope, just got in."

"Got a place to stay tonight?"

"Not yet." John shoved his glass forward for another pour from the bartender.

"Hell, you two can stay with my daughter's family and me. There's plenty of room and the food's good. Come on." He turned and headed toward the open door. John gulped the drink, shoved the glass back, and dropped some coins on the counter. He grabbed Micah by his shoulder and pushed him forward. Hustling across the room, he stepped out into the quadrangle.

Joe Walker walked eight feet ahead of them, his strides long and harefooted. John jostled Micah in order to keep up, ignoring the boy's complaints. They exited through the fort's entrance and headed for the Indian lodges. Horses, dogs, children, and Indians mingled freely, enjoying the evening activities of conversation and games. Weaving through the circle of teepees, Joe stopped in front of a beautifully painted lodge facing east. A soft flickering glow radiated through the covering.

Micah touched the dwelling, made of buffalo hides stitched together, with animals and figures of men painted in brilliant colors on the skins. "How come they paint all over their teepee's like this?"

"It's a story of bravery in battle. This skirmish shows my daughter's people fightin' the Cheyenne," Joe explained. "This here's a picture of me and some of my adventures."

Micah stared at the figures riding horses, some lying on their backs with arrows stuck in their bodies. Symbols and colorful designs marched across the bottom edge, mesmerizing him.

Joe scratched on the lodge wall. He flipped the furry hide door open and stepped inside. "Daughter. We have company," he shouted.

John and Micah entered the spacious lodging. A cloth covering the ground rose five feet up the side of the walls and was tied securely to each support pole. Feathers, beadwork, and painted pictures decorated the covering.

In the center of the teepee, a beautiful young Indian woman knelt in front of a small fire. Her fawn-colored buckskin dress displayed seed beads stitched across the neckline and on the shoulders. Fringe hung from the sleeve and at the hem of her dress. Her long, coal black braided hair hung over her shoulders and down her chest, almost reaching her waist. Blue, yellow and red quillwork adorned her moccasins.

She stirred a buffalo-paunch cooking pot held upright by four short stakes. A small fire of buffalo chips covered by evenly stacked hot stones lay next to her. She picked up a hot stone with two sticks and gently placed it in the paunch to heat the soup.

The delicious aroma caused Micah's stomach to growl. Neither he nor his father had eaten since breakfast.

Raising her head, she gave a welcoming smile to her father's guests.

Joe introduced his daughter, "This is Singing Woman. Shoshoni, from the Snake tribe. She is a good daughter."

Singing Woman lowered her eyes, blushing in light of her father's loving praise.

"She doesn't speak much English, but she understands," said Joe.

The woman nodded her head in agreement. She moved to the front of the lodge. An assortment of bowls lay on a piece of hide next to a neat stack of firewood and buffalo chips. She quickly brought two more wooden bowls and spooned out the corn soup.

She gestured to the floor around the pot.

Joe sat down. "Come on and eat."

John removed his hat.

Mouth open, the boy stood staring at the woman.

"Sit down, Micah."

He sat down between to Joe Walker and his father.

Alerted by low mewling sounds, Singing Woman moved

across to the other side of the teepee to attend a small child. Sitting on the bedding, she unlaced the front of the soft, buckskin sleeping bag, removed the baby, freeing his arms and legs. Then she undid the rawhide strings of her bodice and began to nurse him.

Dipping the spoon into the bowl and moving it to his lips, Micah's eyes followed her every move.

John nudged his son. "Pay attention to what you're doing, or you'll be wearing your food."

The men laughed at the lad's embarrassment.

John noticed a white cradleboard leaning against one of the poles. An old prospector once told him a white painted board meant a male child. "I see you have a grandson. Congratulations."

Smiling, Joe said, "My pride and joy. Lost a grand daughter about three years ago."

"I'm sorry."

"Smallpox," Joe said.

John shook his head. "Bad disease."

Turning to his daughter, Joe spoke in her language, "These are my friends from back east, many moons from here. They will be staying with us tonight." Then he reached for a water bag hanging from a pole, made from a buffalo's stomach, and passed it around to his guests.

"Where's your son-in-law?" asked John.

"Out gathering horses. He'll be here soon."

The hide door flipped open and a tall brave with jet-black braids handing over his shoulder stepped in. His eyes shined like ebony coals as he scrutinized the guests. A small beaded bag hung from a rawhide thong around his neck, caressing his wide bare chest. He wore buckskin leggings overlaid with a red loincloth edged in yellow. Encircling his waist, a belt displayed designs in blue, yellow and red beads. Dusty buckskin moccasins covered his feet.

Joe rose to greet the brave. "Horse Man. This is my friend, John Anderson, and his son, Micah. They have come far and are guests in your lodge tonight."

The Indian raised his hand in acknowledgement, and then hung his bow and quiver from one of the poles.

"This is my son-in-law, Horse Man," said Joe.

Micah looked up at the big man, his mouth and eyes opened wide. Words stuck in his throat.

John stood up to greet the young brave. "Pleased to meet you."

The brave signed a welcome. "Sit. Eat."

Walker and John sat down and continued their meal while Singing Woman scurried about, gathering a water bowl and cloth for her husband. Before returning to the baby, she dished out more soup for her guests.

With spoon held in midair, Micah sat spellbound as the tall Indian hunkered down to wash his arms and face. The muscles in Horse Man's back rippled. Sensing the boy scrutinizing his every action, the brave smiled at Micah.

"Micah," whispered John. "It's not nice to stare. Eat."

"He's a real Indian brave."

After supper, John followed Joe outside. Stars blanketed the black velvet sky. The moon glowed like a silver medallion.

Ambling toward a group of men sitting around a large fire, Joe explained, "These are Horse Man's people. I don't mind campin' with them. When they leave tomorrow, I'm headin' for Green River."

"What about your daughter and grandson?" John asked.

"They'll go with Horse Man. He'll take good care of them. Besides, two of my other young'uns are up at Green River."

"And your wife?"

Joe looked down at his feet. "She died a couple years back. So did a son and daughter. Cholera."

"Sorry."

"Come winter, I plan to go south," Joe announced. "My brother Joel's in Conta Costa, Californy. I might stay there for a spell. Who knows? Haven't told my daughter, yet."

Joining several men around a small fire, Joe Walker introduced his friend, each nodding a friendly greeting to John. Removing a pipe from a pouch he carried, Joe filled the bowl with tobacco.

"It might be a little strong for ya. It's an Indian mixture called kinnikinnick." Joe lit the pipe, took a drag from the stem, and passed it to John.

John took a puff and passed the pipe to his left. Coughing, he tried to catch his breath. "What's in it?"

Chuckling, Joe answered, "Don't ask."

An Indian smiled and snickered. "It bites good."

"You can say that again," replied John.

Conversation rambled from one subject to another. Man That Rides Hard told of the fine horses his son had captured two days ago. Little Elk was more interested in where winter camp might be. Others told jokes and discussed hunting. The discussion shifted to some of the changes made at the fort by the Army.

"Did you know the fort has a new name?" Joe asked.

John stared at his friend. "No."

"They've renamed it Fort Laramie. Us old timers can't seem to remember it." Joe handed the pipe to John.

"Fort Laramie. It could be worse. What's wrong with the old name?" John glanced at the pipe, and then passed it along.

"Nothin'. Guess it was too long."

Joe nodded pursing his lips together. "The Army bought the fort from the company. Bridger came up and camped out on the other side of the river, keepin' an eye on the changes being made. Some say he's headin' back east somewhere, other's say he goin' back to his fort, southwest of here."

"When did the Army personnel get here?" asked John.

"Last week. Only a handful of men right now. Expecting about a hundred Infantry soldiers in the next three months or so. Busy place. Too busy for me and my family."

"Well, with more and more folks traveling to California these days, I guess the Army feels they need protection. What they don't know is that protection is mostly from themselves."

All the men sitting around laughed and bobbed their heads in agreement.

John asked, "Who's in charge of the fort?"

"Right now, a man by the name of Lieutenant Woodbury. Only here to look the Fort over."

"Not staying long, huh?" said John.

"Nope. Word is a Major Sanderson's comin' in to rebuild the fort. Army's not happy with the way it looks. They're puttin' up some quarters and other buildings. Right now they're working on those wide gates ya saw when ya came in. Guess there'll be close to 200 troopers here later this fall."

John looked around at the men sitting near him and quietly asked, "How're the Indians taking all these changes?"

Joe lowered his voice. "Not too good. Lots of unrest and anger." Then raising his voice, he said, "Not at all happy about the whites moving in. Their hunting grounds are disappearing, like the buffalo."

John took in the stony expressions and nodding heads. He understood their apprehension about the Army bringing in so many troops. He didn't blame them for being skeptical. With all the people coming in, they were stripping the land fast of trees and animals.

Changing the conversation, Joe asked, "Where ya headed?"

John smiled. "Going back to California with my partner. Got a claim there."

Joe glanced over his shoulder at the teepee. "Kind of a small partner you got with ya."

"Yes, but all heart."

Joe continued reminiscing about the old days and his adventures with Captain Bonneville, traveling through California, and guiding a wagon train in '41. The two men exchanged stories about the rendezvous at Green River, Joe with his experiences and John with stories he'd heard.

"When I get to Californy, I'll look ya up," said Joe.

"Good, stop by. Be glad to have you. We'll be at Tracer's Point, outside of Hangtown." John gazed at the stars overhead. The sky seemed to be the same no matter where he sat.

Joe tapped his pipe against the flat stone at his feet, a signal to turn in.

Entering the lodge, Joe said, "Singing Woman's made up beds for you and your son. Looks like he's already in the land of dreams."

Joe pointed to a bed of buffalo hides with a willow-rod backrest on the far side of the room, opposite the door. "Your bed's back there. Singing Woman and Horse Man will sleep over here. I have the other bed."

John thanked him. As a guest, he was given a place of honor to rest tonight. The bed against the back wall had more room and belonged to the host. Sitting on top of the buffalo robe, John removed his shirt and boots, and set them aside. Cold from a small draft, he burrowed between the warm hides. He listened to Micah's soft snoring. Off to the side, the papoose's breathing kept rhythm with the gentle breezes brushing against the hide walls.

From the other side of the lodging came unspoken activity. Singing Woman and her husband were enjoying each other's intimate company.

John's thoughts turned to Caroline. He wanted to run his

hands over her delicate shoulders, feel her soft cheek with the back of his hand, cup her chin, and kiss her sweet luscious lips. The thought of holding her in his arms close to his chest, smelling the gentle lavender scent of her hair made him hard. Tormented by his desires, loneliness filled his heart. He took in a deep breath and rolled over with his back toward the fire pit, trying to ignore the rhythmic movement near him and the ache in his groin.

Chapter Eighteen

In the morning, Micah stepped outside to view his new surroundings. Joe Walker and John Anderson had left early, venturing off to God knows where. Singing Woman was busy bathing the baby. Micah wandered about, at a loss what he should do or where he should go.

With his hands in his pockets, he observed the activities around him as the village came alive. Several women and girls gathered buffalo chips for fuel and collected what wood they could find. He shook his head. *Yuk, buffalo chips.* Not his idea of a chore he'd indulge in.

Wandering between two lodges, he came upon a woman stirring a thick paste in a gourd bowl. The contents had an unusual smell.

"What's that you're makin'?" he asked.

Tapping the bowl, she smiled, scooped out a small dollop, and extended it to him.

"Ah, no thanks."

She shoved her hand toward him again. "Eat."

He took the sample from her and nibbled from the glob on his fingers. "Nice," he said, gritting his teeth together.

He didn't want to swallow the mealy pieces in his mouth, so he turned away and headed around to the back of the teepee. Spitting out the offensive mixture, hc shook the gook from his fingers. Taking the end of his shirt, he wiped his mouth, rubbing the cloth across his teeth and tongue.

Raising his head, Micah caught sight of several boys, practicing their skills with bows and arrows, to improve their marksmanship. Some of the boys were very good and hit the center of the target every time.

He ambled toward the group.

One boy walked up to Micah. "You try."

Micah strung the arrow, raised the bow, pulled back on the string, aimed and let it fly. Two Indian boys hit the ground as the arrow soared passed them, wide of the target, striking a lodge.

"Not good," said the Indian boy, pointing to the teepee, grabbing his bow back, while the others roared with laughter, some holding their bellies and rolling in the dirt.

Embarrassed, Micah replied, "You're right. I guess I need a little more practice."

"Lots," came a retort.

Micah chuckled. "Yep, I think that's more like it." He figured he better quit before he hurt someone. The Indian boys went back to their practice.

Rounding one teepee, he discovered four small girls playing with strange looking deerskin and straw stuffed dolls. They hollered for him to join them. He shook his head and skirted around the group. He had better things to do than to play with girl stuff.

Glancing to his right, he noticed a group of older men sitting in a circle on blankets, smoking a pipe and rolling dice made from buffalo bones. They grew louder with each throw. Micah peered over one man's shoulder.

The old Indian looked up and flipped his hand. "You. Go."

Weaving his way among several lodges encircling the grounds, he marveled at all the colors and designs. Scanning the horizon, he noticed another group of Indians camped north of the fort. *Probably a different tribe.*

The intimidating fort loomed ahead of him. Micah gazed at the high, pointed logs anchored to the red-bricked walls and bulging blockhouses standing guard overlooking the Laramie River. The busy hum of men, women and children held his attention. Civilians and military personnel moved in and out of the stronghold, transporting animals and supplies to the wagons camped on the other side of the river. Indians rushed toward the travelers near the fort to trade beaded moccasins, bear-claw necklaces, and decorated deerskin pouches for coffee, shirts, and knives.

As Micah stood mesmerized, two Indian boys ran up to him. One boy about his age stepped around him, checked his boots and clothing. The boy sniffed his hair, then picked at his twisted locks. Finally satisfied, the Indian said, "What you called?"

"Micah Anderson. What's your name?" He twisted around trying to face the Indian.

"Boy Who Spits Far," he said, standing tall and patting his chest. Then he pointed to the younger boy on Micah's left. "Him Little Badger." They both bobbed their heads and smiled.

The boys wore beaded moccasins and breechcloths, no shirts. Their coal black hair hung long and straggly. Dark eyes, sparkling with mischief, peeked out from under long lashes.

"Come," the older boy said, beckoning with his hand. When Micah didn't move, both Indian boys grabbed his arms and pulled. "Come."

They pointed to a large group of boys and girls playing a game with long handled 'J' shaped sticks. He knew this game. He played stickball back in Independence. The three boys ran to join the others.

On the ground lay a ball made of buffalo skin. Micah picked it up and squeezed it.

"Hair inside," said Boy Who Spits Far. Handing a playing stick to Micah, he knocked the ball from Micah's grip and smacked the missile into the center of the group.

As Micah ran with the boys, swinging at the ball, someone knocked him down and trampled him each time he tried to hit it. The game turned into a melee of sticks and bodies. The players rushed each other, forcing their opponents to jump or be hit. No one touched the ball with hands or body. Micah puzzled over the rules. This was nothing like the game in Independence. *Crack! Bam!* Yelling and shouting reached a crescendo, rivaling a stampede. Everyone crunched together trying to get the best advantage to score over the opponents designated line.

Sweat ran down Micah's face. His hands perspired. Dirt clung to every part of his body. "Jeeze!" he yelled as a larger boy shoved him aside. Determined to go the limit, he scrambled to regain his balance and plunged back into the unruly pack, shoving and swinging his stick.

Returning to the lodge, John found Micah sitting cross-legged on his bed, his elbow resting on his knee, holding an herbal poultice to his forehead.

Two Indian boys stood inside the doorway, jabbering away to Singing Woman, gesturing with their hands, vying for her attention with their story.

"What's goin' on here?" Joe bellowed, stepping through the opening.

Singing Woman began explaining, first pointing to Micah and then to the two Indian boys. One of them held a curved stick. John didn't understand her language or how the stick was involved, so he waited patiently for an explanation from Joe.

Boy Who Spits Far stood over Micah bending close to touch the wound on his head.

"Ouch," hollered Micah. "Don't touch it. Leave me alone."

The boy laughed, shaking his head. "He cry like girl." He said something to Joe Walker, which caused him to chuckle. The Indian boys made a quick exit outside.

Joe scratched his head. "Seems your son made a good connection with a shinny stick. He has a small gash on his forehead. My daughter wanted to stitch it. He won't let her touch him. He's a bit leery of all the attention he's gettin'."

"It's all right," Micah insisted. "It's when I got hit with the stick, I couldn't see anything for a while. Every time I tried to get out of the way, someone kept steppin' on me. That hurt worse than my head."

John lifted Micah's hand. "The gash ain't too deep. We'll bandage it back at the fort. Next time, duck."

"I tried. These Indian kids are fast. I totally misjudged the game. Thought it was like the one back in Independence. Wow, it's nothin' like that game at all."

John gave him a quizzical smile. "We need to get going."

Micah got up and walked to the door opening, holding his head. "Thanks."

"Don't mention it." Joe reached for John's hand, giving it a healthy shake. "Maybe we'll meet up again someday."

"Could be. Thanks for the hospitality."

"Pleasure's all mine," said Joe.

John nodded to Singing Woman. She smiled and shyly lowered her head.

Crossing the parade grounds on foot with his pa, Micah waved to Boy Who Spits Far. "Ya know, those Indians are rough. They play for keeps."

"It's called survival, son. These children learn at an early age what will be expected of them. Their life isn't easy by any means. Many of them you played with today will never reach adulthood."

"Why?"

"White man's diseases are killing them. Their way of life is being altered and destroyed. They aren't adjusting to the changes."

"That's sad." Looking back, Micah saw Boy Who Spits Far raise his bow above his head. *Tomorrow his friend might not be around*. "That's real sad."

During the afternoon, John and Micah canvassed the fort for accommodations. They spent some time watching the soldiers at work on the narrow entryway, readying the opening for two tall wooden gates.

John left Micah standing by the store with the saddlebags and gear for about an hour. When he returned, he said, "I've found us a room. We'll be sharing it with seven other men."

"*Seven*." Perturbed, Micah stared at his father for a moment. "Guess I get the floor?"

"We won't stay but one night. There's a few things I need to see about."

Taking a wide stance, his hands in his pockets, Micah glared at his pa. "I heard about the poker game in the back room of the public house."

"It's a nice quiet game, son, and the stakes are good. Just can't let the lieutenant know about it."

Exasperated, Micah shook his head. *This man is impossible.*

Picking up the saddlebags, John took Micah by the shoulder. "Let's go put our stuff away and take care of your head."

Shouldering his gear, a scowl on his face, the boy walked beside his pa, thumping his boot heels hard against the hard ground.

Pushing the flimsy door open, Micah glanced about the simple, sparsely lit eight-by-ten foot room. One bed occupied the room, next to a chair, and a small table with a lantern. He scuffed his boots across the rough-hewn wooden floor.

Spying the uncovered four-paned window, he said, "Nice."

Gear from other occupants lay helter-skelter on the floor, against the wall, and on top of the bed. Micah threw his things in the corner next to the window and collapsed.

He crossed his arms, leaned back against the wall, sticking out his lower lip. "What am I supposed to do while you're out enjoyin' yourself? Chase rats?"

John took his one and only good shirt from his saddlebags and shook out the wrinkles. "You look like a baby when you do that."

"Thanks. I can always depend on you for a compliment!"

"You're mighty testy today."

"Bored is more like it."

"All right. You can go out into the quadrangle. Don't go past the fort entrance. Do you hear me?"

A smile lit Micah's face. He jumped up and saluted. "Yes, sir."

Giving Micah one more paternal look, John said, "Now, let's take a look at your head."

* * *

Later that evening, John left the small room and headed for the public house.

From the window, Micah had a good view of his father as he disappeared inside the building. He stuck around two minutes to be sure John wouldn't reappear, and then slipped out the door. He wanted to investigate everything in the compound: the buildings, the stables, and the stairways to the parapet wall of rooftops. The surrounding noise of animals, civilians and soldiers moving about the quadrangle excited him.

He passed the first doorway. The door was half open. A man stood there in his birthday suit, buttocks facing the opening. Turning, he caught Micah staring at him and threw a shoe at him. "Get out of here, ya little nigger. Go peek in somebody else's room." He slammed the door.

"Phew," Micah muttered. "That wasn't much to look at. What a belly."

Two men leaned against the wall of the next house, passing a bottle back and forth. Neither noticed Micah. Deep in discussion, they talked about how to get their burros west and over the mountains.

Micah started to pass a small dark open space between two houses, when an arm came out of nowhere, wrapped around his neck, and dragged him into the alley. He got up swinging, moving around and punching out with his fists. He couldn't see his assailant, but he heard breathing.

"Come on and fight like a man," he yelled. "What, are ya afraid of me?"

"No," came an answer.

A blow on the top of his head stopped him in his tracks, made him see stars. Whacked at his ankles, a jolt of pain shot up his leg as he fell to the ground. Each time he tried to stand, strong hands shoved him down again. Finally Micah recognized a familiar face in front of him.

"Boy Who Spits Far? What are you doin' here? You'll get into trouble. Indians aren't allowed in the fort after dark."

"I come see you. I want go with you and man."

Micah rubbed the goose egg on his head. "Ya nearly killed me. Did ya have to hit me so hard?"

"You soft." The Indian boy hit Micah again in the chest.

"Quit." Micah scooted back away from the Indian boy. "You can't come with us. Your parents will have our scalps if you do."

"No parents."

"Where are they?"

Boy Who Spits Far pointed to the sky. "With good spirits. Died of pox." Silence hung in the air for a moment. "Me stay with you, yes?"

"Not a good idea. My pa hasn't totally cottoned to me yet."

"What cotton?"

Micah got to his feet. "Never mind." He brushed the dirt from his trousers and pointed across the way. "Let's go over by that buildin'. We can talk better there. We need to think this thing out."

"Yes, you think."

"Sure, give me the hard work. What a mess."

"I no mess, I clean." The Indian boy stood up tall next to Micah.

"I know, I know. Be careful. Stay close to the buildin'. If we see anyone, hide the best you can."

Boy Who Spits Far disappeared into the dark shadows.

"Hey, wait for me. If ya get caught, they'll string ya up," whispered Micah. No answer. "This isn't good."

Next to the back room of the public house, Micah entered

the small dark area, feeling his way along the wall. Squatting in the corner next to the rain barrel, Boy Who Spits Far waited for him. Boisterous shouts and loud music escaped through the thin walls, from the drunks and gamblers inside. With all the noise, Micah knew they could talk without being disturbed.

"Now," said Micah. "Tell me about your family."

Suddenly, two soldiers walked into the dark alleyway.

"Shhh," whispered Micah. Both boys ducked behind the barrel.

"The lieutenant's really pissed," said one soldier.

"Yes, and if he knew about the card game in there tonight, he'd probably hang a couple of those yokels."

"Did the scouting party come back yet from surveying the northern section up by Laramie Mountain?" The older soldier undid his trousers and began peeing on the barrel.

"Nope. That's why Lieutenant Woodbury's pissed. They were expected back around suppertime, but the runner came in and said they'd be back in the morning. Some kind of trouble up there." The younger soldier lit a cigar and threw the lighted match against the wall.

"Well, let's stay out of his sight." The older soldier fixed his trousers and they moved out onto the quadrangle.

"Ish!" Micah said. "He sprayed me. I hate that."

The Indian boy sniffed Micah's head and shoulder. "You smell like piss."

"No, I don't. Let's go over to the other side. It's smelly here. Stupid asses"

"Language bad."

Micah growled, "Don't you start. I need to think."

They sat in a dark corner away from the barrel and hatched their plans. Micah knew fooling his pa was going to be a major task, and traveling without a horse for Boy Who Spits Far would be near to impossible.

Suddenly, the sound of gunshots and shattered glass startled the boys. Stumbling to the front of the building with the rest of the crowd, Micah and the Indian squeezed inside the doorway, engrossed in the fistfight inside the public house. Several soldiers elbowed their way into the room to stop the melee, but they were punched and thrown back out the door.

Making his way into the room among the battered bodies of sweat and blood, Micah saw John held by two ugly individuals, a white man and a mean-looking half-breed.

"Cut him, Crow," hollered Pete Conway, one of the poker players.

A knife slid out of the half-breed's sheath. Leering at him, Crow held it high above John's head. Micah and the Indian boy raced across the room, dodging the drunken fighters. Reaching the half-breed's side, Micah jumped onto his back. His thumbnail cut the side of Crow's eye while the boy clamped his teeth onto the man's ear, biting through the gristle. Boy Who Spits Far grabbed the half-breed's legs and wrapped a piece of rawhide around his ankles. The half-breed fell down, dropped his knife, screamed, and whipped his arms around his head, trying to dislodge Micah.

John pulled back his free arm and landed a solid punch into the other man's face. Blood splattered his shirt.

Staggering backwards, Pete Conway grabbed onto another man trying to steady himself. He pulled a pistol from a bystander's holster and turned, aiming it at John.

Spying the gun, Micah picked up Crow's knife and threw it at the man, burying it up to the hilt in Conway's chest. He stood there for a moment in disbelief, holding his chest, before dropping his weapon. Conway grasped the edge of a table, pulling it over before he collapsed to the floor.

John grabbed Micah by the shoulder and dragged him through the doorway outside as additional fights started. Boy

Who Spits Far jumped across the top of a table and dashed after them.

"There's an Indian in here," a voice shouted above the din. "Grab him before he escapes." Several men lunged at Boy Who Spits Far. He bolted out the door.

"Grab our things. I'll get the horses," John shouted. He ignored Boy Who Spits Far behind him.

Micah and the Indian boy snatched up the saddlebags and personal gear from the room, and headed for the corral, struggling with their burdens to reach the horses. As they passed one dark alley, the Indian boy grabbed his parfleche, bow, and quiver.

The confused crowd emptied into the quadrangle. Lieutenant Woodbury rushed to the Public House. "How did the fight begin? Who started it?"

"Four kids involved and one of them has a gun," said a grizzly looking fellow with a split lip.

A few troublemakers shouted, "There's two dead men inside and that Anderson fool killed them both."

George Crow stood in the shadows, a sneer on his face. "Yep, he did it."

Someone yelled to the lieutenant, "Anderson should be put in jail."

Billy Conway chimed in, "The Indian kid was the cause of all the trouble. He killed my brother." Several men voiced their agreement.

"Yep, he's right. The Indian started everything," one man hollered.

John saddled the two horses. Throwing his bags across the rump of one and climbing on, he shouted, "Hurry up, Micah. We don't have much time before they close up the entrance."

Micah climbed onto the fence and leaped into the saddle. Boy Who Spits Far jumped on behind Micah, landing on the horse's hindquarters behind the saddle, grabbed a death grip on Micah's shirt, and hung onto his parfleche. They took off, made a caracole right turn, then raced around the adobe corral wall.

Several men with flaming torches raced to the fort entrance after them shouting, "There they go. Get 'em."

It was too late. At a full gallop out the archway, the three desperate fugitives pushed their horses into the darkness. Escaping westward, the full moon overhead lighted the trail for them.

Billy Conway leaned against the fort gate and concentrated on the dust trail swirl in the air, dissipate into the night. Cursing John Anderson, he vowed to avenge the death of his brother, Pete. "I don't want the kid who threw the knife. I want John Anderson."

George Crow stood behind him. "Want me to ride with ya to catch that varmint?" He mopped his eye with a dirty handkerchief. Then he held it to his bloody ear. "I want to get my hands on that brat of his and the Indian kid. Teach them a lesson or two. I can't even see right."

"We'll leave in the morning. I'm sure we can catch up with 'em. Anderson's got two pieces of live baggage with him." Billy smirked and turned slowly, sauntering back into the quadrangle. He had plenty of time on his side. The pain he planned to inflict on Anderson would be gratifying.

Stomach tumbling and churning, Micah followed his pa, driving his horse toward the mountain range. Boy Who Spits Far hung on for dear life. His legs gripped the horse's flanks to keep from bouncing with every hoof fall.

Micah's mind was overwrought. Never in his life had he hurt anyone, intentionally. His body felt numb and lifeless, limbs unattached. The pain in his head traveled down his back to his tailbone. The impact of what took place at the Fort hit him hard. Tonight, he'd killed a man.

Chapter Nineteen

Independence, Missouri

The muddy streets seethed with activity. Humidity clung to the air. Alexander could taste it. As he rolled up one side of the canvas to air out the wagon, James leaned over the side.

With his eyes closed, he breathed deep. "Whew. That's better, Pa. It's hot in here."

"Once we're on the trail, you'll be walking. So enjoy the luxury of riding, son." Alexander flipped the brim of James' floppy brown hat.

"I'd walk now, but Ma won't let me. She's afraid I might get dirty."

Sarah sat on the tent, giving her a good view of the Courthouse Square. "Ma, did you ever see so many strange people? That black man over there has a purple shirt on and bright green pants. Do you think he's going to California?"

"I suppose he is," Caroline answered. The congestion in

the streets was overwhelming. "No one seems to know where they're going."

"Wow! The wagons stretch all the way around the Courthouse and back again," James exclaimed. "I tried to count 'em. They just keep moving and adding more."

Alexander removed his hat and gazed about him. "Everywhere you look there's horses, oxen, and wagons. The only thing keeping the animals off the grass is that white rail fence. Don't blame 'em. That grassy area would end up looking like the streets, mud up to your eyebrows."

James pointed, "Hey! Look at those funny little carts. I could push those."

"That's a hard way to travel west," replied his mother. "They'll walk the whole way, pushing or pulling them."

Alexander rolled up the other canvas side. "When I'm finished here, I'm gonna mosey over to the inn. I'll be right back," he mumbled to Caroline.

Caroline nodded.

"Ma, look." James dangled over the wagon side, holding onto the hickory bows supporting the canvas covering.

"James, get back in here. You'll snap the bows. It'll serve you right if you fall into the mud head first."

"See, I told you so," taunted Sarah.

James wrinkled his nose, making a face.

The children continue to enjoy the excitement around them. Men led oxen down the street and drove livestock through town, dogs were running amuck, and children threw mud balls at each other. Some of the older boys aggravated a few donkeys by tickling their heels with willow sticks, making them kick and buck.

"Here comes Pa." James hopped off the back gate to greet his father. *Splunk!* The brown muck splashed over the tops of his boots and onto his trousers. He took a step and the mire sucked at his boot.

"Hey, watch this." He pressed his boot into the mud, making a print, letting it fill up with dark oozy muck.

Sarah wrinkled up her nose. "Yuck." Her brother's antics didn't impress her.

"James, don't. You're getting mud all over you and your clothes." Exasperated, Caroline pointed to the boardwalk. "Go over there and start scraping the filth off your boots. I don't want it in the wagon."

Alexander glanced at his son. "Can't I leave the wagon for one minute before you're into trouble?"

James hung his head. "Sorry, Pa." He trudged over to the walkway, stepping carefully to keep his boots on his feet, and picked up a small stick next to the steps. Sitting down, he scraped off a hunk of mud, flung it into the street, to see how far it would fly.

"James." Alexander gave his son a dark stare, then shook his head. Looking up at his wife, he said, "I checked around to see if John was here."

Lifting one eyebrow, Caroline asked, "And?"

Alexander cleared his throat. "Seems there was a bit of trouble at Noland's Inn where John stayed. During a card game, a gambler by the name of Big Mike tried to shoot him."

"Oh, nothing surprises me. What did John do?" she asked.

"He won and the man accused him of cheating."

She feigned surprise. "Not John."

Alexander smirked. "I know. He's not really honest at cards. Anyway, the desk clerk told me, he and a black boy lit out during the night."

"The young boy from St. Louis?" Caroline's mouth fell open in shock. "Your brother has that black child with him?"

"Yes. Sure is strange. Wonder why John connected up with him? He must be the *small problem* he mentioned in his note. Anyway, the desk clerk told me the two of 'em are headed west."

"I guess we're on our own, again." Caroline pursed her lips together and shut her eyes. *Count. Don't lose your temper. It's not Alexander's fault. It's that stupid brother of his and his harebrained idea of adventure.*

Alexander saw the look on his wife's face. "We've handled it by ourselves this far without any big disasters. I know it hasn't been exactly trouble free, but we're still close to being on time. What we need to do now is solve a couple of problems before we go on."

"Only a couple?" Caroline narrowed her eyes at her husband. "What are they?"

"It looks like we'll have to wait a spell before heading west. If the rain holds off, we might get started in about a month or so."

Caroline shouted, "A month!" She sat in disbelief with her mouth open.

"We'll have to wait and see." Alexander placed both hands on the wagon, looked down at his feet, and scraped the mud from his boot onto the wheel

He grabbed the reins from the hitching rail and climbed up into the seat. "There's another alternative. We can go on to Westport and make a connection there. A man inside said we might get lucky."

Caroline could tell by Alexander's expression that he wanted to go on. Was Westport any different than Independence? Probably not.

"Is this place far?"

"Nah, shouldn't take long."

Sarah stood up behind her pa. "Just sitting here is boring."

Alexander looked at Caroline. "What do you say? Should we try it?"

"Why not. I don't relish waiting here a month. It's crowded, muddy, and a bit too rowdy. Maybe Westport will be better. Now, what's the other problem?"

"We need to buy oxen to pull our wagon over the trail. Horses aren't sturdy enough for the mountains and dry desert conditions ahead."

"Didn't John tell you about needing oxen?" she asked.

He shook his head, "No. It's one of those things he forgot."

"Huh. Only one of the things he forgot? So, what'll we do?"

"There's a few outfitters up ahead. We'll find one on our way out to Westport. Maybe we can sell two of our horses, and with the money we get, we'll be able to buy three or four yoke of oxen. That should get us to California."

"More expenses. Do we have enough money for this purchase?"

"Depends on what we get for the horses." Alexander turned and shouted to James, "Climb on board, son, and bring your stick. You can sit in back and clean your boots. We're heading out."

"Yahoo," James shouted, sliding his boot on. "We're on our way."

"Don't be so loud," said Sarah. "I just want to see the sign that says, *'Trail to California'*."

Alexander urged the team forward, dodged wagons and children, and finally made a right turn onto Maple Street. About two blocks away, he located the outfitters of McCulloch and Sons. After haggling for the best trade, he purchased four yoke of oxen in exchange for three of his horses and an additional twenty-five dollar payment. McCulloch's two sons helped Alexander hitch up the oxen. Ready to move on, he tied the one horse he had left to the back of the wagon and headed out Lexington Street.

Disappointed with Westport, Alexander remarked, "It's like Independence, only smaller."

Caroline stood next to her husband, amazed at the crowds. "I wonder if there's anyone left back East."

"I feel like I'm batting my head against a barn door. Look at all the time we've lost today with buying oxen and getting here. We better find an inn before the sun's down. If we can't find a room, I'm afraid we'll have to sleep in the wagon tonight."

"No!" shouted Sarah. "I don't want to sleep in that stupid tent."

"Sarah, enough. I'm doing my best." Alexander was in no mood for tantrums.

Caroline gave her daughter a stern look.

Eyes wide, Sarah clamped her mouth shut and pouted, turned her back to her father, and leaned against the sideboard.

"The children are tired," said Caroline, "and they need to eat."

"We'll stop over here and see if we can get a room," he said, pointing to the Stone Inn. He wrapped the rope around a railing, and disappeared inside.

A few minutes later, he returned, shaking his head. "Nothing available in town. The desk clerk says all the inns and hotels are filled to capacity. There's a small campground by Cave Springs on the other side of town. We can set up there."

He turned to his children. "We'll sleep in the tent tonight, build a nice fire, maybe meet some new people and dance. How's that sound?"

Sarah frowned and climbed into the wagon.

"I'm hungry," said James.

Alexander chuckled, "That's not a surprise, son."

About a quarter of a mile out of town, smoke rose from campfires surrounded by wagons and tents. Off to one side of the road, horses, donkeys, and oxen were hobbled for the night.

Livestock grazed nearby. Children and adults milled around the camping area. Alexander selected a spot close to a few trees, giving them some privacy.

Untying the lead rope from the oxen, he shouted, "James, help me with the animals. Sarah, help your Ma set up the tent."

The children eagerly scrambled out of the wagon, while Alexander gave a hand to Caroline, helping her down from the seat.

"How are your ribs?"

"I don't hurt much anymore. Only a pinch ever so often. I feel stiff and a bit flat on my backside, though." She placed her hands on the small of her back, trying to rub the ache in her behind.

Alexander grinned as he reached around her. "You need some help."

Playfully, slapping at his hand, she said, "Behave yourself."

He laughed. "Come on, James, before I get in trouble with your ma."

Caroline and Sarah pulled the tent from the wagon and began setting up camp. A woman strolled over from the next wagon.

"Hello. Can I help you with the set up?"

The woman was of average height and slender, with blond hair coiled down to her shoulders. A smile played across her face.

"Yes, if you wouldn't mind. I'm Caroline Anderson and this is my daughter, Sarah."

Sarah smiled, then bashfully cast her glance down to her feet.

"I'm Amanda Young. We've been camped here about a week. My husband, Albert, is over at the post checking on our spot on the list."

"Where you from?" asked Caroline.

"Franklin, Missoura. Don't have any children yet." She rubbed her stomach. "One's on the way. Probably be born in California."

Caroline smiled. "How nice. We have two children. Sarah and James. Our son is with his father right now."

"Well," said Amanda, "let's get your tent up. We can talk while we work."

The women set up camp while discussing their trip across Missouri and the crowded conditions in Independence.

After Amanda left, Sarah said, "Ma, she's real nice and pretty. Did you see the big bruise on her cheek? It's green and purple."

"Yes, Sarah. But, we need to mind our own business. Now, let's not worry about Mrs. Young. We need to get supper ready."

Later that evening, Caroline sat on a log in front of their campfire. "Sounds like a fiddle and a mouth harp over there."

James jumped up, hopping from one foot to the other. "Let's go join 'em." Off he ran.

"Don't be in such an all-fired hurry," yelled Sarah.

Alexander stood up and dusted his trousers. "Good idea. We need a bit of livening up." He extended his hand to his wife. "Shall we, Mrs. Anderson?"

Sarah giggled behind her hand. "Oh, Pa. You're so funny." Then she dashed in the direction of the dancers.

During the night, Caroline awoke to shouting from the Young's wagon and a man's angry slurred and vulgar voice. She lay there listening. Muffled cries and screams of pain resounded into the night.

Sitting upright, Caroline shook her husband. "Alexander, wake up. I think that nice Mrs. Young I met today needs help. It sounds like her husband's beating her."

Alexander sat up and listened. He gently patted her hand. "He's probably drunk. There's nothing we can do tonight."

"He's beating her."

"Maybe, but we can't interfere in their troubles. We'll check on her tomorrow. Now lie down and try to get some sleep." He pulled her down to him, holding her close. He kissed her forehead. "Try not to think about Mrs. Young."

Sleep did not come easy. She lay there listening to the muffled cries and soft whimpers drifting into the night.

The next morning, Alexander left to talk with the wagon master, upset over Young beating his wife. Tired and lethargic, Caroline tried to keep her mind on her work. First, she straightened the bedding inside the tent, and then handwashed two shirts and a pair of trousers. Afterwards, she put aside beans to soak and bread to rise. Finally, she thought about getting acquainted with the area before setting out the noon meal, especially since the children were nowhere in sight. Still curious about Amanda, she strolled over to the Young's wagon.

The young woman stood with her back to Caroline, hand washing a few items and laying them across the wagon wheels.

"Hello," said Caroline.

At first, Amanda didn't face her. When she did, Caroline saw her left eye was black and her bottom lip was cut and swollen. "I fell."

Caroline stood stock-still and tried to smile. "I'm sorry."

There was silence for a moment, then tears welled up in Amanda's eyes and her hands trembled. "He didn't mean to. He was drunk. I know he loves me."

Caroline made no comment.

Amanda tilted her head. "Besides, he has the right. He's my husband."

Fuming, Caroline said, "Husband or no husband. He shouldn't beat you like that."

Amanda snapped, "It's none of your business!" She turned to finish her wash, ignoring Caroline.

Caroline stood aghast, mouth open. *Is she so stupid? How can she cover for that man the way he beats her?* Angrily, she stomped back to her wagon. Grabbing a dry shirt off the wagon wheel, she crumpled it up and threw it into the back of the wagon. Her mood grew blacker as she stamped around the campsite banging pots, lids, and metal dishes as she worked. When the children showed up for noon meal, sensing her frame of mind, they grabbed a few biscuits and escaped to safer quarters.

Alexander stayed away most of the day. Caroline finally came to grips with her encounter with Amanda. The bruises and cuts on the lady's face haunted her. Realizing the horror and fear Amanda must feel day in and day out, Caroline was grateful for a husband like Alexander.

After the children bedded down, Caroline joined Alexander by the fire. Cuddling up close to him, she wrapped her arms around his left arm. Laying her head against his shoulder, she watched the embers float skyward.

Tossing a stick into the fire with his free hand, Alexander tilted his head to rest on hers and patted her hand. "Your thoughts are far away." He pulled her close. "You cold?"

"No. Thinking how lucky I am. You treat me well."

He cleared his throat. "You're my wife." He paused for a

moment, slightly embarrassed. Stammering the next statement, he said, "I…love you." Hurriedly, he continued, "I know I don't say that very often."

She looked up at him, searching his face, and gently placed a kiss on his cheek. "You're a true gentleman. I love you, too."

"I'm glad," he replied, winking at her. "Otherwise, I'd have to go looking for the man who held your heart."

Caroline caught her breath. "Oh, Alexander. You know better than that." *Did he know about John? No, he couldn't.*

"I feel bad when I don't consult you on some of the decisions I make," he said. "It's not that I don't want your opinion. It's just that I don't think ahead on most things."

"At least you're kind and don't beat me."

"I'd never do that. Does this conversation have anything to do with Mrs. Young?"

"Yes."

"Caroline, don't get between Mrs. Young and her husband."

She stared at the flames of the fire. "I know. The old law says a man has a right to beat his wife as long as the stick's no thicker than his thumb, if he thinks she deserves it. Mr. Young uses his fists and does it out of meanness."

"Caroline."

She moved off the log and sat on the ground between his legs. Leaning back against his body, she placed her head on his bent leg. His arms encompassed her, pulling her close to him. He kissed the top of her head.

"Isn't this better?" he asked.

"Mmmm," was her response as her eyes closed, and a smile played across her face.

Alexander looked down at his wife. Her beautiful auburn hair cascaded over his leg. Firelight softly illuminated her angelic face. Wisps of hair escaped across her forehead. He twisted the loose strands around one finger. He traced the soft contour of her cheek with the back of his fingers, following the outline of her jaw. He nimbly caressed and brushed her lips with the tip of his thumb. She nibbled it, tasting the salty sweat. Leaning forward, he slid his hand over her chin and down her throat to her chest. Cupping one breast, he playfully ran his thumb over the nipple.

Catching her breath, Caroline's body immediately responded to his touch, her chest thrust forward, tightening her bodice. Kissing the nape of her neck, he deliberately moved his thumb around and across her erect nipple, sending titillating sensations to the sweet part between her thighs. She felt warm and alive. Her appetite whetted, she arched her back. Squeezing her knees together, she tried to ease her excitement. Her breathing quickened. The fire crackled when a log shifted, like her emotions exploding from the pleasure Alexander aroused within her. She wanted to bed him now.

Horrendous screams and vile yelling jarred Caroline to her senses. Jumping to his feet, Alexander shoved her forward. Ranting and ravings echoed loudly. The Young's' wagon shook violently from the carryings-on inside

"Alexander. He's gonna hurt her again," Caroline gasped.

He adjusted his trousers and commanded, "You stay here." Taking several long steps, he met two other men rushing forward.

"What should we do?" asked Hans Yoder.

"We can't let this go on. He's been drinking all week and he gets real nasty," said another man. "One of these days he's gonna kill her."

"You know she's with child," remarked Yoder.

High-pitched screams caught their attention. Then a gunshot rang out. Everyone froze. Quiet settled around the wagon.

Caroline jumped up and rushed to Alexander's side. "That was a gun."

"Get back. We don't know what's going on in there." Motioning to the two men, he said, "Let's go."

Before the men took two steps, another shot rang out. Then dead silence.

Zachariah Miller and Tom Poston, both wagon masters, pushed through the crowd gathering around Yoder and Anderson.

"Everyone stay back and let us handle this." Pulling his gun from his holster, Miller cautiously made his way toward the wagon, followed by Poston. Reaching the back, he yelled, "Young. Everything all right in there?"

No answer.

Miller pulled the canvas aside and pointed his gun into the interior. He stood for a few moments. Dropping the canvas, he slowly turned and lowered his gun.

Poston quickly looked in. "Oh, my God. What a mess." Sick to his stomach, he turned away and vomited.

Miller faced the crowd and shook his head. "They're both dead."

Caroline covered her mouth to stifle a cry, tears slid down her cheeks.

James and Sarah stuck their heads from the tent opening. "What's that noise?" asked James. "Sounded like a gun."

Caroline rushed toward them. "Just a little misunderstanding. Get back inside and go to sleep. I'll be in soon."

"What're you crying for, Ma?" asked Sarah.

"I'll explain later. Now cover up and please, go to sleep." Caroline closed the flap. Wrapping her shawl around her shoulders, Caroline trembled.

Miller and Poston took the men aside. "Nothing we can

do tonight. We'll bury them in the morning. Maybe we should put a guard on duty to keep the critters away?"

"Good idea," said Alexander. "Two of the single men would probably be good."

Poston walked into the crowd. "Everyone, go back to your tents and get some sleep. Tomorrow we'll handle this. Mitchell, Jones, you two stand guard."

Waiting until the people left, Miller walked away from the wagon, motioning for Alexander to follow. "I appreciate the help you gave me with the wagons yesterday."

Lowering his voice, he said, "Young and his wife were supposed to leave tomorrow. If you want his spot, be up at four and ready to pull out by seven. Keep it to yourself or you'll start a row I won't be able to put down"

"I'll be there and thanks," Alexander said.

Zachariah touched the brim of his hat and strolled away.

Alexander's heart beat faster. Tomorrow they'd be heading west into the territories. He hated to think good fortune came his way because of tonight's tragedy, but he'd be damned if he'd miss this opportunity.

Chapter Twenty

Around dawn the next morning, Caroline stood by the graves of Albert and Amanda Young. The sky was hazy gray, a cold wind whipped her skirt about her legs. Chills played up and down her spine, as Zachariah Miller performed the brief service and Mrs. Abernathy sang a hymn.

"Burying them along the roadside doesn't seem fitting," whispered Caroline. She huddled closer to Alexander. "What are they gonna do with the Young's' wagon?"

"Miller says they're gonna burn it. Too messy to clean up. Besides, no one wants to get near it."

"What are they gonna do with the oxen?"

"They'll roam with the rest of the livestock," said Alexander. "Can't let good animals go to waste." He wrapped his arm around Caroline's waist and grasped James by the shoulder, pulling him close. Sarah stood partially hidden behind him, crying softly, tears sliding down her red cheeks.

After Miller closed with "Amen," he shouted, "Okay people. Listen up. We need to get these wagons moving.

Daylight's coming over the horizon and times slipping away. So harness up your teams and break camp. We're leaving in half an hour."

"I'm hungry," complained James.

"You only ate an hour ago. Sarah, get a couple of biscuits out of the box and give them to James. You can have some also."

Alexander sighed. "That boy's growing."

"I can't seem to fill him up. This day's starting bad with a burial and all."

Alexander placed his arm across her shoulder. "Nah. It's a good day. See the sunrise. Remember, we're on our way."

She smiled at him.

At eight o'clock sharp, thirty wagons pulled out, one after the other, heading toward the western territories. A drove of donkeys, a dozen livestock driven by three lone riders, and the Young's oxen completed the train entourage. The organized departure amazed Caroline.

Morning passed slowly as somber silence plagued the Andersons'. Although she was only a brief acquaintance, Amanda Young's death reminded them of the perilous journey ahead. Even James wasn't his jovial self.

After the noon meal, Caroline and the children walked the prairie trail of flowery flat lands, mixed with rolling hills of green grass. Wagons spread across the trail five wide with adults walking, children running about, while drovers kept the slow-moving livestock last to avoid trampling anyone.

Suddenly James bolted away from his mother. "Don't take off too far," hollered Caroline. "Stay within seeing distance."

He waved his hand, acknowledging her statement.

"Do you think he heard, Ma?" asked Sarah.

"Let's hope so." Caroline eyed her daughter. "I've been meaning to ask how your quilting patches are coming along."

"I have four completed. Two more are cut and ready for sewing."

"I would have thought by now you would have more finished. Maybe tonight we can sit together and work on 'em."

"I'd like that," said Sarah. "Oh, there's Malinda. I'll be back," she called over her shoulder, running behind a passing wagon.

Caroline's heart almost stopped. "Sarah, be careful. You'll get yourself run over."

As her daughter caught up with her friend, Caroline thought how easily children adjusted. *Tragedy seems to fade quickly for children.* Looking around, her mind raced. *So many changes. Can we handle all of them? I wonder what California is really like? To hear it from John, the streets are paved in gold.* She grimaced thinking how her brother-in-law duped her husband into this adventure. *Your due is coming, John. What an ignoramus. Once I get to California, you will pay.*

Caroline tried to picture the river crossings ahead and the mountains they'd have to climb. What bothered her most was what actually waited for them in California. Every time she thought about digging and panning for gold, she wondered if her family could handle the physical labor.

By evening camp, she was exhausted from walking eighteen miles in the sun, inhaling the dust kicked up by all the animals. With the tent pitched and the meal eaten, she couldn't wait to crawl between the covers for a well-earned sleep. Sarah's quilt patches would have to wait for another time.

"How in the world are we to cross here?" asked Caroline as she viewed the turbulent Kansas River with skepticism. Limbs and small woody plants floated in the swirling water. To make matters worse, they would have to navigate the steep bank to reach the sandy bottomland.

"I need to talk with Poston and Miller. Wait here." Alexander jumped down from the wagon to join the men, deep in conversation.

Standing in the middle of the circle, Miller held up his hand. "Okay, quiet down. In answer to some of your questions, crossing the river isn't the hardest part." He paused for a moment. "The challenge is getting the wagons down the slopes and up the other side."

"It looks treacherous," declared Hans Yoder. "With thirty wagons, it's gonna be a big job."

Everyone chimed in at once, voicing concern over the downhill descent.

Miller raised his hands and shouted, "Quiet!" The men ceased talking. "I don't want any complainin'. I've done this before, so listen up. We'll take ropes, coil them around a tree up here, and lower the wagons one by one. You drivers will handle your own oxen. No need to unhitch the animals. Once a couple of wagons are down, the Indian brothers will ferry them across."

"And how many can be loaded on this here makeshift ferry?" questioned a large man in the back.

"The brothers say they can load two to three wagons plus some of the smaller livestock. The rest will have to swim across. The single men and drovers will get them over. Now let's get goin'. We're wastin' time."

Alexander returned to his wagon and climbed aboard. "We're heading down the bank one at a time. I'm taking our wagon. I want you and the children to make your way to the bottom the best that you can. Stay together. There's a ferry down there that'll take us across."

"Is it free?" asked Caroline. "It should be, the way it looks."

"No. It's gonna cost about four dollars and forty cents for our passage."

"Is it safe?" asked Caroline.

"I'm sure these Indians have been doing this for some time."

James stretched his neck to view the raft. "Pa. There's canoes tied together under those boards."

"Don't worry. We'll get across just fine. Now everybody out. I need to get in line."

Caroline and the children descended the steep sandy hill. Reaching bottom, they waited with the other women and children off to one side as the men work.

At the top of the hill, Tom Poston tied one end of the rope around the iron axle assembly under the first wagon, coiled it around a stout tree, then handed the loose end to Alexander and the other nine men.

Parallel to Poston's group, Zachariah Miller set up another group. Two wagons would be making downhill trips at the same time.

"Ready, drivers?" shouted Miller.

"Ready" came the answer.

"Ready on the ropes?"

"Ready" chorused both groups of men.

Slowly, the drivers edged their animals downhill while the men held onto the ropes, letting them out a little at a time. Caroline watched them roll and skid down the steep bank. Reaching bottom, they were pushed onto the ferry.

Another two wagons began a downhill descent.

"Hey. Somebody grab the kid," yelled Mr. Peterson from the ferry.

Caroline screamed, "James. Get back!"

Bent on hands and knees, James grabbed grass and dirt, attempting to scale the hill in the path of an oncoming wagon. The wagon shifted in the dirt and headed in his direction. One man near the front wheel staggered over to James, grabbed him by his shirt and pushed him to the side. Tumbling after him, they both reached bottom end over end.

"Jones, stay with that wheel. Push, men, push. Straighten it up. Don't let it tip over," yelled Posten.

The wagon wobbled from side to side, making its way down the hill, pushing the oxen to the bottom. Peterson grabbed the lead yoke as the wagon stopped sharply at the water's edge. Two men unhitched the oxen and moved them down stream with the other animals, then seven men rolled the wagon onto the ferry.

Irate, Jones stood up, surveyed the wagon, and then stomped toward Caroline. "Let me see that kid," he ordered. "Young man, you almost got yourself and me killed. Stay out of the way." Then he strode back to work, mumbling oaths under his breath.

Alexander stood at the top of the hill. Miller approached him.

"Anderson. You've got to keep that kid of yours under control. He's gonna get people hurt or killed around here."

"Yes, sir. I'll take care of it," said Alexander. "Sorry for the trouble."

"All right. You're next. Get ready." Miller shouted as he walked away. "Anderson's next, let's get goin'."

"Jones, get back up here. We need you. Ms. Anderson, put your son somewhere other than in this area."

"I will, Mr. Miller," yelled Caroline. With a scowl, she faced her son. "James, I could strangle you. Get over on the far side of those trees. I don't want to see you over here or in any more trouble. Do you hear me?"

He hung his head. "Yes, Ma."

"You're so stupid," whispered Sarah. "You could have been killed."

"I've already been told that." He picked up his floppy hat and headed for the trees.

Caroline looked up and caught her breath. It was Alexander's turn to make his descent.

"Jones, Rogers, steady that wagon," shouted Poston. "Anderson, pull back on those oxen."

Men on both sides of the wagon rolled it over the large rocks and pushed it out of the ruts. Caroline waited for the rope to break as the wagon swayed dangerously from side to side. She held her breath. Finally, Alexander made his way to the bottom.

Caroline sat stiffly on the wagon seat, the rapid Kansas River swirled by. There were no protective railings on the ferry, and every bump to the raft caused the wagons to creak and moan. The width of the water didn't scare her as much as the depth. The two Indian brothers poled the ferry out into the current, staffs disappearing into the dark waters. With only a foot of the shaft appearing above the water line, the men propelled the ferry across the water.

James stood next to the wagon side. He rotated a fist-sized rock in his hand. Quickly, he tossed it into the water.

Kerplunk!

Sarah stood up in the middle of the wagon, eyes as big as saucers. "James fell in," she shrieked.

"No, he didn't," bellowed Alexander. "He's only thrown a rock." He turned to his son. "Get in the wagon, James. I've had all I can take from you today."

James wiped his hands on his pants and proceeded to climb onto the back gate.

"Stay put and keep out of mischief. I don't want to see you out here again."

James hung his head. Grasping the gate with both hands, he swung his feet.

"You scared me," said Sarah.

"Ah, be quiet and quit complaining." He lay down on the gate, placed his hat across his face, folded his arms under his head, and bent his knees.

A partially submerged log suddenly hit the ferry with a loud bam, jarring the wagons and passengers.

The boat floundered in the current as the Indians tried to gain control. Alexander steadied himself, keeping his balance.

Flowing back into them, the log hit again. The wagons lurched and slid sideways. The passengers floundered as the ferry swung about in the water.

"Pa!" screamed Sarah. She fell against a tub, cutting her forehead. Sliding across the floor, she grasped the rocker's leg. The chair tipped over, tossing her against the wagon wall. Quickly, she grabbed the sides with both hands, clinging to the boards and screaming, "Help me! Help me!"

Caroline pitched forward. Tightening her grip on the wagon seat, her knuckles whitened. She stiffened her legs against the footboard to keep from plunging over the edge of the seat into the raging river. Crashing over the ferry flooring, water sprayed her from head to toe. "Sarah! James! Hang on."

James rolled off the gate and grabbed the hinged edge. Losing his grip, he tumbled onto the slippery ferry floorboards and crashed onto his knees. Water gushed across his body, washing him near the ferry's edge. Another drifting log bumped against the boat, the wagon moved sideways, throwing him into the cold, turbulent water. He gripped the flooring's edge, trying to grab the wet ropes used to tie the canoes together, but missed them.

Water sloshed over his head, choking him. "Pa, help me," he screamed, dangling in the water.

Throwing himself onto the wooden floor, Alexander sprawled near the water's edge. "James! Grab my hand!" Clutching his son's small wet fingers with one hand, Alexander stretched his other hand forward for a better hold. James slipped from his grasp, splashing backwards into the current.

Alexander screamed. "Hold on, son!" Then turning to the shoreline, he yelled, "You on the shore, get my son. He's in the water. There. Over there." He pointed in the direction where James struggled to keep his head above water.

James thrash in the swift current, arms and head above water, then only his hands.

Men on shore climbed onto their horses. Some tried to ford the river with no avail, while others galloped down the line, dodging boulders and trees.

Caroline screamed, "Oh my baby! Save my baby!"

"Woman, stay in the wagon," shouted Alexander. "Sarah, get up to the seat by your mother and stay there."

Alexander clutched the wagon sideboard, his knuckles white from his grip. All he could do was watch his son being swept away in the tumbling water. By the time the ferry reached the opposite shore, the riders and James were out of sight.

He plunged knee-deep into the water and splashed to shore. He leaped on the first available horse and galloped down stream along the river's edge.

Caroline and Sarah disembarked while several men rolled their wagon on shore, hitched up the oxen, and drove it up the embankment.

Hysterical, gasping and choking, Sarah cried, "My brother. He's gone. Oh, Ma."

Taking her daughter into her arms, Caroline hugged her close, bonnet askew on her shoulders, tears streaming down her face. "How can this be happening? Oh, God, help us," she whimpered. "My James. My poor baby."

Miller walked over to her, hat in his hands. "Miz Anderson, ya need to climb up above where it's safe. This landing site is mighty dangerous. Don't you fret none. Several men are searching with your husband. They'll bring your son back. You wait and see. Come on up and rest a spell while we get the rest of the wagons across."

Caroline crawled up the bank and stumbled toward their wagon, pulling Sarah behind her. Her knees wanted to buckle, her stomach churned, a chill crept over her body. Bitter bile rose in her throat. She fought the urge to vomit. Keeping a steady vigil, she stared across the horizon, as Sarah clung to her.

Once all the wagons and animals were safely across, Miller shouted, "People, round 'em up. We're campin' here tonight."

Poston came up to Caroline. "Miz Anderson. I'll put your wagon in line for ya. You and young missy sit over on those chairs I set up for ya."

"Thank you," she muttered, in a flat, lifeless tone.

Several small fires lit up the darkness surrounding the campsite. Tents crowded the area. Two women soon brought food to Caroline and Sarah. The plates lay untouched.

Fires banked, the travelers drifted to their tents, silence enfolded the area. Caroline sat in a chair next to the tailgate, waiting, waiting for news. Sarah fell into a restless sleep in the wagon, moaning fitfully.

In the distance, Caroline heard horses. Several riders

appeared out of the inky darkness. A man rode toward to wagon and dismounted. Gripped in one hand was a wet, floppy brown hat.

"Here, ma'am. This is all we could find," he said. "I'm truly sorry." Touching his hat brim, he turned to leave.

"What about my husband?" she asked. "Have you seen him?"

"Yes, ma'am. He's still out there lookin' for your son."

Sarah sniffled and jerked in her sleep, then rolled over onto her side.

Caroline held James' hat in her hands, running her fingers over the soggy brim, her heart heavy and body drained. Numb and exhausted, her mind comprehended nothing except the need to sit and wait for Alexander.

Several hours later, a lone rider approached. Her eyes strained to penetrate the darkness. Jumping to her feet, she rushed to the edge of the campsite. Slumped over the horse's neck, the reins drooped from Alexander's hands. She ran to him and grasped his leg. He raised his head and shook it.

"Can't find him," he whispered. "I tried and failed." He dismounted and leaned his head against the horse's neck, grasping the mane. "I've failed James. I've failed you." He turned and shook his fist into the air. "Because of my lust for gold, I've killed our son. My pig-headed desires for adventure. All my fault."

She wrapped her arms around his shaking shoulders. "No, Alexander. It isn't your fault. You didn't shove him overboard. It was a terrible accident."

"No, no," he mumbled. "I couldn't hang on to him. He needed me and I wasn't there for him."

Zachariah Miller stood off to one side. Walking over, he picked up the reins where Alexander had dropped them. "I'm sorry for your loss," he said. He turned and led the horse back to its owner.

Caroline placed Alexander's arm across her shoulder, grasped him around the waist, and pulled him along toward their wagon. "Come. Let's get to bed. Sarah's asleep. There's nothing else we can do tonight. We'll deal with this in the morning."

With a heavy grief-stricken heart, she hugged her husband close, for what little consolation he could provide until he fell asleep.

Finally, she rolled onto her side. With tears trickling down her cheeks, she prayed, "Lord, save my son and protect him. If he is dead, may he rest in your arms. If someone finds James alive, please let them care for him as I would. For in my heart, he will always be with me."

Chapter Twenty-One

Oxen plodded blindly ahead one step at a time, stirring up dust with each step. Despondent over the death of his son, Alexander walked with the lead rein in his hand, oblivious to his surroundings. *I'm to blame for James' death. I'm the father. It's my job to care for my children. Why couldn't I have held on a bit longer? Why?*

Casting his eyes upwards, he glanced at Caroline sitting straight as a board, staring ahead, expressionless. Spirit broken, she had stopped speaking except when spoken to and had taken to walking by herself. *How can I support her, when I can't even help myself?* His head ached and his chest hurt. To make matters worse, from trudging in the frigid water, searching for his son, his cold hung on.

The haunting sound of Sarah crying herself to sleep every night broke his heart. His little girl, now an only child, sorely missed her younger brother. A black shroud enveloped the Anderson wagon. He didn't know how to resolve the situation.

Twelve days out of Westport, they reached the Alcove Springs campground, south of the Big Blue River.

Alexander coughed and spit into the dirt. "We're gonna camp here tonight."

"Fine," Caroline replied, climbing down from the wagon. "Your hacking sounds terrible. You need another dose of medicine."

"Nah, I'll be okay. Some days it's better than others."

Alexander ambled to the river's edge where the current swirl past the bank. Caroline joined him.

"The water's at flood stage," he said. "Miller thinks we'll probably cross in about three days. Depending on whether or not we get more rain."

She stared at the water, and then closed her eyes, pain and horror evident on her face. Each crossing reminded her of James.

Alexander poked the toe of his boot into the ground, making dirt clogs roll down the bank. He looped his arm around his wife's shoulders. "You'll have to sit in the wagon and hold Sarah. She'll be hysterical, but we have to get her across." He didn't look forward to the crossing. In fact, he now hated all the rivers in their way.

They reached Fort Kearney and pulled in front of the general store. The Fort consisted of rambling sod and adobe buildings, tents, with some clapboard sheds.

"Need anything while we're stopped?" asked Alexander.

Caroline pondered for a moment. "We could use more flour."

Coughing and holding his chest, Alexander stumbled to the back of the wagon and reached over the gate. Clinking a bottle against the wall, he withdrew the cork and downed a good swig.

She didn't know how many bottles were left. It didn't matter. His cough concerned her, so she made no comment.

"I'll be right back. While I'm there, I'll check to see if John left a message for us." He trudged away, heading for the general store.

"Ma, do you think Uncle John will be there, when we get to California, or is this one big joke he's playing on Pa?"

"Why would you ask that?"

Sarah tilted her head, "He's never where he says he's gonna be."

"I would like to believe your uncle is true to his word. If not, your Pa will be hurt. Let's pray there's a message waiting for him here."

They spied Alexander exiting the Post Office carrying an envelope.

Caroline gave an audible sigh of relief. "Well, what do you know? There's actually a message for your Pa."

Alexander climbed up into the seat. "You won't believe this. I asked for any mail for Anderson and the postmaster gave me this envelope. It's addressed to Sarah."

Sarah's mouth fell open. "Me?"

"My goodness, Sarah," Caroline said, "open it. Let's see who it's from."

Sarah gently slid her finger along the flap and opened the letter.

Dear Sarah,

I know you didn't expect to hear from me so soon, but I think about you all the time. Ma wanted me to write and tell you what has transpired here. That was Ma's word. Anyway, John is an apprentice for Mr. Levi and doing quite well. He made Ma two oak chairs and a table. They look real nice.

Elizabeth is going to school and can read and write. She has decided she wants to become a teacher like Mrs. Peters.

I think she would make a good teacher. Joshua is still himself and misses James a lot.

She stopped reading and gulped. "I guess I have to write the O'Briens and tell them about James. Will you help me, Ma?"

"Yes. Now go on."

I am taking on odd jobs. I like working at the stables and with the horses. Mr. Randolph told me I had a way with them. One day he's gonna let me break the wild ones when they come in.

Ma is doing fine. She misses Pa a lot, but keeps busy helping Mrs. Broadhurst at the boarding house. Since Ma is a good cook, she makes all the meals and gets paid. We're gonna get a small house soon. I haven't forgotten my promise, Sarah. One day when I get enough money saved, I will come to California. I promise.
Patrick O'Brien

"That young man is sweet on you, Sarah," said Alexander. "He sure is determined. Wonder if he knows what he's getting himself into?"

"Alexander," reprimanded Caroline.

Sarah stiffened her back and raised her chin. "Pa, I'm gonna marry Patrick one day." Clutching the cross hanging around her neck, she pressed it to her heart, gently stroking it with her thumb.

"Right now we need to think about getting ourselves to California." Caroline looked at Alexander. "I guess we don't have a message from John."

Shaking his head, Alexander took a deep breath, choked, and coughed violently.

"Are you all right?" asked Caroline as he clutched his chest. He coughed and hacked, spitting bright green phlegm over the side.

Wheezing, he bent over and picked up the lead rope. "Let's go."

For three long, tiring days, Caroline walked next to the oxen while Alexander slept fitfully on a pallet in the wagon. His coughing grew worse and his appetite dwindled. Sarah sat by him, staring out through the back canvas. No one spoke. There was nothing to talk about.

Following the narrow Platte River road along the bluffs, with three yoke of oxen, did not come easy for Caroline. Her hands burned and her feet hurt from walking all day. Blisters covered her fingers from gripping the rope so hard. Miller loaned her his extra pair of work gloves for protection. At night she salved and aired her hands, trying to heal them.

She kept her mind busy, mentally checking over her supplies or trying to calculate the mileage to the next stop. She had plenty of everything, including insect bites. The pesky mosquitoes were everywhere, welts covered most of her exposed skin.

Today, the little nippers swarmed after Sarah, while she walked. She waved her hands about her face, trying to brush them away.

"Ma," she said, "these bites really itch."

Caroline swished her free hand around her daughter's head. "Get some mud on them. It'll stop the itching. Don't scratch them anymore. You're causing them to bleed."

"Mud makes my skin dry and itchy."

"Sarah, I have all I can do to take care of these oxen. Get some mud on those bites and go collect some buffalo chips. Tonight we'll burn a few in the wagon and smoke those annoying buggers out."

Keeping the mosquitoes out of the food while she cooked proved to be the major problem. Last night, the stew had looked heavily peppered.

Her daughter made a face while picking up the chips, placing them in her apron. "Get more buffalo chips, Sarah and leave the bites alone."

Sarah mumbled to herself. "Can't wait until we get somewhere decent. I hate all these bugs and dirt."

"What?"

"Nothing, Ma." She stooped for more chips.

"We'll be stopping soon."

"Ma, my shoes have holes in them and the rocks poke up inside."

"We'll fix them tonight. Now dump those chips in the back and collect as many as you can."

"Yes, Ma," Sarah mumbled. "Buffalo chips. Meadow muffins. What a stupid name for cow poop."

"Caroline," Alexander hoarsely called.

"Sarah, your Pa needs you. Grab the whiskey bottle and take it to him."

Sarah dumped the meadow muffins from her apron and climbed into the wagon.

Caroline's anxiety deepened. Weak and developing a fever, Alexander's cough grew worse. Tonight, she would put some cloves and cayenne pepper in his hot tea. Maybe a steaming piece of flannel placed on his chest might help break up the congestion.

"Sarah," Caroline whispered, "if your Pa's asleep, come on back outside."

Several hours later, a stiff breeze kicked up, swirling the dust around. Loose debris and hats flew through the air, hitting the oxen and wagons. As the winds picked up, massive black clouds rolled across the green sky, blanketing the sun. Darkness surrounded her. Dogs barked, oxen bellowed, and horses nervously kicked up their heels and whinnied.

Panicking, she halted her team and walked around the wagon. "Sarah, where are you?" Dust blew so hard she couldn't see. Sand stung her face like needles. Suddenly, she bumped into her daughter.

Sarah spit. "Ma. This stuff is awful."

"Take my hand and keep your mouth shut," ordered Caroline.

"I can't see."

"Cover your face with your apron. Protect your eyes." Caroline pulled her daughter along struggling to locate the wagon.

Someone yelled, "A tornado's a-comin'!"

Alexander tumbled out of the wagon and fell to his knees. In a frail voice, he called, "Sarah, Caroline." His words were lost in the blowing gale. He crawled until he reached a wheel. Pulling himself up, he peered into the piercing wind. Spotting his wife and daughter about five feet away, he hobbled toward them, tried to grab Caroline's arm, before falling face down.

With Sarah's help, she lifted Alexander up and steadied him.

He pointed ahead, "That way." Wheezing and stumbling back to the wagon, he dropped to the ground. "Squat down. We'll get drenched. Maybe it'll miss us. Stay near the axle, but don't hang on it."

Jagged fingerlings of lightning struck the ground near them as sounds of thunder resounded over and over. The animals dashed around the area in a wild state of fright, bumping wagons and trampling people. Yoder's horse broke loose and galloped out into the open. As the man raced to catch his horse, lightning struck him, hurling Yoder to the other side of the trail, killing him instantly.

Screams and cries sounded like tormented souls. Sarah covered her ears and shrieked. Caroline wrapped one arm around her daughter while holding onto the wheel rim with the other. The wagon jerked and rocked, almost upending several times.

"We're gonna die! I don't want to die."

"Hush, Sarah. We'll be fine." Caroline sat cross-legged in the mud, her head ducked to avoid collision with the floorboards. She clasped her daughter close to her bosom, stroking her hair. In a shaky voice, she hummed a lullaby close to Sarah's ear.

Alexander pointed, "Look."

Caroline saw a large funnel shape slowly descend from the sky, twisting as it touched the ground, dancing wildly to its own music, side to side. Everything loose went swirling through the air. Furious winds, rain, and hail beat the wagons unmercifully, tearing the canvases to shreds. The choking dust made it hard to breathe.

The funnel whipped around picking up people, and even a few oxen. A roaring sound whisked past the Andersons, shaking their wagon violently. Then as quickly as it came, the funnel receded back into the black clouds and the winds calmed down. The hail stopped, as rain drizzled lightly.

"Stay here," said Alexander.

"Let me go."

"No," was all he said. He wheezed and shook his head. "I'm gonna ...check our wagon. See if ...we've lost anything." Slowly, he crawled from under the wagon to the metal rimmed wheel. As he pulled himself up, he had a coughing spell. Stumbling with each step, holding onto the sideboards, hand over hand, holding himself up, he made his way to the front.

In the wake of the storm's path, several people and animals lay scattered about the area like useless pieces of waste. "Ma, there's two dead people over there," Sarah whispered.

Caroline turned her daughter's face toward her. "Close your eyes. Listen to how peaceful it is. No more storm." She began to hum another song.

Sarah interrupted her. "I'm wet through and through. Can I change my clothes?"

"Soon. Now shut your eyes while we wait for Pa." She uncrossed her legs to stop the tingling. *One catastrophe after another. There always seems to be another calamity just around the bend, waiting to bear down on us. When will it end? If it weren't so far, I'd turn around and head back to Virginia.*

Soaked from head to toe, many of the travelers emerged from their hiding places, trying to comprehend the scope of their losses. Petrified, children hung onto their parents.

Alexander dropped to the ground next to her. "Fourteen wagons destroyed. Many others damaged. Some are filled with water."

"How is our gear and animals?"

"Canvas torn. Lost one of the oxen. We're..." He collapsed into her lap.

"Someone, help me, *please*."

Rushing to her aid, Miller lifted Alexander over his shoulder and placed him on the back gate.

Climbing inside, Caroline and Sarah pulled Alexander onto the wet pallet. "Sarah, see if you can find any dry blankets in one of those chests."

Zachariah Miller walked around, talking with the men and assessing the damages before calling a meeting.

"First of all, we need to bury the dead. The best place is on the trail. We'll let the wagons roll over the graves."

People began to object venomously. With indignation, one lady shouted, "That's a sacrilege."

Mrs. Peterson shouted, "How dare you do such a thing?"

"Wait," Miller yelled, holding up his hands. "You don't understand. If we don't bury them this way, wild animals will dig them up. Worse, the Indians will unearth them for their clothing."

The people settled down, stunned by disbelief in what they heard. Miller waited for a few minutes, and then continued. "After we bury our dead, we need to burn the animal carcasses."

He rubbed his hand across his chin. "Since it's too late to move on, we'll camp here tonight. We have work to do, so let's get going." The group disbanded in silence.

Four days later, Caroline walked the trail, driving the oxen. With another storm brewing, sweat trickled down her face. Dirt stuck to her clothes and body. Her feet hurt from walking and she was exhausted.

"I'm tired of rain and blowing wind. When will these storms quit?"

"What did you say?" asked Sarah, half asleep in the wagon.

"Nothing," answered Caroline. She wanted to feel clean and alive again. She dreamed of a long warm soapy bath to ease her aching body. Maybe use some of the pretty lavender soap she had hidden in a box behind the seat.

Later that afternoon, Alexander took a turn for the worse. His high fever made him too weak to sit up. Sarah stayed in the hot wagon, tending to her father.

Totally disheartened and weary, Caroline looked over the horizon of rutted, scrubby-brown landscape and lifeless vegetation. No green grass or tall-canopied trees anywhere, only brown nothingness. Ahead lay Windlass Hill. Several miles into the valley below, the brown world blended into a spread of trees, a small creek, and beautiful green grass of Ash Hollow. First, they needed to tackle the treacherous downhill descent.

Reaching the hill crest, Zachariah Miller and Tom Poston gathered everyone together. "There are three trails down, cut deep with swales from previous travelers. We'll be using the last one, north of the hollow. The descent is about 200 feet and very dangerous. Everything needs to be fastened down tightly in the front of your wagon. Otherwise your belongings will spill out."

"How are we gonna get the wagons below? Look how steep it is. I see wagon parts at the bottom," asked a man in the back.

"If you listen to me," replied Miller, "you won't have any trouble. We need to detach the oxen or horses, one wagon at a time. Then we'll lock the two back wheels with Peterson's chain and wrap it through the wheels so they'll drag."

"How long do you think it'll take?" asked Caroline. The men became silent.

"All day," answered Poston. "It's not an easy job. If we all work together as a team, we'll get down safe and sound. Don't you worry, Miz Anderson. One of the men will help you with your wagon. Stay in line."

"Thank you. I appreciate that."

"Have you ever been down here before, Poston?" asked a short stout man.

"Twice," he replied.

"All right." said Miller. "I'll need twelve men at the top to handle the rope that we'll fasten to the wagon's axle, just like last time. You four men will hold the wagon tongue to steer it down. Stay with the wagon and stay clear of the wheels. We don't want ya to git run over."

Mr. Peterson stood up. "Why can't we use the oxen to get the wagon down? Holding the tongue is dangerous."

"The oxen can't stop a runaway wagon. If you lose your oxen and crash your wagon at the bottom, you and your family will be walkin' the rest of the way. Besides, no one will get hurt if you listen to me and Poston." He paused a moment to get his point across. "I'm gonna need two men on each side to help ease the wagon across those ruts."

Standing next to Mrs. Peterson, Caroline looked over the edge and spied the trees in the distance. Beyond lay the sweet water creek and luscious green grass.

"We'll finally get to fill our casks," said Caroline. "With nothing but alkaline water for the past three days, fresh is gonna taste good."

"I can't wait to wash this filth off my children," Mrs. Peterson said. "They look and smell like a litter of pigs. Thought I left the farm behind."

Caroline smiled weakly. "Wouldn't it be nice to sit in a tub filled with warm soapy water right now?"

"My goodness, it's been so long. My hair's a mess, my hands look like my husband's, and I won't mention my nails."

"I know what you mean." Caroline sighed, "We're not even half-way to California yet."

"We're going to Oregon and it's a little farther. Poston's taking us there. We'll be splitting up at Fort John."

"Miller told us last night they changed the fort's name. It sounds French." Caroline thought for a moment. "Fort Laramie. That's the name."

"I guess, before we can think about the Fort or taking on fresh water over there, we have to tackle this here hill. Sure looks dangerous. It's straight down. Lord, I hope my man's careful."

"Good luck," replied Caroline.

The two women fell silent for a moment.

"I should be getting back to my family. Looks like the men are still discussing this hill."

Mrs. Peterson spied her children. "Arthur, get down from there. Ann, pick up your little brother so he doesn't eat any more dirt. Next thing you'll know, he'll be turning brown. Thank heavens the baby's sleeping."

Caroline chuckled. "You certainly do have your hands full. Your oldest is seven?"

Mrs. Peterson and Caroline strolled back to the wagons. "Yes. They're seven, five, three, and one. They're all healthy, just tired, dirty, and a little cranky, like their mother."

Caroline shook her head. "You can't keep the dust off your body or out of the wagon."

Descending Windlass Hill took all day and into the close of the evening. When Tom Poston reached the bottom safely with her wagon, Caroline heaved a sigh of relief. Next, the men made a litter to carry Alexander down the steep embankment. Four men hoisted the end posts onto their shoulders, trying to keep it level. Strapping Alexander down to keep him from sliding off, the men sat down into the dirt, digging their boots into the ground as they made their way toward the bottom.

Caroline gasped as the men tried to keep their balance. Dirt and rocks flew over their pants' legs, but no one dropped the litter. Finally, reaching bottom, they carried Alexander to his wagon and placed him on a pallet. Caroline tucked him in, gave him some cool water laced with quinine to help him sleep.

She put her arm around her daughter's shoulder. "We need to get something to eat."

Tom Poston approached her. "Miz Anderson, your wagon's all lined up and oxen unhitched for the evenin'."

"Why thank you Mr. Poston. Sure does a body good to know you're around."

"No trouble, ma'am. In case you're interested, people are gonna gather tonight for some music. Be nice if you and little Miss could join us."

"We'll see, Mr. Poston. It all depends on Mr. Anderson."

Tom Poston tipped his hat and then walked away.

Early the next morning, Caroline rose, tired and exhausted. She'd spent most of the night attending to Alexander. Bending over him, her heart filled with despair. His breathing was still labored and his face lacked color. His condition deteriorating, she agonized over every aspect of the journey again and again, trying to decide what to do. Coming to a decision, she left the wagon in search of Zachariah Miller. She found him alone on the other side of the campground, saddling his horse. She stood about ten feet behind him for a moment. Was she making the right choice? Weary from the arduous journey and all of the hard work these past few weeks, she came to one conclusion.

"Excuse me, Mr. Miller. I need to speak with you."

"Yes, ma'am, what's troublin' ya?"

"Alexander has lung fever. I've been trying to nurse him, with Sarah's help, but handling the oxen all day and doing camp chores takes away from my caring for my husband. His fever is constant and his pulse weak. Most of the times he's delirious. I've decided to pull out of the train and stay here until Alexander is better. I don't want to lose him."

"Are ya sure this is what you want ta do, Miz Anderson?"

"Yes. I believe continuing down the trail will worsen his condition. Every bump is excruciating for him."

"We'll be takin' on fresh water before we leave. But we could stay one day."

Caroline shook her head. "No, we'll need more time than one or two days. Besides these wagons must get through the pass before the snow flies. We'll probably be here at least a week, depending on my husband and how fast he recuperates. I'll join up with the next group coming over the hill. At least they can get us to the Fort where we'll winter over."

Miller paused for a moment and scratched his head. "If you've decided to stay put, we'll move your wagon down the line to Ash Hollow in the morning. There's wood for your fire, good water, and plenty of grazin' area for your oxen. We don't want you campin' here. The next train comin' down the hill might run over ya."

Caroline followed the wagons along the valley, then turned off the trail and headed to the edge of the trees near the creek. Tom Poston rode along to make sure she was set up and settled in before he left.

"Ma'am. This here is the best place for you to camp. Water's near by and the shade'll make it cooler for ya. The next wagon train should be coming over that hill in four or five days. Don't know who's guidin' it. If you tell him what happened, I'm sure you can trail with 'em."

"Thank you, Mr. Poston."

"Yes ma'am. Now, is there anything you'll be needin' before I take off?"

"No. You've done enough."

He touched the brim of his hat, climbed into the saddle and rode away.

"Be safe," she hollered after him. "Be real safe," she whispered.

He galloped across the open field to catch up with the wagons.

Alone and edgy, Caroline took a small pistol from under the bench seat and placed it in her dress pocket. *Never know when I might need a gun.*

Chapter Twenty-Two

On the Trail from Fort Laramie

John pushed his horse to a gallop, leaving Fort Laramie behind him. Luck was on his side so far. The full moon slid out from behind the clouds, lighting the trail.

Come morning, Conway and the half-breed would be in hot pursuit. The two desperados knew this territory better than he did. Being the prey out here wasn't good. He also had a small living burden riding behind him.

Slackening his speed to a lope, he shouted over his shoulder, "Slow down." He knew driving the horses too hard could be devastating in the dead of night. "No sense in wearing the horses down. Might break a leg or something. Don't want to walk to California."

Looking over his shoulder, he checked on Micah. His son rode like a true veteran. John shook his head and muttered, "Must be having trouble with my eyes or just plain tired. I'd swear I'm seeing double back there." Pointing ahead, he yelled, "Up ahead is Register Hill. We'll stop there."

"Okay," Micah answered.

Dismounting, dust swirled about as John swished his hat across his trousers legs. Micah pulled up beside him and Boy Who Spits Far slid off the horse's rear.

John's mouth flew open. He grabbed the Indian by the scruff of the neck. "What in tarnation are you doing here?"

Micah quickly dropped to the ground and flung himself at his father, grabbing his arm. "Wait, Pa. He saved your life back there. Besides, he needs us. He's got no place to go."

Jaw muscles twitching, John stared at both of them, face red with anger. Releasing the Indian, he shoved the boy away and scowled. "Look. I want the two of you to understand something. I can hardly take care of myself let alone two boys. We don't have enough food or horses and your horse can't handle two riders."

Boy Who Spits Far squared his shoulders. "I run."

John narrowed his eyes. "What do you mean you'll run? Where are you gonna run to?"

"I hold horse's tail. Run fast." Then he slapped Micah on his chest. "We switch. I ride and he run."

Micah waved both hands in front of him and shook his head. "Hold on a minute. I don't hold any horse's tail and run. Not me."

"Hmmm. You act like girl. Need teach you things."

"Well, let me teach you…."

"Hold it!" John shouted, separating the boys. "I'm tired and I don't want to hear this crap right now. We'll discuss it later. At the moment, you have a couple of jobs to do. First, grab some of the dry stuff around here and make a fire. The moon's bright enough for you to see. Then, take care of the horses before you rest."

In the darkness, the two boys picked up pieces of kindling. "Just wait," said Micah. "My pa'll come around. He can't send you back now without a horse."

"Watch out for snakes!" John shouted.

Micah dropped his bundle. "Snakes? This trip ain't getting' any better. We'll be lucky to see California alive." He carefully poked at the wood with the toe of his boot. When nothing crawled out, he gathered everything up and hastily returned to the campsite.

"Snake good. Yum"

Micah scrunched up his nose. "Yuck. Remind me never to let you cook."

Spits Far knelt on the ground, opened the strike-a-light bag hanging at his side, and took out his striker and flint. He motioned to Micah. "Put grass here." Micah placed a handful of dried grass on the sandy dirt. The Indian boy nestled his hands close to the grass and struck the stone against his knife several times. Sparks ignited the grass. As it smoldered, he placed his hands on the ground, leaned over and carefully blew into the smoke. Once the flame caught, he added a few sticks, one at a time.

"Now take care of the horses," John said, nodding toward the animals.

Working together, the Indian boy held up the stirrups while Micah undid the cinch. "See, I told you my Pa would settle down. Be quiet. Let me do the talkin'."

John placed his tack on the ground and growled. "When you're through, hobble my horse, too. If you're going with me, you'll both work."

The boys stared at each other and smiled. When they finished their chores, they returned to the fire.

"We've only put about eight miles behind us. Get some rest. We'll be moving on soon." John didn't have to repeat himself. The boys flopped onto the ground, their heads against the saddle, and fell fast asleep.

Several hours later, John kicked their feet. "All okay, let's go."

Micah jumped up, eyes wide, ready to fight. "Where are they?"

Boy Who Spits Far moved swiftly to his feet. Taking a wide defensive stance, he waved a knife in front of him.

John chuckled. "You two a little edgy? Settle down and put the knife away. Nobody's here."

Micah scratched his head and grabbed his hat. "I guess we fell asleep."

"I'd say ya did." John saddled his horse. "Come on. Gotta get going. Not enough mileage between us and the Fort."

Micah grabbed the saddle and waited for the Indian boy to throw the blanket over the horse's back.

Spits Far pointed. "You ride. I run."

"Can you really do that? Sounds half-witted to me."

"Let him be, son." John mounted his horse. "Indians learn early how to travel on foot. He'll do fine. Now listen up, you two. The trail's gonna get a bit rocky in places so follow my lead. Micah, if you get tired, don't fall off your horse."

Micah pursed his lips together, eyeballed his father, and mumbled several indistinguishable words. The Indian boy smirked.

"Quit talking, let's go." John shouted.

After Register Hill, John and the boys rode toward the old Ward and Gerrier Trading Post. John hailed the cabin. "Hello in there. Anybody up?"

At first, no one stirred, then a light flickered inside and the door creaked open. A seedy old man in red wool-flannel underwear held a lantern high. "Who's out there? Don't ya know what time it is?"

"Sorry to bother you so late. We're in need of a horse. Got one for sale?"

"You wanna buy a horse tonight? Are ya crazy or in trouble?" The old man walked to the edge of the porch, stretched his neck to view the riders. "Who ya got behind ya there? Looks like young'uns to me." He scratched his scrawny neck with his free hand and turned, facing the door. "Ya might as well come in. Need to get the boy up to get a horse for ya. Need tack too?"

"Yes. My boys are riding double and we have a long way to go." They entered the two-room cabin. The sparsely furnished smaller room housed a table, two benches in the center and a bed in the corner. The other room served as the post for supplies.

"Hmmm. In trouble, are ya? Sit down and have some coffee. At least I think it's still warm. Can't say much for the taste. Been there a few days. Strong enough to grow hair on your tongue." He walked to the loft ladder and shouted, "Lucas, get your bony ass down here and git this man a horse and saddle."

The boys sat down on the opposite bench from John. The old man tossed three metal cups onto the table. "My name's Seth Ward. Help yourselves. Service quit three months ago when my partner left for supplies in St. Louie." The man shouted again, "Boy, ya stirrin' up there?"

Ward sat down on the bench next to John. "Ya know this here horse is gonna cost ya for getting me out of my warm bed."

"How much you talking about?"

"Humph, like you got a lot ta deal with." He scratched his grizzly beard and eyeballed the boys. "Let me see now. Nothing too big or too wild." He paused for a moment. "Forty dollars."

"Forty dollars," shouted John. "No horse out here is worth forty dollars."

"Take it or leave it." Ward got up and poured himself some coffee.

The boys kept quiet, but stared at John as he haggled with the old man.

"I'll give you twenty five and that's top dollar."

"Nope, won't take less than thirty five." He thought for a moment. "If ya leave the Indian kid here with me, I'll sell you the horse for thirty."

John looked at the boys.

Micah dropped his empty cup. "Pa!" His father waved his hand.

Ward smiled. "Got yourself a real mix goin' for ya there fella. Indian and a nigger. You must have been pokin' all sorts of women."

"Ain't none of your business. Now, about that *golden* horse you're wanted to sell me." Rolling the empty cup in his fingers, John's temper began to show.

"Well, I'll tell ya what. You stay the night, throw your stuff over in that there corner and the boys can help Lucas with the chores tomorrow. Then I'll sell you a horse for thirty dollars."

"No, we can't stay. If they catch us, they'll kill my Pa."

"Micah, be quiet."

"Sounds like you got yourself into a parcel of trouble there, Mister. So, you got a good-for-nothing chasin' ya, huh? Dang blame it, I'll give ya the horse at twenty-eight. No lower, ya hear me? A body's got to git some sleep around here and I ain't about to haggle all night."

Lucas stood at the bottom of the ladder, arm resting on a rung, listening to Old man Ward haggle with a stranger over the price of the horse. "You want me to git the little gray mare for this man?"

"Yes, she'll do fine for one of the kids. She's sure-footed, tame, and flies like the wind. Bet your Indian would like to ride her. You want a saddle? That'll be another twenty five dollars."

Boy Who Spits Far stood up, face stern. "Blanket."

John looked at Ward. "Changed my mind. All I need is a blanket."

"Didn't think he'd use a saddle. Got a nice blanket for two dollars." The old man rose to his feet and shuffled over to the corner. He picked up a dingy horse blanket from off the floor and began beating the dust off. "Like brand new."

"It looks brand new. All right. Get the gray mare and we'll take the blanket. You boys get yourself some coffee because when he brings the horse around front, we're leaving."

"Suits me fine. Ya gotta pay first, before Lucas gits the horse."

John counted out thirty dollars. The old man recounted the money, placed it in a box over the fireplace then took a drink from his cup. "Lucas, git the mare. Toss in a bit of rope for the kid to have a bridle. Can't have him hangin' onto the mane all the way to wherever he's goin'." Then he tossed the blanket to Boy Who Spits Far. "This here's for you."

Ward swirled the coffee in his cup, took a sip, and then cleared his throat. "You needin' supplies? Or are ya all gonna eat grass and sand on this here trip?" His smile spread from ear to ear, devious and sure.

John cringed. He hated being clipped by a wizened old man who had him by the balls. "Let's see what you have and how much these supplies are gonna cost me."

Ward set down his cup, ambled over to the shelves, and began stacking beans, coffee, and cornmeal on the counter.

After dickering over the bill, John and the boys packed up their bags and stepped outside, followed by Ward. When

Lucas came back, he handed the rope to the Indian. Deftly, the Indian boy looped it, fashioning a makeshift bridle, before tossing the loose ends up over the horse's neck. Micah flung the blanket over its back.

Moving close to the porch, the Indian boy took one deft leap onto the back of the little gray mare. "Horse named Moonlight. Shines like silver. Good spirit."

"Yes," said John, "and expensive." He threw a heavy saddlebag over Moonlight's hindquarters and did likewise to Micah's horse. "Whatever you boys do, don't lose the supplies."

Reaching up, Micah adjusted the additional supply load behind the saddle cantle, placed his bedroll and his personal gear on top of the bags, and lashed it all down with the saddle ties. Then he climbed onto the porch, placed his foot into the stirrup and mounted his horse.

John threw the new pouches across the saddle horn.

Ward leaned against the doorjamb, lantern resting on the porch flooring. "Who's comin' in the mornin'?"

"An ornery, nasty fellow and a half-breed," replied John.

"Well, I ain't seen ya, if you're interested. Just get those young'uns somewhere safe."

Lucas stood by the little mare rubbing her nose. "She's a good horse. Take care of her."

Boy Who Spits Far nodded then made a sign with his hand. Lucas returned the gesture.

"Let's go. The sun'll be up soon and we have to make a few more miles tonight." John touched the brim of his hat to Ward.

Lucas waved as the three rode off into the night heading west.

* * *

Billy Conway and George Crow rose early, ate a good breakfast then headed for the public house.

Conway flipped a coin onto the bar. "Barkeep. Set one up for me and my friend here." The taverner grabbed a bottle off the shelf, poured two drinks, and picked up the money.

Crow leaned close to Conway. "I've been checkin' around, askin' about this Anderson fella. Seems he's headed to the California hills, near Hangtown. Has a piece of property there."

"You get the name?"

"Yep. Tracer's Point." Crow downed the shot.

"Think we can get there before he does?" His smiled deviously. "Want another?"

"Yep."

Billy shoved his glass toward the barkeep, holding up two fingers.

"We'll catch 'em," said Crow. "I can track better than any man in this territory."

"What about this place in California?"

"We'll find them. People can't help seein' a man and two boys, one being an Indian."

"Good." Billy took a large swig and wiped his mouth on the back of his hand. "Then all we have to do is get our gear together and head out. No need to rush. With that extra live baggage tailin' behind him, Anderson ain't goin' nowhere fast. Three people and two horses make for a slow trip."

Crow smiled. "If they make it at all." His smug attitude showed in his face, confidence riding high.

Both men laughed.

Conway enjoyed a good hunt, especially human prey. He downed the last of his drink, paid the barkeep, and grabbed his hat. "Let's go."

Outside, they picked up their equipment off the porch and headed out to the corral for their horses.

"Let's get out of here before the lieutenant wants to talk to us again. I'm tired of his questions. We'll get some supplies before we cross the river," said Conway.

"Word is, he's leavin' sometime this week. He don't want no more paperwork."

"I want to make sure we're out of here before he starts his rounds."

The two men saddled their horses, left the Fort, and headed across the parade grounds for the Sutler's General Store.

Several miles from the Fort, Crow said, "There's a tradin' post up ahead. Ya wanna stop?"

"Yep. Anderson might have stopped there last night."

An old man sat in a beat up old chair on the post porch.

"Hey, you," yelled Conway. "You seen any riders last night passing this way? Maybe a man with two kids?"

Ward took draw on his pipe and blew the smoke out real slow. "Nope," and stuck the pipe back into his mouth.

Billy Conway eyed him wearily. "Seems strange ya didn't see 'em. You sure they didn't stop here?"

Ward shook his head.

Lucas walked through the doorway, hands in his pockets.

"Boy. You seen any strangers travelin' through here last night?"

"Nope," Lucas said and walked back inside.

Conway narrowed his eyes. "These two are pissin' me off. Let's go."

As they rode away, George Crow asked, "You want me to go back and stick the two of 'em?"

"Nah. We got better things to do."

"Yep. Like cuttin' that little bastard's balls off."

"Easy, Crow. First, we get Anderson, then the two brats. I want Anderson ta know who he's dealin' with."

"Long and painful?"

With a cunning smile, Conway repeated, "Uh-huh, long and painful."

John and the boys stopped at the Cottonwood Camp Grounds around midnight. Only a couple of campfires smoldered in the center of the wagon train ring. They took care of their horses, threw their bedrolls under a couple tall trees, and collapsed into deep sleep.

A trumpet blast brought the two boys to their feet. "What was that?" yelled Micah.

They stood wide-eyed in the chilly air.

"Settle down," said John. "The trumpeter is only waking up the wagon folks. Get yourselves presentable. Maybe we can grab some homemade food from some of these nice people."

The boys scrambled to roll up their bedding.

Stars were still visible in the hazy gray sky, and shades of pink tipped along the horizon. Early morning campfires dotted the area.

"Morning comes too dern soon." John reached up and rubbed the itchy stubble on his chin. *Might as well let it grow. No sense in whacking if off.*

Children scurried by Micah yelling at each other. "This place is wild as St. Louie."

A large German lady waved to the three. "You come eat vhile the food is varm. Fill dose boys out. Come," she beckoned to them.

Micah and Boy Who Spits Far turned to John. "Can we?"

"Why not. Make yourselves presentable."

Micah dusted off his trousers, rubbed his hands across the seat of his pants and headed toward the delicious smells of breakfast. Boy Who Spits Far, followed closely, straightening his loincloth as he walked.

A tall rough looking man moved to block their path. "Where do ya two pukes think you're going?"

Micah sneered at the man and lied. "We ain't pukes from Missoura. We're gold miners on our way to California."

"Okay, and I'm the King of England, nigger." He took two steps in Micah's direction. "Ya know, I could..."

Suddenly, the man sprawled face forward into the dirt.

"You don't touch dat child. Do you hear me?" The German lady stood over him with a skillet in her hand. "Next time, I knock your brains out. Now, you two boys scoot. Go eat before it gits cold."

Without being told a second time, Micah and Boy Who Spits Far raced to the small table, each grabbed a metal plate and began loading up the food.

John walked up to the lady. "Thank you, ma'am. Couldn't have done better myself. My boys haven't had it easy this trip. Your kindness is appreciated."

"Vell, I don't take kindly to cruelty to animals or children." She wiped her hand on her big white apron, and then extended it. "My name is Hermione Schmidt. My husband over dere is Heinrich. Ve go to live vith our son in Oregon."

"My name's John Anderson."

"Vell, come eat. You're skin and bones. Need some fillin' out, too."

Mrs. Schmidt followed John. As she passed the man grabbling in the dirt, trying to get to his hands and knees, she stepped on his hand. "Oh, sorry."

"Ahhhhh!" he screamed. "That fat thing broke my hand."

"Fat indeed." Holding the skillet in both hands, she said, "I'll have ya know I'm vell formed."

Meekly, the man lay there, rubbing his hand, nodding his head in agreement. "Yes, ma'am."

"Dat's better. Now, I have vork to do," she said, heading for her wagon.

"Hermione, you could have hurt him." Mr. Schmidt kept one eye on the man in question. Turning back to face his wife and he shook his head, chuckling, "Oh my, vhat a voman."

"Vell, next time he von't pick on someone smaller. Fat indeed." Mrs. Schmidt waved her hand. "Now, sit, eat. Da food is getting cold."

"What's that?" Micah asked, pointing to her small square cook stove.

"My Heinrich made dat for me. It is vhat I cook on."

Her husband smiled at the two boys who sat shoveling food into their mouths. "I was a stove maker in Prussia."

"That's a real nice thing to have on this trip," said John.

"Yes, indeed," replied Mr. Schmidt. "Vhere are you headed?"

"To California. I have a piece of land out there in the hills. My brother and his family are behind me a bit, in a wagon. They're coming out to help me work my gold claim." John filled his plate with fried potatoes, a hunk of ham, several eggs, and two buttered biscuits. On the table sat two jars of homemade jam.

"Mmmm. This is real fine, Miz Schmidt. Haven't eaten like this since I don't remember when."

With eyes wide and mouths full, the boys nodded in unison.

Mrs. Schmidt poured each of them a tin cup full of milk and smiled. "Ve have a cow. She gives good milk."

John couldn't move the fork fast enough.

"Get your wagons together. We leave in half an hour," yelled the wagon master. He stopped at the Schmidt's and stood eyeballing John and the two boys.

"You joinin' up with us? If so, you pay me. We're headed for Oregon." He stood waiting for an answer.

"No, we're headed for California. Just stopping through. Happened to see your campfires last night and decided it was safer to bunk the boys here than out yonder."

"I guess it won't cost ya anything since you're not headed our way. You can ride with us a-ways if you want. We'll be slower than what you can travel by yourself, especially when we hit the mountain passes." The wagon master turned and walked away, shouting orders to several of the men standing around.

"Are ya sure you don't vant to travel vith us?" Mr. Schmidt asked.

"Oh, yah. Ve vould like to have you join our travels. Heinrich could use da help."

The two boys' eyes pleaded with him.

"No, ma'am. We're traveling fast and need to get going, but thank you for the invite."

He placed his plate and fork on the table, shook Mr. Schmidt's hand. "Enjoyed the lovely fixings. Never had better."

"Yes, ma'am. They were real good," said Micah, wiping his mouth on his sleeve.

Boy Who Spits Far nodded and made a sign.

"I guess he liked the food, too," said Mr. Schmidt, laughing as he ruffled the Indian's hair.

"We have to go. You're mighty hospitable."

The two boys and John walked away, gathered up their belongings, and saddled their horses.

As they rode away, Micah turned and waved. Memories of Black Molly flashed before him as Mrs. Schmidt stared after them, wiping her hands on her big white apron.

Chapter Twenty-Three

George Crow and Billy Conway eased their hunger with a late meal of stale biscuits and a hunk of roasted rabbit from the makeshift spit. Warming themselves in front of a dwindling fire, they passed dessert back and forth, a bottle of cheap whiskey. There was no need to hurry, they'd find Anderson.

Conway made others pay for their mistakes. Only this wasn't a big mistake. The bastard had murdered his brother.

He settled back, talking about this 'human' chase, making plans on how he'd deal with his prey when he caught John and the two boys. The more he drank, the meaner he talked, dreaming up excruciating torture. Hatred ruled supreme. His thoughts grew wilder with each sip.

He waved his hand in front of him in a zigzag pattern. "I'm gonna cut him first. Make him real sorry for what he did to Pete. Not enough to kill 'im, mind ya. Just enough to make 'im bleed and hear 'im howl."

"Then what?" Crow took another swig, his piercing dark eyes glistening.

"Then, I'm gonna bury him in the sand up to his neck like you Indians do in the desert and trickle molasses around his head."

"Uh-huh. Uh-huh. Go on." Crow grew excited as he imagined the pain and terror in John's eyes. He wiped the drool and liquor from his lips on the back of his sleeve.

"Then all we have to do is wait for the ants to...."

Crow interrupted. "I'm gonna take and hamstring him like my Pa did to a fella once up in the mountains. This fella stole one of his horses, made him real mad. So Pa cut the man good. We all got excited as he twitched and cried, jerkin' about on the ground. Then we strung him up in a tree with a rope around his chest. The man hung there all day in the sun waitin', twitchin', and moanin'. That night, the animals came and, and..." He closed his eyes, a cruel smile on his face, and flopped sideways onto his blanket.

"We'll get that sonofabitch. Kill my brother, will he." Conway leaned his head back against a tree. The warmth from the fire and the soothing liquor inside mellowed him. "You wait, we'll get 'em. Yep. He'll...be sorry." The bottle slowly slipped from his grip.

The gradual ascent into South Pass proved to be easy for John and the boys, the long climb spreading twenty miles wide from mountain range to mountain range. Ahead the ground met the sky, clouds resting on the horizon, touching the dividing line, blending land and sky. The fat puffy clouds tumbled across the horizon in front of Micah. Ahead the wagon swales disappeared into the distance, the land stuck between snow-covered mountains. The air, thin and crisp, a cold gusty wind tugged at him, flapping his jacket tails sideways.

"Are we gonna stop soon?" asked Micah. "Seems to be gettin' colder."

His Pa nodded and pointed ahead.

Spits Far rode silently beside him. He wasn't much company today.

"Hey, where ya at?" asked Micah.

"Mountains remind me of home."

"You miss home."

"No. Mountains." The Indian stared ahead.

"Where?"

"You talk too much."

"What're you mad about? I only asked a question." Micah hated it when his friend was testy.

They rode in silence for a half an hour with only the sound of the swirling wind across the land. The big red sun edged toward the mountaintops. Cold and hungry, Micah's butt felt swollen and his knees hurt from chaffing against the saddle. If only his legs were a little longer, he could grip the horse's belly better.

Ahead, his pa eased up and sat waiting. Elated, all Micah wanted to do was fall out of his saddle, put his feet on steady ground, and eat.

John checked behind him. He knew the boys were ready to stop, especially Micah, but he wanted to get closer to the end of the plateau. Daylight ebbed, vanishing beneath the surface of the horizon. Every day, every mile counted. He needed to get the boys to safety in California. Tosetti, his partner, would help him. Italians were family men.

He hooked his leg over the saddle horn and waited for the boys to catch up. How did he ever get so many snarls in his life? This venture had started out easy. Go to Virginia to convince his brother that gold waited for him, stop off in St. Louis to say hello to D'Alene, then back to California to work the gold claim. A straightforward, easy plan. Suddenly, life had turned on him, dealing him a difficult hand he hadn't planned on playing. Now he was saddled with two young'uns and snarled up in a bad card game that had turned into murder.

The worse part is the two ignoramuses tracking me are armed and dangerous, not to mention crazy .One extremely, life-threatening situation. Conway is blood thirsty, and hot on my trail. I have to be daft and losing my grip. I must have taken a wrong turn back there somewhere in life. The problem is how do I backtrack to straighten out this mess?

"Hey, boys." John pointed ahead. "Let's camp over there. Sun'll be down soon. No sense pushing the horses."

Dismounting, John hauled the food pouch with him. "I'll set up the grub while you boys tend the animals. There's cold fixings tonight."

Later, John sat cross-legged on the ground in front of the fire's dying embers, gazing out over the soft curves of the land lying between the two white-tipped mountain ranges. He closed his eyes and clasped his hands together, resting his forearms on his legs. A soft muffled whinny, a clop of a hoof, whispers of young male voices, and sounds of the night drifted with the cool breeze. Picking up a stick beside him, he fiddled with it, drawing circles in the sandy soil, back and forth. Soft, gentle curves. His longing for Caroline grew. He felt hollow inside. What did his life really amount to?

The sun glowed a brilliant red as it inched behind the mountains. He envisioned Caroline's auburn hair flowing down to the gentle curves of her shoulders, her breasts full and rounded under her close-fitting bodice. His felt a hardness thrust against his Kentucky jeans, making him uncomfortable. Every thought of her made him miserable. He loved her, yet she could never be his, and life wouldn't be the same without her. Tonight, when the darkness arrived, he knew his shell of a frame would be cold and aching for the touch of her body, the warmth of her velvet skin. Tonight and forever, he had nothing.

"Red sure is a pretty color on a woman." Micah stood behind him.

"Red what?" asked Boy Who Spits Far.

"Red hair." Micah grew testy. "You're always asking questions."

John laughed. "You two sound like you're married."

"Ha. That'll never be, thank goodness." Micah sat down next to his father. "You miss her, don't ya? Do you think she's still comin' with her family?"

"Yes." John stared ahead.

"Who?" Spits Far crossed his ankles and nimbly sat down next to Micah.

"A redheaded woman from back east." Micah shook his head at the Indian. "Ya know she'll never belong to you."

"I know that." John scanned the horizon. The last of the sunset turned the sky blood red.

"He wants woman. We steal him one." The Indian threw a stick into the glowing embers.

"Nah," said Micah. "He's in love with this lady from Virginia. Problem is she's married to his brother."

"Bad stuff. Another man's woman. You need own woman. Strong Indian squaw. One good in bed."

"Yep, one that's good in bed," repeated Micah.

"Where's all this advice coming from? I can't believe I'm talking to you two about women, and you who haven't even started shaving." John paused for a moment. A snicker escaped, then laughter rolled out as he slapped his knees. "An Indian squaw! Hell, that takes it. I have enough trouble with two half-pint boys, let alone a woman."

The boys laughed and shoved each other, tumbling in

the dirt while John sat shaking his head. *Maybe it isn't half bad having 'em around. They certainly keep life interesting.*

He shot the boys a look as they romped beside him. "You know, I was sitting here thinking my life didn't amount to much. I plum forgot I have two ungrateful sons to take care of."

"Ungrateful?" Micah stuck his chin out. "We're the best thing you've got right now."

He reached out and ruffled his son's hair. "Yes, I agree. It's time to call it a night. Go get some shut-eye. Morning comes mighty early. From here on in, the trip's gonna be rough. We have some nasty terrain to cover and water will be scarce."

The boys left without being told a second time. John put out the fire. Rough wasn't the word for the rest of the trip. Water was scarce and most of it was rancid. The alkaline desert waiting out there for them would be a challenge.

The cold was blowing in off the mountains that surrounded them. Micah and Boy Who Spits Far scrunched their bodies close for warmth under a couple of blankets. He needed to come up with something to cover the Indian's worn moccasins. The responsibility for the two boys weighed heavily on his mind. There was no doubt the three of them would make the digs. He only hoped they'd get there before Conway.

Two and a half miles down the steep 300-foot descent of South Pass brought John and the boys to Pacific Springs. Dark green grass moved across the horizon in a pleasant wave, a beautiful peaceful sight.

Dismounting, Micah shouted, "Look, the grass moves." He pressed a toe of his boot into a small mound of green and it quivered. "Never saw grass do that."

"Strange place," said the Indian boy.

"Be careful," warned John. "Watch where you…."

Spits Far took one step and sank quickly up to his thighs.

John bolted past the horses toward the Indian. "Don't move, don't wiggle, hold still," he commanded, as the boy struggled in the bog. "You'll only make it worse."

The boy sank to his buttocks.

Micah stood stock-still, not knowing what to do. "What's that?"

"Quagmire, like quicksand." John flopped onto his belly and stretched out toward the Indian boy. "Micah, hold my ankles while I try to grab him. Son! Do you hear me?"

Micah jumped into action. "Okay. All right." He knelt down and grabbed both of his Pa's ankles, holding on for dear life.

"Good. Now, when I say pull, do so, as hard as you can." John reached his hands out to the trapped lad. "Stretch out your arms and tighten them. I'm gonna grab you under your armpits."

Spits Far did as he was told.

John reached around the boy's chest and clasped his hands together. He pulled and inched his way backwards with Micah's help. The quagmire made a sucking sound as the Indian boy eased out of the miry grass, onto solid ground.

Dragging him toward the horses, John said, "You're a bit sticky, my friend."

The Indian boy lifted one foot. "Moccasin's gone."

Glancing at the boy's waist, John nodded, "That's not all you lost."

The Indian lowered his head, and then quickly clasped his hands together over his exposed maleness. His loincloth was missing.

"Well, you can't call your backside shiny," remarked Micah standing behind the two of them.

"Humph!" was Spits Far's indignant reply, as he moved away from their open stares.

"Let's get the dirt off and we'll...." John spotted a small protruding object sticking out of the miry grass. Kneeling down, he grabbed a stick, stuck it a couple of inches into the mud, and slowly retrieved a length of muddy cloth. He extended it toward the naked boy. "Here, I believe this belongs to you."

Micah stretched his hand and grabbed the cloth with two fingers. "I'll hold it for him. Seems to have his hands full right now."

"Not funny," replied the Indian boy, walking stiff-legged in a straddled gait. He tried to extract some gooey clumps by shaking one leg.

"Better get the mud off before it hardens," said John. "Might have to drag you to California."

"Need any help?" Micah roared with laughter.

They spent the next half-hour cleaning off the muddy mess from the boy's body. Then, filling two canteens each to the brim with sweet spring water from the creek, they rode away. The Indian boy squirmed a little in the saddle, trying to adjust the wet loincloth between his legs, making a squishing noise beneath his bottom.

"Uncomfortable?" asked Micah.

"Yes."

"I have to say one thing." Micah gazed toward the Indian's lower body. "You're something, all right."

Spits Far sat straight, squaring his shoulders, a proud look on his face. "Me Indian."

"Oh, ya," replied Micah. "Well, I'm Creole." He pursed his lips together and gave a cocky nod. Then he broke out into a giggle as both boys eyeballed John.

Hearing their snickers behind him, John turned in the

saddle to face the boys, suspicious of their sudden merriment. "Now, what are you two talking about?"

"Nothing," they chorused, breaking out into fits of laughter.

"Let's settle down and move a little faster," he called out over his shoulder. "We've wasted too much time. Still have a full day's ride. Need to put some miles behind us. It'll be warmer up ahead in the basin. May do some walking later to help the horses out."

He chuckled and shook his head. *Boys discovering themselves. What a trip this is becoming. Next they'll want to use my razor, or worse, girls. I know I'm not ready for any of this.*

Ahead lay the Big Sandy, a dry streambed tainted with alkali water. It was the dry season. John knew you had to dig deep for drinkable water.

"Hey. There's a large wagon train camped there. Maybe we can get some warm fixin's again," said Micah.

"We'll see. Have to be over sixty wagons circled. Not sure we want to get involved with this group. Let me do the talking."

They rode into camp greeting people along the way. The response was less than friendly. Tired from a hard day's grueling work and hungry, the families weren't anxious to talk with strangers. John rode off in search of the wagon master. The man sat on his horse giving directions to two men finishing a water dig.

He stared John down as he approached. With the back of his hand, the wagon master pushed up the brim of his hat. "Who are you?" he asked. "And what d'ja want?"

John responded, "Anderson's the name. I'm bringing my boys to California with me."

The man glanced in the direction of the two boys, sitting on their horses a few yards away.

"I thought maybe we could stop with your group tonight." John took his hat off, wiping his forehead with the handkerchief he kept stuffed inside.

"Country's free. Find a place and stay out of the way. We've been digging this here pit most of the afternoon, looking for good drinking water." He pointed behind him to a square hole in the ground filled partially with pearl-colored fluid. "Don't let your horses step in it and no bathing."

John returned to the boys. "We'll stay here tonight, but don't expect any handouts. They're in a foul mood. Let's find a place away from all this noise." Tired and hungry, the boys followed him toward the east end of the campground.

Passing a wagon surrounded by four small children, a woman hailed John.

"If ya got your own food, you can use our fire. Don't have extras for three more mouths."

"Thanks, ma'am. I'd appreciate that." John returned with one small pot of water and food in hand. He placed the pot on the hot coals, cut up the minuscule pieces of leftover meat from a couple of meals ago and dropped them into the pot. The lady, standing near by, handed him a sliver of onion.

"Might make it taste better."

"Yes, ma'am. Not much of a cook myself."

He added a pinch of salt and pepper from tiny pouches and stirred the contents with a stick he kept in the supply bag. Reaching into the canvas again, he retrieved one wrinkled carrot he'd picked up from Mrs. Schmidt and cut it into bits. When the water steamed, he gathered his belongings.

"Here, take these three biscuits. They're fresh. Might make the broth more agreeable."

John smiled, "Thank you kindly."

She nodded and turned away to attend to the cries of her children.

"Ain't much, boys," John said, returning. "I got a couple of fresh homemade biscuits for you."

Micah waggled his eyebrows at the Indian. "Smells good. Love biscuits. How come you can't make 'em like this?" he asked his pa, as he stuffed another chunk into his mouth.

"Slow down. There's only one apiece."

Micah shut his eyes, enjoying the soft fresh, flaky taste. Black Molly use to make biscuits for him in the morning, with sweet butter and blackberry jam. His throat lumped up as he thought about her and his *maman*. No one was left back home. No one. Tears welled up in his closed eyes. He bit his lip to keep from crying in front of the Indian and his pa. Did this man really care about him? He peeked at John from beneath his half-closed eyelids.

John reached over and patted Micah on his head. "Enjoying that biscuit, are you? Maybe we have to try our hand at getting some more. I'm sure we will meet up with other wagon trains and nice ladies. Smile a lot, boys. Women like that."

Then he tore his biscuit in half and shared it with the boys, popping the other half into his mouth. "Eat up. You deserve it." He got up and wiped out the pot and cup with his shirttail. "Tomorrow night, we'll eat better, I promise." He reached over and gave Micah's shoulder a good tug and smiled.

Crow stooped and retrieved what looked like a piece of scrap cloth sticking out of the bog.

"Hey, would you look what I have here," he said holding up a mud-covered moccasin. "Guess we don't have to guess who this belongs to."

"I'd say they're about a day ahead of us," said Conway.

"Yep." Crow tossed the moccasin back across the grassy quagmire then brushed his hands across the seat of his pants. "They're probably movin' at a good clip, tryin' to stay out of our reach. No need to catch up with 'em. Not until Anderson reaches his claim."

Crow adjusted the crotch of his pants before climbing back into the saddle. "What are ya thinkin' about? Pannin' for gold?"

"No sense in goin' back to Fort Laramie when we got ourselves a claim to run. Everything's there. Equipment, stream, claim and three dead bodies that won't tell. Hell, Anderson won't need it."

"You betcha, he won't," Crow roared. "We gonna push on or stop somewhere tonight?"

"Sun'll be settin' soon. We'll spend the night here. No need to be out there in the dark." Conway pointed ahead. "Let's settle in over there. Plenty of water and it's fairly level."

"Sounds good. Got my sweet belle right here," he said, patting the liquor bottle through his supply bag.

Chapter Twenty-Four

Ash Hollow, Nebraska Territory

Caroline bathed Alexander's flushed face and arms, before placing a cool wet cloth on his forehead. He labored with each breath through dry cracked lips, gasping for air. She placed the back of her hand on his cheek. His temperature had increased again after being down this morning. *When will this up and down battle end? He's got to get better.* Pinching the skin on his forearm, it stuck together. *He needs more liquids*. Placing her arm under his shoulders, she helped her husband sip a cup of sweetened tea laced with ginger, cayenne pepper and a few drops of quinine. With his appetite gone, his strength was waning and his temperature was taking a toll on him.

Gently lowering him to the pallet, she called, "Sarah, bring me another blanket. The green one on the line. We need to break your Pa's fever."

Sarah crawled through the opening, blanket wadded up in her arms. "Phew, it's hot in here. Can't we pull the canvas back?"

Caroline tucked the cover around her husband's body. "No. The breeze might give him a chill."

"Is Pa gonna get better?"

"Yes, but it might take..." The snap of a twig caught Caroline's attention. "Shhh. Be still."

Carefully, she pulled the canvas aside from the wagon back and peeked through the opening. Thirty feet away stood four Indians surveying the campsite.

"Sarah," she whispered. "Stay in the wagon and help your Pa. I'll be back in a minute. Don't come out until I call you. Do you understand me?"

"Yes, ma'am."

Caroline climbed out of the wagon and stepped around to the side. The Indians stopped dead in their tracks when she emerged. No one said a word. Sticking her right hand into her pocket, she caressed the cold barrel of the small gun. It was half-cocked and ready. Removing her hand, she smoothed her apron, her stomach muscles tightened into knots.

The Indians scrutinizing her, the wagon, and the animals caused her knees to shake. She placed her left hand on the sideboard to steady herself and smiled bravely.

"Can I help you?" she asked.

No answer. The silence increased her anxiety.

Cautiously, she moved away from the wagon and drew closer to them. "Hello. Can I help you?" There was no response, so she waved her hand in a greeting.

"We trade." A tall middle-aged Indian held up two dangling rabbits. He pointed to a shirt draped over the wheel. "Want red shirt." His ebony hair hung wild and free to his shoulders. He wore a skin shirt, brown moccasins and a blue cloth hung from his waist in front and back. His legs bowed wide enough to shoot a cannon through.

"Trade," he said again and smiled.

"Okay, trade," said Caroline. Alexander had two other shirts. He wouldn't miss one. Besides, fried rabbit would taste good tonight and they looked fresh.

She picked up the brightly-colored shirt, folded it, and extended her arm. He quickly thrust the rabbits at her and grabbed the shirt. She carefully draped the rabbits across the front wagon wheel.

"Salt, tobaccy," said the second Indian. He was dressed similar to the taller man, but his chest was bare. He stood eight inches shorter then the other braves. His scarred face was weather-beaten and a band covered his right eye. When he smiled, several teeth were missing. Pouring a hand full of berries from a doeskin pouch, he extended his arm, stirring the berries with one finger.

Caroline pointed to the wagon. "I go inside. Get salt and tobacco. You wait here."

An older Indian with graying hair shouted, "Sugar, animals." Standing in a proud and threatening stance, he pointed to the oxen.

"No oxen. We need. I give you sugar. Wait here."

He gestured again to the animals, talking with the Indian standing next to him.

Caroline kept repeating, "No oxen. We need. No trade."

A man with red painted zigzag lines across his nose to his jaw mumbled something. His hard piercing eyes scanned Caroline from head to foot. Finally, he lowered his head and spoke to the older warrior, making several gestures. The two Indians turned their attention to the oxen. Taking several steps toward the animals, the sinewy muscles of the red painted brave's arms and legs glistened.

"Ma."

The Indian stopped in his tracks and swiveled, staring mesmerized at the canvas opening.

Caroline froze. Her gaze followed his. Sarah's head stuck through the opening, red hair flying around her face, an apparition of flames. Fingerling sunbeams touched her hair, creating a soft flaming halo.

The painted warrior pointed at Sarah. "Trade horse for red-haired girl." His eyes gleamed as he spoke, never facing Caroline.

"No trade," she said, frantically waving her hands to get his attention. "My daughter. No trade." She shook her head from side to side, to make him understand.

Silence mounted, sending chills up and down her spine. Could she defend herself and protect Sarah if this brave decided he would take what he wanted?

Without moving a step, she commanded, "Sarah. Do as I tell you. Go back inside, right now." She tried to remain calm, afraid to turn her back on the man. She placed her hand into her pocket, ready for action.

Sarah quickly disappeared.

The painted Indian stood erect, waiting for the girl to reappear. He took one step forward.

Caroline sidestepped in front of him, blocking his path and straightened her shoulders. "No Trade," she said evenly.

He stood his ground and pointed to the wagon.

She shook her head and again stated, "No."

His hostile eyes glared at her, face showing contempt. He grunted several words, and then with one last glance, backed away to stand behind his fellow warriors.

Caroline calmly walked to the back of the wagon and stuck her head through the canvas. "Sarah, hand me the small pouch of sugar, one quilt patch off the chest, and the tobacco tin over there. Hurry."

"Ma, that's my quilt patch."

"Sarah!"

Gathering the items from her daughter, Caroline lifted a small bag of salt from the back of the wagon gate and returned to face the Indians. Placing the salt and tobacco on the wagon seat, she opened the sugar bag and poured some into the center of the quilt patch. She handed it to the old warrior. He smiled big. Happy with his trade, he turned and headed toward the horses.

Placing the bag on the wagon seat, she picked up the tin, stuck her hand inside, withdrawing a fist full of loose tobacco. The eye-patched brave hurriedly dumped the berries into a bowl next to the fire and opened his doeskin bag hanging from his waist and accepted the gift. He stood facing her for a moment. "Salt."

Exasperated, Caroline put down the tin, picked up the salt, and poured a hand full into another pouch he had strung at his waist. Grinning, he walked away.

The painted Indian stood, arrogantly, staring at the wagon rear. He was the only one left to deal with. Holding the salt bag at her side, Caroline stood her ground, chin held high. Outwardly, she was brave and strong, but her insides were jelly and knotted. He sulked for a few minutes, before briskly walking away.

Caroline kept an eye on the four of them as they mounted their horses and disappeared through the brush. Her knees shook and a bitter taste bubbled in the back of her mouth. Collapsing, she sat on the ground for a minute, shaking and exhausted. Finally, getting to her feet, she grabbed the rabbits, hung them across a low tree branch. She puttered around the campsite cleaning up, moved the berries to the food box, before returning the tin and pouches to the wagon. Checking on Alexander, she found Sarah fast asleep, curled up next to her father. She pulled the canvas shut.

A soft whicker caught her attention. About thirty feet away, behind a dense patch of brush stood an appaloosa horse tied to a tree. She looked around cautiously. Were the Indians hiding, skulking in the bushes? Was this a trap? Sticking her hand into her pocket, she caressed the gun and slowly approached the animal. Caroline reached out to touch him. He shied away and pawed the ground.

"Whoa, there. I won't hurt you. What a beautiful animal you are." He whinnied and moved away again. Pulling the rawhide rope to her, she gently rubbed his soft velvet nose. He tried to back up, but she held the leather strip close. "Easy, now. Easy." She searched the brush again for the warriors. Only the soft breeze ruffled the foliage.

Undoing the thong from around the tree, she led him back to the campsite and tied him to the back wheel of the wagon.

Opening the canvas cover, she whispered, "Sarah. Wake up. Come see what I have."

Sticking her head through the opening, Sarah was awe-struck. "Oh, Ma. He's beautiful." She jumped down and walked toward the horse.

"Be careful. He's wild."

Sarah reached out to touch his neck, he lifted his head and side stepped away. "Can I have him?"

"We'll talk about that later. Right now I have some rabbits to dress and clean."

She followed her mother. "Those Indians were scary. Weren't you afraid?"

"Yes, I was." Caroline reached out and hugged her daughter close, running her fingers through her hair.

Sarah wrapped her arms around her mother's waist. "What did they want?"

"Just to trade a couple rabbits for one of Pa's shirts. The bright red one caught their fancy."

"They were really ugly, the Indians, I mean." She snuggled closer to her mother. "Especially the one with red paint on his face. His eyes looked mean."

"Yes, I agree." Releasing her daughter, she grasped Sarah's face between her hands and tilted it toward her. "Promise me you will stay close to the wagon until your father is better. We'll join the next group coming over the hill. So, don't venture away. Promise me."

Sarah hung her head and made a face.

"Promise me, Sarah."

"I promise."

She patted her daughter's cheeks, then turned and lifted the rabbits from the tree limb. "Now, we won't give those Indians another thought. Tonight we dine on fried rabbit."

Sarah opened her eyes wide. "Fried rabbit. Yum."

Caroline gutted, skinned, and quartered the rabbits, and placed the pieces in a pan of water to be parboiled. Searching through her spices, she selected a few sprigs of dry sage to get rid of the wild taste. Stoking the fire, she lay on more buffalo chips and brush, and hung the pot over the fire.

The earlier encounter had made her nervous. The painted Indian's piercing eyes haunted her. The look on his face when he saw Sarah chilled her heart. She knew he'd be back, he was a determined man. She didn't look forward to the confrontation. *Oh, Alexander. Please get better. We need you*, she prayed.

Red Knife watched the white woman lead away the horse he had left. He was sure the stupid woman would accept the animal. It wasn't the best animal from his group, but she didn't know the difference. She was not a Crow. Now, the ugly white girl with glowing hair would be his.

Much sadness had entered his teepee the past three years. Hunkering down behind a thicket of bushes, memories raced through his mind of that terrible night when renegades raided his village, killing his two beautiful young daughters. His heart ripped open over the loss, leaving wounds that never healed. The sadness of his wife, Beaver Woman, was hard to endure. She could bear no more children.

When he first saw the flaming hair of the white girl, a vision came to him. He would bring his wife a captive, one she could beat if she wanted to. The ugly white girl could help scrape many buffalo skins. With so many things to do during hunting season, his woman needed an extra pair of hands to help. His wife would work her hard.

He waited patiently. Since his brother-in-law and two cousins were happy with their trade, he convinced them to go on ahead, he would catch up with them. Red Knife sneaked through the brush and made a small area to settle in for the night. Comfortable, he removed some pemmican to eat. The captive girl would be an honor to his venture. There would be many things to teach one so young. Time was on his side. He looked once more, gazing at the horse now tied behind the wagon. The sacrifice of an old animal was worth it for his trade would last a lifetime. Besides, he had plenty of horses. Three were hobbled in the ravine waiting for him, and ten more were back at his lodge. Tomorrow he would be on his way with a slave.

The fried rabbit was delicious, even Alexander ate a couple of bites. Sarah collected the dirty dishes and went outside. Caroline sat next to her husband, wiping his face with a cool rag. Then she gave him some whiskey laced with quinine. He fell back to sleep, breathing more evenly.

She slipped out of the wagon. "Now the dishes need to be washed." To her surprise, her daughter had already set up the water.

"My goodness. You seem to have things under control tonight."

"Oh, you were busy with Pa, so I thought I would help. Besides, the wagon's hot." Sarah stood quiet for a moment. "I really miss James, Ma. It's boring without him."

"Yes, I miss him, too." *Two children passed. Losing one was hard. Losing two was too many. Now only Sarah is left.* She smiled at her daughter. "You're growing up so fast on this trip. It seems like only yesterday you sat in the middle of the trail covered in mud."

"Oh, Ma."

Caroline kissed her on the forehead. "It's true."

Sarah took the small bucket from the fire, poured water into a cooling pan, and added a bar of soap. "We'll make it to California, won't we?"

How many times has my daughter asked that question? "Of course we will. Even though it's taken us a little longer than what we expected, we'll get to Uncle John's. Remember, he is waiting for all of us."

Squatting in front of the wash pan, Sarah swished the plate in the water, then into the rinse water, before handing it to her mother. "Will we be able to get through the mountains before the snow?"

"Of course, we will. After we get these dishes done, why don't we sit and do some stitching on your quilt pieces?"

"Let's hurry." Sarah handed her mother another tin plate.

Her daughter's question bothered her. Would they be able to cross the mountains and beat the snow? What if Alexander didn't get better? Where would they stay?

"If we don't go to California, can we go back to St. Louis or even St. Charles?" Sarah looked up at her mother.

"Maybe."

"If we do, can we visit the O'Briens?"

"The O'Briens, huh." Caroline smiled, placing the dried plate into the storage box.

"Yes, and maybe I could buy a pretty yellow dress with lace." Standing with a plate in hand, Sarah made several turns in the dirt. "If there was a dance, I could twirl all night."

"Enough twirling. Get the dishes finished."

"Wouldn't that be fun, Ma?"

"Yes, it would be fun. Now, hand me the tin."

"I might even see Patrick, and he'd ask me to dance."

"Oh. We're thinking about Patrick again?"

Sarah blushed. "He's so handsome."

"You keep dreaming, my love. Only time will tell. Now, finish the dishes and I'll bank the fire. The sun's going down and we need to get some sewing done."

Sleep did not come easy for Caroline. The ground was hard and rocky, the sagging tent roof, billowed and flapped in the wind, collapse was evident any minute. Her thoughts drifted to the red-painted Indian with piercing dark eyes. Was he out there waiting? Would he come back? Tomorrow she needed to have a good talk with Sarah. Until Alexander was back on his feet, they would have to be very careful.

Snap! Every muscle in her body jerked involuntarily. Each small noise set her alert.

Crunch...

Rustle...

Snap!

Unable to fight sleep, Caroline closed her eyes.

Chapter Twenty-Five

Sarah struggled out of the tent, squinting at the bright light. "I hate mornings." Miserable and dirty, she grumbled to no one in particular. Morning arrived too early for her. She watched the sun peek over the ridge.

Pushing her hair away from her face, she grabbed the damp red hair, gathered it at the back of her neck, and tied it with a crumpled ribbon. A few loose strands escaped, plastering themselves to her neck. Brushing her pinafore and shaking off the loose dirt, she looked around the campsite. "Work. Work. Work. Never time for fun anymore. I'll be so glad to get to California," she muttered.

The horse stood tied behind the wagon. She slapped his hindquarters. "Phooey, you sure made a mess." He ducked his head and shied away from her. "Don't step in it, stupid. Augh!"

Caroline stuck her head outside through the canvas opening in the back of the wagon. "Good morning, sunshine. I see you're up and moving about. We have work to do. First of all, move that animal and tie him to a tree over by the oxen. Then clean up his mess so we don't step in it."

"Oh, Ma."

"Don't be disagreeable. Help me, okay? I'm with your Pa. He seems to be doing better. His fever is down."

"All right, but I'm hungry."

"We'll eat as soon as I'm through. Before you start your chores, hand me the pan of water over there." Caroline pointed behind Sarah. "Then take the coffeepot off the hot coals before it burns."

Caroline ducked back inside.

Placing the pan of water on the tailgate, Sarah set about moving the coffeepot.

"Ma, did you hear that bird?"

"No, Sarah, I didn't. Take care of the horse like I asked you to. I'll be out in a minute. There's a bit of rabbit left from last night in the food box. We'll have it for breakfast."

Sarah opened the box, picked up a piece of meat, and took a bite. "Ma," said Sarah, her voice muffled from a mouth full of food. "There's that bird again. It's kind of strange. Listen."

Caroline hopped down from the wagon and stood listening. "I don't hear a thing, little miss."

"Well, it was close and real strange." She tried to imitate the sound.

"I'm sure it's nothing. There'll be plenty of new sounds we never heard back home." Caroline filled a cup with coffee and selected a piece of rabbit, placing both on a tin plate. "I see you found something to eat."

"Mmmm. It's good. Can I have another piece?"

"Yes, but save some for me. I'm gonna take your father his breakfast. When you're through eating, finish your chores."

After devouring the second piece of rabbit, Sarah moved

the horse. She took down the shovel from the wagon side and cleaned up the mess. Next she set a bucket of water on the hot coals for dishes. Bored and not ready to tackle another task, she walked around the campsite collecting brush for the fire. Wandering farther into the woods and coppice, she caught sight of a small rabbit skittering in and out of the brush. Chasing him became a game.

"Oh, little rabbit, where are you?" She heard him rustling in the thick shrubs in front of her. Picking up a stick, she beat the bushes ever so lightly, poking into the denser vegetation. The rustling stopped. She knew the rabbit sat inside, waiting. She shook several bushes, hoping the animal would hop out. "Bunny, bunny. I won't hurt you."

Snap! The sound came from behind her.

"Sarah! Stop." Panic stricken, Caroline jumped from the wagon back and waved Alexander's dirty shirt to catch her daughter's attention. She saw the back of Sarah's dress disappearing behind some trees. "Come back here now!"

Returning to an opening in the brush, Sarah yelled, "I'm only chasing a rabbit, Ma."

Rustle. Rustle. Snap! Sounds came from the far side of her now. She turned her head to see what made the noise behind her in the hedges. Probably a bigger animal.

"No, come back now, I said."

Puzzled over her mother's outburst, Sarah hit the bushes one more time with the stick, then hurried back to the campsite. Was her mother losing her mind? Maybe she was coming down with the fever.

"Ma, I was only—"

Caroline grabbed her daughter and shook her. "Remember your promise to stay close? Don't disappear like that. It's dangerous."

"Oh, the Indians. I forgot." She dumped a handful of

brush on the ground. "I thought you were comin' down with the fever, yellin' like that."

"Caroline," called Alexander.

"I'm coming'." Still rattled, Caroline looped one arm across her daughter's shoulders and hugged her. "Now stay close. Don't make me worry about you. I'll be right back."

Inside the wagon, Caroline tried to appear calm, but her stomach was tied up in knots. She lifted Alexander's head, gave him a sip of water, and then lowered him gently to his pillow.

"Ah, it feels cool." His voice barely audible, he said, "Weak. Arms heavy."

"You've been very sick."

"You and Sarah—all right? I heard you call her."

"Yes, we're fine." She gave him a big smile. "You seem to be better today."

Slowly, he lifted his hand. "Terrific."

"I'm sure you are." She pushed a few stray strands of hair from his face, and then brushed a kiss on his forehead. "Would you like something to eat? I have a bit of food for you."

"Yes, I'm a little hungry."

She tore the meat into tiny pieces, and then stirred his coffee. "When you're finished eating, I'll clean you up and give you some medicine."

"Our medicinal kind?" He raised his one eyebrow and smiled mischievously.

"Of course, Mr. Anderson." She laughed. "You must be feeling better."

Caroline placed a small morsel of rabbit in Alexander's mouth. He chewed with great effort. In between, she gave him sips of coffee to wash the food down. He managed to finish some of his breakfast.

After she cleaned his arms and face, she moved the pan of water and rags to the back of the wagon. "You're cooler to the touch now, and your color's coming back. Maybe we'll be able to travel in a few days."

He tried to grin, as she fussed over him.

She straightened his bedding and plumped his pillow. "Now it's time for your medicine. Let me see. Was it a sip of whiskey you wanted, Mr. Anderson?" Pouring the liquor into the remaining coffee, she added a few drops of quinine. Lifting his shoulders, she placed the cup to his lips.

"Ah. Golden elixir." Lying back, he shut his eyes.

Sitting next to him on the floor of the wagon, she took his hand and kissed each finger. Freeing his hand, he touched her cheek. No words passed between them for a moment. Placing her arm across his chest, she laid her head next to his. The closeness was overpowering. She needed comforting and she was stealing the moment the best she could.

"Are you, falling asleep?" His question caught her off guard.

"No. I'm enjoying the peace and quiet. Would you like to sit up for a while?"

"Yes."

Caroline stacked some clothes under his pillow. Placing her arms under his armpits, she propped him up.

"There," she said, "how does that feel?"

"Fine. I do feel better."

"Well, I'm glad you're awake and finally eating'. Sarah and I have been so worried about you. Would you like me to comb your hair?"

"No. I think I'll rest now." He closed his eyes and drifted off to sleep.

"Sarah, come get this pan of dirty water for me." No answer. "Sarah? Do you hear me?"

No response. Chills ran down her spine. "If she's playing a trick on me or ventured away, so help me." Caroline's voice trailed off as fear crept into her heart. She fled the wagon, kicking over the pan of water. The campsite's suffocating stillness stifled her breathing. Her daughter was nowhere in sight.

"Sarah!" she yelled. "Where are you? Answer me."

The horse was still tied to the tree next to the hobbled oxen. She checked under the wagon and inside the tent. Wild and frantic, her anguish grew. *Where can she be? She can't have just disappeared. She has to be here somewhere. She has to be. Oh, dear Lord, please help me find her.*

She thrashed around the thick-growing brushwood, like a crazed woman, sloshing through the creek bed, screaming. Her insides convulsed. She fought the urge to vomit. Her knees buckled, causing her to fall several times.

"This can't be happening," she sobbed, pulling her hair. "Oh, God, please help me find her. Please, oh please." She pleaded in desperation. No answer. No one heard her pleas. There was no one to help her.

Gone! Her daughter was nowhere to be found. Only a small scrap of her dress hung on a short scruffy branch near the thicket where she was last chasing the rabbit. Holding the material in her hand, Caroline staggered back to the wagon, ranting to herself. The red-painted Indian had returned for her daughter.

Alexander woke from a hazy dream world, shattered by high-pitched screams and cries. He crawled to the tailgate and lowered himself to the ground. His head buzzed and his legs wobbled as he grabbed onto the sideboard. Standing for a minute, he took two steps. Losing his balance, he fell to his knees. Holding onto the wheel, he pulled himself back up.

Several feet away, Caroline knelt in the dirt, pounded

the ground like a wild woman, screeching unintelligibly. Eyes mustang-wild, hair totally disarrayed, her face stained by tear rivulets to her chin, she wailed hysterically, "Sarah's gone. They've got her. Those thieving Indians have my sweet baby. Oh, Lord, help us." She crumbled to the ground in a heap, clasping her hands to her head, rolling on the ground.

"You're babbling, Caroline." Alexander couldn't comprehend what she was trying to tell him.

"They've got her. The Indians. They've taken our daughter."

"What Indians?"

Rising to her feet, she said, "The four Indians. They came to trade. First they wanted a shirt. That was fine. Then they asked for salt, sugar, tobacco."

"What does that have to do with Sarah?" Alexander clutched his fists, his impatience building.

"It was that ugly painted beast," she shouted. "He wanted Sarah. I told him no. I kept telling him, no trade. He wouldn't listen. I know it was him. He came back for her."

In her outstretched hand she held a scrap of cloth. "Look, this is all that was left."

Suddenly, Alexander realized what Caroline was trying to tell him. Indians had kidnapped their daughter. Spying the Appaloosa, Alexander asked, "If you didn't trade, where did we get the extra horse?"

"He was tied to a tree over in the dense brush. I brought him over to the wagon."

"Caroline, the Indian gave him as a gift in exchange for Sarah." Grasping for breath, Alexander grabbed his wife by the shoulders. "When you took the horse, you accepted his trade."

She stammered, "No. He was just tied there." She stood

stock-still, eyes and mouth wide. "No. Oh, Lord, no," she screamed. She collapsed against his chest and slid down to his feet, grabbing his leg and pulling him over. "I didn't know. I truly didn't know. Oh, God, forgive me."

Untangling his leg from her grip, Alexander struggled to stand. Rage welled up inside him. He couldn't breathe. Extremely weak and his face red with anger, he staggered to the wagon.

"I'll get those mangy savages. Take my daughter. They can't have her, she's mine," he gasped.

Hanging onto the sideboard, hand over hand, he made his way toward the horses, drenched in perspiration. His head pounded, his ears rang, and his knees buckled with each step. His energy began to wane, but he knew what needed to be done. The savages had carried away his jewel and he was going to get her back.

"Get my rifle," he shouted. "Some ammunition, my shirt. Hurry."

Caroline rushed to his side. Her husband wasn't fit to ride out after the Indians. She grabbed his arm to steady him. "You can't go. Look at you. Your legs won't even hold you up."

"Leave me be, woman," he shouted, wrenching himself loose from her grasp, stumbling forward. "Help me onto the horse."

"You're not well enough yet to travel. You won't be able to stay in the saddle, let alone track the Indians. I'll go."

"You go? You'd be worthless out there. A half-witted hindrance. What do you know about tracking?"

"At least let me go with you. Together we can find her." She stood in front of him, trying to block his path.

He grabbed her shoulders and shook her hard as he spoke,

"She's my daughter. I'll go after her. You stay here." He narrowed his eyes and in a threatening tone, shoved her against the wagon, "Get out of my way."

Shocked at her husband's rage, Caroline leaned against the wagon, fearful of his anger.

Alexander held onto the wheel, trying to get his bearings. He lifted his fist, shouting at the heavens, "She's my daughter, my baby. God help me. Give me strength. I'll kill me some savages today."

Caroline caught him as he stumbled again. "She's my daughter, too."

He gritted his teeth and glared at her.

Holding onto his arm with both hands, she frantically asked, "What if you don't come back? I'll lose both of you."

He looked at his wife. "I'll be back. Sarah needs me now more than ever." Alexander grasped her hand, disengaging the death grip she had on his arm. "Let go."

Caroline released his arm, dropping her hands to her side. Realizing he was going alone, she left to get the necessary items for his trip. Returning, she helped him on with his shirt.

"Do you want to take the Appaloosa?"

"No. A pox on that damn horse." His eyes glared at her. "Shoot the stupid animal if you want. Now help me saddle our mare. She'll get me where I need to go."

She helped Alexander ready the mare, then gave him a foot up. He slumped over the pommel, gripping the reins with one hand and the horse's mane with the other. She slipped the rifle into the side holster and placed the ammunition in the saddlebag on back.

"Now, where did you find that piece of dress?" he asked.

Caroline pointed to the dense brush at the north end of their camp. He headed for the thicket, never looking back, searching the ground for clues. Suddenly he took off in a gallop. She froze as he rode away. The horse and rider diminished to a speck, disappearing altogether over the horizon. Cold with fear, Caroline knew her world had disintegrated into pieces, never to be the same. Would he come back? Could he find their daughter?

She stood alone in this God-forsaken, deserted landscape. Where were the other wagon trains? Why didn't someone come to help her? She stood hoping to catch a glimpse of a returning rider. Nothing, just a pathetic dullness.

Walking to the fire, she added the last of the brush and sticks. It would be dark soon and she needed to keep a constant vigil until her husband returned. She searched the surrounding area for more firewood.

Returning to the campsite, Caroline sat with her back against the wagon wheel. Removing the pistol from her dress pocket, she examined it to be sure it was properly loaded and laid it on the ground next to her. Bending her knees, she wrapped her arms around them. She hugged them tight to her chest and dropped her head down to rest. Darkness slowly surrounded her, isolating her from everything except the fire dancing in front of her. Waiting in the dark was all she could do. Wait and pray.

Chapter Twenty-Six

Caroline opened her eyes, staring straight ahead. The hairs on the back of her neck tingled when she heard a snap. Someone was hiding in the brush to her left. Her heart beat against the wall of her chest. Should she move? It was too late to put out the fire. The stalker already knew she was alone. Straining to see into the darkness, Caroline lowered her right hand to the ground, picked up the black powder gun, and placed it in her lap. She only had one good shot.

Glancing sideways into the obsidian night, she tried to look casual and relaxed. It might be Alexander. No. He would have ridden in and made himself known. Maybe the Indians were back. Her stomach lurched. Was this the end? She gripped the pistol handle. If she went down, one of them would go with her.

A sudden movement from her left startled her. Mustering all her courage, she jumped to her feet, raised the gun, and fired. The commotion that followed completely unnerved her.

A grotesque apparition in ragged hide dashed out of the

darkness. It zigzagged and ranted, throwing rocks and buffalo chips. She screamed and turned to escape from the onslaught of the attack.

"Woman," bellowed the barbaric shape, "don't shoot me! Gawldern it, put the gun down."

She couldn't understand what he said, as it was undecipherable. She turned toward the beastly-looking creature and raised the weapon as a club. The man leaped into the air and landed on top of her, toppling both of them onto the ground. With the pistol raised over her head, they grappled for control. Gaining the upper hand, the man tried to pry her fingers loose from the gun. She bit him twice.

He howled, swearing unidentifiable blasphemous words. Hissing through his beard, he shook her hand. "Let loose of the pistol. Do you hear me? And, don't bite me again, ya blasted female."

She thrashed around, making it hard to pin her down. Finally, he dropped flat onto her body, face-to-face, rough smelly beard against her chin. Breathing hard, he wrenched the gun out of her hand.

"Pooh, you stink," was all she could think to say as she lay there shaking, the weight of his body making it difficult to breathe. He was the ugliest human being she ever saw. His putrid breath gagged her.

"Well, thank ye kindly, ma'am. Is that why you tried to shoot me, 'cause I smell?" Growling, he sprang to his feet and extended a hand to help her. "Come on. Get up and don't try nothin'. Didn't figure ya'd try to shoot me, dang-nabit."

Rolling to one side to avoid his assistance, Caroline stood up, brushing the debris from her dress. "Who are you? What do you want?"

"I came—"

"My husband'll be here at any minute so you better go. He's real nasty when he's mad."

"Yes, ma'am. That could be."

She tucked loose strands of auburn hair behind her ears. All the while, she kept a good eye on the vile creature, as he retrieved a fur cap lying on the ground. His graying hair, long and unruly, connected to a wiry, bushy beard, hid his neck. A short deerskin jacket, fringed at the seams and along the bottom, covered his upper torso. His pants, made from the same skins, were filthy, splotched with who-knows-what. High-top leather moccasins laced up his calves with rawhide thongs. An encased knife dangled from his waist.

"What's your name? You looked like something left over from a dung heap and you smell just as bad."

"Humph! I come to help ya and all I get is insults. My name's Ben Wilson."

"Mr. Wilson, I don't need your help and I want my pistol back." She stuck her hand out, palm up.

He raised one eyebrow and slid the weapon into his waistband. "I think I'll keep this here thing a while longer, thank ya kindly. Don't rightly appreciate being shot. Now, let's talk a bit."

"I don't want to talk to you. Go away. This here's my campsite."

He took three steps in her direction.

She screamed, "Leave me alone."

"Ain't gonna bother ya none, ma'am. Don't get your breeches in an uproar."

She opened her mouth, shocked at his last statement. "Honestly, Mr. Wilson."

"Yes, ma'am. Sorry. Answer me this. Where'd your husband go?"

"If it's any of your business, he went after our daughter. She was kidnapped by an Indian this afternoon."

"Injuns, huh? Well, that tells it all." He shook his head, then spit a spot of brown tobacco juice onto the ground. "How many?"

"How many what?"

"How many Injuns were there?"

He was getting a bit testy, so she took a defiant stance. "Four."

"Ma'am, you're one contrary woman. Listen to me and keep your mouth shut," he said. "Ya understand?"

She started to say something, and decided not to when he raised his hand. His squinty eyes told her she didn't want to tangle with him again. Dirt on her dress and pain in her back reinforced her decision. She'd bide her time.

"I have bad news and more bad news. None of it's pretty. Your husband ain't comin' back, ma'am."

"What? I don't believe you. How do you know that?"

"Tarnation, woman. Be quiet. I ain't gonna tell you the gruesome details, but I buried a man up yonder." He reached into his jacket pocket. "This here's a piece of his shirt. Ya recognize it?"

Her face blanched, her hands trembled. Taking the fabric, she smoothed it between her fingers. Tears welled up in her eyes, her lips quivered.

"That does it." He slapped his forehead. "You start cryin' and I'll have to cuss and git real mean. I hate it when women cry." He didn't know what to do with them.

She raised her chin, blinking back tears. "Thank you for burying my husband."

"You're welcome." He removed his hat and racked his fingers through the few gray strands sticking up. "The problem is, if these Injuns or whoever killed your husband knows you're out here alone, they'll come lookin' for ya."

Hands dangling at her sides, Caroline stared at him, expressionless.

"You heered what I said?" he asked.

"Yes." Her answer was barely audible. "Did you find a rifle? It's new, a Sharp's Carbine."

"No, ma'am. No horse, no nothing, only his body shot through with an arrow."

He scratched his head, and then replaced his beat-up fur hat. What a picture she made standing there, her loose hair falling about her shoulders, resting on her full bosom. By golly, she was one handsome woman. But, he could tell she was gonna be a parcel of trouble.

"What's your name, ma'am?"

"Caroline Anderson."

"Miz Anderson, ya can't stay here without protection." He paused for a moment, a look of great pain on his face. "I know I'm gonna regret this. I know I am."

"Regret what, Mr. Wilson?"

"Ben's the name." He paused for a moment, scratched his beard. "Okay. I'll take you to the closest fort where you can get some help." He put it to her matter-of-factly, no pussy-footing around. "That's the best I can do for ya. St. Louie's waitin' for me and my pelts. I ain't gonna miss goin' there this year for nothin'."

"But—"

"No buts. Change into some pants and get yourself together. Ain't takin' no blasted woman in a dress on horseback. We need to head out of here fast. The Injuns could be back in the mornin' and they'll be after you this time."

Caroline couldn't believe her ears. This filthy, unkempt man must be completely insane. He'd just wrestled her to the ground, told her that her husband was dead. Now he wanted her to go with him.

"Wait. I'm not going anywhere with you. This is all wrong. I have to go get my daughter back. Besides, a wagon train is due over these hills any day now."

"Is that so? Well, you can stand there and argue with me all ya want. I'm tellin' ya to get dressed 'cause I'm leavin' in a few minutes. Then you'll be out here in no man's land all by yourself. Don't bother me one way or the other. I can head on East." He turned and walked toward the fire, poured himself a cup of coffee and sat down. "That wagon train you're waitin' on might not get here before the Injuns do. Believe me, them devils'll be back for ya."

The audacity of the man amazed her. Was he real or was she dreaming? She pinched herself. It wasn't a dream. In the far distance, she heard a howl. Did she want to stay here by herself? What protection did she have? Maybe at the Fort, she could get help to find her daughter.

Ben finished his coffee, got up, and tossed the cup into the dirt. "Well, I'm a-goin'. The Injuns'll love your pretty red hair. It'll make a nice trophy." He tapped the brim of his hat. "Good night, Miz Anderson, and good luck."

He took ten steps before Caroline rushed to his side. "Wait. Don't go. You don't understand."

"Yes, ma'am, I do." Taking her by the shoulders, he shook her. "We don't have much time. Ya need to change into some ridin' clothes so we can make tracks before sunrise. Now, git yourself dressed 'cause we're leavin' in five minutes."

She stared at him, dazed.

"Git," he hollered.

She hustled into the wagon. She returned wearing Alexander's shirt, two sizes too big, and a pair of his pants. The trousers didn't fit any better and they felt strange. She could see between her legs. How could she dress like this in front of a stranger? What was happening to her self-respect?

"You'll need a hat and a coat. Roll up a couple of blankets for a bedroll and grab some vittles. We'll need easy eatin' food. Any money you have, bring it along. Move woman.

Move." Then as a last minute note, Ben added, "Grab yourself a piece of rope so you can hold up your britches. Don't' wanta see them hittin' the ground before we get ya to that there fort." Then he muttered, "That should get her craw."

Caroline blushed, then squinted her eyes and pursed her lips. "I heard that." Man's pants. Of all things to be wearing. Whoever heard of a woman wearing trousers? Except for old lady Smith back home and she was half-crazy. "They are kind of comfortable."

"Move, I said." Ben yelled. This daft woman was wasting his time. "Ya act like ya've never seen your legs before."

Hustling back into the wagon, she stuffed powder and shot, along with linen patches into her pants and jacket pockets. Spying a small rolled rug lashed with a rope, she untied it. Picking up a pocketknife from James' stash box, she cut the rope into two pieces. The short one she threaded through the pants loops, the longer length she used to tie up two blankets for a bedroll before she slipped the knife into her pocket. Stuffed behind the flour bags, she grabbed the money tin. Reaching in, she withdrew five dollars and some change. She had no idea where Alexander had hidden the rest of the money. Grabbing her husband's jacket, she made her way to the back of the wagon.

Passing the chest of drawers, she picked up a quilt patch and tucked it into her jacket. Her fingers touched something metal, Alexander's watch. Her heart lurched. The timepiece was an anniversary gift five years ago. Gently pulling it from the pocket, she turned it over to see the engraving, "With love, Caroline." Tears slid down her cheeks.

Why was she out in this God-forsaken land? Why was she putting her life into a stranger's hands? Who was this old man waiting for her outside the wagon? Could she really trust him? For some reason, she believed she could. Anyway, there was no one else.

Returning the timepiece to her pocket, she wiped the tears from her eyes with the back of her hand. Standing next to the rocking chair Alexander had so lovingly made for her, she tenderly rocked it, listening to it creak back and forth in the cramped space. Next to the chair was a curved top trunk. Inside were her children's clothes folded and neatly waiting to be worn. Sitting on the trunk, she bowed her head. She was leaving everything. Taking a deep breath, Caroline stood up, picked up an empty pillowcase, straightened her back, and left the wagon for the last time.

Outside, she went to the food box and filled the pillowcase with vittles needed for the trip. Hefting the bag over her shoulder, she plopped James' hat on her head and gave her pants one more upward tug.

"I'm ready. What fort are we going to?"

"Fort Laramie," he said. He headed to the edge of the campsite and disappeared into the darkness. Caroline took one last look around and ran to catch up with him.

"Shouldn't we put out the fire," she asked, struggling to keep up with his long strides.

"Nope."

"Why?"

"This way, no one'll notice the camp's empty. By mornin' the embers'll burn themselves out."

They walked a short distance to where he'd tethered his horse and pack mule. Taking her things, Ben secured them on the back of his horse. Then he rearranged his supplies and pelts on the mule to make room for Caroline.

"Get on."

"You expect me to ride a pack mule? I have a perfectly good Appaloosa tied at the wagon."

"Yep. If ya want to be kicked to death, you try ridin' him. We don't have time to break him. So git on my mule or walk."

Indignant, she mounted the animal with his help. Straddling two large compressed bundles of pelts, her legs stuck straight out each side.

"This is not comfortable or dignified," she shouted

"Woman. Be quiet or every livin' thing around will know we're leavin'." Ben mounted his horse and rode out.

Darkness concealed the rough terrain. Caroline thumped and bumped like a loose wheel. About a half a mile out, she fell off the mule with a thud.

"Darn. I hate this animal." Picking herself off the ground, she rubbed the sore spots on her buttocks with both hands. "This won't do. No, this won't do at all." She had more aches and pains, and her body felt bruised.

"Hush, woman. Your voice is shrill enough to wake snakes." He dismounted and retied the pelts lower on the mule. "Gawldern it, woman, complain, complain. There's nothin' I can do about these here bundles. They're goin' with me, so make do. Maybe I should gag ya and throw ya across the saddle."

She raised an eyebrow and clenched her jaw. "You wouldn't dare?"

"Jo-fired." His patience lost, Ben began cussing. "I swan." He reached over to help her remount.

Caroline dodged his arm and put up her fists.

"What's that fer?" asked Ben.

"I thought you were going to hit me."

"Hell and damnation, woman. I ain't gonna hurt ya. I just wanta help you up on Sassafras." He patted the mules rump and then extended his hand again.

"I can do it myself, thank you very much." Caroline jumped high and lay across the pelts on her belly. As she eased her legs around the rump of the mule, the bundles shifted and she fell to the ground on the opposite side of the animal.

Ben roared with laughter and slapped his knee. "Yep, you climbed on just rightly, ma'am."

"Never you mind." She hated his laughter at her expense. Grabbing her hat and plopping it on her head, she pulled it down over her ears. Only her nose and chin stuck out from under the brim. She wasn't going to lose it, no matter what. The hat was her son's and it belonged to her. She lifted her chin and stared at the mule, rubbing her hands together. Determination showing on her face, she leaped across the bundles, landing on her stomach, grabbed onto the mule's short mane, and righted herself into a sitting position. Triumphantly she glared at Ben.

"Are ya ready this time?" Ben scratched his whiskered chin. "Yep, I'm gonna be sorry. You're a parcel of trouble, woman. I don't want to hear nothin' from ya until we reach the fort."

"How far do we have to ride?"

He climbed on his horse and trotted off, calling over his shoulder, "Far enough."

Caroline's anger seethed. *Be quiet until they reached the fort? Just you wait, you ugly old man. My turn is coming.*

Four days later, Ben stopped at Robidoux's Trading Post in a basin between two bluffs.

The old trapper had pushed her and the animals hard to reach this place. Hot and dirty, Caroline dismounted, working out the sore spots while she got her bearings. To her right, stood a shabby log cabin housing a blacksmith's forge. The next two buildings, stuck together, housed a grog shop and a small grocery store.

In front of an Indian lodge, three women busily stretched

skins. Children ran about playing games, while two dogs trailed behind, barking and yapping at their heels. Several deserted wagons sat idle while men dressed like Ben moved about the area.

"Ma'am. You stay put. I'm gonna get you a horse if the price isn't too steep." Ben looped the reins over the hitching rail, grabbed a bundle of pelts off his mule, and entered the post.

She was sure his interest was more in the grog shop than purchasing an animal. A bit beyond the building ran a small creek. She went to investigate the area and found the cold, crystal-clear water. Bending down on her knees, she cupped her hands and scooped some to her lips. Refreshing and delicious, it almost made her cry with delight. She closed her eyes and let the water dribble down her chin, feeling coolness touch her chest, relieving the heat within her body. Taking another handful, she splashed her face and raised her chin to let the sun caress her skin. The feeling was heavenly, cool and soothing.

Startled by a young Indian boy tugging on her sleeve, she almost fell into the water.

"You sick?"

"No," she said, getting to her feet, "only thirsty."

"Then drink water. No wash in it."

"Yes, you're right."

He shook his head. "Funny lady."

"Miz Anderson." Ben beckoned her with the wave of his hand.

"Gotta go." Flapping her felt hat against her pants, she strolled over to join the old trapper.

"Got you a nice mare. Cost me most of my pelts. You're more expensive than a cow, and it gives milk."

"What! Comparing me to a cow? You hateful old duffer."

He loved when she got her dander up. He pointed, "We'll camp over there. Get the fire goin' while I go git your horse."

An hour later, Ben arrived with her horse in tow, a beautiful sorrel mare with white stockings and a patch on her forehead, complete with tack and saddle. This was going to cost her but she didn't care. Good-bye Sassafras.

"She's all yours. Think I did pretty good, if I may say so myself." He looked around. "So where's the eats?"

Bristling, Caroline yanked the reins from his hands, led the horse away without an answer, and tied the animal next to the mule.

"Work hard and have nothin' to sup on. Guess I'll have ta fix my own vittles."

"You're the most impatient man I ever ran across. Sit down and I'll get it together for you." Caroline rummaged through the supply bags.

Ben settled down cross-legged in front of the fire, pleased with himself. He loved ruffling her feathers. Her temper matched the color of her hair. He withdrew a small liquor bottle from underneath his jacket and took a swig. Staring at the bottle, he wondered if his whiskey supply would last him through this trip.

"If you fill up on liquor, you won't want to eat. Or worse, you'll fall asleep."

"Doubt it. Never missed a good cooked meal in my life. That is, if the cook ever gets around to fixin' it."

She began slapping mud around the potatoes, muttering to herself. "Maybe he'll choke on these. Maybe he shouldn't eat at all, ornery old bag of wind."

"If ya keep talkin' to yourself like that, people will think you're addlepated."

Caroline glared at him and dropped the potatoes into the fire.

"Best move those to the coals before they burn," he said, wiping his lips with the back of his dirty hand.

After supper Caroline spread her bedroll out in front of the fire. Ben sat in the dirt, inebriated, his empty bottle on the ground between his legs. She lay there knowing he wouldn't last long as he swayed back and forth, trying to stay awake. He soon keeled over on his side, snoring and snorting.

"Serve him right if he freezes to death." Her conscience kept nagging her. She got up and covered him with a blanket. "Sleep tight, you malicious old coot." Returning to her warm covers, she curled up on her side.

Listening to the wind whispering through the tree branches, the sorrowful sound of a coyote baying at the moon stabbed at her heart. She could identify with the animal. Her lips quivered and her shoulders shook, tears trickled down her cheeks. She covered her head with a blanket to keep from waking Ben.

Alexander, I miss the tender touch of your hand, the feel of your strong arms holding me. What I wouldn't give to hear your voice again. Oh, God, help me. My family doesn't exist anymore. I'm alone and afraid. Why, oh, why is this happening to me?

In Virginia I was happy, settled, content with a loving family, a warm cabin, and a comfortable bed. Now I sleep in a bedroll out in the wild, in the middle of nowhere, at the mercy of a dirty stranger. My life is empty, like a cast-off bucket. No one seems to care whether I live or die.

Loneliness was slowly killing her. She needed to harden her heart, like a marble statue in a winter blizzard. What was the use? She didn't care what happened anymore.

That wasn't absolutely true. Back in the dark reaches of her mind, a sliver of an idea slipped forward. John was going to pay for his well-laid plans of enticing her husband to pull up stakes and head west.

A slow evil grin graced her lips. "Beware John Anderson. Revenge is coming on horseback."

Chapter Twenty-Seven

"How much further do we have to go?"

"We're one day from Fort Laramie." Ben nodded his grizzled head. "Yes, siree. Only one more day. Peace and quiet comin' my way."

Ignoring his remark, Caroline scrutinized the trapper leading the way, contemplating how to finagle him into guiding her to California. She'd tried last night at camp. He stopped her short, turning a deaf ear before she could have her say. She needed a good, convincing plan.

"How long are you going to stay at Fort Laramie?" It was best to be cordial at first, so she smiled. Caroline was determined this conversation was going to take place here and now. She wanted him to understand he *was* going take her to California and not to some dreary old fort. John was waiting in California.

"Not long. Just enough to taste the whiskey, play a little poker, and get some good shut-eye in a soft bed."

"Mr. Wilson. I need to talk to you about where we're headed."

"Nope."

She paused for a moment then continued. "I need you to take me to California and…."

Ben shot around in his saddle so fast he almost fell off his horse. "You want me to what?" he roared.

"I want you to take me to my brother-in-law's place in California," she said, sitting straight in the saddle, head held high.

"Ain't that nice," he replied sweetly. Then he curled his lip. "There's no way I'm gonna take you to Californy. Who do you think you are, the Queen of England?"

He swiveled forward and shouted over his shoulder. "I'm goin' to St. Louie with or without ya."

"Ben—"

"Silence. That's the last of it, woman." Stiffening his back and shaking his head, he fell silent, mumbling to himself.

She could hear him growling in low, clipped tones. "Ben." He ignored her. "Hey, you nasty old man. Talk to me."

Ben stopped his horse, spun around in the saddle, and glared at her. "Woman, enough's enough! You're more trouble than you're worth."

The glare in his eyes stopped her dead in her tracks. Maybe now wasn't the time.

The rest of the day was miserable. Neither talked. To make matters worse, an annoying drizzle blanketed the area. Chilled to the bone, Caroline buttoned her wet jacket, pulled up the collar, and tucked in her damp hair. Holding the reins in one hand, she pulled the other into the sleeve of her coat. James' old felt hat protected her face from the rain, but as water dripped off the brim, a small trickle dribbled down the back of her jacket. With her pants soaked, her chaffed numb legs ached from gripping the horse's belly with her knees.

"If misery likes company, Ben must be tickled pink with

today's weather," she grumbled. She didn't have to worry about his answering her. He was stone deaf to any conversation, especially from her.

"That old coot is one ugly human being. All he ever thinks about is St. Louis, liquor, and women. I need a foolproof plan he can't afford to turn down. One way or another, he's taking me to California. No matter what."

Later in evening by the campfire, after the eats were finished, Caroline decided to try one more time to persuade Ben to guide her to her brother-in-law's claim.

"Have you ever thought about how nice California could be?"

Sitting cross-legged, he spit into the fire. Bowing his head and leaning forward, he clasped his hands in front of him and rested his forearms on his legs, ignoring her question.

"Ben, please reconsider taking me to California."

"You gonna start that stuff again?"

"There's gold there."

"Don't need gold." He spit into the fire again, then laid back on his bedroll, covering his eyes with his furry hat.

"You could get rich and buy all the liquor and women you want."

He jolted to an upright position, tossing his hat on the ground. "In a gold field? Ha. Woman, you have no idea. Out there pannin' for gold is a dirty, lonesome job. And what do you get for all your hard work? Nothin'. When you want some vittles, they charge you ten times the goin' price. Most of those tinhorns die before they hit pay dirt. No, Californy is not for me. Now, if you want to go back to St. Louie, I kin help you there." He licked his lips in anticipation of the big city resting next to the Mississippi River.

"Otherwise, we'll be at Fort Laramie sometime tomorrow. Understand?" He squinted one eye, indicating the conversation was over. Grabbing his hat, he laid down on his bedroll, his back to her.

At least, Caroline accomplished one thing. He did talk to her. That was the longest speech she ever heard Ben make.

She curled up next to the fire. At a loss about her future, her destiny, Caroline watched the crackling embers sail skyward, floating free in the wind. She was exhausted to the marrow of her bones. She missed her loved ones. Distorted images flitted through her mind. She banked the fire and covered herself with a blanket, praying for sleep.

Maybe her dreams would console her.

When they arrived at Fort Laramie, early the next afternoon, they found the fortress brimming with activity. Trappers, Indians and farmers, thrown together, created a bustling commotion. Two wagon trains were camped outside the fort. Travelers moved back and forth, taking on supplies, repairing wagons, preparing to push onward. Indians milled around outside the gate creating more congestion. Military personnel paraded across the grounds, weaving their way in and out of obstacles. Soldiers, building barracks and repairing other structures, added to the din and confusion. Amid all this maze of disorderly turmoil, dogs and children ran yelling among wagons and teepees, stirring up the dust and dodging bodies. The nauseating smell of dust, sweat, animals, and food hung in the air.

Leading the supply mule, Ben snaked his way through the Fort entrance, into the enclosed yard, making for the water trough so the animals could drink

Caroline slid from the saddle and tagged closely behind. She walked stiff-legged, her bottom sore from wet pants.

Sassafras, Ben's mule, halted in front of Caroline, raised her tail, and did her business. She dodged the smelly pile and stopped next to Ben as he finished conducting business with the liveryman.

"Nope, don't know how long I'll be. Feed 'em. I'll settle up with you before I leave."

"Stabling is free for the military. You civilians have to pay. I want two dollars now, in case you don't come back or you come back broke."

"I told you, I'd pay you later."

"Out! If you don't pay now, take your animals and git."

Caroline stepped forward. "Just pay him, Ben."

"Woman! Keep your nose where it belongs." Ben glared at her as he reached into his pocket, took out the money.

Ben pointed outside. "There's two wagon trains headin' west. Go see what you can do about gettin' on one of 'em. Maybe they'll be nice enough to take you to Californy."

Without so much as a see-you-later, he turned and headed for the public house, mumbling to himself, "Dad-blame women. They should stay at home and have kids. Who needs 'em? Bah!"

Caroline was amused by Ben's actions as he made his escape, stalking off to sulk like a small boy, reprimanded for bad behavior. He moved his hands about as he talked to himself. Once he looked over his shoulder to be sure she wasn't following him. *Cantankerous old fool.*

Leaving the stables, she headed toward Army Headquarters. Her first objective was to get the commander's assistance in finding Sarah. Six men milled around the small cramped office. A distinguished military officer sat at a desk in the far corner, reading some papers while a soldier stood at attention in front of the desk. At first no one noticed her.

"Excuse me. Can someone help me, please?" All eyes turned in her direction.

"Yes, ma'am. My name's Major Winslow Sanderson. How can I be of service?"

Aware of her unorthodox appearance, she staunchly approached the desk. "My name is Caroline Anderson. I arrived this afternoon and need assistance in finding my daughter. She was kidnapped by an Indian about four or five days ago in Ash Hollow."

"Mrs. Anderson, we are short-handed here. We have a detail out in the mountains cutting timber and the rest of the men are constructing living quarters. Until my additional company of soldiers arrives by next week or so from Fort Kearney, I don't have enough men to create a search party for an Indian with a four or five day head start."

"My husband is dead and my daughter is missing. Please, can't you send out a few soldiers to hunt down this savage?"

"No, ma'am. I understand how you feel."

"No, you don't," screamed Caroline. "That's my daughter out there. Maybe she's dead or lying hurt somewhere."

Major Sanderson stood and beckoned to a man in the shadows, leaning against the back wall. "Ma'am, I'm trying to help you. This is Jim Castor. He's more familiar with this country than I am. I've only been at this post for two days."

Castor sauntered out of the corner. "It won't do any good to go chasing after the renegade, Miz Anderson. By now he's probably traded your daughter for a horse, knives, or even beads."

Caroline placed her hand over her mouth, stifling a cry.

"The only thing we can do is have you fill out a report," said the major. "Then while we're out on patrol, we'll be on the lookout for your daughter. I'm not making any promises. It might take months, or even years."

Her hopes crushed, she wiped her tears with a handkerchief she pulled from her jacket pocket. "Can't you do anything at all? Sarah is so young."

"No, ma'am, we can't." Major Sanderson clasped his hands in front of him. "Not at this time."

Taking a wide stance, she stared the major down. "Maybe I'll just go hunting this beast down myself."

"Can't let you do that, ma'am."

"Why?" She glared at the major.

"It's too dangerous. Besides you wouldn't know where to start looking, and then someone would be filling out a missing report on you."

"Ma'am." Castor cleared his throat, then looked squarely into her eyes. "We don't get many kidnapped children returned by the Indians. They sometimes adopt 'em, and raise 'em as their own. Most the time, they're given to older Indians as slaves. Best thing you can do is go on where you were headed. Leave some type of address, so if she does turn up, we can get in touch with you."

Tears rolled down Caroline's cheeks, her lips quivered, but she refused to break down. "Thank you for your suggestions. I don't have an address right now. My brother-in-law, John Anderson is in California somewhere."

Major Sanderson snapped out of his chair, the room became very quiet.

"Did you say John Anderson?"

"Yes, sir I did." She stared at the commander. Something was wrong. "Why?"

"He wouldn't have two young boys with him, would he?"

"I don't know."

"From the report in my files, he left here several weeks ago with two riffraff trailing him. One of my men heard he was headed for somewhere called Tracer's Point."

"Is he in danger?" She nervously twisted the ring on her left hand.

"Oh, you might say that. Card game in the public house

went bad. A man was killed. The brother of the dead man is hunting him and the boys. I'd be careful if I was you, ma'am."

The news galled her. Another card game and this time he involved two boys. "Thank you for the information. Now, I need to fill out a report on my daughter."

"Yes, ma'am. Sergeant Peoples will help you." A young soldier guided her to a desk.

"Mrs. Anderson, when you've completed your information, leave it on the desk, I'll make sure the commander gets it."

"Thank you, Sergeant Peoples."

"By the way, Miz Anderson," said Castor. "If you're interested in joinin' a wagon train, ya might ask at the sutler's store, right outside the gate."

"Thank you."

Leaving headquarters, Caroline crossed the quadrangle, making her way to the sutler's store. Ben might be right. Maybe she should head west with another group. Entering the store, she received chilly stares from the women, questionable looks from the men. It had to be the pants.

Going up to the counter, she asked, "Do you know the name of the wagon masters of the two wagon trains outside the fort?"

"Yep. There stands one right over there." He pointed to a tall man near the door.

"Captain Braddock, this here woman needs to talk with ya."

"Yes ma'am. How can I help you?"

"I would like to inquire as to your destination."

"We're headed for the Willamette Valley in Oregon territory. Should be leaving in the morning."

"Do you happen to know where the other group is going?" Caroline was disappointed, but determined. She needed to get to California, no matter what.

"Yes, ma'am. They are headed for California. Wagon master's name is Johnson. Jess Johnson." He pointed to a tall man in a light blue jacket and black pants. "He's over yonder, heading out to the gate."

Caroline's heart skipped a beat. She ran out of the store, hollering, "Mr. Johnson. Please wait. I need to talk with you."

Jess Johnson stopped. "What can I do for you, ma'am?"

"I understand your wagons are headed for California."

"Yes, ma'am, we are."

"I would like to join you. I've lost my family, everything I own." He turned away. She grabbed him by the arm. "Please listen to me. I'll not be an inconvenience to you. I can work and pull my own weight. I own a horse and have some supplies."

"First of all, we don't allow single women on a wagon train. Causes too much trouble."

"I promise I won't be any trouble. I have to get to my brother-in-law's."

"We don't have anyone that'll take you in. You're dressed like a man, the women would object. It'll only cause trouble. No, ma'am, can't have that on my wagon train. Maybe the next one through will take you." He tipped his hat and continued on his way.

Embarrassed and degraded, Caroline went back to the fort, headed for the public house. Why was there always an obstacle blocking her path? Feeling totally worthless, she meekly pushed open the half-swinging doors, stepping into a dirty, smoke-filled room. She knew she'd find Ben in here.

Marginal rays of light filtered through the grimy front glass window. Dust rose and swirled in the air. The smelly bodies of unwashed men almost gagged her. Travelers, trappers, and military alike jostled one another for drinking space at the bar, made of two huge casks and a ten-foot-long flat piece of wood. She inconspicuously selected a table in a dark corner and moved a chair in position to keep an eye on Ben. He sat at a round table, littered with money and drinks, playing poker with several boisterous men.

For several hours, people entered and left the public house. All the while, Caroline took care to remain in the shadows. She thought about the embarrassments she'd endured: the donkey, the rejections, the snide remarks. Was there no end to the torment?

I'll be damned if I'm going to put up with this treatment anymore. I'm not going to let anyone put me down ever again. The devil with men and their bigotry. She was going to wear pants if she wanted to. And Ben wasn't going to dump her at this filthy fort. He was going to take her to California. She stared at him from under the brim of her hat. *Beware, Ben. You've met your match.*

Mulling over a plan, she placed her hands into her jacket pockets. She fingered Alexander's pocket watch, nestled in her pocket, gently rubbing her thumb over the case, reminiscing about that special Christmas. It had taken all of her egg money, plus a year of dressmaking to purchase the timepiece. The look of surprise and smile on Alexander's face made all the tedious stitching worthwhile. In the darkened saloon corner, a tear rolled down her face.

"Keerist it, Ben. Play cards," said Castor, eyeing the older man.

Ben scratched his beard. "I'm a-thinkin'."

A fat man pounded his fist onto the table, causing the money to rattle. "No, you're not. You're stallin'."

"Bet he jus' run out of money." Crude laughter came from several of the men.

"Are you playin' or not, Ben?"

"All right. All right. Hold on a minute. There's no need

to rush." Ben folded his cards and looked down at the table in front of him, all the while running his thumb nail across the top of them.

"We ain't got all day. Little Mike called and Joe raised. So, what are ya gonna do."

"Barkeep, bring me a whiskey." Ben opened his cards, one at a time, carefully placing them side-by-side. "Need to wet my whistle."

"More like ya gotta wet your brain to play your hand." Little Mike cackled at his own joke.

"What's the matter, Ben? You got a good hand and can't play it?"

Ben stared at his cards. He spit his chaw into the urn next to the chair. "I'm a-thinkin', I tell you." He reached into his pocket. Empty. What a time to run out of money. The only thing he could do was to bet Sassafras and no one wanted a mule.

Over his head dangled a gold timepiece in a gorgeous case. A soft feminine voice sung through the noise. "Could this be used as collateral for a wager?"

Greedy eyes locked onto the swaying pendant held above the pile of money. Desire spread across their faces.

"I'd say," Josiah cleared his throat, "that's more than enough to cover Ben's bet. What do the rest of ya say?"

Heads bobbed in agreement, keeping an eye on the gleaming gold watch, gently swaying in front of them.

One of the players reached his hand forward. Caroline quickly palmed the timepiece. "Wait," she said, "there's one condition attached to accepting this stake. If Ben agrees to use this timepiece to cover his bet and he wins, then he must promise, before all of his 'friends', to take me to California."

Ben jumped up, knocking the chair over. "What! Ya want me to what? No, gawl-dern your hide. Won't do it. Jus' won't do it, woman."

"All right." She smiled smugly and started to walk away.

Ben glared at her, then looked at his cards again. "Hold on. Ain't decided yet."

Caroline opened the case covering the face. The anxious men stared at Ben, impatient to get back to the card game.

"What's wrong with ya, Ben? Lost your mind?" Josiah reached out to stroke the prize.

As his fingers were about to touch the timepiece, Caroline slipped it into her pocket. "I guess Ben isn't interested in playing his hand." With a haughty shrug, she stepped away from the table.

The card players' shouts of protest resounded against the four walls. All eyes were on Ben as he reached out and clasped her wrist, anger written across his face. "Woman, you are one conniving— You drive a nasty bargain." Pulling her toward the table, his hold on her wrist tightened, pain shot down into her fingers.

She stolidly stood her ground, never showing the agony she was experiencing. "California or no watch, which is it gonna be?"

"She's gotcha there, Ben," said Castor.

Silence enveloped the room. Ben glared at her as he stood, gripping her wrist in one hand and clutching the cards in the other. All the plans he made the past two years were whisked away by a scheming woman and a poker hand.

Ben yanked her close, until they were chest to chest. "Californy," he hissed between his teeth,

She pushed him a little farther. "Louder. Promise me in front of all of your friends."

Shoving her away, he yelled, "Dang it, woman." Chawing one more time, he spit into the urn. "I *promise* to take you to Californy. Now hand me the watch."

Placing the timepiece on top of the money, he leaned across the table and glared at Castor. "Call."

Castor studied Ben for a moment, shook his head, and threw in his cards. He'd played enough poker with the old trapper to know he wasn't bluffing. Eyebrows raised and surprised looks spread across the faces of the other players as Ben placed his cards face down. No one challenged to see the winning hand as he racked in the money.

Pleased with herself, Caroline strutted back to her chair. She had challenged the ornery trapper and won. It had cost her Alexander's timepiece, but it was worth it. Trail life with Ben and his rotten disposition...she might as well forget *pleasant* until he calmed down, which of course might be the entire trip. It didn't matter, she'd won. She was going to California.

Chapter Twenty-Eight

Fort Bridger

"Where're we headed?" Micah asked, shifting in the saddle.

John pointed ahead. "Fort Bridger. Up ahead about five miles."

Micah didn't care how many miles away, he wanted to get off this darn mare, sit on a bench, and eat at a table. He was anxious to reach California and quit traveling by the seat of his pants. If he didn't see the animal for a month, it wouldn't bother him at all. He was a city boy, not cut out for this wilderness crap. He wondered how come the Indian never complained.

He caught Boy Who Spits Far riding with his eyes shut. "How do you do that, keep from fallin' off your horse while you sleep?"

"Not sleeping. Listening. Wind talks to me. Tells me secrets."

"Okay. I hear things, too."

"Stop grumbling, Micah. You're beginning to sound like a fussy female."

"I'm tired, hungry, and every part of my body hurts. We missed breakfast this morning because of the rain and ate our nooning meal in the saddle, which didn't amount to much."

"That's because we need to make Fort Bridger before nightfall. This isn't good country to bed down in. We should be seeing some green grass country up ahead, lots of tall timber, and plenty of fresh water."

"You keep pushin' us, but we haven't seen hide or hair of those fellas from Fort Laramie."

John looked over his shoulder. "Quit complaining and…"

Suddenly, his horse reared, danced around on his hindquarters, and threw him to the ground. The frightened horse neighed and bucked, kicking his back legs behind him before taking off in a gallop.

"Ahh!" John cried out iin pain, scrunched up in a ball held his right lower leg.

Micah pulled his horse to a halt and slid off, landing both feet hard on the ground, kicking up the dust.

"I get horse," yelled Spits Far, taking off at a full gallop.

Micah fell to his knees next to John. "Pa, are you all right?"

"Watch out. There's a rattler over there somewhere. It spooked my horse. Here, help me up. My ankle feels like hell."

Facing his pa, Micah placed his arms under John's armpits, while the man grabbed onto his son's shoulder to pull himself up. Struggling to his feet, John attempted to take a step. Excruciating pain shot from his ankle to his groin. He collapsed to the ground. He groaned."I think I broke my leg."

Micah reached over to hike up the pants leg. "Let me see."

"Don't touch it. We need to make a splint. Unbuckle

my belt and pull it through the loops. Then give me your suspenders."

Micah unclipped his snappers and handed them to his father. Riding up behind them with John's horse in tow, Spits Far slid off his horse.

"A rattler scared the mare. We think Pa's right leg is broken. Don't see any bones sticking out. He can't stand up."

"You boys are gonna have to get me to Fort Bridger. But first, we need to get something to make a splint. Can't be riding with this leg flopping around. You two look for anything fairly straight that we can use."

The boys scoured the desolate area and managed to find several meager pieces of wood.

"This one's kinda scrawny but it'll have to do. The rest are worthless. Bring my rifle over here. We'll have to use it. Now listen up. This is how you're gonna do it," said John.

"Me see this fixed before. I strap you down." The Indian boy placed the rifle on the outside of John's leg and a piece of wood next to the inside of his leg. "Micah, sit on belly, not hard."

"What?" John protested.

"Don't want you move." Spits Far took the belt from Micah. "Keep down."

"Here, I'll hold those straight for ya." Micah scooted forward and pressed the pieces against his Pa's leg.

"Easy!" yelled John, grabbing at Micah, trying to push him away.

"Pa, lay still. The Indian knows what he's doin'. Go on and finish. Pull the belt tighter," Micah directed, holding the splint pieces.

"Use stretchy thing at bottom." Boy Who Spits Far eyed Micah, giving him the sign not to move. He grabbed John's foot and tugged a little.

John screamed, arching his back on the dusty ground, as

the Indian boy wrapped the suspenders around the splint and tied them into a knot.

"I'd give anything for a swig of whiskey right now. Hell, my whole body hurts." He fisted his hands, trying to control the pain.

Micah got to his feet. "How are we gonna get him on his horse?"

The Indian pursed his lips and shrugged his shoulders. "Me think."

"All right you two. Now listen to me," said John. Pain, again, shot up into his groin. Sweat glistened on his forehead, trickling down his temples. "If you bring my horse over here, I'll grab onto the saddle horn while you two push me high enough so I can get my left foot into the stirrup. Once up, I'll be fine. You'll have to take turns riding next to me so I don't fall off and hit the ground."

John leaned over, grasping the mare's mane with his left hand, gripping the reins tightly in his right hand. Bouncing in the saddle shot the pain through his body, straight up into his shoulders, and he fought to keep from passing out. He swayed, drifting to his right.

Micah grabbed a handful of his shirt and hauled him back upright. "We'll be at the fort soon, Pa. Hang on."

"Look," shouted Spits Far, "smoke comes from lodges."

"Hear that, Pa? There's the fort."

"Good," was all John managed to answer. Horrific pain, from his leg slapping against the horse's belly, cut like a knife wedged under the skin.

The ground lay flat and green along the trail leading up to Fort Bridger. A stony brook of fresh water ran alongside the palisades, through abundant grass and off between patches of trees. The unkempt small fort was surrounded by a few Indian lodges and several wagons. The boys looked at each other, disappointed. It definitely wasn't like Fort Laramie. They rode through the wide square entrance. A few rough-hewn log cabins made up the better part of the fort, along with a blacksmith shop and a supply store.

They halted in front of Bridger's Store. Micah jumped down and tied his reins around the porch post. Charging into the store, he yelled, "Do you have a doctor around here?"

The sutler lowered his head and looked over the rim of his glasses. "We don't rightly have a doc. Old Man Bridger does most of the doctorin', but he's not here right now. He's up at Fort Laramie, finishing up business."

A bit testy, Micah's patience ebbed with the long-winded man. "Is there anybody around here who knows about settin' a broken leg?"

"Hmm. Let me see." The man looked up at the ceiling while he scratched his small beard.

The storekeeper had pushed his luck too far. Micah tapped his foot against the counter, his intolerance with the old windbag growing thin. "Well?"

"Maybe Mary Not Afraid of Wolves could be convinced to help you. But you'll have to give her something in return. Got any beads or ribbons? Maybe a mirror or a nice piece of material?"

"No. I'm not carrying anything like that."

"Well, sir, you're at the right spot. Looky here. I have some nice beads. Colorful aren't they? And here's some pretty ribbons, all sizes. Take your pick."

Micah reached for a long yellow ribbon. The sutler grabbed him by the wrist. "Let me see your money first. Ya know these aren't free."

Micah yanked his hand from the man's grasp. "I'll be back." He ran out of the store, mumbling to himself. "Ribbons and beads. Can't these people help somebody that's hurt?"

"You find doctor?" asked the Indian boy, jumping down from his horse.

"Not exactly. The man inside says there's an Indian woman named Mary something who can help, but we have to give her some ribbons or beads in exchange for her services. We gotta buy these. I don't have any money."

"In my saddlebags, right one. You'll find a small doeskin pouch," John moaned.

Micah unbuckled the saddlebag and reached in.

"The left side. Take what you need." John fell over the horse's neck. Both boys jumped to catch him before he slid off the animal.

Retrieving the small pouch, Boy Who Spits Far grabbed it from Micah's hand. "I trade."

Micah cocked his head to one side, and gave the boy the go-ahead hand sign, palms up. Soon, Spits Far and Mary Not Afraid of Wolves exited the store. Three ribbons and a strand of blue beads dangled from the woman's hand.

She stopped next to John's horse, talking fast, giving hand signs, then headed for one of the old cabins at the far end of the square.

"She say, follow."

Micah grabbed the reins of his horse and his Pa's, making their way behind the woman. "Where did you find her?"

"In next room. She help sutler's wife," said Spits Far, striding easily beside Micah.

"I hope she knows what she's doin'. She can't even speak English."

At the cabin entrance, the Indian woman called out and waved her hands. A big bearish white man threw open the door, his black wiry shoulder length hair and beard wrapped around his face. Ducking his head to step outside, his buckskin-clad girth filled the doorway.

"What do you want, woman? Can't ya see I'm busy?" Noticing the travelers, he stood astride on the porch. Mary Not Afraid of Wolves spoke to the man in her native tongue.

"I'm Roger McDougal. Let me get your Pa off his horse and into the cabin. You two young'uns go to the other side of the cabin and feed and water your horses. While you're there, you can take care of my horses, too. When you're finished, grab the ax and go chop some wood for tonight's fire."

Micah put his hand on his hips. "You want me to...."

"Do it," yelled McDougal, narrowing his eyes. "It's your pay for supper. My Mary will take care of your Pa. When you're finished, get back here in case we need your help. Now scat." Then he lifted John from his horse and carried him through the doorway.

"Come," said Spits Far. "Mary first-class healer. We finish fast. Supper good."

Returning to the cabin, Micah brought in an armload of wood from the pile stacked outside and dropped them next to the fireplace.

"How's my Pa?" He bit his lip, hoping for good news.

The Indian woman spoke to her man. Then she made some signs and shook her head.

The boys stood quietly as they listened to her explanation.

Micah opened his eyes wide. "What's wrong?"

"Nothin'," said McDougal. "She tells me this here splint you boys rigged up was first-rate. All she had to do was clean up his leg a little and give him some of her healin' powders to drink, to ease his pain and help him sleep."

McDougal extended his hand. "Here, you can have the belt and pants' snappers back. No need for 'em, since Mary redid the splint. Your rifle's over in the corner. Might want to put it away."

"Ya didn't say how my Pa was?"

"He's healin' good. My woman says it'll probably take about six weeks before he can walk the trails again. Mary's good, plenty smart."

The Indian woman grinned. Three front teeth were missing.

Micah extended his hand. "Thanks, ma'am, for lookin' after my Pa."

She nodded toward Micah, and then spoke to McDougal.

He translated, saying, "She's happy to help. Now, are all the horses taken care of, plenty of water and feed?"

"Yep," the boys said in unison.

"Then it's time to eat. We're not fancy here. One table, two chairs. You boys take the mats on the floor. You'll have to eat with your fingers. Grab a bowl and go get yourselves some soup and meat off the spit. Eat hearty for today there's plenty. Shot an elk last night. Good eatin'." McDougal grabbed his bowl and headed for the fireplace. The boys followed his lead.

"Have you ever had elk before?" Micah whispered.

The Indian boy nodded. "Good, but not like buffalo hump. Yum."

"You eat the buffalo's hump?"

"Best part is liver. Eat raw. Good spirit."

Micah gagged. He made no attempt to continue the conversation.

They filled their bowls and sat down on their mats. Micah raised the bowl to his lips and sipped the broth slowly, and then he wiped his chin with the back of his hand, and dug the meat out with his fingers. It had a gamy smell but didn't taste half bad. Mary brought each of them a hard biscuit, nodding as she handed it to them. They thanked her, then got up and went back to the kettle for seconds.

She took a bowl of broth to feed John. Kneeling next to the bed, she carefully spoon-fed him. Exhausted, he fell back against the pillow and went to sleep.

"When you boys finish, put your stuff on the table and go get your bedrolls," said McDougal. "You can bed down by the fireplace, don't burn your backsides. Mary and I'll sleep on a pallet tonight. We'll leave your Pa where he is. Tomorrow night we'll move him."

The boys retrieved their gear from outside near the door. Micah spread his roll near the fire. Tired but elated, he snuggled under the covers and rested his head on his bunched up clothes. Tonight he was sleeping indoors. No bugs, no snakes, no rain, no…

Micah and Spits Far spent the next week doing chores around the cabin. John stayed in bed a few days until boredom set in. Mary helped him move to a chair on the porch to observe the daily activity around the fort.

One morning, John announced, "We'll be leaving in about a week. Can't wait too long. We need to get over the mountains and on to Tracer's Point before the snow flies. Besides, all this sitting around is making my butt sore."

"Mary says you'll be good enough to ride in about a week or so," said Micah. "Can't wait to leave. It's 'boy do this' or 'boy do that.' I'm tired of cuttin' firewood, takin' care of all McDougal's animals, and everythin' else that comes along."

"Plenty work. Woman bossy," said Boy Who Spits Far.

John laughed. "All women are bossy. Remember that."

McDougal walked out on the porch. "Saddle your horses, boys," he ordered. "We're goin' huntin' for buffalo."

Micah started to say he wasn't goin', but McDougal

lowered his head and stared at him from under his dark bushy eyebrows.

Mounting up, McDougal headed out the gate at a slow trot, followed by the two boys and a wagon driven by three men.

"How long are we gonna be gone?" asked Micah.

"Don't know. Maybe a week. Depends on the buffalo," McDougal said.

"A week?" The boys hung their heads.

After the boys left with McDougal, the cabin was quiet. John lay awake on the mat, aware of Mary, shuffling around the cabin as she worked her chores. She replenished the wood by the fireplace and filled the water bucket. She reminded him of Caroline, with the way she moved softly across the floor.

What did he have to offer his sister-in-law? His housing was a dilapidated shack with one door, no windows. The wind blew through the cracks in the walls. Right now it would house two men and two boys all right, but that was no place for a lady and her family. Maybe when he reached California, he could talk his partner into helping him build a better cabin, one with at least two rooms and a loft. Alexander and his family deserved better.

His deceitful plan had worked in convincing his brother to join in his get-rich scheme for gold. Alexander gave up everything to come to California. For what? John laughed. He'd worked the claim with Tossetti and his pockets were still empty. It had played out early, but he had hoped maybe, just maybe there was something still there waiting to be found. When Alexander finds out about his deception, he'll despise him forever. John felt lower than a snake's belly.

"Leg…" Mary tried to ask him, but could not find the words.

He simply shook his head. "No hurt."

Mary gave him a puzzled look.

He placed his hand over his heart and frowned.

She smiled and said, "Ah." Then she returned to her work, ignoring him for the rest of the day. He found his noon meal on the table, but he didn't have the stomach to eat. He'd misled his brother and compromised Caroline. He was a rotten bastard from head to toe.

Five days later, the six hunters rode into the fort with a butchered buffalo cow in the back of the wagon. The boys dismounted from their horses, corralled them, and headed for the cabin porch. John rose from his chair, hopping on one leg, and leaned against a post. Mary ran to meet the wagon.

"Where've ya been, in a battle?" asked John. Micah's shirt and trousers were blotched with blood, his face haggard. "Tired, are ya?"

Micah puffed out his chest. "Kinda, but we got us a big buffalo. Helped skin, gut and butcher that cow out in the valley."

Boy Who Spits Far shuffled his moccasins in the dust.

"You should have seen him," said Micah, pointing at his friend. "He ate a piece of raw bloody liver, right out of the buffalo. Just bit into it. Never cooked it at all."

"Good medicine. Give strength."

John laughed. "I heard that's supposed to be the best part."

Micah gave him a disgusted look. "Yuck. It was nasty."

McDougal stepped onto the porch. "Buffalo liver is the best tastin' stuff. Nothin' like it."

"Think I'd pass," said John. "You boys need to clean up. Go get your gear and wash up in the brook."

The boys dashed into the cabin.

Mary Not Afraid of Wolves walked toward the men, carrying a pouch of intestines. Another Indian woman walked closely behind with the hide rolled up and tucked under her arm.

She spoke to her husband, then disappeared into the cabin. "She'll clean and scrape the hide later," said McDougal. "She wants to start preparing the hump for supper. She'll cook it over the spit."

The Indian boy raced out the door, passing the two men. "We eat hump," he shouted over his shoulder.

McDougal gave a boisterous laugh. "Ya aren't hungry, are ya, boy?" Leaning against a post and scratched his back. "We shot the buffalo yesterday morning. It took us all day to cut it up into travelin' pieces. Worked well into the evening, skinnin' and guttin'. The boys worked hard. Ya got a couple of keepers there, John."

John nodded and dropped into his chair. "Thanks, they're a handful, but good boys."

Several Indians joined John and McDougal around the porch. "Gus. Henry. Pull that wagon over here. We need to distribute some of this meat to these folks comin' over."

"Ya gonna give it away?" John asked, as the people gathering around.

"Indians think when you share your hunt, you're a big man. Puts you in good standing with the natives," said McDougal, winking at John. Then he joined Gus, passing out the meat to eager, waiting hands while Henry and another man stood in the wagon cutting off large chunks of buffalo.

As they finished doling out the meat, McDougal waved to the men in the wagon. "All right. Let's get these saws and hatchets cleaned up. Clear out the wagon. Then you three men grab yourselves some meat." With that said, McDougal yelled to his wife and headed around the back of the cabin with a couple of tools. Mary walked out to the wagon with a large wash pan and loaded it with buffalo chunks. As she passed John, she smiled.

"Strange people, these frontiersmen," said John. "You spend almost a week hunting, then turn around and give it away. Rough men but good-hearted."

Micah took his bowl to the fireplace. Mary ladled the soup, then dropped in a large chunk of buffalo hump from the spit. He carried the bowl to his mat, not sure if he could eat the steaming broth. All he saw in his mind was the big ugly animal they'd butchered and the bloody hump now part of their supper. He stirred the soup, and looked at Spits Far sitting, next to him, gulping down the broth and tackling the meat.

"Try," he said to Micah. "Sweet. Good. You like." He sucked each finger clean. Rising from the mats, he went back for a second helping.

Micah stared at his bowl and sniffed the contents. It didn't smell bad. He sipped a taste. A little spicy. He drank more, and then placed a tiny sliver of meat into his mouth. Mashing it with his teeth, he wrinkled up his nose, waiting for a strange taste to gag him, like the spring tonic of greens he ate once, but the meat was sweet. He took a bigger bite. Soon his bowl was empty.

"Good," he said, smacking his lips.

Mary smiled at him and nodded.

Spits Far lay back against the cabin wall and rubbed his stomach. "Good buffalo spirit. Stomach full."

"When you boys have eaten enough, I want to talk to the two of you and John outside." McDougal crossed the room and stepped through the doorway. The boys put their bowls on the table and helped John outside to the porch.

McDougal lit his small thin pipe, took a deep draw, and

blew the smoke into the air. "I want to tell you about two strangers that came through here a couple days ago. They stopped at the sutler's store to talk with Jamison." He took another draw from his pipe and continued. "Seems they were lookin' for a man and two boys, one of them being an Indian."

Micah stared at Boy Who Spits Far. John asked, "What did they say?"

"Oh, not much. The sutler told me they kept pretty much to themselves. Just moseyed around the area. Jamison thought I might like to know about them. Are you three in some kinda trouble?"

John rubbed his chin. "Had a little run in with a man at Fort Laramie. He didn't like losin' in a card game."

"Yep, and he tried to kill my Pa." With that, Micah and Spits Far began telling their version about the card game and fight at Fort Laramie.

When they finished, McDougal took another draw from his pipe then tapped the bowl against his boot to dislodge the ashes. "Jamison told 'em he hadn't seen ya. They left early yesterday mornin' headin' south. Since you need to stay another week, I'm sure you're safe enough here. They won't be back."

"Thank the sutler for us, will ya?" John shook the man's hand. "Appreciate all your help."

"Another thing. I wanted you boys to know ole Butch Means took to carvin' your Pa a cane. When you leave, your pa'll have somethin' to help him get around. Now Ole Butch doesn't have any family and can't do many things for himself. So, I'd suggest that his woodpile be stacked and his water barrel filled by tomorrow night." McDougal stuck his pipe into his shirt pocket and headed for the door. "It's time to bed down."

Chapter Twenty-Nine

"Hate ta see you boys go. Seems our firewood pile's never been so well-stocked."

John knew McDougal couldn't resist teasing the lads. He played along. "I'm sure the boys are unhappy about leaving."

Packed and ready to hit the trail at first light, Micah impatiently shifted in his saddle and eyed Spits Far, but didn't say a word.

McDougal stepped off the porch and extended his hand up to John. "Hope you travel safe and get where you're goin'. Keep an eye out for those two desperados. They're ahead of ya now. Be careful with that leg, too. You should be able to take off the splint in about two weeks."

"Thanks for the hospitality. Your wife did a real good job taking care of us. Appreciate the food she packed. It'll come in real handy, especially as I can't do too much hunting."

"She's a good woman. Here she comes now. Has a little somethin' for ya."

In her hands, Mary held three small beaded pouches attached with thongs. She stood in front of the horses, raised the pouches above her head, eyes closed, swaying and chanting in a sing-song cadence. When she finished, she smiled and handed them each one.

"By golly, you must be special. My Mary made those especially for ya. Seems she's taken a likin' to ya."

Mary interrupted him for a moment, talking rapidly. McDougal translated. "She tells me last night she took those bags to the medicine man out yonder. Says they hold magical charms that'll protect ya on your journey. Ward off evil spirits. Mary's a healer in her tribe."

The boys and John thanked her and placed the rawhide strings over their heads, so the pouches rested on their chests. Sitting tall on his horse, Spits Far made a sign with his hand.

John touched the brim of his hat. "Thank you, Mary. We need all the help we can get. We have to be on our way."

Extending his hand to McDougal, he said, "Thanks again."

They left Fort Bridger in single file, well-supplied with food and water. Mary Not Afraid of Wolves had packed chunks of buffalo, pemmican and other unidentified dried meats. McDougal gave them three water bags each and sold John a pack mule to carry supplies he bought from Jamison. Everything they needed to get them to California was strapped to the mule's back.

Four days later they navigated the steep muddy banks of Thomas Fork Creek. The swift-running cold water dragged the horses and riders sideways as they struggled to ascend the slippery incline.

"Tonight we'll camp at Smith's Trading Post. It's about thirteen miles ahead. We'll be able to get out of these wet duds," John announced. "I guess I'll fit in real good with the trader."

Micah asked, "Why's that, Pa?"

"'Cause Old Peg Leg Smith owns that post. Story goes he had to cut off his own leg to survive."

When they reached Smith's Post, John and the boys selected a site and settled in, changing into dry clothes as light faded in the west. They ate a cold supper before laying out their bedrolls close to their small fire. With two wagon trains in the area, noise from all the bustling activities was horrendous. Finally, the fires died down, quiet surrounded them as the travelers burrowed deep into their blankets.

At four o'clock the next morning, a trumpet's blast jolted John from a deep sleep. Startled, Micah jumped out of this blanket, ready for trouble, only to find the area buzzing with excitement, people preparing breakfast and getting ready to pull out.

Micah adjusted his trousers, sat down and yanked on his boots. "Where's Spits Far?"

John pointed to the bushes. "He's doing his business."

"Oh. Guess I'll grab myself somethin' to eat." Rolling up his bedroll, Micah tied it behind the cantle on his saddle.

"Grab me some of the dried meat in that large bag in the back."

"Do ya know what kind of meat this is?"

John chuckled, "No, but I'll try it and let ya know."

Micah selected several pieces of dried pemmican for himself. Gingerly opening the large bag, he looked inside. "Whew, it stinks. You sure you want to eat this?"

"Just bring me a large piece, Micah," John's voice sounded testy.

Picking out the top chunk of dried meat, Micah closed the bag, and handed it to his pa.

Spits Far ambled out of the bushes, adjusting his loincloth. Grabbing his rolled-up bedroll, he flopped it over his horse's back before taking two pieces of pemmican and a small chunk of buffalo from the saddlebag.

"We'll be back," Micah called over his shoulder, as they wandered off in the direction of the crowded campgrounds, leaving John alone to eat his breakfast.

From behind, a dark shadow extended over him and across the grass. "So, where're you from?" a gruff voice boomed.

Surprised, John twisted around and tried to get up, but couldn't reach his cane.

"Here, let me help you, young fella." The gray-haired man handed John his cane and assisted him to his feet. "The name's Thomas Smith, better known as Peg Leg Smith."

"John Anderson. Glad to meet you." John recalled a couple of stories McDougal had told him about this man.

"Where you headed?"

"Back to California."

"Why don't you come on up to my cabin and sit a spell? Got some good whiskey and breakfast is a-waitin'."

"Got my boys with me."

"Oh hell, bring 'em along." Smith hobbled back toward the creek in an uneasy rolling gait.

Spying the boys, John waved them over. "Would you boys like a warm breakfast and some interesting conversation?"

Micah raised an eyebrow. "Sure. Where're we goin'?"

"Follow me." Limping, John headed to the cabin.

"Come on in," yelled Smith, spying his invited guests. "Help yourselves to some food, then sit down over here."

"Boys, this is Thomas Smith and his wife."

"Hello," said Micah, as he grabbed a bowl off the table and headed for the fireplace. Spits Far followed close behind. The aroma was enough to kill for, their stomachs growled in anticipation with each step. Both boys loaded their bowls and escaped, sitting against the wall next to the doorway.

Peg Leg plopped into his a chair at the head of the table, pulled off his wooden leg, and propped the stump on a stool next to him. "I'd say they was a mite hungry."

"Traveling like we are, we don't get too many homecooked meals, especially tasty ones. But we aren't starving."

Smith passed the whiskey jug to John, who filled a tin cup two fingers high. After taking a sip, John gasped for air, his eyes watering. "Whew. There's some nasty stuff."

"It's made the old-timers' way, creek water, grain alcohol, a little tobaccy and some pepper. That's the way they used to make it at the rendezvous up at Green Mountain."

Smith poured another drink, downed it, and poured another, all the while talking about the old days when he rode with Sublette, Williams and Bissonet, trapping for the American Fur Company up in the mountains. The boys moved to a bench and leaned on the table, listening to the yarns Peg Leg wove. Then he told about the fateful day he was shot by an Indian at the North Platte River while looking for beaver. Inching forward, Micah's eyes grew wide. Spits Far sat straight as an arrow.

"Yes, siree, there I was hiding in the bushes, when a stray arrow struck my left leg, just above the ankle. I'll tell you, the pain was bad because it shattered the bone. Right then and there I shouted, 'someone's gonna have to cut my leg off'." He paused for a moment to refill his cup. "No one volunteered so I took up a butcher knife and cut it off myself. They all thought I was crazy and gonna die, but here I am, healthy as a horse." He gave a wicked laugh, then sputtered and coughed.

Micah looked at his pa. "Wow. Don't think I could do that to my leg." The Indian boy sat still, saying nothing. He didn't even blink an eye.

"I think it's about time we headed out. It's getting late. We need to put some miles behind us." John grabbed his cane, got up, and extended his hand to Smith. "Thanks for the vittles and the story. Enjoyed both."

"You're welcome. Don't mind if I don't get up." Then he reached for the whiskey jug and poured another drink.

Outside, Micah talked about Smith and the loss of his leg.

Finally Spits Far said, "Him windbag. Make Indian look bad. Him not brave, him stupid."

"You're probably right. Last night, I ran across a man down by the creek right before we bedded down. He told me Smith was a notorious horse thief. Actually the story goes he lost his leg in a battle with some Spanish ranchers while stealing their horses. It's told an Indian assisted him in cuttin' off his leg."

Micah stopped in his tracks. "You mean he was lyin'?"

"Don't know, Micah. Who's to tell the truth of one story against another. We'll never know. You got entertained while you ate a good warm breakfast."

"I guess so." Micah bowed his head and shuffled his feet. "Sure can't believe everything a person tells ya these days."

Headed for Hudspeth's Cutoff, John and the boys stopped once to take on water. Ahead lay the California Trail. Covered with dust from head to toe, they made another stop at Hot Springs where they found the water too hot to bathe in. The only solution was to dip their shirts, air cool them, and wash their bodies quickly.

With his back toward the others, Micah stripped off all of his clothes, shaking each piece vigorously. "I can't believe all this dirt. It's even between my teeth and up my nose. I'm glad you made me cover my face with a handkerchief, Pa." He retrieved the bright red cloth from his hat, and snapped it in the air.

John relaxed on his bedroll the best he could, propped against his saddle. His feet hurt from walking, but his bad leg was holding up well.

"Still chew dirt." The Indian boy sent a wad of spit into the air.

Micah turned around in time to see the hunk sail pass his head. "Hey, that was great. Is that how you got your name? Do it again."

Standing in the open, buck-naked, the boys took turns spitting, trying to outdo each other. Lying back with his hands behind his head, John grinned. *What a view. Only a man could appreciate this scene.* "You boys better get yourselves dressed, before some of those ladies in the wagon train ahead see you."

Micah stretched his neck. "Ah, we can barely see their wagons from here. Wow, where did all these gallinippers come from all of a sudden?" Micah dove for his bedroll, slapping at the mosquitoes, forgetting all about his clothes.

"Get some shut-eye now. Morning's gonna come quick, and we need to beat those wagons out. Unless you want to eat their dust all day." With that, he turned over, tried to get comfortable, swatted at the horde of mosquitoes, then pulled his blanket over his head. "I think I'm getting too old for this sort of stuff."

Micah wobbled in the saddle, tired from bearing the heat of the sun all day with only a handful of water to drink. His dream was to end this beastly journey.

"We just lost the Humboldt River," John said.

Micah shot up straight and looked around. "How can you lose a river?"

"It vanished underground into a sinkhole." John dismounted, took off his hat and beat the dust off his trousers.

The boys slid off their horses.

Micah shaded his eyes with his hand. "What are those round things out there, Pa?"

"Those bubble-like sand hills are called the hummocks. Beyond them is sixty-five miles of desolate desert."

The boys' spirits dropped.

"That's not pretty," Micah said.

"No," John agreed "It's not pretty. I'm taking off this splint. It's going to be hard enough walking in this heavy sand. Don't need an extra burden."

Spits Far stood holding his horse's reins, moving one foot back and forth in the sand. "Lips dry. Feet hurt. Bad spirit."

Feigning disbelief, Micah said, "I can't believe it. You're finally complaining?"

"Enough, boys. I can sympathize with Spits Far. My lips feel thick and my eyes itch from all this dust. Take a drink, but conserve your water."

Micah mumbled to himself, took a sip from his water pouch, then poured a small amount into his hat for his horse to drink.

John climbed back into the saddle. "Let's go. The longer we stay here, the longer it'll take us to cross this hellhole. We'll ride a while, and then walk to give the horses a break."

Several days later, they crested a hill.

"Fresh water below boys," announced John.

Heading down the steep hill, holding the reins in his

hands, Micah struggled to keep his balance. "All right, fresh, cold water. I can taste it now."

John and the Indian boy cautiously followed him. At the bottom, Spits Far began disrobing.

"What are ya gonna do? Swim in that little spring?" asked Micah

"Me wash body. Clean body, clean spirit."

"Wash, but don't drown in it."

John took off his hat and wiped his forehead with the back of his sleeve. He bent down and slurped a drink, letting the cool water run down his chin, dripping onto his chest. Removing his shirt, he tossed it on the ground then splashed water onto his face and chest, one handful at first. Scooping with both hands, he tossed water at Micah. His son whipped his hands across the top of the water, splashing both Boy Who Spits Far and his father. Suddenly the boys were in a full-fledged water fight.

When darkness surrounded them, they burrowed into their blankets to ward off the cold desert air. There was nothing available to make a fire. Overhead stars filled the sky.

"I'm proud of you boys," said John. "You stuck with me. Sorry it's so hard and dangerous. I promise you, once we get to the cabin, we'll be a family forever."

Micah rolled over. "We're already a family. Ever since we left Fort Laramie."

"Strong family. We look alike."

"Oh, sure we do." John laughed. What a mix-matched group they were.

Micah hooted. "We're twins."

Both boys belly laughed until their sides hurt, their voices echoing through the valley.

John nestled down into his blankets, listening to their tall tales and funny stories well into the night.

* * *

With sore bodies and feet, exhausted from struggling through dirt and sand, the boys stood awestruck by the lush green valley at the base of the Sierra Nevada Mountains. The snow-capped mountains, with irregular peaks, stretched across the horizon, in uneven rows.

"Look at that, would ya? Them's the Sierra's you been talkin' about?" asked Micah

"Yes," nodded John. "Beautiful, aren't they? Bet you two never thought we'd make it this far."

"Can't believe we're seein' green grass. Almost forgot what it looked like."

"Mountains tall," Spits Far said. "How far we go up?"

"All the way over two summits, down into several valleys, and across the Pass to the other side."

"How far is it?" asked Micah.

"As the crow flies, probably twenty miles."

Micah squinted. "And the way we're going?"

"Far. High. Rocky," answered Spits Far.

"Figured that."

"I'd say about seventy miles up to the summits, counting the valleys, and eighty miles over the western slopes into the Sacramento Valley," replied John. "We'll camp soon and begin climbing early tomorrow morning. First, we need a good night's sleep."

"I'll enjoy sleeping on the soft grass," said Micah. "I could do with somethin' to eat."

"Soon, Micah," was all John said.

"Be back." The Indian boy jumped onto his horse and galloped off, disappearing from sight.

"Where's he goin' in such a hurry?"

"Oh, I believe we are going to have fresh meat for supper."

"Maybe rabbit?"

"Probably."

At dawn they broke camp and headed for the mountains, passing a wagon train campsite. Climbing the eastern slope of the Sierra Nevada, they rode single file on narrow trails and scaled several rock formations before dropping down through a tight canyon into an open valley. Once they reached the ridge at Corral Flats, they followed a deep-sided twisted trail down the western slopes into the valley below.

John smiled. "Boys, you are now officially in California."

"Yahoo," they yelled.

"We'll follow the south fork of the American River to Hangtown. Be there in about two days."

Riding into town was a great disappointment to the boys. After crossing the desert, riding dusty trails, and conquering mountains, their dreams of a real town were shattered. A river wove its way between two mountain slopes into a haphazard town of rough-board buildings, tents and mud streets.

"This is a crazy place," said Micah. "Looks like people flung a building anywhere they wanted. Why even the road zigzags every which way."

John noted the frustration on his son's face. "Remember, this is a mining town. Not a fancy city. But, the vittles are good. I'm sure we'll be able to find some soft comfortable beds for the night."

"A bed?" Micah shut his eyes, a goofy grin split his face. "Tonight we don't have to sleep on the ground."

John stepped into the lobby of Sadie's Hotel and Bathhouse. The buxom woman dashed from around the counter, grabbed him, and gave him a big jovial hug.

"Where you been, honey?" said Sadie. "Phineas and I missed you. Didn't we?"

The big black man sweeping the floors looked up. "Yes, ma'am, we sure did."

"Sadie, these here are my two boys and they're starving. I promised them one of your famous meals."

Sadie raised a questioning eyebrow. "Your boys? Let's get these young men fed." She led them into the dining room and began setting out tin plates and utensils. "Now you three sit here and I'll round you up a meal you won't forget."

After eating roast beef, boiled potatoes, brown gravy, and buttered corn, John announced they needed a bath.

"You just follow me and Phineas, honey. We'll fix you right up."

She led them down the hallway and into a large, unpainted back room with six big metal tubs. The big, black man began filling three tubs with warm water from buckets off the wood stove, while Sadie set out soap and towels on the chairs.

"I'm gonna make up your room. Enjoy," she said, pulling the door closed behind her.

Phineas picked up several empty buckets and disappeared out the back door.

John and Micah undressed quickly and gingerly stepped into the water. Slipping down into the tub, each gasped as the steamy water enveloped their bodies. Boy Who Spits Far undressed and stood looking at the tub.

Micah waved a wet hand. "Get in. You'll like it."

"Strange thing." He toed the tub then stuck his hand into the water.

"Hey, Spits Far. It won't bite ya." Micah shook his head. "You chase things, fight mean, and eat raw liver. Now, you're afraid of a tub."

The Indian boy screwed up his face, pursed his lips and stepped into the water. Shrugging his shoulders, he slipped down into the tub.

"Tonight, we are gentlemen," announced John. "All I need right now is a good cigar and a glass of whiskey."

Eyes closed, Micah laid his head back, resting his hands on the side edges. "Ah, this is great, Pa. It's like stealin' a pig and bein' able to eat it without gettin' caught."

"Enjoy, boys. This is the best pleasure you're gonna have for awhile. Tomorrow we leave for Tracer's Point. Can't wait to see Tossetti's face when I tell him I'm a father."

"Need woman," replied Boy Who Spits Far.

"We can work on that," piped up Micah.

"Whoa. We have plenty of time for matchmaking. Let me get this father routine working first." John made himself comfortable and shut his eyes. "Yes, sir, it's gonna be a big surprise to my partner when we all show up tomorrow."

Chapter Thirty

On the Trail to California

"Why are you so darn nasty, Ben?" Caroline rotated the hot coffee cup between her cold hands. "You've been downright grumbly and ugly since we left Fort Laramie."

"Woman. Ya got what ya want. Now leave me alone." Sulking, he turned his back to her.

"All right. So I tricked you back there at the card game. But that's been over two and a half weeks ago. Most of the time you act like I don't exist."

"Ya don't, as far as I'm concerned."

"Ah, Ben, you know you really wanted to help me get to California. If you had left me at Fort Laramie, you'd never have forgiven yourself, especially if something happened to me. Anyway, how would I have survived?"

He mumbled something indistinguishable, all the while sitting on his blanket Indian style, sucking on his liquor bottle.

After a moment of silence, he faced her. "Do you know what you've done to me? I worked hard gettin' those skins together. Campin' in freezin' weather, fightin' nasty critters, always bein' cautious 'cause I wanta keep my scalp, just so I kin go to St. Louie. Sacrificin' for what? To take ya to Californy? There's nothin' there but more hard work."

"But, Ben—"

"No *buts* about it. Ya got this notion in your head you're goin' someplace special, all pretty and wonderful. Well, it ain't. It's ugly, dirty, and it'll probably kill ya in three years."

She stared hard at him, realizing he was probably right. Why was she going on to California? John! She narrowed her eyes. She had an ax to grind for the misery he'd caused her. The losses she had endured. All because of his harebrained scheme for gold.

"You're right. I don't know what lies ahead of me," she said. "And, I'll probably be sorry once I get there." She gritted her teeth and glared into the fire. "I have to go."

"You hate him that much? Woman, you carry a grudge far and above anyone I know."

"Yes, and when I'm through with him, my brother-in-law won't be worth a plug." She kicked her heel toward the fire. Grasping her knees together, she hugged them close to her chest.

Ben took another swig, wiped his mouth with the back of his hand, and corked the bottle. "Let me tell ya somethin'. That hate'll eat at ya until there's nothin' left inside. I know. It took me most of my life to realize that."

"What are you talking about now?"

"My pa was lots older than my ma. Hell, she was barely weaned when my pa married her. They had a cabin near her folks. One day he heard an ax choppin' too close, neighbors movin' in, so he up and took her from Virginy, over the mountains to Tennessee. They walked the whole way, carryin' everything they owned on their backs. He cleared a little bit of land in the deep woods, built a cabin, picked up his rifle, and left. He was a 'long hunter', spent most of his days huntin' in unknown territories with a black powder muzzleloader, sometimes stayin' away for a year.

"Oh, he came back all right. While he was gone, my Ma did everything for herself, huntin', choppin' wood, keepin' herself alive. She was young, strong, and determined. That kinda life takes the youth out of ya for sure. Anyway, come the third year, she had me and Pa was gone again. Don't know how she did it, but she managed birthin' me all by herself. He came back and acted like it was nothin', what she did, then he was off again."

Ben grew silent for a moment. She scanned his face and could tell he was liquored up and his mind was far away.

"So, what happened?" she asked.

"One day, when I was about seven, he left and never returned. My ma aged from all the hard work. She took to walkin' in the woods for hours, returnin' home just before dusk. One day a wagon came by, a family on their way to Illinois: a man, woman and two young girls. My ma was half crazed by that time. She gave me to them and off I went, cryin' and screamin' for her. She turned her back and walked into the cabin. Never waved nor said a kind good-bye to me."

Caroline sat there stunned. "How could she do that to you?"

"I told ya, she was half crazed. I worked for those people like a slave, doin' the work of a horse. Those two girls sat around nettlin' me and tellin' me what to do. When I was about fourteen, I decided I'd had enough so I ran away to St. Louie, earnin' enough money doin' all kinds of jobs and learnin' everythin' I could."

"Oh, Ben I'm so sorry."

"Don't want your sympathy. Ain't tellin' this to get ya feelin' sorry for me. I'm relatin' this to ya, in hopes you'll understand. There's a lot out there that'll tear your heart out, but as long as you're alive, hell, you can do anything ya want."

She glared at him. "It's not the same, Ben. I lost my family because of my brother-in-law."

"You think he planned to kill off your family? Woman, that was his brother. He might get rid of you, but not his brother, that's blood. Did he send those Indians to get your daughter or throw your son in the river?"

She took a deep breath, fighting with her feelings inside. "No, but—"

"Ya ain't listenin'. Sure, he schemed to get ya all out to Californy. Sure he's an asshole for that. Ain't sayin' he's not guilty there. But it's the country and elements ya should be hatin'. That's what did ya in, not your brother-in-law."

She shut her eyes. She didn't want to hear anymore. It *was* John's fault she lost everything, it had to be. *Somebody* had to bear the blame for her pain.

"I'm turning in." Taking off her boots, she borrowed down in the blankets, covering her head. Tears slowly trickled down her cheeks, she sobbed softly, her shoulders shook, and pain filled her chest as she gasped for air. With Alexander gone, there was no one to comfort her. She missed his strong arms to protect her. She was on her own and she hated it. *Oh, Lord. Help me.*

Ben noticed her covers shake and heard the faint sobbing noise. He knew grief and hatred consumed her. He uncorked his bottle and took a big gulp. He could handle fighting and cussing. Why, killing didn't even bother him. But he wasn't accustomed to soothing broken hearts or knowing the right words to help with sorrow, especially when it came to a woman. He'd spent too many years in the backwoods of the mountains. Harsh times were part of his life. What should he say to her? Traveling with this female was taxing his nerves. He took another swig, and then another before putting out the fire, and slipping into his bedroll. *It's better to be drunk and not hear her cry.*

Two days later, they arrived at Fort Bridger. Ben dismounted and entered Jamison's store. He was gone quite a while, so Caroline decided to walk around the area. Finally Ben emerged from the building, shaking his head.

"Ya won't believe what that there sutler's been tellin' me. What a story."

Caroline returned to the hitching post. "What?"

"It seems your brother-in-law and two boys were here for about three weeks. The story goes, he broke his leg and stayed over there with the McDougals until he could ride again. I think I'll go over and have a talk with him. You sit a spell on the porch in the old rocky chair. I'll be back soon."

"I'm going with you."

"No, you ain't. This here McDougal is a mean frontiersman, a rough, ornery Scotsman. I remember him from the old trappin' days."

"I'm not sitting in some stupid chair, waiting for you. I'm going along." She headed for the cabin. Darn if he was going to leave her behind while he asked questions. She had a few questions of her own.

Ben knocked on the cabin door. It squeaked open with each tap. He pushed it wider and stuck his head in. "Hello. Ya home? Hmmm. Nobody's here."

Halfway across the compound a voice boomed, "Get

away from my door, you old windbag. Where's your manners?" McDougal strolled toward them, leading his mare, followed closely by an Indian woman on horseback. He slipped the reins over the railing, stepped onto the porch and eyed Ben, hands on his hips. "I'll be. If it ain't Old Ben Wilson. I thought you were dead by now. Heard you lost your scalp up around the Columbia River."

Ben removed his hat and ran his hand through his greasy hair. "Does it look like I was scalped, you grog-drinkin' Scotsman? You believe everything ya hear?"

"Nope, but it looks like it needs washin', you cussed old fool," said McDougal. He shoved the door open wide. "Come on in and bring in your woman. Don't know why she picked you to stay with."

Caroline flushed, "Oh, no, I don't belong to him. He's taking me to California, as my guide."

Ben slapped his knee with his cap and laughed, "Me with her? Well, that's a pip. Not on a dare. Been hog-swaggled into takin' her to her brother-in-law. Seems he stayed with you for awhile, with two young'uns."

Bending over at the fireplace to ignite a straw to light his pipe, McDougal straightened up when he heard Ben's statement. He stared at the two visitors. His Indian wife stopped in the doorway, three rabbits dangled from her hand.

"What's your brother-in-law's name?" he asked gruffly, suspicious of the lady in front of him.

"John, John Anderson. We were told by the sutler that he broke his leg and stayed with you for a time."

"Have to talk to Jamison about spreadin' lies." McDougal walked over to the table and took a seat in his chair. His wife dropped the rabbits on the other end of the table. "Come on and sit down. This here's my wife, Mary Not Afraid of Wolves. She's gonna skin these scrawny rabbits and make us some stew for supper. Now tell me about this man you're lookin' for." He leaned back, puffing on his pipe and waiting for an explanation.

Caroline sat down on the bench. She started by telling about the letter from John, the trip from Virginia, and how she came to be by herself with Ben. McDougal listened, quietly smoking his pipe.

When she finished, he said, "So, she hoodwinked ya into takin' her over the Sierras. Poker's gonna be the death of ya yet, ya old coot. One day somebody's gonna shoot ya. A gold, pocket watch to cover your bet. That's one game they'll talk about at Fort Laramie for awhile."

"Did you say John Anderson was here?" Caroline suspected McDougal was stalling for time, trying to figure whether he wanted to tell her the truth or not.

"Yes, ma'am he was, with two young boys. Those young'uns worked hard while they were here, fillin' the water barrel and cuttin' wood. They even helped old Butch Means over there." He pointed out the window, took another puff off his pipe, and then stood up.

"I don't usually ask many questions. I listen a lot. Seems to me you're in a hurry to catch up with Anderson. I'd say ya might catch up with 'em if ya leave right away."

Mary spoke to her husband at some length then McDougal translated. "My wife says the man's leg is healed by now and they are probably makin' good travel time. She also reminds me that she gave each of them a medicine bag to protect him from evil spirits. She's a healer. Had a vision that terrible trouble was waitin' for them in California. Two people were gonna die and she wanted to be sure it wasn't the boys. She took a likin' to 'em."

Ben pulled the bench forward on the other side of the table and sat down. "Do I have to twist your scrawny neck to get the full story out of ya?"

McDougal looked first at Caroline. Then he glared at Ben. "All right. Be quiet and I'll tell ya what I know. From what I can recollect, John was playing poker at Fort Laramie. Turned out to be a dishonest game." He gave Ben a look from under his bushy eyebrows.

He cleared his throat, spit in a pot on the floor, and continued. "Anyway, as the story goes, there was a fight and a man got killed. Two desperadoes are after 'em, with killin' on their minds. The rest ya know."

Ben removed his hat, plopped it on the bench next to him and asked, "How long have they been gone?"

"They left about a week or so ago, headin' southwest to Hudspeth Cutoff. They'll pick up the trail along the Humboldt River in order to cross over Carson Pass. He called the name of his place Tracer's Point. Said he had a partner, can't remember his name. That's all I know."

McDougal leaned back in his chair and looked at Ben. Mary spoke to her husband. He removed his pipe from his mouth. "Oh, my woman reminds me that two evil men rode in one day lookin' for a man and two boys from Fort Laramie. They only stayed one night before riding off to California."

Caroline exhaled slowly, "Major Sanderson at Fort Laramie told me about the card game and the two men after John and the boys. Maybe your wife is right about someone getting hurt." She turned to Ben. "We can only stay one night. I'd like to push hard. Maybe get there before something happens."

"Now you're worried about your brother-in-law? Back yonder you wanted to cut him up into little pieces and fry his brains out. Don't understand ya at all."

"I'm worried those two men might harm the boys. They shouldn't be held accountable for what John's done. They, at least, deserve a chance."

McDougal poked Ben, "She available? I'd be willin' to take on another wife. Mary could use the help."

Caroline glared at McDougal. "No, I'm not available."

The Indian woman chuckled while she skinned the rabbits near the fireplace.

An hour later, Ben disappeared for awhile. When he came back, he carried a bundle under his arm and slapped it down on table in front of her. "Here, this is for you. Don't say I never give ya nothin'." With a mischievous look, he grabbed a cup and headed for the coffee pot at the fireplace.

"What's this, a peace offering?"

He strode over to the table and plopped onto the bench. "There's no peace between us, woman. Call it a bribe if ya want."

"And what are you bribing me for?"

He propped his elbow on the table and placed his chin into his open hand. "Just open the gawlderned package, woman. Questions and more questions. That's all I git from ya."

She untied the string, unrolling the small piece of hide. Caroline's mouth fell open. Inside was a .31 caliber colt pistol, holster, and ammunition. For the first time since they started this trip together, she was speechless. "How...."

Ben yanked his hat off his head and slapped his thighs with it. "Ooh, weee, can't believe she's finally lost that tongue of hers. Dang-nabit, woman, I can't have you runnin' around in the California wilds without protection. That little old powder shooter you have in your saddlebags takes too long to load."

She stood up, reached over the table, grabbed him by the sides of his beard, and planted a kiss on his forehead.

Shocked, Ben blushed and sat back on the bench, trying to make light of the situation. He plopped his hat back on his head. "Woman, you're embarrassing me." But a small smile crept across his lips.

"Hell, Wilson, when was the last time a female kissed ya?" asked McDougal.

Ben smiled and lifted one eyebrow. "Ain't tellin'."

"How much did Jamison sock you for the pistol?"

"None of your business."

"Thank you, Benny," she whispered.

Ben waved his hand in front of his face. "Stop that, woman. No need to get all mushy over a gun. You keep this up, McDougal'll get the wrong idea."

When supper was ready, the men dug into the rabbit stew and biscuits. Once their bellies were full, the men stepped outside to smoke. Finally, Caroline and Mary sat at the table and filled their plates. Clean up chores would have to wait. Their conversation was mostly one-sided. Mary nodded and smiled while Caroline talked.

When McDougal announced it was time to get some shut-eye, Caroline retrieved their bedrolls while Ben left to care for the animals.

"Spread your stuff over by the fireplace, but don't kick over the coffee pot," McDougal told her. "One more thing. I wouldn't spread your blankets too close to that nasty duffer. He's mighty sneaky and smells worse than a skunk." Chuckling out loud, he turned his back to the door as Ben entered.

"I heerd that, you ornery toadstool."

The next morning the two men stood on the front porch discussing which route to take to the California Trail.

"I believe takin' the Hastings Cutoff will shorten your trek. The goin's rough, but the two of you can make it. Be sure you stop at the springs to take on water. That desert can make you mighty thirsty."

"Yep, we will. Gonna push hard. If we're lucky, we'll cross the Sierras before the snow flies. We're already well behind reachin' it in time." Ben chewed a chaw of tobacco then spit over the rail. "Your story about John and the boys upset her enough to make her worse than a wet cat in a water hole. First, she's madder than a hornet to get her evens with the man. Now she's worried somethin' will happen to him. I'll never understand this gawlderned woman and don't ever intend to."

"Well, she's all yours."

"Humph. Once I deliver her, she ain't mine no more."

Caroline and Ben mounted their horses and left Fort Bridger, riding southwest. Taking the old trader's route from Salt Lake City, they headed for the Humboldt River. Passing through Echo Canyon, they rode single file up the narrows, crossing Weber River. Ascending the Hogsback Summit, Caroline turned to look back at the Wasatch Mountains. The view was breathtaking. Once they descended into Emigration Canyon, they camped near Salt Lake City and purchased supplies from the Mormons' Desert Store.

The next day they arrived at the Salt Lake Desert. A flat, encrusted land of salt crystals spread across the horizon.

Ben squinted against the glare, judging the distance. "We can cross this here desert and reach the springs at the base of Pilot Peak in about seventeen hours, if we push the animals hard." He turned in the saddle to look at Caroline straight on.

"I can do that," she said. "How many miles across is it?"

"Over fifty but less than seventy. You ready?"

Eighteen hours later, they arrived at the springs and collapsed, exhausted and hot. The three animals survived the grueling ride, but struggled over the last five miles, carrying their heavy loads.

After setting up camp, Caroline grabbed some dried buffalo meat, a pouch of water, and sat down on her bedroll. Ben flopped down next to the small fire, chomping on a chunk of meat.

"Ben, what's your full name?"

He stopped and looked at her from under his eyebrows. "Ain't a tellin' ya." He gnawed off another piece of meat.

"Ah, come on Ben. My full name is Caroline Anne Bready Anderson."

"That's nice." He kept right on eating. Silence fell between them for a few minutes.

"Alluissius Nebednego Potter Wilson."

Caroline raised her eyebrows. "What?"

"You heerd me and don't want to see ya smiling either."

"Potter, huh."

"Yep."

"Nice long name, Ben." She ducked her head to keep him from seeing the smile creeping across her face. Alluissius Nebednego. Good night. His mother must have really hated him.

Ben sat growling. He was unfit company the rest of the evening.

After Caroline finished eating, she crawled between her blankets. The next thing she knew, Ben was shaking her awake.

"Need to go. Long way to the river."

They rode, passing through mountains and canyons. Reaching the Humboldt River, they followed it until it disappeared into the Sinks.

Ben pointed ahead. "There lies the nastiest part of this trip."

Caroline sat in disbelief. "That is the ugliest place I've ever seen. Makes me want a bath with soap and plenty of water. I hate this grit between my teeth." She sat on her horse, covered from head to foot with dust. Sweat rivulets slid down her neck and into her cleavage. Her shirt clung to her back and under her arms. Mopping her face with her sleeve, she smeared the dust across her cheeks and nose. Miserable and exhausted, disillusionment set in. This was a trip from hell.

Much later they finally reached the base of the Sierra Nevada Mountains, the level valley of green grass bordered a wide stream. A welcoming sight to the trail-weary travelers. Fresh water had never tasted so good.

"Stay here, I'm washing this filth off." She dismounted and dashed toward the stream. Undressing behind a few dense bushes, she plunged into the cold water. With no soap or towel, she rubbed her body to rid it of all the trail dust and ugly memories, hoping to leave them behind.

When she returned dripping wet and smiling, she asked, "So, where do we go from here?"

Ben pointed upward

Her gaze followed his finger. She dropped her head. "Another mountain. Why can't men stay put and be happy with green pastures and flat land."

"You mumblin' to yourself again?"

She didn't answer. What was there to say? Sitting in the grass, Caroline begrudged the comforts that the women from a wagon train camped near them enjoyed. She felt jealous of their families and their security. Maybe someday she would have all of that again. Maybe.

The next morning Ben and Caroline began the ascent of the first summit and continued down into a valley, only to begin another climb. They rode through Carson Pass, and reached the ridge of Corral Flat.

Ben sat staring down into a haze-covered valley. A light snow began to fall. "Didn't make this pass too soon. In a few days, nobody'll get through."

"It sure is cold up here. Is that really California down there?"

"Yep."

"How far?"

"About eighty miles straight down. That's Sacramento Valley, what you can see of it. We better get goin'. If the weather gets worse, we could be gettin' into real trouble here."

They reached the valley and followed the South Fork of the American River into Hangtown. Caroline gazed about the misaligned town, not believing her eyes. The men in the streets ogled her as she rode by. One man grabbed her by the leg, pulling her toward him.

"She's mine. I saw her first. Marry me, lady. Stay with me. One day I'll be rich."

Ben took his rope and beat the man until he turned loose of Caroline's leg. "Get away from her, you drunken sot. Go find yourself a hole to crawl into."

More men sauntered into the streets, stared as she passed by, mouths open, some removing their hats. She felt like a dirty queen entering a town of misfits.

To her right, she saw a clapboard hotel advertising baths. "Ben, I need to stop there."

"Let's find a stable first. Then we'll get us a couple of rooms."

Another man made a mad dash for Caroline. Ben rode his horse directly in front of him, cut him off and knocked him to the ground. "If ya know what's good for ya, you'll take your worthless self elsewhere. The lady don't want nothin' to do with any of ya," he yelled.

"Ben." Caroline pointed ahead. Three buildings down stood Kennedy's Stable.

Chapter Thirty-One

Tracer's Point, California

"Hello in the cabin. Tossetti. You there," John shouted.

No answer. The trail led past the cabin, following the rise on the mountainside, snaking back toward the building. An eerie silence settled around thc area. Passing the Long Box, he noticed a shovel stuck upright in the dirt.

"Strange. He usually works until supper."

Micah pointed down stream. "Look. There's two men standin' down a-ways. Maybe one of them's Tossetti."

"Nah. Those are the German brothers. Not too friendly." John dismounted, tied the reins to a low limb and headed toward the cabin. He pushed the door open. Debris was scattered everywhere. The table lay knocked over, chairs broken, mattress ripped apart and the rest of the contents strewn across the floor.

"Looks like a herd of buffalo stampeded through here," remarked John.

Micah peeked around his father to get a better view. "I'd say someone put up a heck of a fight."

"Conway, Crow here. Bad medicine," Boy Who Spits Far said. He backed away from the cabin door, cautiously scanning the trees and brush along the ridge.

Stepping inside, John sifted through some of the mess.

"What ya lookin' for, Pa." Micah kicked at a couple of loose boards at his feet.

"I had a cash box with some papers in it on the shelf when I left. It doesn't seem to be here."

Blood splattered the floor next to the bed and on the walls. John lifted one corner of the mattress. Nothing. "You boys go on outside and look around, but keep your eyes peeled. I believe Spits Far's right. We've got unpleasant company."

A few minutes later, Micah returned. "Pa. We found a man behind the cabin."

John followed his son. His partner sat tied to a tree with a rope around his neck, cuts over most of his body, some fingers missing, and scalped.

He removed his hat, clutching it tightly in his hands. "You boys go get your horses. I'll join you in a minute."

Micah stared at his father. "Aren't we gonna bury him."

"No bury. Crow know we here."

"He's right," said John. "If we bury him, they'll come looking for us. Right now no one knows we've been up here and that gives us a chance to stay alive, until I can get a plan together. Now, go mount up. I'll be right with you."

John removed his hat and bowed his head for a moment. Tossetti had been a good partner, not much talk and all work. He didn't deserve this type of treatment. John narrowed his brows and crushed his hat in his hands. He'd find the son of a bitch who did this.

He spun around and headed toward the boys. Climbing

into the saddle, he said, "We're going to take the mountain trail to the top. On the other side is a cave I found years ago. We'll stay there for a while."

"Here I was lookin' forward to a nice warm bed to sleep in tonight."

The Indian boy raised his eyebrows. "Cabin. No bed. Sleep floor."

"Yes, I saw that, too. How come you only got one bed in the cabin?"

"We took turns sleeping. Sometimes one of us would sleep on the floor, if we had to."

Climbing the mountainside was difficult. The trail narrowed down in several spots and boulders seemed to rise out of nowhere. The steep side fell into a deep ravine and tree limbs hung over the path, making travel toilsome. Finally crossing over the ridge, John led the boys down the other side to a cave. The rocky entrance was hidden by dense overgrowth.

Pushing the brush aside, Micah whistled low. "You can ride a horse in there." His voice echoed back and a grin spread across his face.

"Hellooo," he yelled, and then waited for an echo again.

"Quit playing around and step aside. I need to make sure we're not sharing this cave with anything else."

"Ya mean like a bear or somethin'?"

Spits Far calmly answered, "Snakes."

"Snakes! Go ahead, Pa, I'll wait."

The Indian shook his head, giving Micah an indignant look. "Humph. Brave one."

"Don't 'humph' me, Indian. I don't fight with snakes."

"Settle down, boys." John stepped inside. The ebony darkness swallowed him.

The boys waited, keeping the horses still. Finally, Micah's

patience vanished. Dropping the reins, he stepped inside the entrance. "Pa?" The echo sounded back. He moved outside and sat down on a boulder to wait. "Think something's happened to him?"

"No."

Suddenly John emerged from the opening. "You called?" He snuffed out a torch.

"What's that you got?"

"A couple of years ago, I placed two torches inside, just in case I might need them."

"Where were ya?" asked Micah.

"Way back in another chamber. We can keep the horses in front by the opening. The cave narrows down too much in back. Take the chamber to the right, it's perfect. Let's get settled in. Crow won't be able to track us here. He and Conway are probably in town getting liquored up on my money, and too busy to give us another thought."

"How come ya didn't take your money with ya when ya left," Micah asked.

"Left some in case my partner needed help while I was gone. Gold claims are strange. Sometimes they pay off and other times they don't."

"Guess Tossetti *needed* more than money this time."

"Yeah." John fell silent.

After hobbling the horses and feeding them, the boys collected some firewood. Boy Who Spits Far found a shallow pit, placed several pieces of kindling into the hole and made a small, smokeless fire, giving some light to the cavern's stark surroundings. The jagged rock walls were damp to the touch. Micah unrolled his bed gear near the fire, next to Spits Far.

John gulped a drink from the water pouch, before passing it on to the boys. "I don't want you two to be raising your voices in here until I can figure out whether we have bats or not."

Micah jumped to his feet. "Bats? What else haven't ya told me about?"

The Indian shot John an impish grin. "Rats."

"Rats!" Micah shifted around looking at the ground. "Was that one?" He pointed, "Over there."

"Sit down, son. Spits Far is only funning with you. Let's get some sleep. We have lots to do tomorrow."

Micah plopped down on his blankets, glared at his friend. Then he cautiously looked around the cave floor, scanning the area quickly. "Rats. I really hate rats."

Deep in thought, John leaned against the cave entrance, peering into the sky as the first light peeked over the horizon. His well-planned trip was a total catastrophe. Nothing had worked out the way he'd intended. Now with two young boys at his side, the situation grew more difficult, if not downright dangerous. And, the idiots gunning for him were probably within shooting range. All the cards were stacked against him. He didn't know how to resolve the situation without getting someone hurt or killed.

Micah lay staring at his father's shadowed outline, emphasizing his broad shoulders and narrow hips. His Pa was a big man, but he looked taller than his actual height. Quietly getting to his feet, he walked up behind John. "What are ya thinkin' about?"

John jumped. "Nothing much. Just thinking."

"You worried about what's-her-name?"

"Caroline?" John shook his head. "No, too much else to fret about. Although, I would like to know how close my brother is. He should be reaching Hangtown within the next month."

"Maybe I should watch for 'em in town. You know, keep out of sight but see everything."

"We'll see. Right now I need to know the whereabouts of Conway and Crow."

Boy Who Spits Far spoke from behind them, "Me find them. Let you know."

"Now that you're both up, let me think for a minute." John twisted his mouth and furrowed his brows. Pointing to the Spits Far, he said, "You ride into town, but stay hidden. I need to know what they're up to. Stay out of the acting sheriff's way. He's a bit slow-witted, but he'd love to get his hands on you. He hates Indians. I'll give you a note for Sadie at the hotel. She'll help you out. In fact she might even feed you, if you cut some wood for her. Micah, I want you to check out the cabin and let me know when those two no-goods get back. You boys be careful and use the old back trail. It's overgrown and a fairly safe route for the moment."

Micah left his horse tethered over the ridge. As he crept closer to the cabin, he heard men's voices. They were back and arguing, but he couldn't make out what they were saying. Suddenly the door flew open and Conway charged outside.

"The hell you say," shouted Conway. "The three of them should be arrivin' anytime now. All we have to do is wait. In the meantime, get your lazy ass down by the stream and look for that gold everybody's searchin' for."

"No," replied Crow. "I'm goin' to town. You keep an eye out for Anderson and those two brats."

Micah knew Conway was exasperated by the tone of his voice as he replied, "We came here to find gold, and to kill Anderson and those two whelps. Now, if you don't want to cooperate, leave."

"I ain't leavin'. Half of all this is mine. I don't search for gold unless you do, too. Why do I have to do all the work?"

They stood three feet apart glaring at each other. The half-breed stomped back into the cabin, then rushed out. He climbed onto his horse and rode off at a high lope. A flash of light caught the boy's eye. The cabin was on fire. Conway stomped around, kicking at the stumps, cussing up a storm.

"Why didja burn the cabin down, you stupid half-breed? We need it to survive." He mounted his horse and took off after Crow.

Micah ducked down behind a boulder, and then crept backwards toward the trail, high-tailed it back to the cave.

"You did well. Since Crow's burned the cabin down, I need to get back there to search through the rubble, but it's going to be difficult without cover. There's a small box buried somewhere under those burnt floorboards. Now is probably the best time to search for it with both men in town."

"I can be the lookout."

"Good. I don't expect Spits Far to return from town for at least a day or so. I hope he stays out of sight while he's there. Let's go. If I can find that box, we'll have some gold to sell."

"What about the other one, with your papers in it?"

"It's gone. They've probably spent the money and have my claim papers crammed in their pockets. Jeeze, I'd love to wring their necks. I worked hard striking this claim."

"You've lost everything: your claim, the money, your partner."

"Yes, but I still have you. We'll find another claim. Never did see much color here anyway. Maybe we'll set up a claim further north." John stood and dusted off his trousers. "All right, we're gonna go the back way, sneak down behind the cabin area. You need to stay on the hillside behind some good cover and keep an eye out for them. Give me a whistle if you see them coming up the trail. Don't get caught. Crow is one nasty son of a... Let's say he'd like to get his hands on you."

"Yeah. Well, I have some ideas of my own," Micah replied. "None of them are nice."

* * *

John edged his way cautiously down behind the smoking boards. Picking up a hot board, he dropped it, shoving it to the side. Smoldering debris covered the floor. Pulling the half burnt mattress aside, he kicked some wood away and rubbed his boot toe, scraping the dirt. Getting on his hands and knees, he ran his hands around the exposed dirt and under a small piece of wood. He stopped scraping with his fingers and grabbed a small scrap of board, pushing and digging at the ground. He was so engrossed, he never heard the whistle from above.

"Looky who we have here."

John fell backwards.

Conway circled him, sneering and waving his gun in one hand. "Mr. Anderson, thank you for dropping in for a visit. Sorry your cabin burnt down. Crow, where are ya?" Crow walked out of the woods, a big grin on his face. "Accommodate Mr. Anderson here with some nice ropes. We brought them especially for you."

John tried to rise to his feet, but Crow jerked John by the hair and bashed his face into the boards, breaking his nose.

Conway waved his hand. "Easy, Crow. We don't want to damage the valuable goods now. Let's see what he was diggin' for."

The half-breed pulled John's head up and stuck a knife to his throat. "Can I nick him a little?"

Conway looked up from his kneeling position. "Just a little." Then he continued to scrape at the dirt with his knife, digging a small hole. "Nothing."

Crow slid the tip of his knife along John's cheek, from his ear to the corner of his lips. Droplets oozed along the thin cut, mingling with the blood flowing from his nose. The half-breed stuck the knife under John's chin, pressing it against his throat.

Standing up, Conway said, in a syrupy voice, "Now, Crow, be nice. What a shame, I said only a nick. Save the longer slices for later." Suddenly, his voice took a hateful edge. "Remember we have all night to avenge my brother's death. Drag him over to one of those trees and tie him up. Now I wanta know. You got something hidden around here you want to tell me about, Anderson?"

Slumped over, John didn't answer. Blood trickled from his nose onto his shirt.

"No answer, huh? Okay. Where've you got those two brats stashed?" yelled Conway.

Crow nodded in the direction of the woods. "Caught me a nigger in a woodpile. He's out cold."

Conway broke into a nasty chuckle. "Now, that's more like it. When you have this one taken care of, bring that bastard kid here and tie him up."

"Move," shouted Crow.

John staggered, trying to keep his footing as the half-breed dragged him backwards by the hair, all the while holding the knife to John's neck. Dropping him to the ground and then slamming him against the tree trunk, Crow tied John against the rough bark, arms around the trunk behind him, staking John's legs spread-eagled. Taking a step forward, Crow kicked him in the midriff. John cried out in pain, his head jerked forward as he tried to curl in a ball.

"Does that feel good? Give you more later. Maybe I'll show you how to skin a skunk tonight. Kids peel real slow."

With John securely tied, Crow swaggered back into the woods. He threw an unconscious Micah over his shoulder, carried him to Conway, and dropped him to the ground with a thud. Getting a rope from his horse, he trussed Micah up like a turkey, arms and legs tied behind his back. Carrying the boy with his belly dragging the ground, Crow tossed him up against the tree and left him lying on his side.

"When he comes to, he won't be able to go anywhere." The half-breed cackled an evil laugh that sent a chill through Conway. "He won't even be able to piss in peace."

Conway walked around the area, rubbing his chin. "Let me see. One. Two. What are we missin', Crow?"

"The Indian kid?"

"Yes, go find him. Don't make me do all the work. If these two are here, the other one is close by."

Crow gripped the hilt of his knife, knuckles turning white. The two men stared at each other. Crow was the first to flinch.

With one hand on the hilt of his pistol, Conway asked, "Are you contemplatin' some type of action? Or are ya thinkin' about how you're gonna find the boy? Since he ain't showed up yet, he's probably in town."

The half-breed didn't answer, as he stood staring at his partner. Finally, he mounted his horse and rode off.

"I guess you two will be missin' supper tonight, but then again, if I leave, you might *be* supper." Laughing wickedly at his own joke, Conway walked to his horse, grabbed a hunk of meat and a water pouch. Finding a comfortable spot, he sat down to eat. Pulling a ten-inch knife from its sheath, he cut off a chunk of meat, and lifted the blade to his mouth.

"My, my, if you could only see your pretty face, the way it's swellin'. By tomorrow, both eyes will be swollen shut. And, your nose. It must hurt like hell. Maybe Crow can cut it off so it won't bother you so much." His nasty laugh echoed through the canyon. "Haven't had this much fun in years." He cut another bit of meat with his knife and placed it in his mouth.

Conway felt a hand on his shoulder. He jerked halfway

around. Bam! Boy Who Spits Far stood over the fallen man with a piece of wood. Picking up Conway's knife, he slit the man's throat. Then he grabbed the dead man's hair in one hand, ran the knife around the front of the skull from temple to temple, and peeled the scalp off.

Raising it over his head, pointing to the sky, Spits Far whooped out a war yelp, "Aiyeeeeeee, ya, ya, yaaaaaa."

Sticking the bloody scalp into his rawhide breechclout belt, he slipped the knife sheath from Conway's belt. He stepped over the body and made his way to John. "Bad man deserves death."

He carefully cut John free of the ropes, then freed Micah. Both lay in pain unable to move. Spits Far brought his horse and boosted Micah across its back. Grabbing two long, thin, half-burnt cabin boards, he tied two ends together, spreading the opposite end wide in a simple V-formation. Using the ropes and bindings, the Indian boy tied two shorter boards crosswise and wove branches he cut from a small tree, making a flimsy travois.

"Help. Me up." John staggered to his feet, but fell to his knees. "Can't see. Pain bad." He passed out.

Spits Far brought the horse and travois to him, and gently rolled John onto it. The boards weren't long enough to attach to the horse and John's legs extended beyond the litter. The Indian boy tied the reins on Conway's horse to his saddle before going back to John. With all the strength he could muster, he picked up the end of the travois and slowly stumbled forward, dragging John behind him.

Finally, Micah sat up as life came back into his arms and legs. He slipped off his horse.

"Here, I can help." Hanging onto his reins and gimping with each step, he grabbed one litter pole. Together, they struggled up the mountainside, getting John to safety, with the horses trailing behind.

Inside the cave, they pulled John off the travois and carried him to his bedroll. Spits Far built a small fire while Micah searched for the medicine bag John kept in his saddlebags.

Ripping off a piece of his Pa's shirt, the boy poured some water onto the cloth and began cleaning John's wounds. "Ya know, when Crow comes back and finds Conway dead, he's gonna be madder than hell."

Spits Far sat back on his heels. "He look for us. Maybe find us, but we fight." The boys realized they weren't free from danger, not with Crow on the loose.

"How come you're back so early? Did Pa's family come to town?" asked Micah.

"No. Sadie want you come to town."

Micah hunkered down next to his pa. "We need to get some help for him. I don't know what to do. The way Crow was kicking him, some of his ribs are probably broken."

"I go back Sadie's. Get help. You stay here."

"Yeah, well you keep an eye out for Crow. He's lookin' for ya."

The Indian boy grinned, "Got catch me first. I find and bring your horse, then leave. Not worry." He slapped Conway's knife sheath which he now owned.

Micah stood up and sarcastically shouted, "Right. Don't worry. Everything's fine."

"You talk funny," Spits Far said, shaking his head. "I go. Need cover tracks to cave."

Micah nodded, then plopped down next to his father. He poured more water onto the cloth, rung it a little, and continued to wipe his father's face. "Pa, ya got to get better. I didn't come all this way to lose ya now. Besides I need ya." Tears trickled down his cheeks. Then he gasped, "I love ya."

Chapter Thirty-Two

Emerging from the bank, Caroline staggered across the wooden porch in a daze. "This is impossible. I can't believe it. No one ever heard of John Anderson."

Totally numb from frustration, her mind shut down, refusing to cooperate. Now what? Where was she to go? This town was the end of the trail. There was nothing here, nothing at all.

Leaning against a post, she surveyed the dirty clapboard buildings, the muddy streets with puddles of water and the shoddy, sagging tents. Animal dung littered the road. Stifling odors mixing with suffocating smells of sweaty unclean bodies filled the air. Her gaze drifted across to the seedy hotel then down to the makeshift saloon. There was neither rhyme nor reason to the way Hangtown was set up. It was stark, naked, and ugly. So, where was the gold?

Men, with long unwashed hair and dirty clothes, roamed around staring at her. She ignored them. Most of them were hunched over from shoveling dirt all day. No smiles, no happiness, and no warmth to suggest they loved the existence they had carved out of the hills. Caroline could only feel the sadness and hardships surrounding her.

Sitting down on the bank's wooden steps, she leaned against the post, dangling one leg off the porch. She'd left beautiful Virginia for this? Life here was barely an existence and her home in Virginia was long gone, never to be reclaimed. Her future lay before her.

"All this way for nothing. No John, no gold, nothing but dirt, mud, and a town of ignorant men. I don't even have money for room and board." A snicker escaped her lips, then a giggle, turning into a belly laugh. She became hysterical.

A rock hitting her shoulder stopped her short. Turning, she glimpsed a head and eyes peering around the corner of the bank building.

"Lady," said the young man behind her.

She rose to her feet. "Did you throw that rock at me?"

"You look for John Anderson?" The Indian boy pointed toward the north end of town. "He coming in."

She narrowed her eyes and leaned forward. "How do you know that?"

"Me know. Follow me. I take you to him."

"What? No, I don't think so. I don't know you and to be honest, I don't trust you."

"You red-headed lady from East? Caroline?"

Flabbergasted, she asked, "Who are you? How do you know my name?"

"Son of John Anderson."

Dumbstruck, Caroline hesitated for a moment. "Son? How many sons does John have these days? He certainly must have gotten around when he left Virginia."

"You come."

"No. If John wants to see me, he'll have no trouble finding

me. I'm probably one of five women here, I think." She turned to step off the porch.

"Wait. Him in trouble."

"He's constantly in trouble and I don't care. Go tell him what I said. I'm not staying in this town very long, so he better hurry."

She hastened across the road, dodged two men on her way to Sadie Jane's Hotel and Bath House.

Ben hastened out of the stables and headed for the bar. His anticipation was getting to him. He couldn't walk fast enough. He wiped his hand across his wet mouth, thinking about the taste of throat-biting liquor. Ah, sweet elixir of life. Then he'd go to Sadie Jane's and have him a....

He spied Caroline on the bank porch, talking to an Indian boy. Ben halted dead in his tracks, his hand stopping in mid air. Yep, that's a heap of trouble standing there. He squinted. "Maybe I should go over to see what she's up ta. No tellin' with that woman. And with an Injun, humph. Whatever it is, they're both up to no good."

He stepped up onto the boardwalk and paused in front of the saloon doorway. "Dadburn woman. She's been nothing but trouble from the start and it looks like it ain't over with yet."

Mad as a hatter, he shoved open the saloon's swinging doors. The comforting noise of the bar enveloped him, bringing a smile to his face. The smoke filled his lungs, the sour smell of unwashed bodies made him happy. He was gonna get lost in familiar surroundings and enjoy himself.

Tapping the counter, he shouted, "Barkeep, give me a glass and leave that half bottle within reach. I need salvation. Time enough tomorrow to think about the pain in the ass across the road." Dropping his money on the counter, he slowly poured himself a drink. His mouth watered as he licked the side of the glass to catch a drop of the delicious elixir trying to escape. Throwing his head back, he gulped the first drink.

The slow, burning sensation traveled down his throat, through his chest and into his loins, warming his body. "Ah, good stuff," he gasped, shutting his eyes. He picked up his bottle and glass, headed for a table in the nearest corner, to lose himself. There was plenty time tomorrow to worry. He sat down in a chair with his back to the wall, placed the bottle and glass on the table. Ever since he met that gawlderned woman, his life had changed. All he had worked for this past two years, gone. He stared into the empty glass, knowing he was never going to St. Louie again. He was looking at the backside of his life. Pouring himself another drink, he lifted the glass. "Here's to all the old trappers who've gone before me. I'll be joinin' ya soon, fellas."

Sadie Jane's was not a fashionable establishment. The sun shining through the one lobby window cast shadows across the floor. Dust and cigar smoke filtered through the sunbeam.

"What's the price of a bath?" Caroline asked.

An elderly blonde lady dressed in a not-too-clean, worn, and wrinkled burgundy dress, manned the front desk. Her rouged and powdered face was a contrast of red and white. Her outward appearance bespoke a wordless tale of tough living, but her soft gray eyes twinkled when she asked, "Honey, whatcha need?"

"I want a warm bath with clean water," replied Caroline. "And a clean towel."

"The bath is two dollars, warm water is a dollar extra," she said, pointing to the sign on the wall. "And the towel is fifty cents."

Caroline felt in her pants pocket to see how much was left. She plunked down the coins. "This is all I have. What will it get me right now?"

Sadie eyed her and counted out $2.75. Smiling, she said, "That'll do. Come on and follow me, sweetie. A bath will do ya good. Heck, I'll even throw in the soap and make sure you have a curtain for privacy."

"Privacy?"

"I have one room for both ladies and gents. If you don't want the curtain just say so. But if I were you, I'd take it. It's up to you," she said with a smirk, as she gave Caroline the once over.

"I'll take the soap and the curtain, thank you."

Caroline followed the woman through the lobby, down the hallway to the last door on the left. The bathing room was fairly large with six tubs spaced around the room. Two tubs had curtains hanging from the ceiling. As she entered the room, three male occupants all but drowned themselves, hiding from her. Then the hollering, hoots, and whistles started.

"Easy there, fellas. This is a lady and she's not interested in you. So, mind your manners and stay away from this side of the room."

Sadie grabbed the soap and towel off a shelf, laid them on a table next to the tub. Phineas began pouring in hot water.

"You here for any special reason? Lookin' for a job?"

Caroline sat on the chair and removed her boots. "No. I was supposed to meet my brother-in-law here."

Pulling the curtain around the tub, Sadie asked, "What's his name? Maybe I know him."

Caroline removed her holster and hung it on the back of the chair. Ben told her to wear it in town. It felt strange on her hip. "John Anderson."

"Anderson," whispered Sadie, as she jerked the curtain shut. "Shhh. Don't talk too loud. These walls have ears. When you're through, we need to talk. Enjoy your bath and when you're finished, my room is the first door in front of the stairs. Knock twice."

Caroline stared at her with her mouth open. Sadie held her finger to her lips and left the room. Phineas emptied the last bucket of hot water, nodded and left.

Caroline undressed, laying her clothes across the chair before gingerly stepping into the steaming water. She shuffled her feet around for a moment, and then slowly submerged her body, except for her bent knees. The tub was not large enough to accommodate her entire body, but it certainly would do. The hot water felt heavenly. For the first time in months, Caroline felt like a lady of luxury. There was no way to explain what it meant to take a bath with clean water and sweet smelling soap. She slipped her head down into the water, sat back up, and scrubbed it well with soap to remove the caked-on dirt, before ducking her head back into the water to rinse. She pulled it back and gathered it to one side, gently twisting out the excess water. *Clean at last.*

Shutting her eyes, she settled back in the tub against the high back, relaxing every aching muscle. A curtain rustled near her, her eyes shot open as she reached for her pistol, lying on the chair next to her. She listened for footsteps, and then relaxed as the noise stopped. Maybe being more alert for intruders would be to her advantage. As the warm water conquered her body, she shut out the world and floated into the peaceful surroundings of her past. She could almost smell the Virginia mountain air, filled with sweet honeysuckle, hear water trickling over the creek rocks behind the cabin.

The curtain rustled again, then opened, jarring Caroline back to reality. Sadie smiled. "Honey, it's time to get out.

Take your time. I'll be waitin' for ya." She pulled the curtain closed and left.

Caroline dried her body, dressed and buckled the holster on her hip. She noticed Sadie had left a comb on the chair. Leaving the room, she walked down the hall to Sadie's door and knocked twice.

The door squeaked open an inch before an eyeball appeared.

"Come in."

John lay on the bed, face swollen and discolored, an ugly cut from his eye to his chin.

Shocked, Caroline stared. "What happened to him?"

"About two days ago, his boys hauled his butt in from Tracer's Point with Phineas' help. They tell me two desperados jumped him up at the cabin. His partner's dead," said Sadie. "They beat John up pretty good, broke his nose, a couple of ribs, might even have lost some teeth. Can't tell with his lips so swollen. I gave him some whiskey to kill the pain, and to get him to sleep. The trip down from the mountains took a toll on him."

Caroline walked over to the bed. "Is there a doctor in town?"

"He's up in the hills right now. With this gold strike, the doc's never in town, especially when you need him."

"What can we do for him?"

"I wrapped his ribs. He seems to be breathing easier. As far as his nose, can't do much. With his eyes so swollen and his lips puffed up the way they are, I figured, let him be. Right now I need to tend the cut on his cheek, then we'll let him be for awhile."

A small tap at the window caught Sadie's attention. She pulled up the up sash, and in crawled two boys.

"What's your name?" Sadie asked her.

"Caroline."

"This here is Boy Who Spits Far and that one over there is Micah. They've been taking care of John."

Caroline nodded to the boys. "Where are the two men who did this to him?"

"I kill one. But half-breed still here."

Sadie shook her finger. "That's why I told you the walls have ears. Crow's a nasty, ugly buzzard." She spoke to the boys, pointing toward the bed. "We need to let him sleep. You two bed down in here tonight, stay clear of the window and keep the shade pulled."

She motioned to Caroline. "Follow me. We're gonna take the room next door, to be close. Just in case there's trouble. You boys lock the door behind us."

"I don't have any money for a room."

"Honey, that's not important. John's a friend. All the time he was here, he looked out for me."

Caroline raised an eyebrow.

"Not that kind of friend," said Sadie, sarcastically.

They left the boys and settled in the next room.

Sadie lit a lantern. "If you'll help me, I'll give you free room and board as long as you stay. I could sure use a hand with these crazy men around here. A lot of 'em come for one warm meal a day. Can you cook?"

"Yes."

"Good. In the morning, the boys will get the wood and water. The kitchen is in the back. I'll tell you what to fix. Plan on twenty for breakfast. There's a gown on the hook over there. Now, get yourself undressed and asleep. Morning comes early around here. I'm gonna lock you in. I'll be back later." She left, shutting the door.

Caroline scanned the room. The bed was adequate, with several covers and two pillows. A lantern sat on a small table by the window. A picture hung on the wall, but it was too dark to make out what it was. She pulled on the window sash. It was locked. Sitting on the bed, she began to undress. Ben would have to fend for himself tonight. Placing her clothes on the chair across the room, she pulled on the gown and crawled under the covers. Snuggling down into the bed's softness, she rested her head on the pillow. It smelled of sunshine and fresh air. The smooth sheet caressed her body as she stretched her legs. Then curling up, she pulled the covers securely around her. *A real bed.*

Early next morning, Caroline manned the front desk. A shabby, dark skinned man sauntered in, dressed in dirty buckskins. Canvassing the room, he sauntered up to the counter. His piercing black eyes cut to her heart. She suppressed a shiver.

"Can I help you?"

"I'm looking for an Indian boy," he replied. "He's a relative. Seen him?"

"No, I don't believe I have." She stared straight into his eyes, never wavering.

"There's another boy that hangs around with him. Dark like me, wiry hair. Nigger kid."

"I haven't seen him either."

He glared at her, then nodded and left the hotel lobby.

Sadie came downstairs, arms full of dirty linens. "How are things goin'?"

"I think that man, Crow, was just in here looking for the boys. The one Micah told us about."

Sadie stopped at the bottom of the landing. "I'll be right back." She headed toward the back of the hotel. Returning, she said, "We need to be very careful. If he even thinks they're here, he'll kill them and us, too. I'll talk with the boys. They can only come out at night and no lantern lights in their room. From now on they'll be eatin' in there too, no more sittin' in the dinin' area. And we'll have to get our own wood from outside. Someone's bound to squeal to Crow. Word gets around this town faster than water runnin' through a sluice box."

"Why don't we tell the sheriff? You do have one, don't you?"

"Yes, but I know he'd turn John over to Crow to avoid fightin' him. He's trouble from way back."

Ben woke up, stiff and sore from the dampness. He sat up and stretched his arms over his head. He couldn't remember how he had made it back to the stables last night. He plucked straw from his hair and beard, then pulled on his moccasins. Standing, he took his hat and beat away the debris from his shirt and pants. After running his fingers through his disheveled hair, he swiped a finger across his teeth. Following a hard night of boozing, he felt like hell. Without searching his pockets, he knew he'd spent a good deal of money. The prices in town were too steep. He'd have to leave soon or be forced to pan for gold.

Looking around he realized Caroline had never made it back to the stable. "Now where can that blasted woman be off to?" He wanted to be angry with her, but deep inside he had to admit he was getting kind of attached to having her around. Besides, she made good coffee.

"Hey, you gonna pay me for using my stall?" The liveryman asked.

Ben picked up his rifle and saddlebags, and sauntered over to him. "Here, I'm payin' for one, since no one else showed up. I need to keep my personal stuff in a safe corner." He handed the man five dollars.

The man pointed to the front of the stable. "Put it over there. It's where I stay. We don't have much traffic this time of the year. Most of the people are up in the hills after gold."

Ben started to leave.

The man stopped him, holding out his hand. "That'll be two dollars in advance."

"What? Just for watchin' costs?"

"Nothing's cheap around here anymore."

Ben left the stables and headed down the street, not exactly knowing where to start looking for Caroline. It was still early. Not too many men were roaming about at this hour of the day. The sky was dressed in early pinks and rose, casting shadows across the buildings. Maybe he should eat first.

Entering the hotel, he stopped at the front desk and inquired about breakfast.

"We'll start serving in about an hour," said Sadie. "You can take a seat over by the fireplace and I'll have someone bring you coffee, if you want."

"Yep, and I could do with bit of sugar, if ya don't mind."

She winked at him and left. Ben stood for a moment, wondering why she winked. He looked down at his shirt and leggings. Nothing was sticking out. A mirror hung in the corner of the room. Walking over, he took a look at himself, moving his head back and forth, lifting his chin. The image wasn't half bad. Maybe he needed to use a comb. He raked his fingers through his long, graying, scraggly hair. Lifting his arms, one at a time, he took a sniff.

"Whew. That could kill a skunk. Need some purty water." He lumbered down the hall to the back room and entered the bathing area. Looking over the shelves, he didn't spy any toilet water, but there was a sliver of soap. Picking it up, he stuck his hand into his shirt, and rubbed the soap under each armpit. Grabbing a rag, he dipped the corner of it in a basin of standing water and wiped his face.

"Now, ain't we somethin'. At least we smell better." Grinning really big, he rubbed his teeth with the rag and spit on the floor. He pulled loose two pieces of fringe from his shirt, tied them together. Gathering his hair behind his neck, he wrapped the rawhide around and tied it tight in a bunch. Straightening his shoulders and puffing out his chest, he went back to the lobby, strutting his stuff.

A steaming cup of coffee waited for him on the table next to the overstuffed chair. The fabric was soiled and worn, but Ben didn't care. It was better than his saddle or the ground he'd been used to. Sitting down, he propped his moccasined feet on the small table in front of him and sipped his coffee.

A voice behind him asked, "Can I get you anything else, sir?"

Recognizing Caroline's voice, he jumped to his feet. "What in tarnation are ya doin' here? I waited up for ya and didn't get a lick of sleep worryin' about ya last night."

"Shhh, sit down. I have something to tell you. Keep your voice down." Caroline pulled up a small chair next to him. "I found my brother-in-law."

She commenced telling him all that had transpired the day before, starting with the bank, adding the boys and Sadie, describing the half-breed and how he had beaten John.

Ben listened, bobbing his head. "How's John doin'?"

"He's taking a little broth, but his face is cut and his eyes are almost swollen shut. We believe his ribs are broken. The boys are with him." She looked around behind her, eyeing the front door and lowered her voice. "The horrible thing is the half-breed was here this morning. He intends to kill the three of them."

"Hmmm. I'd say you got yourself in a pickle. Maybe I'll take a look around for ya after breakfast. See what I can come up with. Stay away from this fella if he comes a-callin'. Don't want ya to get yourself shot or sliced up."

Sadie walked over. "Breakfast will be ready in a few minutes. That'll be three dollars."

"That's highway robbery, woman. Why, no eggs and bacon are worth that much. Do I look like I'm rich or somethin'?"

"No," said Sadie, "but you are kinda handsome. Maybe if ya stayed around a while, we might talk cheaper prices."

Caroline rolled her eyes.

A smile spread across Ben's face as he puffed out his chest. "Yes, ma'am. I might be doin' just that. Thought about it some."

"We do have rooms available, if you're interested," said Sadie, sending Ben a coy look.

Blood rushed to his face. He opened his eyes wide and grinned.

"Ben." Caroline shook his shoulder. "*Ben!* Listen to me. Crow is very dangerous. Killing is what he likes to do best."

"I understand, but right now I'm gonna eat in that there dinin' room. After that, I'll mosey down the street and over to the saloon. Some people get loose-lipped when they're all liquored up. Now, don't you nice ladies worry none about me. I'll get back with ya sometime this afternoon." He strutted into the dining room to eat his breakfast.

"Ya know, he's sorta cute in a rough way," said Sadie.

"Oh, yes, real cute," Caroline replied.

Later that evening, Ben returned and sat in the lobby, chewing on some jerky

"Ben," said Caroline. "What did you find out?"

"Seems this here Crow feller is lookin' for gold he thinks your John has. Lots of gold."

"That's crazy," replied Caroline. "All he's got, according to the boys, is his claim and a burnt down cabin. From what they described, it isn't much to look at."

"I'm tellin' ya what I heerd. Now my strategy is to get this brother-in-law of yours out of town, say maybe up north around Three Forks. It's on the other side of Feather River. The barkeep tells me, not much is developed there yet. Could be Crow wouldn't think of his gettin' out of town as broke as he is."

"I don't know. I don't want John dead, maybe hurt him a little more."

"Woman, I'd say he's hurtin' a-plenty right now. Ain't nice when someone breaks your ribs."

Sadie interrupted their conversation. "Why don't we sleep on it, make a decision in the mornin'? It's gettin' late and the men'll be here early for breakfast."

Caroline nodded, said good night and headed for her room.

Ben shuffled his feet. Looking up at Sadie, he smiled. "Well, I need to be gettin' back to the stables, unless ya got an extra room I could rent tonight. Don't have much money left."

Sadie grinned, slipped her arm through his, pulling him close. "I got just the room for ya, Benny. And it's real cheap, sweetie," she whispered close to his ear, walking him toward the stairs. "You can get your stuff from the stables in the mornin'."

Ben grinned from ear to ear.

Chapter Thirty-Three

Micah slipped outside and squatted behind the bushes. The outhouse was too far to go and he didn't want anyone to see him. He heard footfalls behind him in the undergrowth. Dropping to his knees, he rolled onto his back. He wiggled into his trousers, dirt and sticks catching in his pants. Putting his arms through his suspender loops, he crawled on his hands and knees to the woodpile. A seven-foot opening lay between where he hid and the building, so he hunkered down, staring into the blackness, waiting. Finally, he made a mad dash for the back door. Inside, he peered through the gauze curtains. Nothing was moving out there. Probably his nerves playing tricks on him. But, maybe he needed to mention it to Sadie.

In the morning, Caroline arrived with a tray of food and set it on the table. John was still asleep.

"When he wakes up, you feed him," she said to the boys, scowling at them.

"Don't you want to be here when he wakes up?" asked Micah.

"No."

Micah rocked back on the chair legs. "Why not? You're all he talked about since we left St. Louis."

She stared at the wiry-haired boy. "Really!" She stiffened her back.

"Do you hate him?" Micah paused for a moment. "He told me how badly he treated you. He left my *Maman,* too. Only he honestly didn't know she was gonna have a baby." He grinned. "Me."

Caroline listened to the boy pleading his case for John.

"He's tryin' to be a father, but he's got a long way to go."

"Do you love him?" she asked.

The boy smiled big. "Yep. He kinda grows on ya."

"What about the Indian boy?"

Micah shrugged his shoulders. "He came along with us from Fort Laramie. Helped save my Pa's life. He doesn't have anyone. So, he's my brother."

Caroline walked over and hugged Micah.

He gave her a questionable look. "What's that for?"

"No reason," she said. "Maybe we can work on getting to know each other."

He stared at her for a moment, then began telling her about the footsteps he heard last night. "I waited as long as I could behind the woodpile. When I didn't see anything, I ran inside. I peeked through the door window to see if anyone was out there."

"You need to be careful. Next time, do your business behind the woodpile, it's safer and closer."

"But you can see me from the door."

"Better we see you than Crow."

He hesitated for a moment, and then nodded in agreement.

Later that afternoon, Caroline returned to John's room

with a dish of soft potatoes and gravy, along with a cup of coffee. He lay on his good side, trying to reach the water on the table next to him.

Setting the food on the table edge, she handed him the cup. “Here,” she said curtly.

He gave her a cockeyed grin. “How long have you been here?”

“A couple days.” She picked up the bowl and stirred the gravy into the potatoes.

“Where’s Alexander?”

She shoved the bowl onto the table, stared coldly at him, and cleared her throat. “Your brother and James are dead. Sarah is missing. I’m all that’s left.” Yanking the spoon out of the bowl, she jammed a dollop of potatoes in his mouth. “I don’t want to talk about it right now. Eat.”

He tried to talk with a mouth full, “My brother—”

“I don’t want to hear anything you have to say *right now*.” She shoved another spoonful into his mouth.

“But…” In went another spoonful. His eyes watered as he almost choked, swallowing hard. His cut lip began to bleed.

“Caroline, I—”

“You don’t seem to understand. I don’t want to talk,” she said, eyes hard and glaring. She tried to feed him another spoonful, but he pushed her hand aside.

He didn’t ask any more questions, but fell back against the pillow.

She picked up the bowl and left the room without a word, slamming the door behind her. Her emotions were about to explode, she wanted to hit something, or maybe break something.

The nasty looking half-breed stood in the lobby, leaning casually against the desk.

She dropped the bowl on the counter. “What do you want?”

He jumped. "I'm still looking for that cousin of mine. Seen him?"

"No. Now get out of here."

He stared at her for a minute, curled his upper lip, then quickly turned and left the hotel.

Sadie entered the lobby. "That nasty fella back again? I think he's suspicious." She walked to the window and pulled the curtain aside an inch.

Crow leaned against the porch post across the street, surveying the hotel. Finally, he swaggered toward the general store.

"He's gone." Sadie pointed her finger at Caroline. "A little testy, are we? Now what's in your craw?"

"Every time I go into his room, I want to strangle him, beat him to a pulp with my fists, and hit him with a chair. I'd love to hear him beg for mercy. Give him some real pain like twisting off his head or any body part that offends me."

"My, my. Sounds to me like love at first sight."

Caroline looked at her, mouth open. "What? Have you been listening to me?"

Sadie smiled, walking toward the desk. "Sure have, honey. Only I hear your heart not your words. But first you need to tell him how you feel, before you mutilate his body. Go in there and rant a little. Call him a few ugly names. Hit him if ya want, just don't kick him in the ribs or touch his face. Men don't understand until you're really riled up. Then it's like a hammer bangin' on their head. But, ya have to git angry enough to git your point across."

"I'm angry enough, believe me."

Sadie grabbed Caroline by the shoulders and turned her around, facing the door. "Then go back in there and give 'im hell. He can handle it. He's a big boy." She shoved Caroline toward John's room.

Caroline yanked the door open, banging it against the wall, knocking the hall tree over. John jumped at the sudden intrusion. His pants hit the floor.

"John Anderson, you're despicable, an absolute bastard. If you weren't hurt, I'd kill you myself." She stepped closer to the bed, hands on her hips. "Because of you I have nothing. The clothes on my back belonged to Alexander, Ben bought me the gun and horse, and the hat belongs to my son. You stole all my dreams, my beautiful home, my very existence. Everything is gone, shattered, left behind on the trail. If it wasn't for some old trapper named Ben Wilson, I'd probably be dead by now."

She swung at John. He ducked quickly, trying to avoid her fist. Stumbling over his trousers, he fell across the bed. She jumped on top of him, pelting his shoulder with her fists. Grabbing her wrists, he rolled over to protect his swollen face and broken nose.

Jerking loose, she shoved him aside. "I hate you, you worthless piece of trash. I hope you rot in hell. Men, I hate 'em all."

Getting to her feet, she grabbed the bedpost. Facing John, she stood her ground and glared at him. "I'm going to tell you a thing or two and you're going to listen to me. So be quiet. First of all, getting to this hellhole was not easy. I lost something very precious on this horrendous trip, my family. Do you know what that's like? I had to stare down Indians, only to have them sneak back and kidnap Sarah. So, I am leaving here and returning to Fort Laramie to find her."

"Sarah?"

Venomously, she spit out the words. "Yes, Sarah, my daughter."

Standing, John extended one arm, trying to placate her. "I'll go with you and help find your daughter."

Caroline narrowed her eyes and placed her hand on her hips. "You are an egotistical fool. What makes you think I need you? I traveled over twelve hundred miles on horseback and made it here without your help. I don't need you."

"Listen to me, please." He shuffled closer, but not within swinging range, his pants still wrapped around his ankles. "Can you settle down and be quiet for one minute?"

Caroline yanked the door open. Turning, she cocked her head. "I don't need you, John."

Pulling up his trousers, he followed her into the lobby, holding onto his waistband, struggling to keep his balance. "I love you. I want to help you."

"You haven't heard a thing I've said!" she yelled. "I-don't-need-you. Not you, not any man in my life." Tears streamed down her cheeks.

"Give me a chance to help you find your daughter."

"Ahhhh!" she screamed. "She's not only my daughter. She's your daughter, too."

John's eyes widened, his jaw went slack. "My daughter," he whispered.

"Yes, you nincompoop. Your daughter." Turning, she dashed out the open doors, fleeing into the street in the direction of the stables.

"Wait!" he shouted after her, wrestling with the buttons on his trousers. "Caroline. Wait."

"Ya need help, John?" asked Sadie, giving him a sarcastic grin.

"Is she right, Sadie? Is Sarah my daughter? Did you know?"

"Yep." She walked from behind the lobby desk and grabbed his waistband with both hands and began buttoning his pants.

Humiliated, he closed his eyes and shook his head. "Women. You're a passel of trouble."

"If you two don't keep it down, that half-breed will be back here," Sadie warned him.

Huddled in the back corner stall, Caroline wept. "What am I going to do?" she wailed. "Oh, Lord. Can I truly make it back to Fort Laramie by myself? I can't stay in this rundown dump of a town. I have to go back. Sarah needs me." She cried and hiccupped, realizing how alone she truly was. *The way Ben's sashaying around Sadie these past few days, even he's abandoned me.*

She heard footsteps approaching the stall. Wiping her face with the sleeve of her shirt, she got to her feet. John stood there looking liked a whipped puppy.

"Caroline, please forgive me," he pleaded. "I never meant to hurt you. Honest to God, I love you too much to cause you harm. You're breaking my heart." He moved around the stall divider and stepped closer. She shoved him away.

"Leave me alone," she demanded. "This is my stall. I don't want anything to do with you. I've got to think. I *definitely* don't need you right now."

He reached out and clutched her close, managing to get one arm around her shoulder. She struggled, trying to push him away. He held her fast, cradling her in his arm.

"I didn't know Sarah was my daughter. I honestly didn't know. Why didn't you tell me?"

"Tell you," she said, laughing through her tears. "You were never around. When you left me in Pennsylvania, I was pregnant. I didn't know how long you'd be gone and I didn't want to face having a baby by myself. So, when Alexander proposed, I accepted."

She paused for a moment. "You only think about yourself.

Just like coming to California. You were constantly on the trail ahead of us, never thinking we might need your help."

"I'm sorry. What a fool I've been. Did Alex know about Sarah?"

She looked away. "No."

He tipped her chin and looked into her eyes.

"You'll never know how much I want to die." She buried her head in his chest, sobbing hysterically. "They're gone. Everyone I loved is gone. What am I gonna do?"

"Caroline, my love, listen to me," he said, caressing her hair, kissing the top of her head. "I love you and always will."

She stepped back and looked up into his face. "I can't trust you. You're never true to your word."

He pleaded. "Please, give me another chance? I'm not asking for your love. Let me make it up to you."

With her eyes closed, Caroline only shook her head in disagreement.

"What about James and my brother?"

She raised her tear-stained swollen face. "James fell into the Kansas River. The water swallowed my baby up as he struggled for his life. Alexander and some of the men rode downstream, hunting for him, but all they could find was this stupid floppy hat I wear." Angry, she tossed the hat across the stall.

"Alexander took lung fever from spending all day and night in the cold water looking for our son. After the Indians kidnapped Sarah, Alexander got up from his sick bed and went looking for her. He couldn't even mount his horse by himself, let alone fight. Ben found his body and buried him on the prairie."

He stayed silent for moment, contemplating all that she told him. "Listen to me. My gut tells me Sarah is still alive. We'll go to Fort Laramie and search for her. We'll ask Spits

Far to help us. And we have Ben. Maybe he'll guide us."

He slid his arm over her shoulders and tried to pull her close. He winced from the pain in his chest.

She snuggled close, careful of his ribs. "Nothing will ever be the same," she said.

"No, but we can try." He brushed stray hairs from her face and kissed her nose, then her eyes, working his way to her chin and finally her lips.

"Wait." She tried to push away.

"I love you, Caroline." He slowly sat down on the straw, then stretched out full length. She joined him and nestled close, cradling her head in the crook of his left arm.

"All I want is you in my arms forever." He tried to lean forward but flinched.

"Be careful. You chest needs to heal. Let me." She placed her lips softly onto his.

He reached forward and undid several buttons on her bodice with one hand.

Her ample breasts pressed against the lace chemise, trying to escape. She moved forward to let him kiss the valley between each delicious mound.

John started as the front stable door creaked. He managed to stand and look over the stall wall. Crow glared at him from the other side, a knife in his hand. The Indian reached across the wooden rail and shoved John, toppling him onto his back.

"I see my hunch paid off. Saw that nigger kid of yours comin' out that back door the other night. I knew something was up. Then when I see you dash out of the hotel, I knew I hit pay dirt." Crow wiped the back of his free hand across his mouth.

The glare of his wild eyes and curled lips caused Caroline to edge backwards against the wooden wall.

John struggled to his knees, using one arm as the other one clasped his chest.

Crow slowly made his way around the divider. "You got somethin' laying there next to ya I want ta try. Looks like a good piece."

As the half-breed stepped toward Caroline, John pushed up and knocked Crow backwards. The force of the impact caused the Indian to lose his balance for a second. Coming unhinged, Crow made a wide swing of his knife, but John dodged the thrust and toppled onto the ground, moaning in pain.

"Guess I'll have to finish ya off, before I use your woman. I can smell her all the way over here."

Holding her shirt closed to cover her breasts with one hand, Caroline shuffled her free hand in the hay, looking for her pistol. It was back at the hotel in her room.

Caroline's movements caught Crow's attention. Stalking her like prey, Crow grabbed her by the hair, yanked her to her feet, and threw her across the stall, slamming her into the wall.

"Stay put, bitch."

As John tried to stand, Crow backhanded him across the face. Blood gushed from his cut lip as he collapsed.

"First, I'm gonna cut you real good. Maybe slice off that manly part. It offends me." The half-breed reached out to grasp John's genitals.

He plowed his head into Crow's stomach, banging him against the wall. Both men fell onto the floor.

Crow jumped to his feet and raised the knife over his head. Lunging toward John, the half-breed yelled, "Aieee!"

Caroline jumped onto his back, gouging at his eyes and biting into his shoulder. He shook his head and backed into the post, knocking the air out of her. She fell to the floor in a heap.

A shot rang out. Crow pitched forward, face down, knife still raised over his head, and landed on top of John, the knife missing his head by inches. Ben stood straddle-legged in the opening, eyes squinting, holding his rifle.

The next morning, before the dawn light crept over the horizon, Caroline and John appeared in the hotel lobby. He leaned on her as he made his way in. No one asked where they'd spent the night. The smiles on both their faces were enough to satisfy doubts anyone might had.

She carefully helped John into bed. He tried to rise up on his elbows. "I need to tell you about Micah."

"We'll talk about that later. Nothing matters right now except your getting better."

"But, you need to know."

"Your son loves you. I can live with that. The rest we'll discuss at another time."

"He's a good kid and I love him."

"Yes, I can tell that. Now rest."

As Caroline left John's room, Ben stood waiting for her in the lobby.

"I talked to the sheriff about the body in the stables. Told him I shot the half-breed in self-defense. The town's gonna bury him." Ben raised one eyebrow up and down. "Seems the livery man saw everythin'."

She blushed, staring at him in disbelief. "He what?"

"Yep. He says it was the best show he'd seen in years."

By the end of the week, Micah and Boy Who Spits Far faced off in the lobby, arguing hot and heavy.

"You ain't no man. You're a kid like me." Micah gritted his teeth and balled his fists at his side.

The Indian squinted. "I man. You boy."

Micah took a swing at him, but the Indian stepped back, dodging his fist and laughing at him.

Ben walked up behind Micah and grabbed him by the neck, shaking him. "Calm down. Ain't worth a fight, whatever it is."

"He says he's a man because he killed Conway and counted a 'cow' on him."

"I think you mean 'coup'." Ben glanced at the Indian. "Did ya?"

Spits Far nodded. "Also got scalp and horse."

"Now that's somethin' for a young buck like you."

Micah jerked loose from Ben's grasp. "So, what's that mean?"

"You hotheaded whelp. He touched his enemy and then took a scalp and his horse. Now a brave that does that deserves a new name." Ben rubbed his beard. "Yep, he's crossed over."

"So," said Micah, "What's that make me."

"Stupid," was Spits Far's answer.

"That's enough. Let's go ask your father. He was there."

As they entered John's room, Caroline sat on the edge of the bed. "What's all the noise out there?"

"It seems the young lad here crossed over to manhood when he did Conway in." Ben pointed to the scalp hanging from the boy's belt. "It's your obligation to rename him."

Spits Far straightened his shoulders, lifted his chin.

John pulled himself up to a sitting position. "Do you have any suggestions? I'm not quite sure what to do."

"From my experience with Injuns, the name has to mean somethin'. Like a spirit or whatever."

John thought for a moment.

"You can call him Chief Pain In the Butt," said Micah, flopping onto the floor.

"Micah, behave yourself," Caroline chided.

"I remember him standing over me up at the cabin once Conway died. He looked so tall, so strong." John thought for a moment. "How about Standing Tall?"

The Indian lifted his chin. "Like Standing Tall. Good name."

"What about me? I deserve a new name."

"Trussed turkey," said Standing Tall with a straight face, then he chuckled.

Everybody laughed except Micah.

Ben rubbed his beard. "Ya know the boy has somethin' there. The two of them saved your life."

"Yes, they did." John looked at Micah. "How about Brave Warrior?"

Micah jumped up off the floor. "I like that. I'm Brave Warrior." He stood shoulder to shoulder with the Indian.

"They make a pair, don't they?" said John.

Caroline took his hand. "You should be proud of them."

"I am. Now I'm tired and need to rest, everybody out." He slid down into the covers, laid back and shut his eyes.

Caroline shooed them out and quietly shut the door.

Three weeks later, John announced, "We're leaving today, so everyone pack up your belongings."

"Are you feeling well enough to ride?" Caroline asked.

"I'll make it as long as we ride easy," came his answer.

The boys dashed to their room, dumped their personal items into their saddlebags, and grabbed their bedrolls. Finished, they dropped everything they owned in the doorway of the hotel, took a seat on the floor, and waited.

Sadie leaned against the hotel porch post and waited. She didn't have much to say as the entourage got ready to leave.

Ben stood with his back to Sadie, packing items into his saddlebags and trying to ignore her.

John knew he didn't want to catch her eye. Ben wouldn't be happy staying in this town and he definitely wasn't interested in panning for gold.

"Hope ya all have a safe and easy trip. Do ya know where you're goin'?" Sadie stepped off the porch and walked in Ben's direction.

"We're heading toward Fort Laramie. Then we'll give it a try around the mountains north of there." John pulled the rope tighter around the last bundles on the mule, while Caroline helped him. "We have to look for our daughter."

Sadie stood next to Ben. "Is that right, Ben?"

"Yep." He just kept stuffing the saddlebags until nothing more would fit. He buckled them down the best he could and leaned his head against the horse's side.

"Ben?"

He stood erect and removed his hat, holding it with both hands in front of him. "Sadie, I can't stay here." He turned toward her. "I'm not cut out for this here hotel business like you. The mountains and free air's callin' me. Can ya understand?"

"Yep, I understand. Sure would've been nice if we could've worked things out, though. But remember, whenever ya come through here, ya always got a room—free—anytime ya want ta stop." She reached over and planted a big juicy kiss on his cheek.

"Darn, Sadie," he dropped his head, crushing his hat in his hands. His heart hurt to leave her behind. "Why can't you come with me? If ya want."

She tilted her head, coyly. "You old codger. I didn't think ya'd ever ask. Wait one minute." Lifting her skirt up to her knees, she took giant steps back onto the porch and quickly disappeared into the hotel.

Surprised, he asked, "What'd I say?"

"I'm not sure," said John. "But I think you got yourself a woman for keeps."

Ben scratched his head and smiled. "I guess it could be worse. I must be good-looking or something."

"I think it's the 'or something' that got her, Ben," teased Caroline.

Sadie burst through the doorway, dragging two large valises. She wore brown coveralls, boots, a red plaid shirt, and a large felt hat.

"You boys go round up my two horses over at the stables. Ben, you and John get down from those animals and help tie these valises on one of my horses when the boys get 'em."

Ben dismounted and stood sheepishly holding the reins.

She walked over to him and threw her arms around his neck. "Nothing I'd like better than to spend the rest of my time with you, you handsome devil."

Ben blushed, tongue-tied, too embarrassed to speak.

She turned to Caroline, "Isn't he just the cutest thing?"

"Oh, yes, real cute."

Once the valises were tied on, Ben helped Sadie up onto her saddle. Climbing onto his horse, he said, "Let's go."

Standing Tall stood on the porch. He gave a whistle and Micah came running around the corner. "Had to go to the bushes."

John gave him a quizzical look. "What? With an outhouse out back?"

"He kiss girl good-bye," teased Standing Tall.

"Didn't either."

"Did, too"

"Enough. Climb up, we're heading out." John shook his head. "I don't think I can handle this."

Caroline chuckled. "We started out small and we've grown into an entourage. I wonder if anyone else wants to join in."

"Wait a minute," shouted Ben. "Sadie, what are ya gonna do with the hotel? Ya just can't leave it like this."

She smiled mischievously. "Oh, I sold it last night, lock, stock, and barrel to my hired man, Phineas Michaels. He and his daughter, Laurie, are already settled in."

"Well, I swan. Ya knew all the time I'd ask ya to go with me, didn't ya?"

"I was hopin', you sweet thing."

John tapped the brim of his hat. "Warned you, Ben. You gotta watch these women."

"You take care of yourself, John Anderson." Caroline smirked, glancing at him sideways. "You're gonna have plenty to handle from here on in."

"Life used to be so easy," he said, shaking his head. "Let's go, we need to get up the trail some before nightfall."

As they moved out in single file, Laurie Michaels stood on the hotel porch, waving.

Standing Tall smiled at Micah. "She waves at Brave Warrior."

Micah slapped his friend's arm with the back of his hand. "Shut up." Facing forward, he dangled his left hand at his side and gave a farewell backwards wave.

John looked at Caroline, riding next to him. "I'm not sure if I'm cut out to be a father."

"Don't worry, you'll learn fast. We'll keep you on the straight and narrow."

"That's what I'm afraid of."

She gave him an impish grin. “What about being a husband?”

He raised one eyebrow and cracked a smile. “Now, that will prove to be an interesting challenge with the right woman.”

~End~

About the Author

A native of Jennings, Missouri, Gwyn Ramsey spent many hours at the library, reading Nancy Drew, Little Women, Treasure Island, Anne of Green Gables, and many others. Stories were important to her, but it wasn't until she was in high school that she tried her hand at writing. She took journalism and wrote for the school paper. When she finished high school, she went out into the work world and eventually married.

She attended the Florissant Valley Community College in Missouri and pursued a Computer Applications Associates Degree. One writing class assignment required that she research and write a final paper. Gwyn's subject dealt with Agent Orange and the effects on our military in Vietnam. Per the Veteran Affair's Office request, the paper was submitted for their files.

As her family grew up, she developed an interest in genealogy. Eventually she published a quarterly genealogy newsletter to share the information she had on file. Research became a hobby that would stick with her through the rest of her life.

When Gwyn and her husband moved to Florida, she left the secretarial field and decided to try writing again, only more seriously this time. As her stories evolved, the characters came alive. Writing is now an important part of her life. She has traveled across the United States during the gold rush with her characters through undeveloped territories, seen the wonders of the west in its magnificence, and eaten the dust from the covered wagons as she walked the Oregon Trail. What an adventure her characters have taken her on.

Now as her novel, *Journey to Tracer's Point*, is published by Treble Heart Books Sundowners division, her determination and love for writing has paid off. Come join Gwyn in an adventurous ride of stories that will thrill you.